LW DAVIS

Lemonade

A Soul-Quenching Southern Saga, Brimming with Magic, Grace, and Redemption

First edition

This book was professionally typeset on Reedsy.
Find out more at reedsy.com

Contents

Prologue

What binds their souls in hate's dark dream?
Beneath the current....
Hear it scream....

—RUN, Rylan... RUN...

The Boy King

The Boy King

The Kingdom

The boy crouched low, his eyes speckled with flames. He coiled like a spring begging to snap. His toes dug in, the creek's bank grounding him as he stared at the cracked face of his watch. The second hand ticked—57, 58, 59—each click a heartbeat, a dare. His breath hitched, eyes narrowed, hazel glints catching the sun's last gold through the trees. 0...

He exploded from the makeshift starting line, a scrawny blur of muscle and grit, sprinting flat-out toward the creek's edge. His legs burned, lungs screaming as he launched himself into the air, arms clawing for the rope dangling mid-flight. His fingers snagged it, rough hemp biting his palms, and he swung hard, body arcing over the creek's ripples like a pendulum gone wild. He dared not fall or let go; the water in the pool below was dark, alive with secrets he was soon to know. The rope's arc peaked—his cue—and he twisted midair, aiming for the fallen oak sprawled across the river like a broken bridge.

His bare feet slapped the old fallen tree, a split-second wobble nearly pitching him into the drink. He caught himself, heart hammering, and grinned—wild, reckless, alive. The tree groaned under him as he bolted down its length, arms pumping for balance. A chipmunk right-of-way stretched ahead and ended sharply at the bank. No slowing down—he leapt again, soaring toward a boulder jutting from the shore like a gray fist punching skyward. His soles hit stone, knees buckling, but he rolled with it, finding his balance in a crouch, chest heaving, eyes darting ahead.

The creek glowed, a ribbon of danger and promise, as he continued to conquer the water walk—stone to stone, each a slick, uneven hop daring him to slip. One—two—three—his leaps were quick, bare feet gripping wet rock like they were born for it. A fourth stone wobbled under him, his arms windmilling, then he launched anyway, landing hard on the fifth with a grunt.

No time to breathe—the last boulder loomed. He jumped and landed it with all the grace of a drunken soldier. He caught himself from falling backward into the creek and dove into a wall of soft, tall foliage on the shore that swallowed him whole. Sporadic clumps of saw-grass attacked him, but he laughed—a short, sharp bark of triumph.

He flattened out, belly-crawling under a thorny bush, its barbs snagging his straps, pricking his back.

"Come on!"

His teeth gritted while dragging himself through the dirt. Thorns drew blood—little red beads on his knuckles—but he didn't care, just kept moving, inching past the bush to a patch of poison ivy gleaming oily green in the sun. **No touching that,** he thought, bear-crawling around it, feet and palms sinking into soft earth, sweat stinging his eyes. His breath came in ragged bursts, but he didn't stop—couldn't stop, not with the watch ticking in his head.

Clear of the ivy, he dropped back down from the crawl and rolled—once, twice—coming up on one knee beside a pile of rocks, smooth and river-worn. His target swung lazily in the breeze: an old coffee can dangling from a pine branch, rusted and dented. He snatched a stone, hefted it, and cocked his arm, still kneeling, chest rising and falling like a bellows. The throw flew wide—cracking against the tree's trunk instead, missing the can by a foot.

"Dag-nabbit!"

His voice cracked, frustration flaring hot in his gut. He grabbed another rock, steadied himself, and struck the pose again—one knee down, eyes locked on that swaying tin. His arm snapped back, then forward, a whip-crack of motion, and the stone sailed true—ping!—smacking the can dead center. It swung violently, a wild pendulum, clanging like a bell tolling victory.

He didn't wait to gloat—somersaulting fast, one after another, ten in a row. The world spun, sky and creek blurring into a smear, his stomach lurching with every flip. He stumbled up on the tenth, wobbly as a pub crawler on holiday, head pounding, vision swimming. A dizzy laugh bubbled out—he couldn't help it, even as he staggered toward the fallen tree, half-running, half-falling, bare feet slapping mud and moss. The creek bank loomed; he pushed harder, legs of jelly but stubborn, breath tearing out in gasps that burned his throat.

He hit the old fallen tree's pinnacle, skidding to a stop, and fumbled for his watch. His hands shook as he squinted at the time—two minutes, thirty-two seconds flat. His personal best, shaved by a hair.

"Yes!"

His fists shot skyward, chest heaving, sweat dripping off his nose. He stood tall on the fallen oak's natural platform above the dark pool spinning under him, slightly counterclockwise, with a faint tremble—a ripple no wind could claim. Pausing to catch his breath, he gazed at the creek's shimmering expanse, its beauty now tinged with an eerie stillness. Bubbles broke the surface, slow and deliberate, each one popping with a hiss. A wisp of steam curled up, thin and ghastly, twisting in the still air. Something shifted below—deep, heavy, unseen—sending a shiver through the current, a pulse that lapped at the tree's roots where he stood. Rylan could hear it trying to claim him, filling his breath with the faint sulfur sting that crept into the breeze. The sound of the pool boiled low, as if it were whispering to him, a growl of heat and hunger rising from its depths.

* * *

Unlike the pool, the Kingdom's creek glittered like a ribbon of liquid glass under the tender embrace of a spring afternoon; its banks were alive with the season's reckless bloom. The air was thick with the scent of wild Honeysuckle and damp earth, a breeze teasing the water's surface into playful ripples that caught the sun's golden slant.

Dragonflies darted in iridescent flashes, their wings humming a soft tune. Red-winged blackbirds trilled from the cattails, their calls weaving into the symphony of life unfolding along the shore. In that moment, to him, the world felt both vast and intimate, a quiet celebration of time turning gently forward.

The trees flanking the creek—ancient oaks with sprawling, knotted limbs and willows unfurling tender, lime-green leaves—swayed in a slow, gentle rhythm, their branches glistening with dew, each droplet a tiny prism catching the morning light. The breeze teased through them, stirring the canopy into a soft rustle—a sound like glass chimes tumbling over stones. Mist-filled rays of light poured through the gaps above, spilling across the creek bed in a shifting tapestry of gold and shadow, painting the silt and pebbles in patterns that danced and flickered, as if the world itself were flirting with the day.

The boy stood poised, arms raised, atop a humongous old fallen tree; his was a story waiting to unfold. The old tree wasn't just a rotting hulk sprawled across the creek bank—it was a bustling Kingdom, a neighborhood of critters teeming with life and secrets. The tree, felled long ago by some forgotten storm, lay like a toppled giant, its gnarled roots clawing at the sky and its splintered trunk hollowed out by time and weather. Moss clung to its bark in soft green patches, and wildflowers sprouted where the wood met the earth, as if the tree still dreamed of spring despite its slumber.

The chipmunks had claimed it as their own, turning the crevices and cavities into a labyrinth of dens. He could sit for hours watching them dart along the tree's length, their stripes flashing like tiny banners. They'd scamper up the broken branches—highways now—and disappear into the crevices that served as doorways. They'd chitter to each other in a language he swore he could almost understand. Inside those hollows, he imagined their world: little rooms stuffed with crunchy acorns and pine needles piled up like blankets, maybe a chipmunk mayor barking orders, or a market where they traded shiny treasures stolen from the creek.

The tree straddled the water's edge, extending out over the pool that bubbled over smooth, color-filled stones. What used to act as a place to dive and flip from, a doorway to the world underneath, had long since been surrendered to what was now lurking deep in the depths. To the boy, the fallen tree was a bridge between his reality and something bigger—a place where the ordinary met the extraordinary.

Down below, the creek sometimes gave a shiver, a dark spinning ripple that didn't match the breeze, and the chipmunks would freeze from a combination of terror and panic. Their whiskers would twitch as if they knew something was watching. Their little world felt full of energy—but shaky. A place that used to tower over everything, now fallen, but they kept going, tough and clever, making their lives in the leftover pieces of something that had been conquered long ago.

The boy loved being a part of it all—the way the air carried the smells, the way the shadows played on the water, the way the chipmunks ruled their tiny Kingdom.

His favorite were the rare Crimson Lotus flowers that he would sometimes see floating past through the Kingdoms waters. He would watch, wondering where they came from and where they would go. Sitting there he would breath it all in, the whole place alive, as if it were whispering secrets just for him, a fragile but busy little Kingdom tucked into the magical woods, but now he watched the soul of his Kingdom throb. A dark, taunting pool bubbled underneath him—a once-pristine hollow, now rippling with a song of demise.

It had been the Kingdom's crown jewel, a haven where summers dissolved into fearless leaps and reckless swings. The rope, knotted to a warped branch, creaked as he soared from its frayed end, cutting the air before crashing into the cool, clear depths with a yell that roused the squirrels above.

Below the surface, a hidden realm unfurled—families of rainbow fish, their scales a fractured prism of ghostly colors, drifted in silent schools, their babies glinting like lost embers chasing after them. Turtles prowled, slow and ageless, shells traced with cryptic moss, while frogs perched on the banks, eyes like dark pearls staring through the haze. Crawdads crept over the bed of colored stones—gleaming through fissures where spectral plants coiled upward, their tendrils pulsing with an unearthly glow of lavender. He would leap from the fallen tree's pinnacle, a natural diving perch, plunging into the water's embrace, the critters cheering from above as he broke the surface, breathless and wild.

It was pure paradise, until that fateful day, marked by a chilling echo that silenced the creek's song.

Fiver Loads

It slunk in like a predator, the afternoon he frolicked too long by the creek's edge. The sun sank low, bleeding the forest in a bruised violet, and the pool's crystal heart shuddered—a backward ripple trembling at its surface, unprovoked by his stones. The air soured, the wildflowers hid, Honeysuckle curdling into something sharp and wrong, and the water blackened, dark as a grief too deep to name. The boy had always wondered why the pool had turned, and that day he knew.

The critters halted—chipmunks mid-dash, frogs mid-breath—their silence an omen the boy felt, but couldn't read. Then it breached, just barely breaking the surface, the first time he had spotted it, copper scales flashing briefly, a warning too fleeting to hold. It was no fish—long and evil, it was a demon, birthed from a fear that gnawed at his edges, fueled by a hatred that craved innocence like a flame craves air.

Somewhere in the stillness, a whisper brushed his ears—faint, like a dark breeze trying to speak, or a low groan rolling off the murk, **words*—he thought, a sound that clawed at the back of his skull, a shroud of torment through generations, a specter of loss lurking just beneath.

The boy had faced it fully only once since then, a night when the forest cloaked itself in pitch, and he'd crept back with a lantern, its flame dancing in his unsteady hands. The pool lay dead, dark, a mirror of nothing, until the water slowly started to bubble, a layer of steamy fog rose across the surface—a form reared upward, vast and blurred, its contours lost in the dark but framing a fire gland throbbing in its throat, a molten glow that burned the shadows back. A soft, slow haunting whisper floated on the searing breeze that he swore said,

"Mine..."

His lantern crashed to the stones, light guttering, and the Dragonfish—named in that very moment—leaving a choke in his throat—slid back, leaving the pool a chasm, its once-bright wonders drowned. That day, that moment, had planted a darkness that would claim more than the water; it was a shadow that would fuel the torment he was destined for.

He had fled, the forest's whispers a howl in his ears, fear, a live wire sparking in his chest. The pool was gone, its rainbow fish snuffed out, its turtles entombed, its plants shriveled under a veil no skip could breach. Now, he stood by the fallen tree, the rope swing swaying limp in the twilight, its end grazing the blackened water like a ghost's touch. The Dragonfish was there, its fire gland a muted ember, watching, waiting.

The boy's fist tightened, nails biting his palm. This thing—it despised the Kingdom, despised the light that had once danced here, and coveted his soul. It had risen once, fully, and he'd barely glimpsed it, but he felt it: a battle brewing, a reckoning tied to that fateful day when the pool turned dark—a day that would steal more than he could bear.

The forest loomed, branches clawing at the stars, and the pool stared back, a pit of dread. He edged closer, the diving spot a phantom under his feet, and the water shifted—a breach, just a sliver of its head, one amber eye surfacing, unblinking, ancient, alive with a hunger that stretched beyond now, beyond him, toward a loss he couldn't yet name. His blood roared, but he held its gaze.

"I'll stop you," the boy's voice a thread in the gloom.

The Dragonfish's eye sank, but a chill gripped the boy—a fleeting vision of the Tree of Life, its roots pulsing with ancient runes, whispering of a battle yet to rise. He shook it off, heart pounding, unsure if it was fear or fate.

* * *

The boy launched himself onto the Kingdom's floor, tucking into a roll with the same reckless flair he'd seen Colt Seavers pull off on the flickering screen of the old Tell A Vision.

He rose up on the crest of the bank, one hand in the air pointing, the other holding a flat skipping stone, his eyes wide and fierce, head tilted back, taking in as big a breath as he could possibly hold. Out here, all his memories were swallowed by the sparrows' chatter and the water's playful Trickle, a sound with which he had fallen deeply in love. The dappled light shifted, brushing the creek bed with its restless glow, and the trees swayed on, dripping life into the stillness. Jumping into action, he crouched near the water's edge, his bare toes squishing into the cool, silty mud, the cuffs of his worn trousers rolled up and already soaked.

* * *

He didn't know how many years he'd held. He thought he remembered that his birthday was sometime in the spring, but he wasn't really sure. It had been a long time since then, and his family had long since forgotten about special days. The last one he could recollect was down by the creek, the sun hanging lazy over the water, painting it gold like a promise. He'd been—what, six? Seven? Too young to care much about counting years, but old enough to feel the day was his.

Mamma and Pops were there, knee-deep in the crystalline pool under the fallen tree, showing little Bubba how to float. The creek was alive that day, same as always—fish flashing silver beneath the surface, dragonflies and flutterbys doing tricks—and that sweet hum of water over stones mixing with the wild Honeysuckle thick in the air. Bubba, all chubby arms and giggles, kicked his tiny legs as Pops held him up, water lapping gently around his belly.

"Keep your head back, Bubs,"

Pops rumbled gently, grinning under his cap, while Mamma splashed alongside, her laugh bouncing off the trees like it belonged there.

The boy had floated too, sprawling around the pool on his back, staring up at the sky through the willows till his ears dipped under and the world went quiet. The creek cradled him, cool and clear, its current tugging soft at his toes.

When Bubba got tired, Mamma hauled out the blow-up alligator she'd snagged from the five-and-dime in town—green, patchy, smelling faintly of rubber and store shelves. She plopped Bubba on it, pulling him around the pool in slow circles, his squeals ringing through the afternoon haze. The boy and Pops watched from the bank, legs dangling over the fallen tree. Every time Mamma paraded Bubba floating past, they would make monster faces and reach their hands out toward him, formed into the shapes of claws. Baby Bubba would just laugh and giggle out loud, riding along on his alligator chariot.

They'd brought lemon cake—Mamma's best, tart and sweet, the kind that stuck to your fingers and made your tongue sing. It sat on a flat rock, yellow crumbs scattering as they dug in, Bubba smearing it on his cheeks like war paint. Pops handed the boy a new fishing pole—bamboo, sleek, with a line that gleamed like spider silk.

"Reckon you're old enough to hook something real now."

His voice was low and proud. The boy grinned, running his hands over it, already picturing the fish he'd pull from that glittering water. It was a good day—bright, loud, full—before birthdays slipped away like leaves, down the creek

* * *

He was a lanky boy with dirty blonde hair, plastered to his forehead from the spring warmth. His hazel eyes gleamed with the thrill of a free afternoon. A handful of six smooth, flat stones that had been personally deemed worthy of weaponization, which he called fiver loads, waited in his sweaty palm.

The sun blazed high, and his hazel eyes narrowed, locked on the water's golden ripples. He'd been at it all morning—persistently developing his weapon: five perfect skips with a hop, the evil Dragonfish's doom. Four skips came easily now, but the Fiver was a beast, taunting him, laughing at him. He was still a little awkward and lanky, but today his chest puffed broader, his voice cracked roughly as he muttered,

"C'mon, you're better'n this."

It wasn't just getting the five skips; it had to have a special twist in the throwing motion so that after the fifth skip, it would lift the stone off of the surface of the water high enough to target the fire-making gland of the deadly beast.

He envisioned his enemy, which lay dormant at the moment but could breach at any time and target him with its poisonous, laser-like flame. He ducked, eluding an imagined advance, and reached into his overalls pocket for a fiver load. He watched intently for a ripple that would give away his enemy's position, stifling its surprise attack. He dropped and rolled across the forest floor and snapped back into his first position on one knee, eyes glued to the water, his Fiver (throwing arm) extended up into the air, loaded, cocked, and ready to roll.

He let out a small *roar* as he launched his first assault, his wrist twisting the motion just so—*plip, plip, plip, plip...*

"Four again, aaaahhhhh!"

A growl rumbled low in his throat, a sound he'd heard from the mill hands, and he slammed a fist into his thigh, stinging himself awake.

"Dang it!"

He stood and steadied himself for another go, breath sharp in his chest. Dropping low, he surveyed the water, then sprang—a tuck and roll, fast as a thunderclap, dirt kicking up under his feet. A fiver load sat heavy in his grip, cocked in the Fiver, primed for something big. He let it fly—plip, plip, plip, plip, plip,—five skips, clean and high, pulling the creek like a blade. A roar ripped out of him, wild and rough, echoing off the trees, and he leapt up, nearly toppling over into the mud. His fists shot high, slinging wet earth in arcs, and his grin stretched wide—untamed pride burning deep in his gut. That Dragonfish was in for it now, and it didn't even know.

He had taught himself to keep his wits keen, eyes and ears open to every rustle and ripple around him—had to, seeing as he was the world's one and only Dragonfish slayer. A relentless knight of special weaponry, armed with nothing but stones and grit. He stood guard over the Kingdom, slinging fiver loads one skip at a time, keeping the dark at bay.

Dragonfish beasts could stretch up to six feet long, with scales that glowed like molten copper, and black spikes spanning from their head and back, down to their long, winding tail. What set the Dragonfish apart was its fiery breath, a gift as unnatural as it was deadly. When provoked, it reared its head above the water and unleashed a plume of laser-like searing flames, hot enough to scorch its enemies to death. Yet, for all its might, the Dragonfish harbored a singular vulnerability—a weakness tied to the warrior art of stone skipping.

Only an expert warrior skipper, a knight of the stone, whose stone dances across the water with five skips or more, and who can execute the specific twist of the wrist in the throwing motion that causes the fiver load to rise after the fifth skip, can hit the Dragonfish in the heart of the fire gland. The secret lies in the rhythm: a perfectly skipped stone, launched with skill and intent. The knight must strike the creature mid-breach, piercing the soft, scaleless patch beneath its jaw where its fire gland hums. The impact erupts its glowing fire gland, causing an implosion of flame and water that reduces the beast to a smoldering husk, sinking harmlessly below the surface to its demise. Lesser throws—four skips or fewer—merely enrage it, inviting a counterattack of flame and fury.

A splash—not his own—pricked the boy's ears, sharp like a snapped twig. His head whipped upstream, heart thumping hard in his chest, every muscle coiled to leap. The Dragonfish? He scoured the water, eyes darting over every ripple, every shiver in the creek's dark skin, hunting for that copper gleam.

When *the girl* broke into view downstream, his whole world slammed to a halt. His breath snagged, stuck somewhere between his ribs, and time hung still as a held note. Slow and deliberate, he eased the four leftover fiver loads into the pouch on the front right of his overalls, fingers steady despite the buzz in his veins. He dipped a hand into the creek, scooping up some cold water, and ran it through his blond mess of hair, pushing it back till it stuck. He licked his thumbs, quick and slick, and ran them over his eyebrows, flattening them down smooth as a millpond. Cupping his hand, he puffed a breath into it, sniffing fast—good enough, no stink to scare *her* off. Then, with a deep breath and a roll of his shoulders, he started toward *her*, strutting like he'd seen Tom Cruise do on Dollar Tuesdays—chin up, grin cocked, a swagger that said he owned the creek and then some.

Her

The boy's eyes stopped, a flicker downstream where the creek spilled wide into the pool, *her* bare feet sunk ankle-deep in the flow. The water curled around *her* calves, soft and clinging like it couldn't let go, rippling gentle under a spring sun. *She* stood maybe a heartbeat older than him, *her* golden hair falling free and wild, catching the light in a glow that spun 'round *her* head—silk threads, shining like something too pure for this world, dancing with every tilt of *her* chin.

Her sundress was hitched up in one fist, crumpled high. *Her* arms browned by days outdoors, and in *her* other hand, *she* gripped a fishing pole—bamboo, old and weathered, its line strung tight, quivering in the current like it felt *her* pull. A breeze stirred, lifting *her* hair higher, and for a split second, he swore he saw a shimmer—faint, white, like feathers nobody else could catch, gone when he blinked. His chest hitched, wonder pricking his skin, like *she'd* stepped outta some higher place to stand in his creek.

The fifth fiver load slipped from his fingers, plunking into the mud, as his breath snagged on something sharp and new, foreign to his world. He couldn't seem to take in enough air to combat what was turning inside of him. It was as though he was being smothered by a very unfamiliar sensation. Not a bad sensation, but unfamiliar for sure. It took a minute before he realized he was actually embracing and enjoying the sinking sensation, submitting to the rush of endorphins that were suddenly infiltrating parts of him that he was not quite familiar with at this point of his reign.

A fish busted through the creek's skin, slick and sudden, yanking the boy's eyes from *her* to the battle brewing downstream. It was good-sized, fat and shiny, thrashing hard against *her* line. *She* let out a yelp—pure, bright delight, *her* voice crackling through the air setting the whole day ablaze. He yelped back, a wild burst tearing outta him, the kind only half-boy, half-man could let loose—loud and raw, heart pounding with the thrill of it. As *she* reeled, a glint caught the sun—not just the fish, but something off *her*, a flicker too quick, like wings shimmering in the spray, there and gone. His shout hitched, eyes wide, wonder mixing with the rush—could *she* be more than *she* seemed...

He couldn't tear his eyes away. *She* yanked the pole with a wild grin, *her* bare arms flexing as *she* fought the fish, breaching the surface with angst, tail thrashing. *She* laughed—a sound so free it made the creek sing in harmony—*she* yanked it harder and reeled it closer, feet steady on the slippery stones. When it finally slapped onto the bank, *she* dropped down beside it in the mud and grass, h*er* eyes—bright as the sky mirrored in the water—blazing with victory.

His chest tightened, then burst open, a flood of heat and wonder crashing through him like the creek after a rain. It wasn't just the fish, though that was a marvel, it was *her*—the way *her* hair fell across *her* cheek, the curve of *her* lips as *she* whooped, the strength in *her* small hands as *she* held *her* prize aloft. His heart pounded, wild and alive, with desires he'd never known—soft, aching, and electric. He wanted to run to *her*, to splash through the creek and cheer *her* on, to feel the damp earth under their feet—together. He wanted to hear that laugh again, to see *her* eyes catch his, to be part of *her* world in a way he couldn't yet name, but that he felt in every trembling inch of his soul.

The boy's stare tugged *her* gaze upward, like *she* had felt it brush *her* skin, and those jade eyes—flecked with gold, tiny sparks glinting like caught sunlight—locked hard onto his. Time dragged out, the creek's gurgle fading to a whisper, holding still as if the world waited. Across the water, they met—no touch, just a pull, a first holding that sank deep into his bones.

She grinned then—bold as a storm, dazzling like light splintering off wet rocks, daring him to move—and waved him over, *her* hand slick with fish slime, smeared with mud and creek water, shining wet in the sun. *She* was near perfect, too perfect maybe, **Lordy, she ain't just anybody,** he thought, chest tightening with a mix of thrill and wonder...

"Hey!" *she* hollered, voice slicing through the spring haze. "You gonna stand there like a stunned trout, or you gonna come see this beauty?"

A grin cracked his face wide open, nerves humming like a struck banjo string. The cold bit hard, but he didn't care—his feet slapped the shallows, pushing him closer. As he neared, a gentle breeze carried *her* scent, sweet and wild like the Honeysuckle nodding along the bank, filling his lungs till he near drowned in it.

She could steer the wind itself if she reckoned to, he thought, half-dazed, feeling the breeze bend around *her* like it was obeying something holy. A soft light danced in her shadows—faint, quick, like a glow spilling from her edges, too pure for just a girl, making his heart skip.

"The Wind blows where it wishes," *she* said with a giggle.

He was confused as *she* seemed to read his mind.... He couldn't breath the smell deep enough to satisfy his desire. A smudge of dirt streaked *her* nose, and *her* hair tangled just so, making *her* look like the Warrior Queen of his Kingdom. *She* cocked *her* head, sizing him up.

"Ever seen a fish this big?"

"Nope, not in person" he admitted, eyes wide. "You're a wizard with that pole."

"Stick around," *she* tossed the fish back into the water with a little dance of celebration... "I'll teach you a trick or three."

He crinkled his nose, watching *her* intently, "Ain't you gonna eat that?"

She looked through his eyes and into his soul,

"I was already blessed with all that I need for today."

He found comfort in *her* aura. They fished side by side, poles dipping into the creek as they swapped wild tales of monster catches and near-misses, their laughter echoing off the water.The fish had abandoned him, bites vanishing like whispers on the wind, and frustration coiled tight in his chest. Beside him, *she* glowed, *her* line singing with life as *she* reeled in catch after catch, each one a gleaming prize, kissed by the water's magic. He watched, jaw clenched, unable to unravel the mystery—why did the creek favor *her* so? What secret did *she* hold that eluded him?

She felt a storm brewing in him, his impatience rippling like the current itself. A giggle danced from *her* lips, soft and bright, and *she* leaned close, *her* voice a melody woven with mischief and knowing.

Her finger traced the eddy, and for a heartbeat, the water glowed faintly jade, as if *her* touch stirred something ancient beneath the creek. Rylan squinted, *her* glow like the springs he had heard spoken of, hidden in a hollow past where the Sound of the Water sang her secrets.

"Cast there,"

She pointed as *her* eyes shimmered with knowing.

"Ain't no fish over there," His tone was rough with certainty. "They ride the current—always have, always will."

She didn't argue, just tilted *her* head with a smile, *her* eyes shimmering like the creek at dawn, and nodded gently—agreement laced with a quiet dare.

He flung his line into the current again and again, each cast a defiant prayer, but the water mocked him with its silence. *Her* words burned in his mind, an ember of doubt and longing he couldn't snuff out. The creek seemed to hum, alive with some unseen enchantment, and *her* laughter—sweet, unguarded—wove through the air like a spell. Finally, when he thought *her* gaze had drifted, he surrendered. With a flick of his wrist, he sent his bait soaring to that still, shadowed spot *she'd* blessed with *her* whisper.

The instant it kissed the water, the creek erupted. A titan burst forth from the depths, scales flashing like molten silver under the sun's dying light. It was the biggest he'd ever caught or seen, maybe ever dreamed of, a creature of myth, summoned by *her* magic and his reluctant faith. It swallowed the bait whole, and the fight was on—his pole bent, his heart thundered, and the world shrank to the dance of a man and a beast. *She* whooped beside him, *her* voice a wild hymn of joy, and when he finally hauled it ashore, they collapsed into laughter, breathless and alive.

The afternoon unfurled like a love song after that, their conquests piling up as the creek performed for them both. Every splash, every tug on the line, was a tapestry of passion and wonder woven between them. The fish weren't just catches; they were gifts from a world suddenly brimming with magic, sparked by *her* giggle, *her* breath, *her* glance–*her* unshakable belief. As the day wore on, he knew: it wasn't just the fish *she'd* lured, it was him—hook, line, and sinker.

* * *

They raced along the bank, dodging roots and leaping stones, and then plunged into a rock-skipping contest—the boy bloated with pride as he hit six skips, then *she* got a seven. He had never even seen a seven except for his Pops...

She spun toward him with a grin that screamed trouble, barking,

"Count me down!"

He blinked, baffled, tilting his head like a confused pup.

"Time me, you goof!"

She was practically buzzing with impatience. He fumbled, glancing at his watch, then back at *her* just as *she* exploded into motion like a firecracker with legs.

She bolted for the creek's edge, all wild energy and zero hesitation, launching *herself* at the rope with a whoop that echoed through the trees. *Her* dress flowing behind *her* like wings of an angel. His breath hitched as *she* snagged it mid-air, swinging in a massive, twisting arc—pure chaos in motion, whipping around like a tornado.

She slammed into the old fallen tree and didn't even flinch, hitting the ground running, she leaped completely across the chipmunk right-of-way like *she* was born for it. Across the boulders *she* flew—no dainty hopping for *her*, just a full-on sprint, each step a dare to gravity itself. Then, with a gleeful cackle, *she* dove into the deep grass, rolling like old Colt Seavers himself...

Under the thorn bush *she* went, belly-crawling like a commando, then popped up and charged around the poison ivy on *her* feet and hands with the lumbering grace of a mamma-bear on a mission. Clearing the ivy field, *she* threw *herself* into two slick rolls, popping up on one knee and snatching a rock in one fluid move. With a flick of *her* wrist—straight out of Pops' old baseball stories—*she* nailed the swinging coffee can dead-on, the clang ringing out like a victory bell.

Not done yet, *she* launched into a chain of ten somersaults, each one tighter and faster than the last, before springing up and sprinting full-tilt to the diving spot at the pinnacle of the old fallen tree. *She* skidded to a stop, whirling to face him with a triumphant smirk, chest heaving, eyes daring him to be impressed.

He stood there, jaw unhinged, eyes wide as saucers, looking like he'd just seen a unicorn wrestle a grizzly and win. *Awe* didn't even cover it—he was downright dazzled, half-convinced she could outrun lightning and whoop anyone dumb enough to challenge *her*. Snapping out of it, he glanced at his watch, then back at *her*, still reeling.

"One minute, forty-nine seconds."

She was certainly a ball of spitfire...

"Fast, huh?"

She tossed him a cocky grin, like *she'd* just rewritten the rules of speed and fun in one go.

The sun climbed, then dipped, painting the sky in pinks and oranges, and still they played, muddy, breathless, and alive, the creek their Kingdom and spring their endless song.

* * *

As dusk crept in, the air cooling and crickets tuning up, they flopped onto the grassy bank. The day's heat lingered in their skin, their clothes damp and streaked with dirt. The boy had already decided he wasn't making it home by dinner... a choice he made fully knowing the consequences of his decision. He dug into his satchel, pulling out a dented canteen—tart, sweet Lemonade, the kind that stung your tongue just right. He unscrewed the cap and offered it to *her*, his heart thudding as *her* fingers grazed his.

"Try this," he said, voice soft in the fading light. "Mamma makes it better than anyone."

She took a long sip, and then leaned back on *her* elbows, staring at the first stars at dusk, just peeking through the twilight. *She* smiled from deep inside and handed the canteen back, *her* eyes glinting with something new—something that mirrored the ache in him.

"What is your name, my new King?"

"Rylan—Rylan Blaze"

"What's your middle name Rylan Blaze"

He rolled his eyes and held his breath...

"Ember...."

She thought for a moment with an obscure look and a tilt of *her* head, and suddenly let out an endearing belly laugh, grabbing his face,

"Rylan Ember Blaze?" Smiling ear to ear. "It's cute... so cute...I just love it!"
"Cute—yeah—great..."

He shook his head, embarrassed and ridden with shame...

She put *her* other hand on his pouting face,

"King Rylan Ember Blaze—I suppose that would make me a Princess."

"Princess?" Rylan questioned...

She sat up and looked him in the eye exclaiming with a very bold expression on her face...

"Well you would have to marry me in order for me to be your Queen..."

They laughed—then laid back, breathing each other in as deeply as they could. The silence was filled with the Trickles of the creek moving on without them and the choir of crickets and bullfrogs serenading their first shared Lemonade. As *she* nestled *her* head back down into his chest, *she* could feel his heart exploding. *She* laid *her* hand on his pounding heart and said,

"You know King Rylan, that's the kind of Lemonade that could make you want for nothing more for the rest of your life."

He was in deep. *She* looked at him with eyes that longed for something unfamiliar to *her* and asked,

"Do you think when we are old, that Lemonade will still taste just as sweet?"

Rylan thought for a moment before replying,

"I guess that would depend on how much of the good stuff you put in the mix."

They lied in the swaying grass together, her head falling onto his shoulder, and they drifted off under the comfort brewing in their hearts.

* * *

"We fell asleep..."

Rylan opened his eyes wide; the words came tumbling out in a panicked rush. "We've gotta get home..."

The spring breeze, and the harmonies of the Kingdom had woven a spell over them, creating a cradle beneath the star-strewn night. *She* stirred, half-lost to sleep, and blinked up at him, eyes hazy with dreams, flickering faintly in the starlight. In that quiet glow, *she* seemed both fragile and fierce—smaller, softer, yet still the wild Warrior Princess with whom he had conquered the day.

Rylan froze, heart thudding like a war drum. He gazed down at *her*, memorizing every curve of *her* face—the damp curls clinging to *her* brow, the smudge of mud on *her* nose—etching *her* into his soul as if *she* were a treasure he might lose to the night. His chest tightened, a dizzying ache blooming there, because amid the fire of *her* laugh and the strength of *her* hands, a truth hit him like a skipped stone: this Princess—his future Queen—who'd stormed his world with a fishing pole and a grin, was still a stranger. He didn't even know *her* name, and that thought carved a hole in his soul.

"Hey..." he whispered, voice low and rough, thick with urgency and something softer. "Don't you need to get home?"

She stretched, slow like a kitten. *Her* body was still molding into his as she propped *herself* onto an elbow. Those eyes glowed with sleepy mischief, catching the stars like they belonged to *her*.

"I'll be alright," *she* murmured, *her* voice soft, a velvet thread, heavy with the edge of slumber. "You can go on without me."

Rylan's brow furrowed, *her* words slicing deeper than a Dragonfish flame. Go on without *her*? The idea felt wrong—like leaving half his heart behind.

He stared at *her* confused, *her* face a map of shadows and light, shook his head, jaw tight. But the clock in his mind ticked louder, each beat a hammer against his ribs.

If he didn't bolt home now, his parents would unleash the hounds—visions of lanterns bobbing, and the sheriff's gruff voice barking his name, the whole town carrying torches and hunting him like a lost little colt, invaded his last moments with *her*. He couldn't risk that, not even for the girl who'd set his world ablaze.

His hands trembled as they slid to *her* face, cupping *her* cheeks with a tenderness he didn't know he had. *Her* skin was warm, streaked with creek mud, and his thumbs brushed that smudge on *her* nose, lingering there as he fell into her gaze. He let his fingers drift, innocently but achingly, threading through *her* golden hair—soft as silk, tangled with the day's wildness; it was a feeling he had never experienced before.

"What's your name?" he insisted, in a raw whisper, urgent and pleading. "And... how will I find you again?"

She smiled—the curl of *her* lips made his pulse race. She leaned into his touch, *her* warmth seeping into his palms and softly spoke,

"*Follow the Sound of the Water.*"

Her words a velvet promise, soft yet carved into the night like an ancient vow.

"That's where I'll be, waiting..."

Before Rylan could catch his breath, *she* tilted *her* head and pressed a kiss to his cheek—gentle, fleeting, a whisper of *her* lips against his skin. Rylan exploded—a fire roared through him, heat and light bursting from his chest, racing down his arms, sparking in his fingertips. His breath snagged, face flushed hot, and for a heartbeat, the world vanished—crickets, creek, stars—all gone, leaving only her, so close, so real. His hands tightened in *her* hair, a reflex of wanting something that he was yet to even remotely understand. He found himself nearly pulling *her* back, craving just a little more of that impossible burn, but the memory of a dark circumstance to his action clawed him upright.

"I—I gotta go..."

His voice cracked as he scrambled to his feet. He didn't want to leave—not *her*, not this moment where the air thrummed with *her* nearness—but he had no choice, as the darkness was already holding him to account. One last look—he burned *her* silhouette, glowing against the creek, stars and moon, into his forever.

* * *

Rylan turned and ran as fast as he could, half because he knew he was most likely in for it when he got home, and half to show off to his newfound Princess just how fast he was. The field sprawled wild before him, the night air sharp in his lungs. His heart hammered—half from the run, half from that kiss, a blaze he couldn't outpace. About halfway, he skidded to a halt and spun back. The creek glimmered faintly, a silver thread under a sky ablaze with stars—so bright they turned night to twilight.

"WHAT IS YOUR NAME?"

His voice erupted, slashing through the silence, raw and desperate—no answer, no laugh, no splash, no echo—just the black void of *her* absence. *She'd* vanished, swallowed by the dark, and his gut wrenched like a wound.

Rylan's mind churned: *Where had she vanished to*? He fought to rein in his imagination, its wild hooves galloping toward impossible places—maybe *she* was a sprite born of the water, or a dream slipped from the stars. More likely, he told himself, *she* lived nearby, some hidden hollow in Eldergrove, *her* parents working late into the night, leaving h*er* free to roam under the moon. But doubt gnawed at him. He'd scoured every inch of this town, from the creek's banks to the fields and beyond. No trailer, no shack could claim *her.* No trace, no echo—just *her*, sudden and blazing, like a comet across his sky.

There was so much he burned to know. *Her* divinity pulled at him, a tide he couldn't name, flooding the hollows of his soul. *She* was a mystery he was too young to unravel—how did *she* move with such grace, wield such quiet power? Why did *her* presence stitch him whole, mending cracks he hadn't known were there? Fear surged then, cold and sharp—what if he never saw *her* again? What if the pull of the town's dark edges drowned *her* face, her voice, until *she* was just a shadow he'd let slip away?

Rylan shook his head, jaw tight, refusing to let that terror take root. Deep down, beneath the panic, a steady pulse beat: their story wasn't done. *She* wasn't just a fleeting spark to be lost to the night. *She* was his Princess, his flame, and they had a lifetime of adventure unfurling in front of them—creeks to conquer, stones to skip, secrets to share. The thought warmed him, steadying his steps, even as the shadow of home loomed closer.

He raised a hand, slow and uncertain, waving to the empty horizon—to the Princess he'd claimed in a day and lost in a breath; as his hand slowly succumbed to gravity he pressed it to his chest, feeling *her* kiss linger there, searing like the flame of a Dragonfish.

He turned toward home as Eldergrove's shadowed roofs loomed ahead like crooked teeth against the night sky.

The Shadow

His house stood silent, a hulking silhouette. Its windows—black as empty eyes staring down at him—judging, waiting. Rylan gripped the trellis, the weathered wood splintering into his palms, thorns from the climbing roses snagging his shirt, tearing at the fabric. He continued, climbing quiet as a thief, toward his second-floor sanctuary.

Each creak of the old boards under his weight was a whisper of doom, but he pressed on, driven by the fading glow of *her* face and the dread of what lay ahead. He reached the window, fingers fumbling at the sill, and pushed—nothing. It wouldn't budge. His pulse spiked, a frantic drumbeat in his throat. He swore he'd left it unlocked—it was *always* unlocked. It was his secret gateway to freedom, and now to *her*. He shoved again, harder, the trellis groaning beneath him, and then his heart sank...

A shadow rose up and loomed from inside the window—tall, broad, dark—a figure filling the frame like a specter summoned from the Lake of Fire itself. It didn't speak, didn't move, just motioned with a single finger. It was a silent command of reckoning, pointing down toward the front porch. Rylan's stomach lurched, his grip tightening on the vines as if he could cling to the memory of his Princess's warmth forever, but that finger was a judge's gavel, and he began the agonizing descent, each step a march to his own execution.

He took his time—every second he could steal, the night air was cool but void of consequence to the sweat on his brow, fueled by the fear in his gut.

The front door stood ajar, a sliver of shadow spilling out like an invitation to a tomb. He paused, chest tight, mind racing. What if he turned back; ran to the creek, to his Kingdom, to *her*—his *Princess* with the golden hair and fearless laugh? Could he vanish into that wild world, let the adults forget him, let the Dragonfish guard their secret forever? The thought flickered, tempting as a flame, but died fast. They'd hunt him down—a lynch mob, the whole town—torches and all. He'd never see *her* again if he was locked away.

* * *

Resigned to fate and certainty, he stepped inside, the dark swallowing him whole, a chamber of judgment awaiting its prisoner. The air hit him first—thick with pipe tobacco, smoke curling in the shadows like a snake poised to strike. The pipe Pops smoked was a family curse, passed down from his father with a grim vow. Pops had always told Rylan that one day it would be his, but Rylan wanted no part of it. His Pops would tell him it didn't matter, that the Pipe had already chosen him, that it was just waiting to be passed on, automatically attaching itself to the next generation.

The thing was eerie—long and warped, like a dark wizard's staff, its blackened chamber tilting forward for an easy light. You could see it's fire brewing deep withing its guts. It reeked of decay—a sour, heavy stench that clung to the air like a bad omen. At night, when Pops sat alone, the pipe's ember would flicker, painting his outline in a dull glow—sharp jaw, black spiky hair, slumped shoulders, a shadowed figure haloed in smoke. That sight was burrowed into Rylan's dreams and would often wake him in a cold sweat, the smell still burning in his nose.

It got worse when Pops would invite Mr. Whiskey home. The bottle and pipe turned him into something different—his shouts or ragged breaths spitting fire, a bitter haze of smoke and liquor that stung the air. It wasn't just the glow; it was the weight of it, pressing Rylan and his mother down, shrinking them into silence. Pops' eyes gleamed, hard and distant, the ember flared in the dark. Those nights, Rylan huddled tight, watching that light, heart thudding as he held on to the memories of *her*. The fear lingered, but deep down, he clung to a promise—**Follow the Sound of the Water**—a thread of hope against the shadow creeping closer.

The old man moved slowly, deliberately, reaching for the kitchen table lamp with the scrape of a match that hissed like a warning. The room bloomed in sickly yellow, peeling back the dark to reveal him fully. A worn Bible was on display, laying open on the table. Rylan knew the exact verse it would display. He stood there in silent judgment as dread clawed up his spine, cold and sharp as a blade pressed to his throat.

"Where you been, boy?"

* * *

The kitchen lamp sputtered, throwing shadows across the table. His father sat hulked in the corner, pipe smoke curling around him like a noose tightening slowly, the cherry glow flaring red in his sharp eyes. Rylan's heart thumped wild as he faced the storm brewing in his father's stare. His mind raced, scrambling for a lifeline. He couldn't spill the truth—not *her*, not the creek, not the storm *she'd* unleashed inside of him. He licked his lips, tasting the memory of the sweetest Lemonade, and stepped forward.

"I—uh—I was hunting, Pops. Down past the oaks, chasing a buck. Got turned around in the thick of it, lost track of time. You know how it gets out there, all man against the wild."

The lie hung thin as creek mist, and his father's eyes narrowed, darting back and forth like the arm of a polygraph. He leaned forward, chair groaning under his weight, and sucked on the pipe, smoke billowing into Rylan's face in a slow, deliberate cloud.

"Hunting, huh?" His voice was a blade, cutting through the nonsense. "You, a scrawny little boy, tracking a buck past dusk with no rifle, no knife, just muddy trousers and a grin, you think I'm a fool, boy?" He tapped the table with his burnt out pipe, hard, the sound of a gavel cracking in the silence. "Try again. Truth this time—or you'll wish you had..."

Rylan tried to swallow his stomach back down, the lie crumbling like wet dirt in his hands. His fingers twitched, still warm with the memory of the smell of *her* hair—golden, tangled, real—and *her* voice whispering in his subconscious:

Water...

He couldn't bury *her*, not under his father's glare. He swallowed hard, voice trembling but firm.

"All right, Pops. No buck. I was... I was at the creek, with a girl. We fished, skipped stones, and stayed late. That's it. I swear."

The old man's brow arched, smoke curling from his nostrils like a monster from beneath the surface, sizing up a kill. He leaned back, chair creaking, and let out a rough laugh—short, bitter, cutting.

"A girl?" Disbelief dripped from every word. "Oh yeah, smart guy? What's this girl's name, then?"

Rylan froze, chest tightening like a trap springing shut. *Her* name—he didn't have it, just a void where it should've been. His mouth opened, then shut, words dying on his tongue. His father's laugh turned cold, eyes glinting with triumph.

"That's what I thought. No way some girl is hanging out with you all day and into the night. That's rich... You're spinning tales again, boy, and I ain't buying it... A girl... you wouldn't even know what to do with one..."

Heat flared up in Rylan's chest—not just shame, but anger, sharp and alive. He shot to his feet, chair scraping the floor and banging loud against the wall.

"*She's* real! *She's—she's* better'n any buck! *She* caught a fish big as my arm, laughed like thunder, called me *her* King—" His voice cracked, fists balled tight, the memory of *her* kiss burning his cheek. "You don't know nu thin about it!"

His father surged up, like lava rising from the cauldron, and in one swift move, his hand clamped Rylan's shoulder next to his throat with the grip of a bear trap. He shoved him back into the chair with a force that rattled his teeth. Rylan struggled to gather himself while his Pops chuckled deviously, but had been reminded once again of who the power player in the situation truly was.

"Don't you dare rise up to me, boy," his father snarled, looming close, tobacco breath heavy, burning Rylan's eyes. "And you'll watch that mouth 'fore I stuff it full of wash rags and soap. I brought you into this world, I can most assuredly take you out."

Rylan glared up, defiance flickering under the sting, but his father's eyes were pure black, stone, unyielding. Times like these Rylan swore he could see an amber glowing, burning under his father's shirt where his heart was supposed to be. The old man straightened, chest heaving, and ran a hand through his black spiky long hair,

"I'm too dang tired for this crap tonight." He pointed a long thick finger, voice dropping low and mean right in Rylan's face... "We'll revisit this when I've had time to think it over—when I ain't so wore out I can't see straight. You'll understand then—mark my words boy."

Rylan's heart sank. Time to think it over meant only one thing—until his pops next bender...

"Bed! Now! And don't think for a second this is done."

Pops eyed him up and down and pointed toward the stairs. It was a promise, heavy as the reckoning Rylan knew was coming. This was the worst possible outcome. Rylan was hoping to get it over with and settled, but now he would spend the next undefined amount of time fearing what was surely in his future...

Rylan stumbled up the stairs, legs leaden, the mud on his feet smearing the steps. He collapsed onto his bed, still in his damp clothes, the scent of creek water, mud, and his new found friend clinging to him like a secret he couldn't shake.

He didn't want to bathe or wash his clothes until he knew when he could smell *her* again... His cheek burned where *she'd* kissed him, *her* words—"*waiting for my King*"—a lifeline in the dark.

Dusty's

Mr. Whiskeys visits usually turned the old man's temper from stern to savage, but sometimes he'd get happy and just chase Mamma around the house. When he'd catch her, they'd wrestle their way into the bedroom where the match would usually get a lot more intense. They would shout at each other, with lots of banging on the walls between heavy huffing, and hollering for God's and Jesus's mercy. Rylan was always baffled at how they would work it all out in the end, and both could come out of the room happy after a confrontation of such sorts.

"Your father's a good man, Rylan, just Old Testament in his ways."

Mamma would say it over and over again a hundred times, as if the more she said it the truer it would become. Maybe it was just her feckless way of trying to protect them all from the monsters that grew inside of him.

She always remembered the young man she had met at the church dance, his shy smile flickering like a candle in the dim glow of the fellowship hall. He was young then, innocent—or so she thought—his eyes catching hers across the scuffed wooden floor as the music hummed. That very afternoon, he followed her home, trailing a few steps behind like a lost pup, and somehow, he just never left.

They were eleventh graders when their story took root, two kids tangled up in a love that felt like fate. High school blurred into stolen glances and whispered promises. They had a history that stitched them tight—flowers pressed into her heart, Valentine's cards scrawled with clumsy devotion, proms where they swayed too close, church socials where their laughter rang out over the hum of hymns.

She could still taste the sweetness of that pie she'd baked for Pops to take to the church's charity auction. It fetched sixty-seven dollars—the highest bid of the night. Peach and Apple Crunch Delight, she'd called it, and Pops had grinned wide as the preacher handed the money to a family whose roof had caved in after a storm, his name tied to something good.

Back then, he chased her with a thirst that had no quench, relentless and wild. Nights when the moon hung low, he'd tap at her bedroom window, his shadow stretching long across the sill. She'd slip out, heart pounding, bare feet brushing the dew-soaked grass as he whisk her away—always back before the rooster crowed, before her daddy's boots hit the floor. They married young, too young perhaps, and Pops took life by storm, a force she couldn't harness nor tame.

There were cracks—even then, if she'd dared to look. The night after prom, when the air still smelled of corsages and cheap cologne, he'd shouted at her over something small—her laugh, her dress, she couldn't recall. Her brother stepped in, all bravado and protective fury, and Pops' fist met his jaw with a crack that echoed in her skull for years. Sometimes he'd make her sit silent for hours, his eyes hard as flint, his voice a low growl while he watched Sunday afternoon ball games. He was pretty set on how he liked things and she told herself it was just his way, that the good outweighed the bad. She'd brushed it off, dazzled by the roses he'd bring the next day, the way he'd pull her close and call her his world.

* * *

It wasn't until Rylan arrived that the shadows grew teeth. Pops had been a whirlwind before, all charm and restless energy, but the baby's first cry seemed to unsettle him. Pops' own father had taken him to Dusty's Club the night Rylan entered the world, while Mamma lay sleeping in the hospital alone, healing from hard labor.

A gruff clap on the back and a bottle between them to toast the new life. After that night Pops seemed to change, Mr. Whiskey sank its claws in deep, a friend that lingered long after the glasses were drained. Pops started coming home late, reeking of smoke and sour mash, his laughter turning sharp, his hands unsteady. Mamma saw it— the way his eyes dulled, the way his voice could cut—but she clung to the boy from the church dance, the one who'd followed her home.

When Pops' father passed, it was a quiet death that left a void he filled with more than grief. The pipe had been handed down. He'd sit by the fire, puffing slow, the smoke curling upward like ghosts escaping a grave. She'd watch him, the flicker of the flames catching the lines in his face, and feel a chill she couldn't name. Something was shifting, something heavy settling in the air between them. The boy she'd loved was still there, buried somewhere beneath, but the man he'd become cast a shadow she couldn't outrun.

Rylan slept in the next room, a soft bundle of hope, but even his coos couldn't drown out the dread creeping into her bones. She'd lie awake, wondering how long she could hold on to the memory of that church dance before the darkness swallowed it whole.

* * *

It was early 1980 something, and Eldergrove had been gutted. At one point in time it was a bustling town of 3,200 souls when the waters through town ran full—before they shriveled down into a slow leak. The steel plants raged like dragons along the riverbanks, their smokestacks belching fire and fortune into the sky. In the 1960s and '70s, the town thrummed with life: mill workers in greasy overalls crowding the diners, trucks rumbling through with loads of raw ore, and families building lives on streets that stretched hopeful and wide.

The farms and ranches surrounding the town were abundant with life and fresh produce, and the markets around town thrived. The plants were the heartbeat, pumping jobs and dreams into every corner—and while the steel plants employed most of the towns folk, the ranches and farmers kept them all fed.

A group of gypsy types had found their way into town and started a little commune out on the edges. They would show up in town on Sunday mornings to the little old Church in the square that had been redeemed, and rejuvenated into something that had been freed from religion. A young man with long twisty hair was it's keeper. His name was Ezekiel Moonchild. He had recently taken over and the first thing he did was hang an old hand painted sign above the door reading, **Jesus Loves Everyone.**

Ezekiel had become the genial landlord of the quaint shops encircling Eldergroves square as well as much of the town's surrounding properties. He had received them all by default from family hand me downs, due to being the only one left of his lines. He would hang around the huge, *Tree* in the center of town, that the locals referred to as the *Tree of Life*. The rumors were that the giant *Tree* guarded the entrance into Eldergrove's deepest secrets.

Ezekiel would push his seat-less bicycle all over, delivering packages and mail to everyone. With a warm smile and a slight bow, he handed fresh-picked wildflowers and small tokens of his admiration to all the ladies, offering compliments—on anything he could find—charming his way into their hearts and the latest gossip. He carried pockets full of candy and new a few magic tricks as well, that would create a fan base of children that would follow him on his daily strolls. He made his rounds, visiting each shop and the weathered Old Church, exchanging pleasantries and news. At day's end, he would settle into the rocking chair on the porch of the square's only vacant shop. He would whittle away at a tall pole out front that he was crafting, its peak destined to bear a gleaming crescent moon. He had the perfect tenant in mind for his empty old shop, but she was still chasing dreams, and traveling time. The seer inside him knew that one day his lifelong friend Zora Thornweaver would wind her way back to him, and he had a place for her in waiting.

By the late 1970s, well before Rylan's small family had wondered into the town in Hotel Chevrolet, the waters that had given life to Eldergrove had all but relinquished, the towns wells had dried up, and the old rusty dragons went quiet, shuttered one by one as the steel industry shriveled and moved overseas. With them went the people. Slowly, year by year, the town emptied out—families chasing work elsewhere, leaving behind sagging porches and For Sale signs that held no inspiration. Now, only 1,260 remained, a stubborn remnant clinging to the bones of what was.

Half of them were the old Gypsy leftovers. Pops called them the *Bohemians*, gray-haired wanderers who'd drifted in over time, drawn by the cheap land and the middle-of-nowhere quiet. They built shacks and trailers out past the creek, tending fields of weed, and distilling liquid gold, under the lax eye of a pretend sheriff.

The other half were homegrown families, some farmers and ranchers, their roots sunk deep into Eldergrove's soil, land passed down through generations, like a family Bible—worn, cherished, and unyielding. These were the folks who stayed when the plants closed, who weathered the lean years with calloused hands and stories of better days, their names etched into the town's crumbling brick and rusted mailboxes.

Eldergrove still had its unique bones—the school with its chipped and worn banana yellow paint, the church with its crooked steeple that had once been blown up by a lightning strike, the courthouse where the clock froze at

3:17 one stormy night and never moved again until one of the Bohemians supposedly climbed up there amid a moonshine bender and set it at 4:20, whatever for who knows, but one place stood out...

A shadow among the faded storefronts: the "Members Only Club," as Pops called it, though the sign out front just read *Dusty's* in peeling red cursive. It was a squat, two-story Saloon built way back when half the men still wore guns around the town. It was wrapped with warped clapboard walls and windows that stared blankly onto Main Street. Its old swingin double doors had since been replaced by a big metal one that you had to knock on and give em your credentials to enter. The boy had been inside once, years back... before Bubba...

* * *

Pop's luck had actually been riding high on a winning streak at the card table—his pockets loaded with "paper" he called it, his grin wide and reckless. There was an ice storm brewin that night and it was too cold for the boy to wait outside in Hotel Chevrolet, so Pops had dragged him in, a skinny little kid in an oversize hand-me-down jacket, through the saloon's creaky door.

Inside, the air was thick with smoke and the twang of guitars. A couple of local Bohemians creating the soundtrack, perched on stools, picking strings and attempting tunes from a band they called *The Dead.* A knot of men hunched over a table, including the bartender, cards snapping against the wood, smoke, laughter and curses rising in bursts. The players taking turns putting money on the table and casting doubtful eyes at each other.

Three women, who looked to be about the same age as Mamma, perched on a sagging couch near the bar. They sat smoking, chatting in low tones, and smiling crooked and inviting like at the players when they could catch a glance. The women's eyes were sharp but tired, and their faces pale under days old makeup. Rylan couldn't figure them out—why were they just hanging around, looking hungry and all worn out? He'd thought maybe they were wives waiting on their husbands to cash out, but then Pops had tossed back a whiskey and returned a smile at one of them. Just like that, they headed up the secret back stairs, disappearing behind a curtain, leaving Rylan blinking at the empty space.

When Pops beat the cards, and got to treat himself to what he deemed **quality time,** he would usually be fine when he came home, but when he lost the games, he would come home and spend most of the afternoon with Mr. Whiskey and the word of the *Good Lord.* He always started off our **Lessons** with the same subject. Rylan had heard it what seemed to be a hundred times at least, and it still didn't make a bit of sense to him...

Withhold not correction from the child: for if thou punish him, he shall not die. Thou shalt punish him, and shalt deliver his soul from Hell.

Pops would read it slow, voice booming, explaining how every lick was God's will, and how it'd make Rylan right. Rylan just figured if Mamma and the Bible said so...

Alone

It had been a week or maybe more since Pops had promised retribution, and Rylan had hoped for forgetfulness. He found himself alone, the air heavy with the ghosts of chaos. Mamma had slipped out hours before, bound for Auntie Lulu's house down the lane—a ritual escape that usually stretched into multiple glasses of the sweet stuff and a sleepover that would leave Rylan alone with the dark currents within their home.

The room around him was a battlefield: the rickety chair toppled near the desk, books splayed open like wounded birds, and an old dented-up tin canteen that had been flung against the wall lay injured yet again. He huddled in the corner, wedged between the bed and the peeling plaster, his body a map of aches—ribs throbbing, stomach tight, hip screaming with every shift.

That was a pretty bad one, his thoughts echoed in his skull, sharp and hollow, **maybe the worst one ever.**

He reached up, hand trembling, and snagged the edge of the quilt from the bed, tugging it down in a slow, heavy heap. The blankets were warm, draped over him like a shield—soft, worn, a flimsy fortress against the cold and darkness seeping in from the world around him. Rylan pulled them tighter, wrapping himself in layers until he was cocooned, swaddled like an infant craving the safety of a mother's arms.

His breath was ragged and shallow, and a hot sting pricked his eyes. Tears slipped freely, tracing paths through the grime on his cheeks, and he cursed himself silently.

Men don't cry—his father's voice, gravelly and unyielding, roared in his head. *Men take it. Men stand tall.*

But here he was, curled small, and the shame burned hotter than the bruises blooming across his skin.

* * *

A few days of false peace had passed, with Rylan continuously on edge. Pops had come home late from the saloon, the soured stink trailing him like a shadow. Rylan had heard the door slam, the boots stomp, the mutter of a man who'd brought home his fury. The afternoon unraveled in shouts and the crash of fists, a storm Rylan couldn't outrun.

It was hours before the house was quiet, broken only by the faint creak of settling wood. Rylan waited, ear pressed to the floor, until the last echo of movement faded, trying desperately not to draw any more attention in his direction. After a few hours, the half-stomping footsteps, and curses had ceased.

He peeled the blankets back, the air biting his damp skin, and tried to lift himself. Pain lanced through him, so hard he bit his lip to stifle the groan. He gripped the bed frame, sitting himself up inch by inch. The taste of blood lingering on his tongue, bitter and metallic, mingling with the memory of Pops forcing cold grits down his throat mid-rage.

His mouth was a desert—parched, sticky like someone had poured Elmer's glue down his gullet. All he could think of was Mamma's Lemonade, that tart-sweet salvation—a lifeline shimmering in his mind's eye. It would wash away the hurt and quench the fire in his throat, if he could just get to it.

Standing up straight was a pipe dream at this point—his spine screamed, bent him double—so he gripped the stair rail and hauled his battered body down, step by agonizing step. Each shuffle was a gamble, his ears straining for the monster's growl, but he knew the routine by heart. Pops would be slumped low in his seat on the couch, passed out cold, a half-empty whiskey bottle tipped over, tobacco spilling like ash from a grave next to his pipe. It was a scene etched into Rylan's skull, a grim still life of the man who'd raised him and broke him in the same breath.

He made it down silently and the kitchen loomed ahead, shadows clawing at the edges of his vision. He eased in and carefully opened the fridge, hinges whining soft as a whisper, and there it was—one last glass's worth in the pitcher, glowing faint yellow under the dim bulb. His hands shook as he snatched it, pouring a sloppy gulp straight into his mouth, no need for a glass. The Lemonade quenched, hitting his soul like Communion—it was tart as a slap and sweet as Mamma's voice, stinging the raw cuts inside his cheeks. He winced, the acid biting deeper than usual, a bitter-sweet burn that mirrored the night.

He choked out a silent laugh, privately, quietly thinking to himself, *Ain't never as bad after the storm, as it feels when you're in the thick of the hurricane.*

The sting lingered, sharp against his busted lip, but courage flickered alive in his gut. He wiped his mouth, wincing as his knuckles grazed the swelling, and limped into the abyss toward the living room. He crept through the doorway, heart thudding like a war drum. He eased his head around the frame, just enough to catch the back of Pops' skull, slouched heavy against the couch cushions.

Some late-night yahoo named Dave was yammering through the static on the *Idiot Box*. Pops was snoring—rumbling like an old classic Shovel Head—passed out cold, whiskey fumes rising off him like heat off asphalt.

Rylan stood motionless in the dim flicker of Pops' old lamp, a shadowy figure swallowed by the night's heavy silence, his breath shallow as he watched his father snoring halfway sitting up, head bobbed down at an angle resting on his chest. He was, defenseless...

Rylan felt it in the pit of his gut, a dark pulse urging him toward retribution. He could strike now. Pops lay helpless, a mirror to the countless times those thick, calloused hands had crashed against him and his Mamma, leaving bruises that faded slower than the fear. The thought coiled tight in his mind, tempting him with its weight, a promise of something horrible yet justified.

His gaze drifted downward, catching the glint of the ember still burning in the half-full pipe.. A thin wisp of smoke still curled from its blackened bowl, faint but alive, like a whisper of the chaos it fueled. He could snatch it, hide it somewhere deep in the hollows, and Pops might never suspect him, but that thought soured fast. Pops would turn that rage on Mamma, and Rylan couldn't bear to imagine the fallout, the way her eyes would dim further under that shadow.

Then a worse notion slithered in, unbidden and cold, as if planted by some unseen hand. Dark to its core, it gripped him—violent, foreign—a stranger's voice in his head whispering of blood and finality. His mind spun, dizzy with the how. What would Mamma say, her voice trembling between grief and relief? Could jail—its cold bars and hollow echoes—possibly be worse than this house, this life, where every creak of the floorboards carried a threat? The question clawed at him: could he push through it, cross that line, become the dark shadow he now cast?

Rylan's gaze swept the room, the lamp light flickered, casting jagged shapes across the walls. There, by the hearth, a poker jutted from its stand like a blackened claw—cold iron whispering of vengeance. His eyes then darted to the mantle, where a tin of lighter fluid glinted dully. It ignited thoughts of flames roaring through the house, devouring every trace of his father's cherished world. His mind raced with all the dark possibilities.

Suddenly something beckoned him... his glossed over stare locked onto the knife. It lay gleaming on the counter top, a blade meant to provide nourishment, now poised to carve out retribution. He was being pulled toward it. He reached out, as though his arm was no longer his. His grip tightened around its handle, the metal cool and unforgiving against his palm.

The darkness guiding him promised freedom for him, for his mother—a chance to escape the suffocating chains of this life. He turned, the knife steady in his hand, and stared at his fathers oblivious figure. The air thickened with the weight of what was to come, and in the dimness, Rylan's thoughts coiled tighter as he stood on the edge of an abyss about to swallow them all.

He stood frozen, the air thick with pipe tobacco and whiskey's sour bite, the temptation swelling like a storm cloud ready to burst. His father's chest rose and fell with every gasp for air, while Rylan's heart thundered, teetering on the edge of a choice that could snuff out the boy he'd been and birth something darker in his place.

Rylan straightened as best he could, a broken boy playing man. He hobbled towards his Pops, each step a quiet defiance. His eyes glared with a burning hate for his Pops, a compromised titan whose chest rose slow and ragged. Rylan's breath hitched, a knot twisting in his throat. He stepped close enough to smell the sweat and ruin, his hands were trembling, not from fear but something deeper, something raw.

He raised the knife, tears filling his eyes and soul, and readied himself for the darkness already written.

* * *

He stood defiantly as his hands moved on instinct, steady despite darkened draw. He placed the knife down on the old coffee table. He capped the whiskey—and slid it onto the shelf where it belonged. He swept the tobacco back into its pouch, stuffing it tight, then lined it up neatly while smothering the pipe and setting it near the matches, just how Pops liked it kept...

Gentle as Rylan had never been allowed to be, he slid his arms around his Pops' neck, leaned him forward, turned him, eased him down, and laid him flat on the couch with a pillow for his head, accepting the risk of a newborn ceremony of wrath if the beast were to be awakened...

His Pops didn't stir, just grunted softly, a sound that might've been peaceful if you didn't know any better. Rylan lifted his feet—one at a time, heavy as sin—slipping off the scuffed boots, leather worn thin from years of stomping through life. He hoisted those legs onto the cushions, careful, like tending a wounded bear that might still swipe at him.

Rylan grabbed Pops' favorite quilt—Mamma's handiwork—the patches read like little candy hearts; Patched with Love, World's Best Father, DADDY with a heart around it. Rylan continued tucking it around his broad frame, careful not to disturb the slumbering giant.

He stepped back, chest tight, eyes burning. Tears slipped freely, hot and unstoppable, streaking through the grime on his face. Shame overwhelmed him. He swiped them off with a rough arm, angry at the leak, but they kept coming—silent, stubborn—a flood he couldn't dam.

Men don't cry.

Pops' voice growled inside his head, but Rylan stood there anyway, baptized in his tears for the father he loved, the monster he feared, the man he couldn't quit.

He reached for the old lamp—Pops' favorite, a relic from better days—and twisted the knob, dimming it to a soft glow that softened the hard lines of the room. Shadows danced across Pops' face, smoothing the rage into something almost human. Rylan picked up the blade calling from the table, looked at his father with his fists tightly clenched, and a breath shuddered out of him.

"I forgive you, Poppa..."

Caged

Time had crawled by slowly since that beautiful day at the creek. It always became blurry in the haze of confinement. That day in the Kingdom glowed in his mind, a sunlit escape he revisited over and over, drowning out the reality of being locked in this door-less cage. Pops had ripped the door off its hinges after that night, a further punishment to ensure Rylan wouldn't run away before he was deemed fit for parole.

Mamma and Pops fought most days and nights now, their voices a jagged chorus. It was mostly about Rylan—his Lessons, his defiance, his very existence. Mamma didn't see the need to imprison him any longer; he'd already taken his beating, she pleaded, but Pops wasn't done being mad. These things took time with him, festering like a stubborn wound that just wouldn't heal.

Some nights, the screaming stretched on until it turned physical—Rylan could hear the struggle, Mamma's gasps for air, the thuds of resistance. Trapped upstairs, he could only imagine, while fighting to block it all out.

He'd focus on the *Sound of Water* instead—her words, a velvet promise echoing from that spring day. He'd picture the creek, its ripples quenching his thirst, its currents hiding both her and the Dragonfish. She was there, waiting, and so was his foe—a beast he'd slay with a perfect fiver shot in his pursuit of his Princess, if it came down to it. The fiver loads and his daydreams were his way back to her, and he clung to them like a prayer.

* * *

After the worst fights, Mamma would creep in, her face shadowed with exhaustion. She'd kneel beside Rylan, press a soft kiss to his forehead, and whisper,

"I love you, Ry. Everything's gonna be alright."

Her voice was balm, shaky but sure, and she'd sing "*Three Little Birds,*" their song.

"Baby Don't Worry.... 'bout a thang... 'cuz every little thang is gonna be alright."

She'd warble off-key, and he'd harmonize equally, his cracked voice weaving with hers. They would laugh fearfully at how awful they sounded, singing in whispers so as not to interrupt a temporary, fragile thread of peace. She'd sneak him scraps of dinner when she could—cold biscuits, a hunk of meat—her hands trembling as she passed them over. She was scared, terrified, but she stayed, rooted in this hell, a battered shield between Rylan and the monster downstairs. He knew it, felt it in his bones: she endured this storm for him, her baby boy, taking the blows so they wouldn't all land on his breaking body. Every bite she stole for him was a quiet sob, a piece of her heart she could still manage to give.

Rylan didn't know why Pops hated him, what spark he'd struck to set that blaze raging in his father's soul. It swelled and crashed like a tide born of some deep, hidden current—wilder with each surge, darker with every breaker—its waves scorching through their fragile lives, scalding Mamma's quiet pleas, searing Rylan's frail frame, leaving embers in the air they all shared. Still, God forgave him, Rylan loved him—Pops, his father, a man hardened by a torment too vast to chart, a violent history with his own monster submerged beneath the surface, its heat festering, waiting to burst forth in a plume of ruin that could turn them all to ash.

Rylan laid there, a prisoner, he wept—tears spilling hot and helpless—not just for his own splintered shell, but for his father, consumed by that hidden pool of molten lava boiling deep in his soul. He mourned the father he'd never know again, lost to a dark fury. Rylan could almost see it flicker, with scales in the dark of his gaze, a beast born of their tie. The bruises would dull, the cuts would mend, but this wound—the why of it, the love scorched into dread—tore open, raw and relentless. No blanket could shield it, no song could hush its roar, no whispered plea could sever the bond that birthed it—a hurt that thundered in his dreams, forged in depths he feared to name.

Mamma Bear

A few weeks had passed by. Rylan lay sprawled beneath his patchwork quilt. A flashlight's beam cut through the dark, spilling gold over the worn pages of *Treasure Island.* Jim Hawkins was just setting sail, the sea calling him like the creek once called Rylan, and he traced the words with a finger, lost within their pull. His transistor radio hummed low, a tinny whisper of old '70s tunes he and his Mamma used to dance to—guitars weaving through the static, a hymn to simpler days. He kept it quiet, real quiet, because the house had ears, and he didn't want Pops' shadow creeping up the stairs. His room still sat gate-less, that doorless frame a mocking boundary.

Rylan's mind drifted, half-dreams flickering like fireflies. *Her*—Jade eyes glinting off the spring, *her* voice a ripple in his chest. He saw *her* in the dark, barefoot by the old fallen Tree, fish swirling at *her* hem, and he wondered if *she* dreamed of him too. Sleep tugged at him, heavy as creek mud, and he sank into it, the book slipping to his chest, the radio's croon fading to a murmur.

BANG!

An echo roared through the house, sharp as a shotgun blast, and Rylan's eyes snapped wide. He near tumbled from the bed, heart hammering like a fiver load slung at a tin can. The quilt tangled round his legs as he froze, ears straining. Shuffling feet—quick, uneven. A shout, low and slurred, then another, higher, fiercer. And then Mamma's voice cleaved the night like a blade through Honeysuckle:

"I AM DONE CARL!"

Rylan's breath caught. He'd never heard her like that—not soft, not hushed, not the gentle hum of her kitchen hymns. This was a roar, a thunderhead breaking over the Kingdom, and it yanked him upright. Something was wrong, bad wrong, and he had to see. He slid from the bed, knees brushing the cool floorboards, and crept to the stairs edge. His hazel eyes peered through the railing's slats, and what he saw lit a fire in his gut.

There she stood—Mother—silhouetted in the dim glow of the living room's single bulb. Her sundress hung loose, stained with flour from supper's biscuits, but she wasn't the quiet woman who'd kneaded dough that night. No, this was a warrior, a Mamma Bear roused from her den, and she was fearsome.

In her right hand gleamed a chopping knife, its blade catching the light like the Dragonfish's amber eye—sharp, unforgiving. In her left, she gripped her brand-new cast iron pan, heavy as sin and most likely lethal, its black curve a shield and a promise.

She'd cornered Pops by the sagging couch, his broad frame shrunk against the wall, and Rylan saw it plain: she'd had enough. Pops rubbed a lump on his forehead, a red welt blooming where that pan must've kissed him good. His eyes were glassy, he'd been dancing with Mr. Whiskey again, drowning whatever scraps of poet he had left, and Mom wasn't letting it slide—not this time. His shirt hung open, buttons popped, and he swayed, one hand raised like he could ward her off. But Mom advanced, slow, deliberate, her bare feet planting firm on the warped floor. Another lump was coming his way.

"You listen here, Carl,"

Her voice low now, a growl that shook the bones of the house.

"You don't let up on Ry, I swear to the Lord above and the Devil below, I'll give you what's comin'. I've borne your storm long enough—your fists, your bottle, your black fire—but you don't touch my boy no more. He's off limits, you hear? Mine!"

Rylan's chest tightened, a knot of awe and fear twisting up inside. She was claiming him and it hit him fierce—she'd been quiet all these years not because she was weak, but because she was waiting. Biding her time, soaking up all the hurt until it boiled over.

Pops muttered something, slurred and mean, but Mom cut him off, knife slashing the air an inch from his chest.

"I'll wait,"

Her eyes blazing, wild as the creek in a storm.

"I'll wait 'til you're snoring, dead to the world, and I'll take this knife—"

She hefted it higher, light dancing off it's edge—

"and I'll remove your most valued possessions. You'll wake up less a man than you ever dreamed of Carl, and I—won't—shed—a—tear..."

She leaned over him with a fire in her eyes that could melt steel.

"You git the hell out of my house. You go sleep it off in the shed, under the truck, in the damn ditch like the animal you are—I don't care. But you're out of my house 'til you reckon for what you've done."

Pops blinked, slow, he rubbed that lump again, wincing, and Rylan saw a flicker—fear maybe, or shame. But Mamma didn't flinch. She stood tall, pan cocked like a cannon, knife steady as the Tree of Life's roots, and Rylan knew she meant every word. She'd do it. She'd carve him down to nothing if he pushed her, and something in that made Rylan's throat burn with pride.

He thought back—days blurring into years—of her softness. Her hands kneading dough while Pops raged, her voice soothing Rylan's bruises with lullabies, her Lemonade stretching to fill empty bellies when the pantry ran bare. She'd been the thread holding them together, stitching up the rips Pops tore through their lives. When Bubba came screaming into the world, she'd cradled him like a miracle, whispering prayers over his crib.

When he'd gone, she'd wept silent, her tears watering the Kingdom's dirt while Pops drowned in his bottle. She'd borne it all—his fists on her arm, his boots on the floor, his curses on the wind—and still she'd poured love into Rylan and into this broken family.

But now—she was done bleeding. She'd snapped, and it was glorious. Rylan saw the woman she must've been—before Pops, before the weight of Eldergrove pressed her down—fire in her veins, who'd danced barefoot in the creek and who'd laughed under the Honeysuckle moon. That person had roared back to life, and she was fighting—for him. She wasn't just Mamma no more—she was a force, a shield, a love so vast it swallowed the night itself.

Pops staggered back, hands up now, muttering,

"Alright, alright, I'll go."

He fumbled for his coat, and lurched toward the door. Mom didn't lower her weapons, not until the screen slammed shut and his boots crunched down the gravel path, fading into the darkness. Only then did she exhale, a shudder running through her, and the knife clattered to the floor. The pan stayed in her grip, like she might need it yet, and she sank down onto the couch.

Rylan crept down a step, then another, heart pounding. He wanted to run to her, to bury his face in her sundress and tell her he'd seen it all, that he loved her fierce and true. But he stopped, caught by the sight of her shoulders shaking—not crying, no, but trembling with the weight of what she'd done. She'd drawn a line, a boundary stronger than any cage less room, and it was for him.

He slipped back to his room, flashlight forgotten, radio still humming. He climbed under the quilt, Treasure Island left open, but his mind wasn't on Jim Hawkins no more. It was on Mamma—she'd turned the Kingdom's quiet into a battlefield, and she'd won. The girl's face flickered in his dreams again, but now it was joined by Mamma's, fierce and unbroken, an angel with a flour-dusted halo.

Rylan knew, deep in his bones, that whatever came next—Pops' return, the creek's whispers, the world beyond—he'd fight for Mamma, 'cause she'd fought for him, and that was a love worth slaying dragons for.

Freedom

Rylan awoke to a house stripped of its usual weight, the air was eerily still, void of Pops' brooding shadow. Rylan shuffled downstairs, ribs still tender, hip creaking like an old hinge, smell of bacon blessing the air. He found his Mamma in the kitchen, her face softer than it'd been in weeks. She turned, her eyes catching the morning light, smiled faintly and said,

"He's gone, Ry—You have officially been released—free to go." Her voice trembled, a mix of relief and warning.

"Officially, official"? He asked smiling, with a grin that could melt a frozen heart.

They both broke out with heart felt, yet reserved laughs. She looked at him and swore she could see his back end wiggling just like a joy filled puppy,

"Just, for God's sake, please just be back by dinner, Ry—don't give him a reason to come looking..."

Rylan nodded quickly, a promise he'd keep for her sake, not his.

Freedom hit him like a lightning bolt—his whole body buzzed, a wild hum racing through his veins. The creek, the Kingdom, *her*—it all flooded back, bright and alive. He tore upstairs, each step a jolt of pain and thrill, and paused at the top grinning like a fool.

He busted out dancing—*The Running Man*—legs pumping awkwardly, dancing white boy face, and free at last. He then twisted into the—*MC Hammer*—arms flailing as he timed it just right—"Hammertime!"—a shout that echoed off the bare walls. The dance was clumsy, pure, joyful, a burst of life chasing away the shadows.

He dove for his bed, shoving a hand under the pillows, fingers closing around his fiver loads—his last stash. He loaded them into the pocket of his war pants—those patched overalls—right where his Fiver loader, could snatch them up quickly.

Outside, the sun blazed high, promising a long, hot day, perfect for the adventure he'd been dreaming of through every locked-down night. He bolted back down the stairs barely laying feet to any of them, calling, "Mom! Lemonade—please!"

She smiled, and filled up his half-collapsed canteen. She handed him his lunch, wrapped up with a note inside—leaned over and kissed him on the forehead. Rylan immediately reached up and wiped it off....

"Hey now..." Mamma did her best impression of taking offense.

Rylan smiled sheepishly at her in return. He was ready to roll, armed with a canteen of Mamma's love, a half a spam sandwich, with government cheese and butter, and a handful of Saltines all wrapped and stuffed into his satchel along with four fiver loads buzzing in his pocket, his fishing pole, and a coffee can half full of night-crawlers, filling out his arsenal...

He ran to the front yard, his canteen hung heavy at his side, Mamma's Lemonade sloshing inside—a treasure he'd rationed in his mind down to the last precious sips. He licked his lips, but he wouldn't touch it. Not yet.

That Lemonade was for *her*—for the Kingdom, for the creek, for the bigger cause whispering through his soul. He'd save it, share it, let it seal their next moment with sweet nectar. His eyes darted to the garden hose coiled like a green snake by the porch. Best water on earth, hands down—cold as a mountain spring, straight from some deep, secret place beneath Eldergrove. Life's Juice, straight up.

He grinned, decision made, and lunged for it, twisting the spigot with a squeak. The hose sputtered for a moment and then exploded like a geyser. Steaming hot water shot out that morphed into warm stale water—then magically reincarnated itself into the icy fresh juice of life that helped define summertime. He was spraying his head and face while biting and slurping at it like a big old dog. He cupped more of it to his mouth, gulping fast and wild, the chill hitting his teeth like a shock. It was so good—pure, crisp, alive—he couldn't stop, drinking till his belly swelled tight against his overalls, sloshing with every breath.

Dizzy hit him hard—too much, too fast. His head spun, vision blurring, and his stomach groaned in revolt. A massive burp rumbled up, loud and wet, half the water spewing back out in a spray that soaked his front side. Rylan staggered, laughing—a sharp, goofy bark of a laugh that echoed off the house.

"Well, that's one way to do it."

He wiped his mouth with the back of his hand, still chuckling at his own dumb glory.

Straightening up, he took a deep breath, the air sharp with Honeysuckle and freedom. He had no clue that a kindred soul was observing his battle with the water hose, but he was ready for the journey lay ahead. The Kingdom called—*her* voice in the water, the Dragonfish's scales glinting in the deep. Rylans hazel eyes locked on the horizon, that wild line where earth meets sky, and he took off—full sprint, legs pumping, heart pounding, a boy unbound racing toward whatever waited beyond.

* * *

Rylan skidded to a halt, his sprint to find her slowing as his lungs screamed for mercy. He collapsed beneath the shade of an ancient oak, its gnarled branches sprawling wide, a fortress against the searing mid-Summers sun. Clouds moved mysteriously through the vast sea of blue, his mind focused upward. He wondered what it'd feel like to stroll across the cotton candy landscape—were they as soft as they looked, plush and yielding underfoot? How did they cradle all that water before it rained, heavy yet floating, defying the pull of the earth? Lightning—where did it come from? Was it really just God shuffling his furniture around, as Granny used to tease, or something wilder, a spark born in the sky's secret depths?

He squinted, tracing their edges, imagining heaven perched just beyond, so close he could almost touch it. The dusty picture Bible they had on the shelf back home, always showed Angels lounging on those fluffy drifts—did that mean paradise was right there, waiting? He grinned, picturing his lumpy bed stacked against a cloud's embrace, and figured even his threadbare quilt couldn't hold a candle to that kind of sleep.

As he lay there watching he saw a snowman melt into a giant fluffy haired dog that then morphed into a giant Pillsbury dough boy. He poked his finger toward its belly while trying to giggle like the pudgy little ghost chef. Suddenly it turned dark with an odd swirling motion about it—almost like a serpent—swimming through the crystalline blue waters that held it. A single bolt of molten colored electricity shot through it exposing what he thought was an eye, seeming to momentarily scan his soul. Then, as quickly as it appeared, it disintegrated, melting into nothingness.

* * *

The creature that now stalked Rylan, was no mortal dog—he was a majestic beast of sheer magnitude, wisdom stitched from starlight and shadow, heart vast as the untamed wilds of the Kingdom. Long ago, under a crescent moon sharp as a blade, he'd slipped from his Mamma's grasp, tumbling from a farmer's rickety truck as it rattled through the night past town. A pup then, barely a whisper of fur and bone, cast into a realm where destiny brewed in secret currents. The land took him in, its creeks shimmering with fish that danced like silver spirits beneath the surface. With jaws kissed by instinct, he quickly learned an awkward method he used to pluck them from their watery lairs and hook them with his teeth, a lone hunter learning to feed his hunger.

In those fragile, fearful days, the forest had unveiled another mystery: a she-bear. Her eyes were twin embers of ancient fire, her cub a shadow at her side. She first discovered the pup trembling, halfway stuffed into an old box behind one of the towns *treasure chests*. He was suffering, freezing, and just seeking shelter from the cold of a looming ice storm, and she claimed him as hers—an act of grace woven with magic.

Her embrace was fierce yet tender, *nurturing*, a mother's l*oving* embrace laced with the wild poetry of the woods. For a season that stretched beyond time, she raised him and her cub as brothers, their spirits bound in a dance of fang and claw. She taught them the art of the wrestle, tumbling through moss and mist until the earth sang; the climb of the fallen pines, the stalk of rabbits, swift as moonbeams, through glades aglow with faerie light. Her wisdom rumbled like distant thunder, teaching them the lessons of survival.

In the creek's deepest pools, she unveiled the secrets of the swim and guided them to snare fish that gleamed like sunken treasures. She ascended fallen oaks to woo the bees, her paws dripped with honey spun from sunlight and storm. The brothers would lick her paws clean like children with batter beaters. Berries she offered—ruby jewels to savor, amethyst poisons to shun—each a lesson in the land's bittersweet embrace. And in the village's shadowed alleys, she taught the fine art of raiding the *treasure chests*—the trash cans brimming with feasts, fit for a bear Queen and her rogue Princes.

Their days were a whirlwind of adventure, racing through brambles, diving into rapids, outwitting the wind itself. Yet beneath it all simmered a romance that beckoned her.

The she-bear's gaze held a longing, a love vast as the horizon, as if she'd once roamed beside a mate now lost to time. For a young girl, it was pure whimsy—the forest a playground of enchanted secrets, but seasons turn, and the bear's fire dimmed. Her spirit yearned for a slumber deep as the earth's core, a mystical renewal whispered in the rustle of leaves. With a final loving nuzzle, she vanished into the dusk, leaving the brothers to claim their fates—two wild hearts set loose under a sky ablaze with purpose.

The dog grew into a phantom of Eldergrove, a grown man's spirit clad in fur—rugged, resolute, a wanderer with an edge honed by solitude. He haunted the barns and shuttered mills along the creek's bank, a spectral guardian of the rusted relics. By night, he prowled the town's fringes, a shadow slipping through the glow of lantern-lit streets, scavenging troves left by souls too hurried to see the magic in their leavings.

By day, he slept in hollows where the earth hummed, dreaming of a companion—a soul to share the untamed symphony of his life. People turned cold, their eyes blind to the mystery in his amber gaze, their voices sharp with dismissal. Yet his heart burned, a quiet inferno of longing, an ache for a bond, a connection to defy the years he'd roamed alone.

Along an old dirt road, dust swirling like a sorcerer's veil, he glimpsed a figure—a boy, locked in a duel with a garden hose, water arcing like a dragon's breath. The boy bit and slurped, a warrior in a teenage epic, his belch a triumphant roar that shook the air. The dogs spirit ignited—this was no ordinary soul, but a kindred flame, a partner for the quests ahead. He melted into the grasses, a furry ninja, stalking with a grace born of bear-taught guile. The wild blades bowed as he moved, his eyes locked on the boy's sprint toward the creek, a path shimmering with the promise of adventure.

When the boy collapsed beneath the ancient oak, sprawling in the grass, he felt the pull of destiny snap taut. He looked for something that would impress the boy, showing him how strong he was. He saw small sized fetching log lying in the grass and he grabbed it in his jowls. His heart thundered, as he stepped forth—back end just wiggling out of control—drool gleaming like a river of stars—a floppy-eared enigma, grinning ear to ear, ready to weave his magic into Rylan's tale.

* * *

Something was crawling on Rylan's arm. He swatted at it fast, rolling over, only to see it wasn't crawling but fluttering— a *Flutterbye* like Mamma called them. Biggest he'd ever seen, wings splashed with gold, black, and a variety of colors to match the sunset. A daredevil pilot defying death with his, flipping, and spinning 360s. Rylan grinned, completely mesmerized, until a loud *thud* snapped him out of it.

He jerked his head and froze. There, not ten feet off, stood a beast—a tiger-striped dog, massive as a mini horse, teeth at least an inch long... significantly bigger than Rylan... muscles rippling under a coat that gleamed in the sun. Quite startling really, but as scary as it first was, Rylan couldn't help but notice the dog's ears—floppy, huge, and loose, like they'd lift him off the ground if he ran fast enough. The thud? A log—not some twig—a full-on three foot long log—the size of one of Rylans whole legs. The dog had dropped it, and then plopped down, staring at Rylan straight, with a grin stretching ear to ear. An uneven spool of drool spilled from both sides of his jowls as it panted in rhythm, tongue lolling freely about 4 inches beyond his chin...

A boy dog, no doubt—a full-grown man, really—sitting there—bare and proud—not a care in the world about it. Rylan laughed, a sharp burst of envy bubbling up. Imagine it—digging in mud, chasing squirrels, lapping creek water, all buck-naked, **Now that's living** he thought.

"Well—who are you, friend?"

At "friend", the dog thrust out a paw—big as a bear's—landing it square in Rylan's hand. Rylan cracked up again, shaking it like they'd sealed a deal.

"Nice to meet you Old Guy—gotta go though—Kingdom's waiting."

He stood, brushed down the dirt, and started off while tossing a wave over his shoulder.

"See ya around Old Guy..."

Fifty feet down the path, he glanced back. The dog was tailing him, that goofy grin still plastered on his face, drool dripping steady.

"I gotta go, mister..." Rylan called. "Don't you need to get home? Good boy—go on."

Old Guy just stared, panting, smiling like he'd heard nothing. Rylan shrugged and trudged on, another hundred feet, then froze mid-step—arms still swinging, body tilted half forward. He held his breath, ears straining. No rustle, no heavy pants, nothing. He spun fast, heart kicking—and there Old Guy was, three feet back, sitting silent as a ghost, drool pooling, grin wide as ever.

"What the—?"

Rylan was half-laughing, half-spooked. It was magic or something—pure stealth—ninja quiet, this hulking beast shadowing him without a sound. Old *Scooby* didn't have a thang on him...

He tested it again—walked, stopped, spun—every time... Old Guy was right there, inches away, grinning like they'd been soul mates forever. Over and over it went just like that, step by step to the Kingdom—together. Rylans new friend soon walking up close, tight beside him, a drooling, floppy-eared guardian watching over Rylans every step.

The Return

Rylan stumbled into the Kingdom, Old Guy at his side, the creek swelling full and wild under the still rising sun. Whispers were abound of Mother Nature's favorite songs—the Toad and Cricket Choir belted out their welcome, a throaty croak and chirp rejoicing at their arrival, and the birds chirped like sopranos carrying different harmonies. Dragonflies and flutterbys were dive bombing each other with the vigor of life. The air thrummed with the sweet smell of Honeysuckle and Tree Moss, thick enough to taste.

Rylans chest heaved from the sprint, he was home—his untamed refuge. He scoped the Kingdom, hazel eyes darting to where he'd last left *her*—that grassy bank where *her* golden hair had spilled across his lap, where *her* lips had brushed his cheek... *She* was absent. Nothing now but swaying golden and sunset colored wildflowers dancing in a sea of Jade windblown grasses. It took him straight back, deep into *her* eyes. The windows into the soul that he had every intention of existing in. While Sitting there still, listening, studying his surroundings, *her* absence became a hollow ache, a fire burning somewhere inside of him.

Rylan shuffled over to the old fallen tree, a hallowed haunt buzzing with the neighborhood of the chipmunks, and offered a friendly nod. Amid their frantic scamper—tiny paws darting, tails flicking—they froze, snapping upright on their haunches like soldiers at attention. They knew Rylan, trusted him through years of quiet visits, but Old Guy was a stranger, may as well of been a small hungry chipmunk eating bear at his side.

A ripple of unease swept through them—soft squeaks and trembles, a low murmur of panic rising. Rylan caught the cue and turned to Old Guy, his voice firm but calm.

"These chipmunks are all critters of this Kingdom—they're off-limits, buddy—no doggie snacks here."

Old Guy cocked his head, a puzzled whimper slipping out, while the chipmunks sat paralyzed, their wide eyes glazed with fear, caught between flight and faith.... cautiously they resumed their pursuits.

* * *

Old Guy was fearless, splashing in the creek despite Rylan's half-shouted warnings, his massive tiger-striped head dunking under the surface, chasing his foes with reckless and relentless glee.

Rylan let his thoughts drift, sinking into a daydream as soft as *her* lips had been—warm, fleeting, a whisper against his cheek that still burned weeks later. He could smell *her* in the wildflowers lining the banks and see *her* in the beauty he'd carved into his memory: jade eyes flecked with gold, mud-smudged nose, that fierce grin as *she* reeled in her prize. His fingers twitched, longing to thread through *her* tangled hair again, to feel that spark. But the creek's surface rippled, pulling him deeper—past *her*, to what lay beneath, the things he couldn't see or quite grasp.

He thought of his Mamma—her shaky voice singing *Three Little Birds*, her quiet hands sneaking him biscuits when Pops turned savage. She was his protector, a shield she didn't even know she held, her love as natural as the creek's flow...

He wondered about Old Guy, how long could he possibly hold his breath—his giant head still submerged, bubbles popping like tiny laughs—and then his mind snagged momentarily. Old Guy really needed to learn about the danger of Dragonfish and it's sneak attacks. He was a big boy but a Dragonfish was a fierce foe. Rylan climbed up onto the back of the fallen tree and perched himself in his favorite sitting spot, overlooking Old Guy playing. His eyes began to become very heavy with the weight of the seasons he had just endured. He sat leaning up against the tree with the sunlight and the breeze encouraging his demise almost as if they had been sent by the Dragonfish itself...

Hotel Chevrolet

Rylan's good memories of Mamma and Pops were scarce as fireflies in a snowstorm, flickering rare and faint against the sprawl of all his bruised years, but there was great times as well—a jewel he polished when the dark pressed too close. Back in 1985 when they first rolled into Eldergrove, they were ragtag trio bunked up in Hotel Chevrolet. That's what they had named Pops rusted-out old pickup truck. Its bed was stuffed with their worldly goods: a dented cooler, a tarp patched with duct tape, Mamma's quilts stitched with love and desperation. They'd been traveling with the *gypsies* for a while then, bouncing from town to dusty town, following some band around. They started looking for a place to call home when Mamma's belly started swelling round with Rylan's baby brother-to-be.

It was late summer—the air thick with heat and the buzz of cicadas—when they'd stumbled on Eldergrove. Pops had spotted quite a few for sale signs, but one grabbed his attention, crooked and peeling, staked in front of an old weathered house on a scrappy plot of land overlooking the creek lands. The roof sagged like an old man's shoulders, windows stared blank and cracked, but Pops saw his own Kingdom rising out of the dirt.

"This is it, Ry,"

His Pops voice booming with a joy Rylan had never heard before, his big hands clapping Rylan's scrawny shoulders.

"Our shot, boy—roots, a roof, a place to call home. I bet there's fish in them creeks." He was lost in his vision. "Heck, there's even an old *Members Only Club* within spitting distance." His grin split wide, tobacco-stained teeth flashing, eyes crinkling with a light that made him look younger than the whiskey lines and belt scars ever let on.

Mamma was glistening as well, her cheeks flushed pink under the freckles, her laugh spilling out like a song as she rubbed her mildly swollen belly.

"A home, Ry," she had whispered, tugging him close, her apron smelling of flour and sweat. "No more running."

Pops brokered a deal with the owner—an old coot with a limp and a handshake—and for a stretch of days, the world felt golden, drenched in a syrupy promise Rylan could almost taste.

* * *

The first time Momma and Pops had stepped into the Kingdom, the creek's wild embraced them, its banks bursting with late-summer blooms. They'd piled onto the big fallen tree, its bark sun-warmed and rough under their legs. Rylan, a child, was perched between them, his bony knees knocking against Pops' thick thigh, Mamma's arm slung loosely around his shoulders. The creek glittered below, a sheet of sapphire glass catching the sun's slant, its *Trickle* a soft hymn that drowned out the road's hum.

Mamma had packed the brand-new canteen—shiny and silver, not a ding on it, a thrift-store treasure she'd scrubbed until it gleamed. She had filled it with her famous Lemonade, a secret recipe that told the tales of generations before. It sloshed into the tin cups, ice clinking from the cooler, droplets beading cold on the metal.

"To us,"

Pops toasted, his voice a rumble of thunder and honey, and they clinked cups, Lemonade splashing over the rims, sticky on their fingers. Rylan gulped his down, the citrus bite chasing the heat from his throat, and grinned as Mamma handed out Spam, Saltines, and government cheese—greasy pink squares and yellow wax slapped onto crisp, bland dry crackers. Mamma called it *Manna* from heaven above, a feast fit for kings in their patchwork court.

They laughed—God, how they laughed—with endless, belly-deep roars that shook the tree and sent blackbirds scattering from the cattails.

Pops was a storm-wrought titan most days—gruff silence, or a thunderous working tornado, but that late-summer afternoon in the Kingdom, he was a man ablaze with something softer. His eyes danced, dark and molten, as he scooped Rylan up in his burly arms, a low chuckle rumbling from his chest.

"Hold tight, boy!" he roared, tossing Rylan into the creek with a whoop that echoed off the oaks.

The rope swing came next—Pops' big hands shoving Rylan higher and higher, the world a blur of green and blue until Rylan let go, flipping midair, plunging into the crystal clear water with a splash that sprayed like shattering glass. Cold shocked his skin, soaking his patched overalls, but he bobbed up laughing, breathless under the sun's golden columns.

Pops wasn't done. He strode up the fallen log, its end jutting boldly out over the deep pool, and leapt—flipping with a grace that belied his size, his broad frame slicing the water cleanly. Diamond arcs fanned out, glittering in the light, gifting them with a temporary rainbow in the mist. Rylan grinned as the spray from his fathers fall slapped him in the face, icy and sharp. Invigorating.

Pops turned his gaze to Momma, and the air shifted—thickened with a heat

Rylan couldn't name, but he felt it prickling his neck. She stood ankle-deep in the creek, a vision in white—a sundress, thin as a whisper, clinging to her curves, her bump just starting to show, but the signs were all there. Her hair, flowing and loose, and tumbled over her shoulders, catching the sun in a halo of chestnut fire.

Pops waded closer, water rippling around his thighs, and splashed her—deliberate, playful, his big hands scooping the creek like a lover's tease. The water hit her squarely, soaking that white dress until it hugged every line of her. She shrieked, "Stoooppp..." a delighted trill that danced with the crickets, her arms flailing as she splashed him back, but Pops just grinned—wolfish, hungry—and let out a low, sultry growl.

"Lord, woman,"

His voice was gravelly with heat, his eyes raking over her, lingering where the wet fabric showcased the swells of her body, rounder now with the baby on the way.

"Look at you—all ripe, and purty as ever. Ain't no man alive luckier'n me."

His words dripped with a raw, reverent lust, and Mamma's laugh turned bashful, her cheeks flushing rosy pink under the summer glow. She swatted at him, water flying, but her eyes—bright as the creek's shimmer—locked with his, sparking with a fire that said she felt it too. They were lost in each other, a current pulling them tight, and for a heartbeat, the outside world didn't exist.

They fished that day with bent rods and night-crawlers dug from the mud, Pops hollering when he hooked a fat one, its scales flashing silver-green in the sun,

"Beat that, Ry!"

Rylan tried, his line tangling more than catching, but it didn't matter—they were alive, electric, a family stitched together by the day's wild joy.

As the day wound down, they stood on the shore and skipped rocks across the reflection of the day moon. Smooth, flat stones were plucked from the creek bed, still dripping as they lined up to skip. Mamma managed three, giggling self-consciously as they sank with a plop. Rylan hit three mostly, and one kind of four, his chest puffing with pride, and Pops was a master—nine skips—each one a perfect arc, the stone skimming like a bird across the water, rippling out forever.

"That's how it's done, son!"

Pops ruffled Rylan's wet hair, his calloused hand gentle, not a fist or a rod. Rylan stared, awestruck, at this giant who could tame the creek with a flick of his wrist, a King in his own right.

They sprawled on the tree afterward, sun drying their skin, crackers crunching between their teeth, Lemonade tangy on their tongues. Mamma leaned into Pops, her head on his shoulder, his arm slung loosely around her, and Rylan nestled between, their warmth a cocoon he'd never known before, and would never since. The creek sang on, dragonflies flirted with the breeze, and for that one moment, the world was right—bright, loud, theirs.

* * *

"Bubba!" Pops bellowed. "Bubba's tough... none of that Carlton fancy prancin'! My boy's gonna skip rocks and wrestle hogs, not dance around like some city fool!"

His dark eyes flashed, daring Mamma to argue, water beading off his shoulders in the sun's glare.

Mamma fired back with a smirk that could melt steel. "Carlton's got soul, you big brute!" She flicked water at him with a quick wrist, her long hair whipping wild in the breeze. "He'll sing, not grunt—and Carlton ain't no dance—it's classy, something you wouldn't know if it bit you!"

Pops snorted, loud and rough, swiping a hand through his spiky black hair. "Class? Carlton sounds like a sissy jig—'do the Carlton!'" he mocked, shimmying his hips in a ridiculous wiggle, while swinging his arms side to side and snapping his fingers. "Boy'll be twirlin' with teacups while I'm teachin' him to gut fish!" He doubled over, cackling, his big frame shaking as Mamma splashed him again, her eyes dancing with fire and fun.

Rylan stood there, ankle-deep in the creek, mud squishing between his toes, watching them like a hawk. Their love was loud, messy, and bigger than the Kingdom itself, but he had his own idea brewing.

"Hulk!" His voice piped high over the crickets, arms flexing like he'd seen in Pops' old comics. "Hulk's the best—he'd smash the bad guys *and* your dumb names!" He puffed his chest, grinning wildly, picturing his brother green and roaring, busting outta Mamma's belly like a superhero.

They froze mid-splash—Pops caught wiggling, Mamma pausing her flick—heads swiveling to gape at her gently swollen belly, then at Rylan, then back at each other. Water trickled off Pops' nose, Mamma's dress hung wet and heavy, and for a split second, the creek seemed to hush. Then they burst—Pops' booming belly laugh colliding with Mamma's high, hiccup-like giggle, both doubled over, clutching their sides like they might split wide open.

"Bubba-Carlton-*Hulk*?!" Pops wheezed, slapping his thigh, sending up a spray. "Lord, woman, we've spawned a circus!"

Mamma wiped tears from her eyes, still laughing, and yanked Rylan into a soggy hug up against her very swollen bumps. He panicked, made a tormented face and struggled to escape her death grip.

"You little nut... Hulk, huh? He's already kickin' like it!"

They all collapsed on the fallen log, laughing, breathless and soaked, Mamma sandwiched between them, Pops' arm slung over her shoulders, his rough hand ruffling Rylan's wet hair. The creek sparkled, the sun blazed, and for that moment, Bubba-Carlton-Hulk wasn't just a name—it was all of them, wild, loud and tangled in love.

Bubba-Carlton-Hulk

Nine months they'd waited—Rylan and Pops orbiting Mamma like she was the sun, tending her every ache with a devotion that felt both clumsy and fierce. Rylan rubbed her swollen feet 'til his hands cramped, grinning through the groans she'd let slip, while Pops fussed over the toilet paper, flipping it to hang just right—over, not under, "'cause that's how Momma likes it." was the theme of most everything as it should have been. They fetched her Lemonade when her throat turned to dust, and they'd hover close, half-laughing, half-worried, as her belly grew rounder than the moon over the creek.

Now, here they were, in the sterile hum of Eldergrove's hospital, a place half-empty, too clean and sharp-edged for their wild souls. Rylan tore up and down the long hall, a football tucked under his arm. In his head, the baby—his little brother—was already the Hulk, a Prince of the Kingdom as well as being destined to storm the football field like a wrecking ball. He'd plow through linebackers, Rylan reckoned, tossing that pigskin farther than the creek could stretch, and Rylan would be right there, hollering from the sidelines, proud as a King. Pops didn't tamp that dream down—not today. His eyes glinted with the same big ambitions, a rare spark unclouded by whiskey or pipe smoke.

"Little Bubba's gonna be a titan," he growled, clapping Rylan's shoulder, and for once, his voice carried hope instead of thunder.

They'd just wheeled Mamma from the waiting room, her sundress soaked dark— sweat or water or both, Rylan couldn't tell, and he figured it wasn't his place to ask. She was hollering, wild and fierce, her voice bouncing off the walls like a storm breaking loose.

"CARL!"

She screamed colorful word's filled with angry affection at Pops, sharp as a skipping stone's edge, and he just stood there, half-green, half-dazed, looking like he'd swallowed a lightning bolt and didn't know whether to spit it out or ride it. The nurses swooped in, efficient as hawks, draping him in a blue gown that swallowed his broad frame, snapping rubber gloves over his calloused hands, and jamming a cap over his spiky black hair. They dragged him off to the birthing room, leaving Rylan alone in the hall, a boy with a football and a heart thumping too big for his chest.

He waited, restless as a chipmunk on the fallen tree. The hall stretched endlessly before him, a runway for his dreams, and he tossed the football to himself, catching it mid-stride, weaving through imaginary defenders. "Hut, hut!" he'd mutter, faking a handoff to the Hulk in his mind, then sprinting ten yards to snag his own throw.

Nurses shot him looks—half-amused, half-exasperated—but he didn't care. Time crawled, thick and slow, each tick of the clock a tease, until his legs burned and his palms stung from gripping the leather. He'd pause, panting, hazel eyes darting to the double doors, willing them to swing wide with news.

Then they did. Pops burst out, glowing like he'd just lit the sky on fire, his grin wild and untamed, the kind Rylan hadn't seen since the days before the pipe took root.

"It's official," Pops roared, voice booming down the hall. "It's a boy!"

Rylan's chest exploded, a flood of joy crashing through him like the creek after a rain.

"Officially official?"

Rylan's grin split wide, and they both cracked up—deep, belly laughs that shook the sterile air. Pops threw his arms out, and Rylan matched him, two fools dancing in the hallway, hopping and spinning like they'd just won the Super Bowl.

"Hit me!"

Rylan yelled, taking off in a sprint. Pops dropped back, eyes glinting, and lobbed it—a perfect spiral, arcing like a comet. Rylan leaped, snagging it mid-air, and bolted ten feet, slamming an invisible goal line.

"Touchdown!" He spiked the ball so hard it bounced off the wall.

They collapsed against each other, breathless, laughing until their sides ached. Pops ruffled Rylan's hair, his hand steady for once, no tremble of rage or ruin.

"That's our Hulk," His pride was thick in his throat. "Gonna tear up the field, just you watch."

Rylan nodded, picturing it—Bubba, broad and unstoppable, charging through life with that same reckless blaze they shared today. The hospital faded, its antiseptic sting drowned by the scent of Honeysuckle on the breeze sneaking through a cracked window, the Kingdom whispering its blessings.

Somewhere beyond those doors, Mamma rested, her warrior's fire banked but burning still, Baby Carlton cradled in her arms. Rylan felt it—the family whole, if only for now, stitched tight by this moment. The creek's trickle hummed in his soul, a song of triumph, and he knew: this was a day the Kingdom would remember, a day when love outshone the shadows, bright as a fiver load skipping five times across the water.

* * *

Time had passed them by, and that next summer, Pops light burned bright, a titan vibrating with something golden, not yet tarnished by the shadows Rylan would later know.

Back then, Pops was still writing, his soul buzzing with stories that spilled from him like a river unbound. Since Rylan could remember, Pops had been wrestling a novel to life, but in those days, it was more—short tales and poems bursting forth, each one a spark from the furnace of his mind. It was this side of him—untamed, brilliant—that had snared Mamma's heart, hooked it deep and fierce.

Before the pipe his own father had pressed into his grip, Pops smoked only cigarettes and the sweet, earthy weed he'd get from the town's gypsies. He would take his notebook for walks down to the creek and perch on a jagged rock or pace the bank, notebook clutched like a lover, scribbling frantic lines, sketching doodles that danced with his words.

He'd mutter and growl, acting out every scene—sword fights, lovers' quarrels—his big frame lunging and twirling as the pen scratched fire onto paper. He didn't just write his characters; he breathed them, lived their joys and broke with their sorrows, a man possessed by the worlds he created. Mom had fallen hard for that kind of passion—headlong, breathless, the kind of fall that leaves a woman dizzy and a man proud to be the cause.

It was romance raw and real—his rugged hands, stained with ink and tobacco, crafting dreams she could feel in her bones; her soft sway as she'd drift closer, drawn by the heat of his spirit, her voice a melody humming along to his chaos. Together, they were a force—Pops weaving tales of heroes and heartbreak, Mom his muse and anchor, their love a wildfire tearing through the ordinary. In those days, they moved through life hand in hand, a rhythm so alive, so enviable, it could make any heart—man's or woman's—ache to chase that same untamed blaze.

The baby brother had come screaming into the world, red-faced and fists swinging, and they still hadn't settled on a name, bickering over Bubba's grit and Carlton's eloquence. So, for the time being it would be, Bubba-Carlton-Hulk, Bubba-Hulk to Pops and Rylan, Carlton to Mamma.

Pops juggled writing with Mill shifts and hauling lumber—all the while hammering together their sagging castle on that scrappy Eldergrove plot, nails biting wood with every swing. At night, he'd cradle Mamma, her body soft and spent from carrying the baby, his rough hands gentle as he kissed her forehead under the kitchen lamp's glow. There was no hint then of the black tide buried inside him. No echo of the father who'd carved torment into his soul, and no trace of the mother who'd borne her own silent scars.

* * *

The darkness Rylan would later face, was a smoldering ghost. Sure, Mr. Whiskey tagged along some nights, turning Pops' laugh sharp and his grip tight, but it was rare—fleeting. Time went on and Pops' "*play*" got rougher, wrestling Rylan hard to the dirt, dunking him under the creek till bubbles burst and his lungs screamed, before yanking him up with a laugh. Pops would roar, with the fire of tobacco and whiskey, breathing hot on Rylan's face.

"Just makin' a man outta ya, boy!"

Mamma would see Rylan's confusion and in her reassuring way would tell him,

"He's golden underneath, Ry. Loves us deep. It's not his fault...."

When she would say it "wasn't his fault," Rylan knew what she meant, his fathers dark hand-me-downs as the origin of the evil they endured. Rylan wasn't fully privy to the stories that she hinted at but he had known of his fathers dark journey.

When Rylan was little—still small enough that his feet dangled off the floorboards—he'd unearthed a relic of his father's past, tucked away in a splintered trunk under a pile of moth-chewed blankets in the back of a closet.

It was a journal, its leather cover cracked like dry creek mud, pages curling at the edges, stained with time and a boy's forgotten ink. Back then, Pops burned to be a writer, a poet—his young hand spilling dreams across the paper, words that danced wild and free, stitching beauty from a world sometimes broken. Rylan pored over them, eyes wide, breath shallow, tracing lines that sang of hope and ached with a scarless soul. But that ember had been smothered—snuffed by a father's heavy legacy, crumpled like so many fragile dreams ground to dust beneath the weight of the years, leaving only echoes in the darkness that Rylan had rights too.

Father loomed, a mountain carved in wrath,
Eyes like coal, burning holes through tender skin,
A belt in hand, a rod to carve the path,
Each lash a hymn to drown the boy within.
"Don't you weep, son," he'd growl, voice like stone,
"Men don't break, men don't bend, men don't feel."
But tears would fall, silent, alone,
A river dammed by shame no child could heal.
The barn was witness—splinters, blood, and hay,
A whiskey breath, a fist that split the dawn,

"Stand tall, you cur," he'd roar each day,
Till love was just the bruise he'd lean upon.
Hate weaponized, innocence, a hard stare,
The echo of a scream he locked away,
A fire glowing beneath, the scales hidden there,
A dragon born of nights he couldn't slay.
He'd crawl to bed, ribs heavy, soul torn apart,
Whispering "I love you" to the dark, the dread,
For that's the curse—our wild, unyielding heart,
To cradle the monsters underneath
when we're tucked safely in our bed.

Rylan kept the old journal, and carried it deep within the satchel he would wrap around himself that stored his most important treasures. A slingshot, specially selected slinging stones, a Swiss Army knife, three sugar cubes, bent fishhooks, a chipmunk-chewed acorn, and from that point forward, an old tarnished journal that had been long forgotten by its author.

Forever

Bubba-*Carlton*-Hulk had woven a thread of radiant joy through the family and community. He spread a sense of goodness , so potent it seemed to cradle them all in his glow. To Rylan, it was as if the baby's first cries had rekindled a hidden ember in Pops, awakening a purpose long buried beneath the weight of old scars—a quiet, fierce determination that shimmered in his eyes like the creek at dusk. Mamma, meanwhile, was a vision of light, her face aglow with a warmth that rivaled the sun itself. Each day, she'd cradle *Carlton* in his stroller and push him through the winding paths of Eldergrove, past the town's shops that still remained, her steps guided by an unspoken rhythm, as if the town itself whispered secrets to her.

Every Sunday, when the sun cracked the sky and spilled gold over the jade grasses, Mamma would scoop *Carlton* from his cradle, his tiny fists punching the air like he was born to rumble. She'd wrap him in a quilt stitched from Pops' old flannels—soft as a prayer, smelling of wood smoke—and hoist him into his stroller, her yellow cotton dress swishing as she slipped out the screen door. Rylan would tag along sometimes, kicking dirt, but mostly it was her and *Carlton*. Occasionally Pops joined, but church was never really his thing. She would parade *Carlton* to the Old Town Church—a hulking shell of Eldergrove's past, its whitewash peeling, its steeple sagging like a tired mule. The flock had claimed it, freed it, and now it thrummed with what Rylan figured Jesus actually intended.

Once a stiff institution, all rules and starch, it'd been the town's pride—

standing tall, oak beams, a pipe organ squat in the corner like a sleeping giant. But the suits and sermons had faded, and the *Bohemian flock and the community left overs had* moved in—Over a hundred freedom-seeking souls and growing, in patched denim and beet-dyed skirts, farm hats and coveralls, too poor for pew cushions but rich in grit. Honeysuckle clawed the walls outside, and the oak door, scarred with a rough-hewn cross, swung wide under a sign: **Jesus Loves Everyone*,* painted bold in red, swaying lazily in the breeze. Mamma would stride in, Carlton gurgling proudly, her boots thumping the worn pine floor as the air would hit her—thick with frankincense and myrrh, sage smoke curling from burning bundles along the sills.

Inside, the church dripped with tie-dye and faith—walls draped with swirling banners, purples and oranges stitched by hands that knew hunger. Silk-screen art splashed the beams. An old statue of a baby lamb curled under a haloed cross still stood. Candles flickered in jelly jars, wax dripping slowly, their glow dancing off brass crosses tilted on shelves, a chipped wooden Jesus leaning beside a loaf of sourdough torn open on the altar—a slab of oak scarred with time. The old pews were gone, swapped for quilts, rugs, bean-bags and half broken down paisley couches sprawled wildly. Up front, the pulpit was just old milk crates under a batik cloth, a jug of wildflower mead and a bowl of creek water waiting to share.

Mamma would plop down near the front, *Carlton* kicking in her lap, his round eyes blinking at the chaos. She would typically sit down next to Zora Thornweaver, a poetically gifted spell binder, as well as a prophetic seer, and man was she good at poker. She had owned the Crescent Coffershop across the way in the square ever since Mamma had come to town in their house on wheels. Zora would await their arrival and ask to be the one to hold him. Mamma would always try and beat her to the offer.

"It's Miss Zora Carlton! Your favorite little Bubba!" and she would immediately hand the little bundle joy right over.

"My little Star-forged Titan, ain't you just so special." Zora squeezed him tightly whispering into his ear, as if she knew he would understand. "Your heart's been hammered into the tome of life that guards the heavens' child, an anchor for the Kingdom when the dark coils strike their worst."

He held still in her touch content with her words. He smiled relentlessly and squeezed her finger as if he knew his why.

The flock would shuffle in and Mamma would glow with pride as they would swoon over her baby boy, taking him off of Zora's hands and passing him 'round while Momma grinned widely.

Mamma would lead the charge today—her turn to speak, her voice rising like the creek at dusk. "He's God's gift," she'd say, cradling him again. "Born to the Kingdom, baptized in love 'fore we got here. Ain't that the Gospel—holdin' tight to what shines?"

No pastor preached—they never needed one. They all just took turns, stories spilling raw. Souls exposing themselves with unrehearsed truths. Mrs. Peesewell hunched at the pipe organ, her knobby fingers waking it with the grace of the *old rugged cross*, or something similar. The notes rolled deep as thunder. The others would join in—really anyone who played an instrument: a banjo strumming fast, mandolin weaving high, and a stand-up bass that shook the floor. The drum circle kids—half a dozen local wildlings—pounded a rhythm on skins stretched tight. The flock would leap up, dancing with mystical movements, worship spilling out in stomps, hands raised to the sky, and claps, singing loose, loud, and alive.

Mamma would sway and swing with Carlton, his gurgles threading through like he was part of the choir. She'd twirl him gently, his quilt flapping, while the flock spun and shouted, the floor trembling under their stomps. Between songs, Mrs. Peesewell would ease into something slow and steady, and they'd hush while Ezekiel would slip in a verse or two from the bible that always seemed to be relevant. With their hands raised, prayers thrummed through their bones—Mamma whispering thanks for her boys, lost and living.

It was faith with dirt on it, simple as Lemonade. They'd light more candles, pass the wine, break the bread—*Carlton* gnawing a crust, drooling proud. At the very end Ezekiel would always close things down with a final prayer.

"Father, bless us with the spirit of gratitude and goodness. Thank you,"

and the flock would join in, yelling out in a chorus,

"AAAA MEN!"

The old church, once a cage of judgment, was theirs now—tie-dye soft, crosses bold, a hippie Jesus wearing a lei around his neck, smiling down. When it all wound down, Mamma would linger, as the flock spilled out, trading hugs and jam jars, making sure they aligned their watches with Johnny Pocketwatch, the churches official door-holder and Eldergroves official timekeeper, ever since the old clock had frozen up way back when.

* * *

Among Mamma's cherished haunts was the ancient Tree of Life, a towering sentinel rooted between the church's weathered wood and the mill's crumbling husk. Rylan swore the tree was older than time itself—hundreds of years, maybe thousands, its gnarled branches stretching skyward like the arms of some forgotten god. Its bark was etched with the echoes of generations, a living chronicle of joys and sorrows, births and betrayals, as if it held the town's soul in its roots. There were rumored to be secret carvings in that tree but Rylan had yet to figure out how to access them. To him, it was no mere tree but a guardian of mysteries, magic, and whispers that carried on the wind, hinting at tales yet untold.

Whenever he could, Rylan would scale its twisted limbs, perching high above like a young eagle, his hazel eyes glinting with curiosity. From his leafy throne, he'd peer down at the townsfolk who gathered beneath in what passed for Eldergrove's heart—a sprawling square alive with murmured gossip, bartered dreams, and the faint hum of something older stirring beneath the cobblestones. The Tree of Life stood as a silent witness to it all, and Rylan felt its pulse quicken under his hands, as if it recognized him and sensed the adventures that awaited. What secrets did it guard? What shadows lingered in its shade, ready to unfurl their riddles? The tree seemed to lean toward him, its branches swaying with promise, beckoning Rylan toward a future where the past's veiled truths would rise to meet him, daring him to unravel them.

* * *

Mamma had been off-limits, a fragile Queen nursing the prized Bubba-Carlton-Hulk, and Pops' attention turned more toward Rylan—little things at first, bumps and nudges, charlie horses, slug bugs and so on...

Pops had a morning ritual, a game he'd spring on Rylan when the dawn still hung soft and gray over their creaky house. He'd twist his thick fingers into that *OK* sign, rough knuckles flexing as he planted it low—on his thigh, maybe his shin—and call out, low and teasing,

"Hey, Ry, check it out."

Rylan, blinking sleep from his hazel eyes, would turn, trusting as a fawn, no shadow of doubt in his small frame. He'd follow Pops' pointing finger down to that circle, see it, and try his fastest to poke his finger in it , which would break it's power, and reverse the punishment, but Pops was always quick as a whip, his face would crack open with a grin.

"Gotcha, boy, gotcha! Heh-heh-heh!"

Rylan would slump, a shy giggle escaping despite himself, caught again in Pops' snare. Pops would slug him in the arm for his prize—not menacing-like, not yet—a playful jab, his big hand hovering there a beat too long, heavy with something unspoken.

"You're my boy, Ry,"

His voice softened, a gravelly warmth wrapping around the words like a quilt over thorns. Rylan felt it deep—Pops' affection, clumsy and loud, a tether in a world that already swayed unsteadily beneath his feet. He'd smile up at him, heart thumping with a love that didn't know better, soaking in that fleeting glow.

Pops had started playing it quite a bit, every dawn a fresh trap—and Rylan's arm began to tell the tale—a bruise blossoming, faint at first, then darker, a tender patch that throbbed quietly. It didn't heal, couldn't, not with Pops' hand swinging day after day, each slug landing a little sharper, a little heavier, a little more intentional...

Rylan would wince sometimes, a flinch he'd hide quickly, but Pops would just laugh louder, eyes narrowing like he saw something Rylan didn't.

"Gotta toughen you up, kid."

Rylan would nod, desperate to believe it was still a game—nothing more. Deep down, a chill crept in, a whisper in his gut he couldn't name, a shadow stretching long and cold behind Pops' grin, promising a day when that hand wouldn't pull back so gentle.

It was those nights that Mamma would slip off with Bubba, over to Auntie Lulu's for the night, her ritual escape with sweet wine and a sleepover, that things started getting darker. Those were the times Rylan learned to vanish—melt into the shadows, breathe shallow, be a ghost. He didn't get Pops, didn't grasp what flipped the switch to those *moments*, but he knew the air thickened when it came, heavy with pipe smoke, Mr. Whiskey's company, and a quiet pacing that cut like a blade.

* * *

It was a steamy afternoon as the family piled into Hotel Chevrolet and rattled down to Eldergrove's church picnic at the Tree of Life. The field behind the steeple was alive with townsfolk: women in floral dresses fanning themselves, men jawing over last night's big fight. Kids darted through the field of lightly swaying Jade, giggling and chasing the scattered multicolored flutterbys. A banner flapped in the breeze...

Annual Baby Crawl-Off

A gaggle of babies, nine months to a year old, squirmed at the starting line, a chalked strip in the dirt. Pops swaggered over, Bubba in his arms, chest puffed like he was entering a prizefighter.

"This here's Bubba-Carlton-Hulk," he bragged to the crowd, voice booming over the chatter and giggles. "Gonna smoke these lil' crawlers—watch and weep!"

Rylan was surprised Pops hadn't taped a racing number on him. He imagined baby Hulk in a full-on uniform with the world-famous number 3 on his suit and helmet.

Pops plopped Bubba down at the line, next to five other chubby contenders, their folks cooing and waving rattles. Mamma knelt down beside Rylan, her sundress pooling in the grass, and whispered,

"He's got your fire, Ry—let's see it shine."

Rylan tilted his head, hazel eyes shimmering like the creek at dawn, a spark of mischief and devotion dancing within them as he envisioned the Hulkster's first fishing lessons. Under Rylan's steady hand, the little Prince of the Kingdom—newly anointed, his tiny crown woven from willow twigs and creek-side dreams, would rise as a fisherman of legend. Together, they'd race through the Kingdom, bare feet kissing the earth, leaping from stone to stone with the grace of young deer, their laughter a melody woven into the wind. They'd cast lines into the glittering water, pulling up bounties kissed by the creek's ancient magic—fish with scales that glowed faintly, like embers of a forgotten spell. By twilight, they'd huddle close, cooking their haul over crackling campfires along the shore, the flames painting the mud smears on their faces in gold as the scent of sizzling fish mingled with the wild perfume of moss and pine.

From the old fallen tree, they'd launch into the air, flipping and twisting like spirits unbound, splashing into the pool's embrace with joyous shrieks. Stone-skipping contests would follow, their fiver loads dancing across the water's surface, each ripple a burst of enchantment, leaving trails of silver light that lingered just a heartbeat too long. And when the mood turned bold, they'd wage epic battles against the grandest of imagined foes—armed with sticks for swords and hearts ablaze with courage. Rylan, the King, and Hulk, his radiant Prince, would stand side by side, their bond a magic deeper than the creek's hidden springs, ruling the Kingdom with love so fierce it could melt the hardest diamond, a tale of brotherhood and wonder that would echo through Eldergrove's soul forever.

* * *

"Go!"

The babies lurched—some wobbling, some flopping, some just bawling. Pops bolted to the finish line, twenty feet away, crouching low, arms wide, hollering, "C'mon, Bubba Hulk! To yer ol' man!" His grin flashed, tobacco teeth gleaming, but Bubba froze. His little face scrunched, sour as a lemon, eyes narrowing at Pops like a dog growling at a stranger, sensing a secret nobody else could see. He sat back on his haunches, arms crossed, refusing to budge.

The other babies crawled ahead—two body lengths, three—while Pops' grin faltered, his brows knitting. "What's this now?" he muttered, hands dropping. Rylan frowned, scooting closer. "C'mon, Bubba, go!" But Bubba just glared, a tiny storm cloud, like he saw scales glinting under Pops' shirt, a flicker the rest had missed. Mamma leapt up and dashed to Pops' side, dropping to her knees at the finish line.

"Carlton, baby, over here!" she sang, voice bright as her smile, clapping her hands. His eyes snapped to her, and he lit up like fireflies, a sour pout splitting into an ear-to-ear grin, baby giggles bubbling like creek water. He launched forward, arms and legs churning, a pint-sized Speed Buggy tearing through the dirt.

The crowd gasped as Bubba blasted past the pack—chubby legs pumping, drool flying—leaving the other babies in his dust. He crossed the line ten feet ahead, a full double-distance lead, tumbling into Mamma's arms with a triumphant squeal. She scooped him up, spinning him high, her laugh ringing out as Pops whooped, slapping his thigh. "That's my boy, the Dale Earnhardt of crawlin'!" he roared, pride swallowing his confusion from a heartbeat before.

Rylan ran over, grinning wildly. "He's fast, Pops! Kid can cover some ground for sure." Pops ruffled his spiked black hair, nodding, while Mamma hugged Bubba tight, whispering, "You're a crawler ain't ya, Little Freebird?"

The picnic rolled on—fried chicken and guitars pickin, everyone gleefully content. Everyone but Bubba. He just kept squirming, eyes darting to the field's edge, toward the creek and the hills beyond, as if he could hear the creek's ripples calling him already. Rylan saw it too—that restless spark, an itch to roam free, wilder than the creek itself. It was a flicker of something big, something that'd soon spill over their lives like water breaking a dam, pulling them all into its current.

* * *

A few Sundays later, the morning dawned normal, soft sunlight casting its palette through the stained-glass window in the kitchen, the house creaking awake. Pops sipped coffee, black and bitter, while Rylan gnawed a biscuit, crumbs dusting his overalls. The front and back doors yawned wide, as always, letting the breeze carry in the scent of Honeysuckle and the haunting ripples of the creek just before a storm.

Mamma bolted down the stairs, her bare feet slapping wood, hair wild, eyes wide with a terror Rylan hadn't seen before.

"Ry—Pops—where's Carlton?"

Her voice cracked, sharp as breaking glass. They shook their heads, slow and confused, peering at the empty crib like it'd cough up an answer. No sign of the baby Hulk—no coo, no rustle, just silence where a baby should've been.

Mamma's panic erupted slowly, then all at once. Pops snapped alive, a coil unwinding, barking orders as he yanked on boots, coffee mug shattering on the floor in a spray of black shards. Rylan stood frozen, biscuit crumbling in his fist, as Mamma dialed 911, her words tumbling frantic into the receiver:

"Baby's gone—missing—help!"

* * *

The search for Bubba-Carlton-Hulk spilled across Eldergrove's fields like a dark tide, the townsfolk calling it *the grid*—a slow, somber march, step by step, through the swaying jade grasses that stretched wide under a sky too bright for such sorrow. They lined up shoulder to shoulder, boots crunching the earth, faces tight with a quiet terror nobody dared name. A pack of dogs trailed them—some floppy-eared mutts that would always welcome Bubba and Mamma on their morning strolls, others lean hounds with noses sharp as sin, the kind folks swore could sniff out a whisper of life in a haystack. The air thrummed thick with Honeysuckle and fear, a sinister hum that prickled Rylan's neck as he watched from the edge, hazel eyes wide and burning.

The hound men, grizzled and grim, called for something of Bubba's—a scrap he'd worn, a thread to cling to. Mamma stumbled forward, her sundress fluttering like a ghost in the breeze, and pressed a tiny knit cap into their hands, her fingers trembling as if it still held his warmth. The men knelt, passing it among the dogs, their snouts burying deep into the wool, snuffling loudly and desperately, tails stiff as they caught his scent—a fleeting echo of milk and creek mud. Rylan's chest tightened, picturing Bubba's chubby fists clutching that cap, his giggle dancing on the wind those mornings when the town waved them by.

Nearly all of Eldergrove's 1,260 souls had turned out, their shadows stretching long across the fields—men in flannel with jaws set hard, women clutching shawls like shields, kids darting nervously at the fringes. They'd all grown sweet on Bubba, that little Prince with his drool-filled grin, hollering, "Hey there!" and waving as Mamma would wheel him past the porches, where most of life happened in a town like that.

The townsfolk moved as one, a ragged choir of hope and dread, voices low, eyes scanning every ditch and hollow. The dogs barked—a sharp, mournful wail that cut through the rustling grass—and the air grew heavier, thick with something wicked, a shadow nobody could shake. Rylan felt it too, a cold claw sinking into his gut, deeper than Pops' games, whispering that the creek's secrets had woken, hungry, and claimed the young Prince.

After a long day, dusk ushered the full moon onto the horizon, its radiant glow dominating the twilight. The luminous Goddess slowly eclipsed the fading, sunlit sky.

Town folk scoured every inch of the property.

As the sun burned the last minutes of the day, a gray-faced farmer slowly drove his old truck up to the house. He got out and shuffled up to the porch, hat in hand, voice low.

"Y'all need to come see something."

Mamma's scream tore loose, a banshee wail that shred Rylan's ears. Pops went pale, skin waxen, eyes hollow. He caught Mamma before she fell and held on tight.

When he finally let go he stumbled out to the old farmer's truck. He put his hand on Rylan's chest blocking him and said,

"Stay here, Ry. This ain't for a boy's eyes."

Rylan begged to go, voice cracking, but Pops slammed the door, tires spitting dirt as the truck roared off toward the creek, a red and blue glow, pulsing across the horizon.

Rylan couldn't resist the pull of his fear, sinking claws into his gut, not Pops kind but something deeper, something true. He ran, faster than ever before, feet pounding the earth, grass slashing his shins. The eight hundred and fifty three steps from his house to the creek, had proven to be miles longer than it ever had been before, a blur, full of dread. Halfway there, he crumbled, knees buckling as he heard Pops' screams piercing the air:

"NO! NO! NOOOOOO!"

Guttural, broken, a beast gutted alive, words drowning in agony that made no sense. Rylan scrambled up to his feet and ran harder, chest burning, he made it to the crest of the bank, and froze. There, by the creek's edge, Pops knelt, a giant felled, cradling a lifeless bundle in an old towel—Bubba Hulk, tiny and still, skin gray-blue like wet slate, eyes shut. Forever...

But Rylan...

The water lapped mockingly, its glitter gone black under the siren's glare. Mamma had just arrived, Zora and Ezekiel were helping to hold her up, her legs barely working, and she crumpled down into the mud beside Pops. Rylan's knees buckled, his scream choking as Pops cradled the Prince—gray-blue, gone... Rylan followed and watched as the coroner rushed the body off; he heard him saying something quietly to the Sheriff about a possible miracle as he sped away, sirens glowing.

As Rylan ran back to his parents, broken and embracing at the water's edge, something breached—slow, deliberate—molten scales catching the dying light, black spikes slicing the surface. A head reared, jaws gaping, and a hiss split the night. Rylan swore it whispered something—a promise of sorts, too low to distinguish—its eyes glowing amber like Pops' rage. No one else noticed the evil lurking. Real, alive, birthed from the dark that took his brother, Rylan's breath seized, terror coiling cold in his spine. He didn't know its name then, didn't grasp its weight, but it seared into him—a beast that changed the creek forever, its waters no longer innocent but stained with loss.

That was the beginning, the night the creek turned black—its song silenced, its banks heavy with ghosts. Pops' cries faded to a numb hum, Mamma's cries a distant echo, and Rylan stood, a boy unstitched, staring at a monster he'd pursue through years of pain, innocence lost to the deep.

* * *

A few days later, the air hung thick and heavy, suffocating with the weight of sorrow as Bubba's funeral crept upon them. Across from the Tree of Life and the church's sagging steeple, a small cemetery sprawled—an overgrown patch of earth cradling the bones of strangers, their names weathered to whispers on crooked stones. Mamma stood at its edge, the stroller she still pushed—empty, her eyes hollowed out by grief, a keening moan escaping her lips. She couldn't bear it—couldn't fathom leaving her baby boy there, alone amidst the silent chorus of the unknown, his tiny soul lost to the damp, unfeeling ground.

Pops was a shadow beside her, his broad shoulders slumped, his hands trembling as they clutched at nothing. Time had stopped for both of them, a cruel, sticky trap of indecision, their voices circling endlessly—broken—broke, and unable to afford even a sliver of stone to mark their son's passing. They were adrift, drowning in the humid haze of loss, unable to anchor themselves to a choice.

* * *

Rylan, with his heart cracked open and bleeding, found a spark in the quiet eye of the storm raging around inside him. While his parents stumbled through their grief, he slipped away, feet sinking into the soft, wet earth as he made for the old tool shed at the property's edge. The shed loomed like a relic, its splintered walls exhaling the scent of rust and memory. Inside was Pops' meager hoard of tools—earned through sweat and years of demand when patching their fractured home. Rylan wasn't sure what it was, but that old shed, which overlooked the Kingdom, had a sense of grace about it. Rylan often thought of it as his retreat from the battles of the real world. He could sit with the doors open taking in the whole landscape, swearing to himself that he could spend an eternity in that very spot.

Rylan's fingers brushed the cold, worn handle of his grandfather's hammer—a family heirloom. It was Pops' treasure, the only hammer he would ever wield, its heft carrying the weight of a thousand untold stories: nails driven into dreams, boards mended through rage and love, a lineage of labor etched into its grain. Rylan clutched it tight, the wooden handle warm against his palm as if it pulsed with the ghosts of those who had swung it before him. He gathered a handful of other weathered tools as well, a chisel, a rusted saw—anything that might serve his aching purpose.

He worked through the night, grief and pride stoking the fire in his chest, his breath ragged in the sticky air. Sweat mingled with tears as he tore into a slab of old barn lumber, its splintered edges biting his hands. With every strike of the hammer, he poured himself into it—his love for The Hulkster, his fury at the world that stole him, his desperate need to give his brother something eternal.

The box, rough and raw took shape beneath his trembling fingers, an eternal resting place for his baby brother, the sweet Prince. He nailed two pieces he had set aside together into a cross, and with the chisel he carved Baby-Bubba-Carlton-Hulk into its arms, each letter a wound, each stroke a vow.

When he presented them to Mamma, her sob broke free—a sound so tender and shattered it could melt the stars. She ran her fingers over the jagged letters, her tears falling like summer rain, and whispered,

"It's perfect."

Pops stood mute, his face a mask of numbness, though his eyes betrayed him—red-rimmed, glistening, a man unmoored by a heartbreak too vast to voice.

Rylan's voice cut through the haze, soft but steady.

"Let's take him to the creek,"

his words trembled with a love so fierce it hurt.

"I'll watch over him there, and he'll watch over me. He won't be alone..."

His parents, lost in their fog, could only nod, their will surrendered to the boy who had become their compass.

* * *

The next Saturday dawned muggy and close, the sky a bruise above Eldergrove. The townsfolk gathered beneath the Tree of Life, their faces etched with shared sorrow, a humid hush blanketing the square.

Old Zeke had stepped forward, his voice a low rumble of scripture and solace, and he said a few words about grace and eternal rest that felt both hollow and wholesome. He told a story.

"One must live paying attention to the dashes. The in between moments. Feasting one's eyes on the little bitty things that make life such a treasure. The big things will create a wonderful sketch of a life, but the small things fill it all up with color. live a big life, while watching for the dashes. And as Pops would put it, LOVE HARD."

Old Miss Peesewell, her strong, gnarled hands from years of coaxing the church's ancient pipe organ to life, led thirteen souls of the makeshift choir in a rendition of "*Amazing Grace.*" The melody rose, ragged and raw, a hymn that clawed at the air—sticky with tears, humid with longing, horrifying in its beauty as it wrapped around the memory of a life too brief.

The townspeople marched through the town to the sounds of the choir, carrying the casket to the creek, a procession of love and loss, the cross held high in Rylan's hands. As they approached the creek, the water glittered, dark and deep, its surface a mirror for their grief, and when they laid Bubba's tiny soul to rest under the big oak by the creek, the whole town seemed to hold its breath. The ripples whispered—a soft, mournful song of welcome—and Rylan felt it: the unbearable ache of goodbye, the searing warmth of forever. His brother was home, cradled by the Kingdom, and though the pain would linger like damp heat on skin, there was love here too.

That was the day Pops broke—leaving Momma holding onto Zora while he silently walked away, the day the Dragonfish sank its teeth into his soul and swallowed him whole, leaving a stranger where his father once stood. The creek's black water mirrored his eyes that night, hollowed out and glinting with something cold, something that turned Mamma and Rylan into shadows he couldn't bear to see. They weren't his anymore—they were the enemy, thorns in a wound too raw, too vast, a grief that crushed his soul and left no room for them. It was all just too much.

Friends

Rylan was suddenly startled back into reality and reminded of where he was. In front of him, a huge mammoth of a beast—wiggling his butt giddily and hopping on his front two legs like a jumping bean, was all smiles. Pride, water and drool flying everywhere. The dog had dropped a huge, slimy fish smack-dab in Rylan's lap, a trophy that was still flopping around. Rylan yelped, stuffing his father's journal back deep into his satchel, and laughed with pure joy. Old Guy had provided a raw, wet burst that shook his tears loose. "You crazy mutt!" he hollered, shoving the fish off, its scales glinting like the Dragonfish's kin. Old Guy kept grinning and pranced around like he was a dancing bear in a circus.

Rylan shoved the hulking fish from his lap, its weight a fleeting shadow of the creek's deeper secrets, and seized Old Guy by the scruff of his thick, matted neck. They tumbled down the bank's slick slope, laughing and growling, a tangle of boy and beast, mud clinging to their thrashing forms as if the earth itself mourned their reckless joy. The creek glittered black below, its surface a silent witness, rippling with the ghosts of what lingered beneath.

Old Guy's tongue lashed out, a slab of wet muscle half the breadth of Rylan's skull, slathering his face with a warmth that felt both alive and ancient—Rylan yelled, "You slimed me!"—a slurp that echoed the creek's lost songs. They barreled after squirrels, their fleeting tails flickers of life in the humid haze. The air hung thick, sticky with the weight of summer and something unspoken, that gnawed at the edges of their play.

Rylan snatched a jagged branch from the damp ground, its bark peeling like old skin, and swung it high—a sword carved from the bones of the forest, a boy's defiance against the dark. He twirled it with a grace born of fury and dreams, showing off for Old Guy, whose amber eyes glinted with a knowing spark. The beast lunged, jaws clamping the wood, and a tug-of-war erupted—primal, fierce. Rylan's muscles burned, his feet skidding in the mire, but Old Guy's bulk was a force unbound, dragging him through the muck as if he weighed nothing at all. The branch groaned, splintering under the strain, a hymn of resistance swallowed by the creek's black maw.

They fought on, a dance of chaos and kinship, their breaths ragged in the heavy air—Rylan, a boy unstitched by loss, and Old Guy, a creature of sinew and loyalty, tethered to him by a thread stronger than grief. The bank bore their scars: churned earth and broken twigs, a fleeting testament to a moment where the Dragonfish's shadow couldn't reach. Yet beneath their howls, the creek whispered still—a mournful lullaby, its waters stained with memory, watching, waiting, as the boy and his beast carved a fragile joy from its haunted depths. Rylan wiped his face and stared at the creek—a black, lucid mirror, hiding its secrets. *Her* lips, Mamma's song, Pops' scales, Old Guy's joy—they all swirled together, a Kingdom of beauty and hurt. He didn't have *her* name or know Pops' soul, but he had this: *the water's song*, a Kingdom, a friend's grin, and a heart too stubborn to break.

* * *

A ball of fire loomed in the sky, baking Rylan's skin, blades of grass tickling his neck as he propped himself on an elbow. Old Guy flopped down beside him, a hulking heap of tiger-striped fur, his massive head resting on paws big as dinner plates. The creek *Trickled* softly and steadily ahead—its liquid glass whispering secrets Rylan swore he'd crack. He squinted at the water, hazel eyes glinting with a season's worth of scheming, then turned to his drooling partner-in-crime.

"Alright, Old Guy, here's the play." His voice was low and serious, like a general briefing his troops. "We're gonna quit wigglin'—you especially, ya big lug—and go dead quiet. Listen for the *Trickle* calling to us—see? That sound's gonna lead straight to *her*. Best plan I've cooked up yet, and I've been stewin' on it since the moon was fat last."

He jabbed a finger at the air, grinning fiercely, his dirty-blond hair flopping into his eyes. Old Guy's ears twitched, one flopping loose like a tattered flag, and he let out a rumble, "Mmmmm," deep and lazy, his tongue lolling four inches past his chin. Drool plopped into the dirt, a shiny puddle forming fast.

Rylan shot him a look—half glare, half grin—and hissed, "Shhhh! C'mon, man, we're in stealth mode here!"

Old Guy blinked, and smiled slow and unbothered, and "Mmmmm'd" right back, longer and louder this time, like he was arguing the point. Before Rylan could shush him again, a meaty paw—big as a bear's, muddy from creek splashing—slammed down onto Rylan's lap with a wet *thwack*. The weight pinned him, Old Guy's claws flexing just enough to say, "*I'm in on this too, pal.*"

"Yeah, yeah, we're friends, yup" Rylan proclaimed using his best Scooby-Doo voice, laughing sharply as he wrestled the paw off and shoved it back to the grass. "Quit it, ya goof—gonna crush my fiver loads!"

He slung an arm around Old Guy's thick neck, pulling him close till their heads knocked together, fur tickling his cheek. With his free hand, he pressed a finger to his lips, locking eyes with the beast.

"SSSHHHHHHH!" he hissed, dragging it out, brows arched high like a stern teacher schooling a rowdy kid.

Old Guy froze, head tilting sharp to one side—those floppy ears dangling at a ridiculous angle, one eye squinting, the other wide and glinting with a look that screamed, *"Seriously, dude? You're shushin'—Me?"* His grin stretched wider, drool dripping faster, a silent challenge in that goofy stare. Rylan snorted, barely holding it together, and tightened his arm around Old Guy's neck, ruffling his fur rough and playful.

"You're hopeless, ya big mutt," he muttered, voice softening, a grin cracking his face wide. "But you're my kind of hopeless. C'mon—lie down proper, huh? We're a team on this."

He patted the ground beside him, firm but fond, and Old Guy obeyed—sort of—flopping down with a dramatic huff, his bulk shaking the earth, paws sprawled like he owned the whole Kingdom. His head thudded onto Rylan's leg, heavy and warm, drool soaking through Rylans overalls in mere seconds. Rylan didn't mind. He leaned back, one hand resting on Old Guy's scruff, the other shading his eyes as he tuned into the creek's Trickle—soft, insistent, tugging at his soul like *she'd* promised. Old Guy's panting slowed, a steady huff-huff syncing with Rylan's breaths, and for a stretch, they just lay there—boy and beast, best friends, listening together. The plan was simple, but with Old Guy's sloppy loyalty and Rylan's stubborn heart, it felt bigger—like they could track *her* to the ends of the earth, Dragonfish be damned.

"Got your back, Old Guy," Rylan whispered, scratching behind an ear, feeling that love settled deep—wild, messy, unbreakable. "We're gonna find *her*. You'n me."

Rylan reached over and scratched him on the butt just above his tail.... "This the spot Old Boy?"

Old Guy "Mmmmm'd" again, softer now, a grumbly agreement, eyes glossed over and half cross eyed he nudged Rylan's hand with his wet nose.

Rylan grabbed his paw—

"Yes buddy... we are friends."

Original Gangster

Old Guy sprawled beside him, flat on his back like a toppled giant, paws stabbing straight up at the sky, belly exposed—a tiger-striped mountain of fur begging for a scratch. Rylan obliged, digging his fingers into that soft underbelly, grinning as Old Guy's legs twitched like he was starting a Harley. Drool ooooozed from his lolling tongue in a steady, sloppy stream flowing from his upside-down smile.

"You're a mess, ya big goof," Rylan's voice was warm with that easy love only a best friend earns.

Rylan's eyes lit up—lightning in his brain.... He had been trying to come up with a name for his newfound friend. Looking at him he just kept being reminded of that story book his Mamma used to read to him about an elephant named *Dumbo*, and as funny as he thought it was, he couldn't name him that...

He suddenly bolted upright, hands flying off Old Guy's gut, eyes wide as the creek itself.

"I GOT IT!" he shouted, voice cracking high and wild, shattering the afternoon's hum.

"Old Guy, how do we find *her*—the *Sound of the Water*? We follow it to the *source*, ya Dumbo! DUH!"

He slapped his forehead and chicken necked his head, laughing sharply.

"It's where it's loudest, the spring—upstream, that's where *she's* at, that's where the magic happens!"

He thrust his hips forward in a hard fast motion and yanked his hands backward, as he'd seen his Pops do a hundred times. "UUUUUHHHHHH!!!" He jabbed a finger toward the horizon, where the creek twisted north, its *Trickle* swelling into a roar and he could feel it in his bones.

Old Guy rolled over, heaving himself up with a grunt, and cocked his head sideways—those floppy ears dangling, one eye squinting like, "*You serious, kid?*" Rylan jumped to his feet, snatching his gear—canteen sloshing, satchel heavy with fiver loads. He propped the fishing pole over his shoulder and tore off upstream.

"C'mon, ya lug!"

Ten steps in, he skidded to a halt, spinning around. Old Guy hadn't budged—just sat there, a drooling statue, head tilted the other way now, staring like Rylan had lost his mind.

"What's up with you, huh?" Rylan called, hands on hips. "C'mon already!"

Old Guy yawned—jaws gaping wide, teeth glinting like a dinosaur's—and he just stayed put, defiant as all git-out. Rylan rolled his eyes, stomping back with a huff.

"Alright, hold your horses, drama king."

He looked around and spotted the fish—Old Guy's slimy prize from earlier, still barely flopping in the grass, scales catching the light.

“Fine, we’ll clean this upstream,” he muttered, scooping it up, its cold weight slick in his hand. Old Guy’s ears perked, and he lumbered after Rylan like a knight trailing his squire, drool marking their path.

* * *

They trekked on, Rylan chattering away as the creek’s song grew louder, a wild pulse under his words.

“You know, Old Guy, I been thinkin’—‘Old Guy’ is kinda lame, right? We need somethin’ with *bite*.”

He stopped dead, spinning to face his pal, who halted mid-step, drool swinging like a pendulum.

“What’s your vibe, huh? Bear? Nah, too obvious. Ralphie? Pfft, you ain’t no Ralphie—too fancy.”

He tapped his chin, hazel eyes glinting mischief.

“Old... Guy...” His eyes began to widen then slowly lit on fire—“Ohhhh Geeeeeee!—OG!”

Rylan tilted his head sideways back at Old Guy and said

“Well?”

He received a smile, a face slurp, and an itty-bitty tail wiggle....

“OG! OG! OG!”

He threw his arms up, whooping like he’d just won the World Series.

"O-RI-GI-NAL GANG-STA! That's IT! That's IT!"

OG plopped his butt down, head tilting so far it nearly hit the ground, his baffled stare screaming.

"*What the heck, dude?*"

He let out an unamused yawn stretching ever wider and it grabbed Rylan's attention—stopping his celebration mid O...—OG's jaws were unhinging, his muscles flexing, teeth massive and gleaming, a prehistoric maw that could snap a tree trunk. Rylan froze, and let out a slow whistle.

"Dang dog... you could chomp my whole head off—one bite—just gone. That's some crazy stuff right there..."

Out of nowhere, the air shifted—sharp and heavy, a ripple of unseen currents tingling along Rylan's spine like the breath of something ancient stirring awake. The creek's *Trickle* dimmed, its song muffled by a stillness that draped the Kingdom like a shroud, the light bending oddly through the trees as if caught in a web of shadow. OG surged to his feet, a guardian roused, every hair on his spine spiking into a bristling ridge that shimmered faintly, as though kissed by some ethereal glow.

A growl rumbled from his chest—deep, guttural, a sound Rylan had never heard, resonant with the echoes of old wars fought in realms beyond sight. It rolled through the earth, stirring the silt, a primal warning that chilled Rylan's blood and set his heart pounding against his ribs like a trapped thing.

"What is it OG?"

His voice cracked, thin with a boy's fear as he gripped the fish tighter, its scales slick against his palm.

OG leapt in front, planting himself like a sentinel carved from the creek's own magic, teeth bared in a snarl that gleamed wet and fierce—a knight clad in fur, his amber eyes alight with a fire that seemed to pierce the veil between worlds. His haunches tensed, muscle rippling beneath his tiger-striped coat, and a howl tore from his throat—a wild, haunting cry that echoed through the trees, carrying a note of something celestial, as if calling forth unseen allies from the Kingdom's depths. Rylan's gaze flicked to the bushes where OG stared, his breath catching as the leaves quivered, parted by a presence too vast, too dark, to belong to the daylight world.

A bear, massive and towering, rearing up on hind legs like a specter had been summoned from the creek's black heart. Its fur was matted, streaked with ash and crimson, as though stained by the blood of fallen souls, and its claws glinted like shards of obsidian, sharp enough to rend the fabric of hope itself. Its eyes burned with a malevolent gleam, twin pits of shadow that swallowed light, radiating a hunger not just for flesh but for despair—a beast born of the same darkness that birthed the Dragonfish, a herald of ruin with the weight of sin in its stride. Its roar was a low, guttural dirge, a sound that seemed to pull at the edges of Rylan's soul, whispering of loss and endings.

"HO—LY...!"

He stumbled back, slipping in the silt, the fish clutched tight as if it could shield him from this evil made manifest.

OG lunged—airborne in a heartbeat, a streak of fur and teeth, his roar a hymn of defiance against the bear's unholy presence. It was a move etched into his bones, learned in shadowed days of battles past, a knight's charge against a fiend.

The bear met him with a swipe of its claw—a brutal arc of darkness that cut through the air, trailing a faint shimmer of malice, as if the very act of violence fed its power. The blow struck OG's flank, sending him tumbling across the bank in a spray of dirt and dust, his body rolling to a stop against a gnarled root with a muted thud. Rylan froze as the bear's gaze swung to him—those shadowed eyes locking on with a promise of oblivion. It dropped to all fours, the ground trembling beneath its weight, and charged—straight for him, a tide of evil surging forward, its breath a rancid fog that carried the scent of decay and broken dreams.

"OG!"

Rylan shrieked, panic clawing his chest as he scrambled back, the fish slipping in his sweaty grip. The bear was close now, its claws tearing gashes in the earth, each step a drumbeat of doom that echoed the beat of Pops' rage, the weight of Bubba's loss—a living symbol of the family's fractures given form. Its jaws parted, revealing teeth jagged and stained, as though it had feasted on the light of better days.

OG staggered up, shaking off the hit, blood matting his fur like a martyr's mark, and launched again—his teeth sinking into the bear's neck fur, a desperate grip to anchor Rylan's fleeting hope. The bear roared, a sound that shook the trees and sent a ripple across the creek's surface, as if the water itself recoiled from its taint. It thrashed, shaking OG loose, his body skidding across the silt once more, but that moment of resistance gave Rylan a sliver of time.

He clambered onto a rock, legs trembling, the moss beneath his feet slick with the creek's tears. The bear loomed closer, its shadow stretching long and twisted, a stain upon the Kingdom's purity. Rylan sucked in a breath, channeling Pops' gravelly lessons—"*Make yourself big, boy!*"—memories that tore from his gut, infused with a spark of the creek's magic, a defiance against the evil before him. He waved his free arm high, the fish dangling from the other like a relic of innocence, and shouted.

"GET OUTTA HERE!"

His voice cracked but carried, a boy's cry woven with the Kingdom's strength, echoing off the water and the trees. The bear paused, its growl deepening, eyes flickering between boy and dog—a moment of doubt in its dark purpose.

Rylan's mind raced—two hands, bigger threat—and he acted, hurling the fish with all his might. It sailed through the air, a shimmering arc of scales and light, a small piece of the Kingdom's grace flung against the bear's malice. It bounced down the hill, splashing into the creek with a soft plop, the ripples spreading like a prayer cast into the void. Rylan stood as tall as he possibly could, with both hands extended up into the air, and screamed with every bit of man he could muster,

"AAAAAAAAAAAAAHHHHHHHHHHH!!!"

The bear froze, rearing up once more, its massive frame swaying as its nose twitched, caught by the scent of the fish—a fleeting distraction from its hunger for ruin. Its eyes narrowed, shadowed pools of doubt, as OG rose again, growling low and steady, a sound that hummed with the creek's own voice, a guardian's vow against this harbinger of despair. His fur glowed faintly in the dimming light, a knight blessed by the Kingdom's magic, and he stepped forward to Rylan's side, amber eyes locked on the bear with a quiet, unyielding fury.

The bear hesitated, its claws sinking into the earth as if reluctant to release its hold on this moment of darkness. Its growl faltered, a crack in its malevolent armor, and then—hunger, the basest of its drives, won out over its deeper intent. It turned, lumbering down the bank with a crash of snapping twigs, its retreat a reluctant surrender as it splashed into the creek after the fish Rylan had thrown, the water spinning into a blackened void around its paws as if mourning its presence.

"OG, LET'S GO!"

Rylan's voice was sharp with urgency, leaping off the rock, feet hitting the silt with a wet smack. OG fell in beside him, fur streaked with dirt and blood, but his grin—wide, wet, and radiant—shone like a beacon of triumph, drool swinging as they moved.

They sprinted upstream, legs pumping, hearts pounding in sync—boy and dog, a blur of mud and resolve against the fading echo of evil. The creek's roar swelled, a cleansing hymn guiding them to the source, to *her*, to safety. Rylan laughed—breathless, jagged, a sound laced with the Kingdom's wild magic—glancing at OG loping beside him, ears flapping like banners of a battle won.

"You're a freakin' lunatic, OG!" He gasped, voice rough with joy, the words spilling out as his lungs burned. "Saved my butt back there—a holy gangsta!"

OG barked—a deep, goofy woof—nipping at Rylan's heels, drool flying as they ran, a salute to their victory over the dark. Rylan reached down, ruffling OG's scruff, feeling that bond tighten—unbreakable, forged in the shadow of evil, blessed by the creek's mystique.

"Me and you, OG. Ride or die, Old-Guy!"

OG's tongue lolled out, a sloppy banner of their shared spirit. The bear was gone, its darkness swallowed by the creek, and Rylan knew OG was more than a friend—he was his guardian, a knight touched by grace, a piece of the Kingdom's magic made flesh. Together, they'd chase the *Sound of the Water* to the ends of the earth, undaunted by the shadows that lingered.

Call of the Water

Rylan and OG pushed onward, the creek's restless *Trickle* cutting a shiny silver path through the growing wild-wood, like a trail pulling them into something special. The world around them felt bigger, as if nature were opening up, showing off its wonders. Tall, mossy oaks stretched toward the sky, their twisty branches reaching out, and willows leaned over the water, their lime-green leaves—dotted with yellow and purple—shaking in a breeze that carried the Kingdom's sweet smell, a mix of Honeysuckle and dirt that stuck to Rylan like a warm hello. Ferns popped up along the bank, brushing his legs with soft little taps, almost like they were cheering him on.

The air buzzed with life, a big, happy sound that wrapped around Rylan like a cozy blanket. Bullfrogs croaked low and strong from the creek's dark spots, cicadas hummed in steady beats that matched his breathing, and crickets sang a high, tinkling tune. It all mixed with the creek's splashing laugh, getting louder as they climbed, calling him forward.

Dragonflies zipped around like tiny lightning bolts, their blue and green wings sparkling, while flutterbys twirled in golden loops above the water, looking like a sunset come alive. White albino squirrels darted through the bushes, quick as ghosts, and chipmunks chattered alongside, their bushy tails bouncing. It was a wild mix of sound and motion, a song that felt old and full of life, like the Kingdom was singing just for them.

Rylan stopped, breathing hard from the hike, his patched overalls sticking to his legs with sweat, the patches Mamma had sewn on holding tight like little hugs. He put his hands on his knees, gulping the warm, thick air, and grinned broadly, as OG trotted to the creek's edge. The Minihorse—Rylan's silly name for him—dunked his big, striped head into the water, slurping loudly and happily, making ripples spread out fast.

His floppy ears dangled like soggy flags, and drool dripped into the creek, shining in the sunlight. Rylan laughed hard, a belly laugh that bounced off the trees, wild and free, and let out a loud, goofy howl that mingled with the crickets. He grabbed his beat-up old canteen, its dings telling stories of the past, and twisted off the cap. Tipping it back, he let a swallow of Mamma's Lemonade pour in, hitting his tongue with a zing that felt like love. He swished it around slowly, enjoying every bit, letting it wake him up like a promise he could taste.

Halfway through drinking, something stopped him. A sound, soft as a breeze, slipped through the creek's Trickle. He froze, Lemonade sitting in his cheeks, eyes squinting as he tried to hear it better. He listened hard, letting the water's noise fill his head, and there it was: a girl's voice, light and pretty, mixing with the creek like a golden thread. His heart thumped loudly, banging against his ribs. Was it real? He swallowed quickly, the Lemonade rushing down cold, and turned to OG, who'd pulled his wet face out of the water, drops falling from his jowls.

"You hear that, OG?"

Rylan's voice was quick and excited, hazel eyes shining with wonder, like he still believed in magic. "I know you do... shhh!"

He stuck a finger to his lips, fast and firm, but a grin peeked out anyway. OG plopped down, his butt hitting the ground with a splash, head tilting sideways. His ears hung like wet rags, one eye half-closed, the other big and curious, a low *grumble* rumbling out—a funny little question, drool plopping into the dirt.

Rylan twisted the canteen cap back on fast, his hands shaking—not from being tired, but from the spark flipping in his stomach, as if flutterbys were waking up. He squinted upstream, his breath catching as the creek changed before his eyes.

What had been a creek had now turned into a cascade of water, spilling down from rocks piled high atop each other like nature's own messy stack of blocks. The stones, smoothed by years of the creek's touch, glistened wet and dark—some mossy—some bare, jutting out in a jagged line that climbed toward the hill's crest. Water rushed over them, fast and free, tumbling in little leaps from one rock to the next, splashing white and foamy where it hit. It wasn't a huge waterfall—not yet—but a lively, bouncing flow, as if the creek were in a hurry to show him something big. The sound grew bolder, a mix of gurgles and soft roars, calling him closer with a voice that felt alive, tugging at his heart.

"Let's go, boy!" he shouted, voice breaking with excitement, feet shifting in the mud. "It's close—I can feel it!"

He started running, steps long and eager, OG right behind him, a drooling shadow bouncing in the spotty sunlight.

"*She's* perfect, OG!" Rylan yelled back, words spilling out as if he couldn't hold them in, his heart jumping around like a crazy bird.

"Just like you, buddy—perfect in all your messy ways! I never had flutterbys like that in my tummy 'til *she* kissed my cheek—swear it, they've been dancing there ever since!"

His cheeks went red, that memory lighting him up—*her* lips so soft, *her* hair tickling his face, starting a flutter he couldn't stop.

OG let out a long, goofy "*Mmmmmm,*" deep and warm, as if he got it, his tail smacking the air in time with Rylan's words.

He slapped OG's flank, his eyes drifting back to the hilltop—just a hundred steps off now. OG bounced up too, shaking off the dirt like it was nothing, his grin wide and wet, ready to move on. The falling creek's song got louder, a big, clear sound that grabbed his heart. And there it was again—that hum, not quiet anymore, ringing out like a bell, a voice floating through the air. Light and perfect, it brushed through the trees, tugging at him with a tune he felt deep inside. His heartbeat sped up, thumping wildly, and he stepped forward, singing along under his breath.

"Don't worry... about a thang..."

OG's ears flicked up, his head tilting fast, drool swinging as he caught the change, his eyes bright with something smart. Rylan breached the hills crest, and stopped, heart exploding from what he saw.

Believe

Across the meadow, he saw *her*, glowing in the sun like silk, *her* shape framed by the water's shimmer. flutterbys circled *her* like a crown—**Three Little Birds** swirled in her breath, sweet and clear, sinking into Rylan's bones as if it belonged there. *She* looked up at him, and everything stopped—the air heavy with something big and quiet, a feeling as strong as the Kingdom. Seeing *her* hurt in a good way, so much he could hardly move.

Right then, he knew—it hit him fast. He knew *her*, as if a locked door in his heart had opened. He let *her* in—all of *her*—*her* beauty, *her* wisdom, *her* strength, everything *she* was. It rushed into him like a river, washing away the bad stuff—the hurt, the dark, the broken pieces—leaving him clean with just *her* look. *She* was like a gift he hadn't asked for, making him feel whole.

She stood in the spring, fishing pole in hand, the line tight, but it wasn't just that. The fish in the clear water didn't just bite—they moved with *her,* swirling like shiny jewels, as if *she* were directing them. *Her* hair waved, her eyes sparkled, *her* voice floated around him—it was too much, but it held him tight, safe like he'd never been before.

His stuff fell from his hands, hitting the ground without a care. His arms flew out, hands wide, reaching over the spring as if he could grab *her* right then. His voice burst out, strong and sure, he suddenly knew.

"TRICKLLLLLE!"

* * *

Trickle turned and smiled—a slow, radiant curve of *her* lips that struck Rylan like a bolt from Heaven. It was an old-soul love affair unfurling its wings, a promise whispered across lifetimes yet untouched. *Her* wave was an invitation, delicate yet fierce. Rylan's breath snagged, his hazel eyes blazing as he spun to OG—his drooling knight, grinning wide—and he took off, heart a wild drum thundering in his chest.

He swore if he ran fast enough, he could run across the top of the water all the way to *her*, his faith a bridge over the water's surface...

As his toes kissed the depths, doubt flickered into his certainty, and he knew he'd be swimming... The spring swallowed his shins, cool and alive, and he plunged forward, a boy reborn in the current of *her* call.

Trickle dropped *her* fishing pole at the water's edge, its bamboo clattering like a discarded relic, and *her* giggle spilled out—bright, untamed, a melody that spun the world into a frenzy. *She* stepped onto the sandbar, a ribbon of gold threading through the spring, the water lapping no higher than the tops of *her* feet. Rylan stood waist-deep and stopped for a moment to catch his breath—he couldn't turn his eyes away...

She traversed along the top of the sandbar out to the point, where they almost touched. The shallows surrounding them erupted—fish boiling at the surface, breaching and twirling in a kaleidoscope of sapphire, emerald, and molten amber. Their scales catching the sun like scattered stars. They mimicked *her* every motion, a shimmering court bowing to their Queen. To Rylan, *she* walked on water—a vision so real his soul trembled.

Trickle thrust out *her* hand, Rylan ran to *her*—warm, slick with spring water, electrified with *her* pulse. He pulled *her* in, with the weight of every aching night he had clung tightly onto *her* memory, and *she* crashed into him, *her* laughter a cascade of light, flirtatious and free, daring him to dive deeper. He stared deeply into the jade-stained windows of *her* soul, flecked with gold like embers of a fire that had burned for him since the beginning. They held him, unyielding, and he surrendered—lips crashing to *hers* in a kiss that shattered the boy he'd been.

He had never felt anything as soft as *her* lips before. *Her* taste flooded his everything—sweet and savory, laced with the tart sting of what he thought was surely Honeysuckle Lemon Sugar.

It was young love's first bloom, wild and reckless, innocent, playful passion, enduring, a vow etched into their bones. His arms tightened around *her*, pulling *her* flush against his trembling, overstimulated frame, every nerve alight with the thrill of her nearness. *She* giggled into a kiss, a flirtatious trill that danced across his lips, *her* body yielding yet commanding, enthralled as if *her* spirit had slipped into his soul and claimed it whole.

The world blurred—they were one, a young and innocent love so vast it swallowed the spring itself.

Hard Love

As Rylan lay drying on the shoreline, he couldn't fathom Heaven or anything being sweeter than this. The spring's shimmer, Trickle, OG's drooling grin—it was paradise so pure—roaring through him like a river unbound.

Pops' gravelly growl echoed in his skull,

"You gotta love hard, boy—""

Back then, those words sank heavily, tales of Pops' *hard love* were etched in bruises and whiskey fumes. But Mom? She'd giggle, *her* eyes soft as creek moss, hearing Pops',

"I'm lovin' on you hard, woman"

She was his everything, good and bad, a lifeline she gripped as if it was *her* last breath.

Now, watching Trickle rise from the spring—water streaming from *her* sundress, clinging to every curve like a lover's caress—Rylan *knew*. His heart slammed against his ribs, a thunderous ache, as *her* bare feet pressed the bank's silt, each step a hymn to *her* untamed grace. She was too much, his senses drowned in the musk of *her* skin, the glint of jade in *her* eyes piercing him like lightning under a storm-lit sky. This was *loving hard*... gut-wrenching, soul-defining, a man's pride swelling in his adolescent frame, fierce and unbreakable.

The three of them sprawled on the bank—Rylan, Trickle, OG. No cares to tether them, the world a distant hum beneath the Kingdom's song. Hunger gnawed, sharp and ravenous after their play, and Rylan's hand dove into his satchel, fingers brushing the paper towel wrap and the dented canteen, two-thirds full of Mamma's Lemonade.

Rylan grinned, a spark lighting his hazel eyes, and declared,

"If there's a God... today he's smilin' on us."

Mamma used to say that when she was praying out loud: "God, please smile upon my boys and myself, sweet Jesus."

Rylan felt it, a divine nod warming his bones. He reached into his satchel, and there it was wrapped in paper towel. He tore off a corner of the sandwich he had wrapped, its crust still soft, Spam, government cheese and butter oozing out the edges, and handed it to Trickle along with a couple Saltines. *She* took it, *her* fingers grazing his, a jolt that made his breath hitch. Another piece for OG—the Slobber Monster—who wolfed it down, one gulp, drool leaking all over. Rylan skipped himself; he'd be fine, he wanted to make sure Trickle and OG got their fill.

Trickle finished *her* bite, *her* lips parting in a silent plea for more, crumbs dusting *her* chin like tiny stars. Rylan's pulse quickened—he reached in, pulled out another corner, with a few more saltines, stunned to feel the satchel still heavy with food. **What the heck?** He thought. He tore a chunk for OG, then gave in and tore one for himself, saltines crunching between his teeth, Spam tangy on his tongue—and still, the bag held more.

It defied logic, a miracle spilling from his hands, and they ate, ravenous, laughing, tearing into sandwich and crackers as if it were a feast from the

Kingdom itself. Trickle shoved four saltines in *her* mouth at once, cheeks bulging, eyes glinting with mischief. Rylan stared, bewilderment twisting his face; *her* mouth so full *she* could barely chew, *she* looked like a chipmunk, crumbs seeping through *her* lips as if a dam were breaking. *She* opened wide and shouted, muffled,

"Got anything to drink?"

They erupted like a volcano as cracker shards sprayed everywhere. They collapsed into each other, howling, rolling in the grass, a tangle of limbs and unrestrained laughter. Rylan swiped saltine dust from *her* cheeks, his grin spanning ear to ear—sympathy, adoration, pride all blazing in his chest. He twisted the cap off the canteen, the tart-sweet scent of *Lemonade* hitting the air, and handed it to *her* with a reverence that made his hands tremble. *She* seized it, tipping it back, gulping deeply, *her* throat bobbing as the liquid quenched a thirst that seemed to echo his own. Water from *her* hair dripped onto his arm, cool and electric, and the spring's hum wrapped them in a cocoon of sound—bullfrogs croaking, dragonflies buzzing, OG's huffing breaths as he fixated on a squirrel darting up a tree.

* * *

They melted into the sandy bend of the creek, sitting side by side—Rylan and Trickle, their faces inches apart, breath mingling in the Honeysuckle-heavy air. Trickle sat knees hugged to *her* chest, *her* sundress clinging wet and bright, golden hair dripping slow beads that caught the sun like molten stars. *She* traced idle spirals in the sand with a twig, *her* eyes drifting somewhere beyond the horizon, a quiet settling over *her* like the hush before a storm.

"You're awful quiet, Trickle," he said, voice soft but probing. "What's got your attention—where are you at?"

She glanced at him, *her* lips twitching into a half-smile—gentle, but laced with something heavy, like a creek stone smoothed by years of current.

"I was home for a moment but I'm back... Just hypnotized by the water, I guess" *she* murmured, *her* voice a lilting thread.

She flicked the twig into the shallows, watching it bob and spin, a tiny vessel lost to the creek's will. Rylan's brow creased, his fingers digging into the grass as if he could root himself to *her* words.

"Yeah?" he said, low and careful, a King coaxing a secret from his Queen. "What's pullin' outta you today?"

Her gaze melted into his, and for a heartbeat, the world shrank to the space between them—the spring's hum, OG's huffing breaths, the rustle of leaves all fading to a distant hymn.

"You first," she leaned in close, *her* voice an alluring whisper, *her* smile sharpening, playful but piercing. "You'll soon know me better than anything you've ever known."

He exhaled sharply, a laugh that wasn't quite a laugh, and flopped down backwards, staring up at the canopy where sunlight speared through in golden lances.

"Ain't fair, turnin' it on me like that."

His voice softened, cracking open like a dam giving way.

"Alright, Trickle. You wanna know? It's Pops. Always Pops. He's... he's a mountain I can't climb, and I'm scared as heck I'm gonna end up just like him."

Her hand stilled in the sand, *her* eyes narrowing—not with judgment but with a hunger to understand.

"How's that?"

Rylan swallowed, and sat up slowly, as if the weight of it was dragging him under.

"He's got this fire in him—used to be golden, bright as the sun off this spring. Wrote poems, built our house with his bare hands, loves Mamma so hard it makes the air shake. But it's twisted now—whiskey and that cursed pipe turned it black, and he... he hurts us, Trickle. Shoves Mamma 'round when the dark takes him. I'm scared I've got that same fire, waitin' to burn me up too. What if I turn into that? What if I can't stop it?"

She shifted closer, *her* knee brushing his, a spark of warmth in the cool silt.

"But you love him..." *she* said, not a question, *her* voice threading through his fear like a lifeline.

"Yeah..."

His eyes swelled, raw and unashamed.

"God help me, I do. He's my Pops—taught me to take care of my Mamma, fish, skip stones, wrestle hogs, a laugh loud as thunder. Even when he's breakin' me, I see that spark—somethin' worth savin'. I think he's still in there, buried under all that hurt. Saw it clear as day when Bubba..."

His voice cracked, splintering on the name, and he clenched his fists, knuckles whitening against the earth.

Trickle's breath caught sharply, a hitch snagging in *her* throat like a thread pulling tight, and *her* hand stretched out, trembling just a touch. It hung there, hovering over his, fingers splayed as if *she* could scoop up the pain pouring out of him—raw, thick, seeping into the air between 'em. *Her* eyes flickered, and Rylan felt it—a warmth brushing his skin, faint as a whisper, as if *she* wasn't just holding space but mending it.

"Tell me about Bubba," *she* whispered, soft as a prayer, *her* eyes locking with his, steady and deep.

Rylan's chest heaved, a sob clawing up his throat, but he forced it down, letting the words tumble out instead.

"When Bubba died, it gutted 'em—Pops and Mamma both. Pops was a titan that day, holding' him up at the crawl-off, braggin' to the whole town. Mamma... she was light itself, singin' to him, pushin' that stroller like he was *her* whole world. Then he was gone—just... gone. Found him by the creek, cold and still, like the water stole him right outta our hands. Mamma crumpled, wailin—Pops... he screamed—deep, awful screams, like something ripped his soul clean out. But in his eyes, past the rage, I saw it—a spark, faint but alive. He was hurtin' so bad, 'cause he loved so hard. That's what I'm prayin' for Trickle—to pull that man back from the dark."

Her fingers brushed his brow, tentative and electric...

"Grief wouldn't even exist if we never had the joy of lovin so hard."

Rylan listened to *her* and replied, trembling with a boy's confusion and a man's fury.

"Bubba's passin' broke me too. He was my little Prince—I was gonna teach him to fish, skip stones, rule this Kingdom with me. I'd dream of us runnin' wild, laughin' 'til the stars fell. Then God just... yanked him away. Didn't warn us, didn't explain—just took him. I don't get it, Trickle. Is God good, givin' us this Kingdom, this magic? Or bad, snatchin' Bubba like that, leavin' us to drown? I blame Him—hate Him some days—but I keep prayin', hopin' there's a reason I can't see..."

His words hung heavy, a storm cloud over the spring, and Trickle moved swiftly—*her* arms wrapping around him, pulling him into *her* embrace with a fierceness that stole his breath. *She* pressed one hand to *her* heart, the other to his, *her* palm warm against his chest where his pulse thundered wildly. *Her* jade eyes bored into his, deep as the creek's hidden springs, glinting with a love so vast it swallowed his rage.

"Ry," *she* whispered, voice a melody of steel and grace, "you ain't alone in this. I'm here—your Kingdom's here. Let it hold you."

Rylan noticed his satchel still lying open from the feast and inside he saw the card his Mamma had sent with his lunch that must have fallen out when he opened up the paper towels, the writing on it hinted:

Dream Rylan—Mamma

The weight of the words—Pops' fists, Bubba's ghost, God's silence—lifted, a burden unspooling through Trickle's touch. Rylan's eyes fluttered shut, and he fell—not into sleep, not into waking, but into a place beyond, a liminal realm where Trickle's presence tethered him. It wasn't *her* body beside him, but *her* soul—golden, unshakable—grounding his spirit to the Kingdom's roots. The *Sound of the Water* swelled in his ears, a lullaby weaving through his bones, and the darkness parted...

Redemption

He stood in a valley drenched in pearl clouds—whimsical, mystical, a vision spun from the Kingdom's wildest dreams. Paths of molten gold wound through emerald glades, lined with willows dripping silver leaves that chimed like bells in the breeze. Springs burst from cliffs in cascading waterfalls, their waters shimmering with sapphire and amber. The most perfect place he'd ever seen—the Kingdom's magic pulsed here, amplified, a sanctuary carved from eternity's edge.

Across the water, a boy stood—small, sturdy, casting a line with a flick of his wrist, his laughter bubbling like the creek at dawn. Rylan's heart lurched—he couldn't place him, yet he knew him, a recognition stitched into his marrow. Trickle's voice brushed his mind, soft as a breeze through the oaks.

"Go,"

He hesitated, then took off, feet pounding the golden path, the air crackling with life.

"Run, Rylan—Run." *Her* words were a spark igniting his soul.

He crested the bank, close enough to see, and stopped dead—breath snagging, world tilting. It was Bubba-Carlton-Hulk—alive and radiant, a young boy now—but Rylan could see who he was. His face glowed with a slicked grin, eyes glinting mischief as he reeled in a fish of legend. Beside him sat OG, massive and grinning, his tiger-striped fur gleaming in the sun, drool swinging like a victory banner. OG's amber eyes met Rylan's, steady and sure, a silent promise...

Bubba turned, waved—warmth flooded Rylan, a tide of life so pure it burned away the grief and the blame. This was Bubba's Kingdom now—a place beyond loss, where the creek's song never faltered—where love reigned unbroken. Rylan stepped forward reaching, tears streaming hot and free, but the vision softened, fading slowly like twilight swallowing the day. The golden paths blurred, the waterfalls hushed, and Bubba's laugh echoed into silence, a melody he'd carry forever.

* * *

Trickle gently guided him, floating weightless through the mist, to a place where he could see a mother sitting alone in the sterile, cold embrace of a hospital room. Her hands trembled, clutching the edge of a crib where her infant son lay, tethered to a chaotic web of bandages and cables. Her face was a map of anguish, etched with the raw, unrelenting grief of a woman who had just endured the unthinkable—catastrophic, an inebriate's reckless cruelty. The collision had stolen her husband and daughter in an instant, ripping her world apart, a fragile thread of life dangling in the wreckage. Now, she sat, forsaken by fate, with no family, no friends, only the fleeting kindness of a stranger to anchor her to hope.

As Rylan watched, a radiant aura that shimmered with ethereal light surrounded the woman. Within it, four faces emerged—man, eagle, ox, and lion—each glowing with celestial grace, as if drawn from a realm beyond the stars. The light bathed her, pulsing with a warmth that stirred Rylan's soul, an enlightened guardian's embrace offering unwavering assurance. In that moment, he felt a profound truth that everything was as it should be, like there was a purpose for it all, and that this was not the last time he would see the Tetramorph that acted as her guardian.

A doctor stepped into the room; a donor had been found—a child of the same age, sex, size, and blood type, whose organs could replace the ones failing within her son. A miracle dangled before her, yet it was laced with a devastating truth. Rylan felt the weight of it crash into him.

How could the Creator, who loved every soul with infinite tenderness, bear the agony of such a decision? One child's death to grant another life—how could even the divine heart reconcile that torment?

Tears burned in Rylan's heart as the realization seared through him. In that moment, he understood the unbearable cost of redemption, the piercing beauty of sacrifice, the bitter and the sweet. He felt the mother's desolation, her desperate clinging to a flicker of hope, and the silent, sacred exchange that wove their fates together. Rylan's soul trembled with the weight of it—love and loss entwined, a divine sorrow.

* * *

A vast ocean emerged, stretching endless and gleaming, its blue so deep it swallowed the horizon whole—somewhere wild, untamed, beyond the reach of a map—they weren't floating anymore; they were soaring, sweeping over the waves, arms flung wide, the wind roaring past them fierce and untamed. Trickle's golden hair streamed wildly, catching a light not born of the sun.

Below, the ocean pulsed with wonders defying names. Whales rose slowly, their backs arching dark and glistening, massive as hills emerging from the tide. Their songs rolled upward, low and mournful, vibrating through Rylan's chest like a chant from a forgotten realm, stirring something ancient within him.

Dolphins flashed in silver arcs, leaping high in spinning frenzies of joy and singing, their laughter splashing the air—playful spirits weaving through the spray. Turtles glided steadily, shells sprawling as wide as old VW Buses, etched with patterns of countless years, moving as if bearing the weight of time. Sailfish pierced the surface, gleaming blue and sharp, breaching with sudden flicks, while reefs flourished beneath—sprawling bursts of red, gold, and violet, glowing faintly, all touched by a ball of flame.

They dove into the deep blue, breaching the water's surface, plunging into its core. The ocean parted around them, clear as polished crystal. The depths—limitless, a blue so fierce it consumed his mind. Schools of hundreds of different varieties of fish shimmered, twisting through kelp forests swaying tall and verdant. Rays swept past, wings flapping slowly and silently, casting shadows on the sandy floor. A shark sliced through, gray and sleek, eyes glinting coldly but passing without pause, leaving Rylan wondering if it knew they didn't belong.

Trickle's fingers grazed his, light as a whisper, and a warmth pulsed through—binding him to this marvel, leading him deeper.

Ain't no dream... this is real, he thought, half-lost.

The water spat them out, and they found themselves standing on a cliffside. Rylan drew a ragged breath, chest heaving, and the air struck him—salty, warm, laced with something sweet, like home distilled into a gust. This wasn't his creek, but it echoed the same song, wrapping around him like a memory taking shape.

A waterfall thundered beside them, a hundred feet tall, its white rush crashing down in a deafening cascade. It fed seven pools below—each one, catching the next—carved into the rock like a staircase sculpted for giants. Mist rose, dampening his face, and Rylan caught rainbows flickering in it—thin bands of color bending toward the sea, faint as a vow whispered on the wind.

Beyond the cliff, the ocean sprawled fierce and boundless, hurling itself against spires of rock rising sharply from the deep—black, rugged peaks, small mountains thrusting out of the blue like guardians of a sunken world. Waves smashing them relentlessly, bursting into white explosions of froth, the sound pounding through the ground like a heartbeat older than his years. Rylan felt it rattling his bones, a rhythm soothing his edges.

Trees leaned over the cliff's rim, swaying gently in the breeze, branches drooping with fruit—mangoes dripping gold, papayas glowing orange—and Lemons, the most beautiful he had ever seen. He plucked one and peeled it. He bit into it, accepting its conditions, the juice bursting onto his tongue, sticking to his chin, tasting as if he were consuming the vision itself. It was both bitter and sweet, as if it had been ordained by father earths own hand and dipped in Mamma's magical Honeysuckle Lemon Sugar.

Roosters strutted freely around the cliff, bold and untamed, combs flashing red, crowing deep and rough, their calls laying a basis for a wild chorus of tropical birds. Bright ones screeched, wings blazing red and yellow, while smaller ones—green, blue, gold—trilled high and free, spilling sound like water cascading over stones. The noise wove around them, lifting Rylan's spirit, and he glanced at Trickle—*her* jade eyes catching the light, gold flecks sparkling, and that glow flickering around *her* again, soft as a breath, making him wonder if *she'd* summoned this song, some angel tuning the air to sing for him.

A Gypsy camp clung to the cliff's edge, poised above a colossal waterfall fed by a mystical spring, as if the rock itself had birthed it. The spring sparkled, its waters so pure they seemed distilled by the heavens, pooling in this sacred hollow to nourish the world below. Its flow stretched beyond Rylan's sight, a shimmering mystery that outran his understanding. On a weathered porch, an elderly couple rocked in chairs polished by time, their silhouettes framed against the setting sun. The man's hair glowed white as the foam churning far below, while the woman's tight braid wove silver threads like rivers through slate. They shared a pitcher of Golden liquid, its radiance alive, smothering the dying light, searing their image into Rylan's soul.

Trickle surged forward, hurling herself against an invisible barrier that rippled like liquid starlight. Her arms stretched through it, fingers grasping at the firmament that held them back, her heart laid bare in a fierce yearning. Tears traced her cheeks, defiant against the radiant, faith-filled smile that lit her face, as if she could will the boundary to dissolve.

Rylan was drawn to them, his legs itching to run, to cross that stretch and sit at their feet, quenching his soul with the Golden Ale, hearing their voices. He stepped forward, heart racing—but something stopped him, solid and unyielding, blocking him and Trickle from drawing closer. His fists clenched, reaching through it, but it stood firm, a barrier woven from the vision's own fabric. Trickle's hand brushed his shoulder, light as a feather, and *her* breath hitched—soft, aching, like *she* felt it too. Rylan looked into her eyes and realized this place held her heart as well as all of her secrets.

The sun dipped lower, spilling red and gold across the ocean, and the scene shimmered—fading slowly, like water slipping through his grasp, leaving him yearning for a place he couldn't reach. The cliffside lingered, the waterfall's roar echoing, the waves' crash thumping, the birds' song twisting through him. He saw the couple again, their faces blurred but warm, sipping the Golden Ale as if it held the world's sweetness. Trickle stood silent beside him, *her* glow dimming but present, a light he couldn't shake. Was *she* drawing him here, revealing her secrets, something beyond his creek, beyond Bubba's loss, beyond the Dragonfish's shadow?

The vision stretched further, letting him soak it in, the ocean's wild dance, the cliff's green embrace, the cabin's quiet promise. He felt the fruit's juice again, sticky on his lips, heard the roosters crowing, the birds singing and the waves roaring. It was a coast raw and alive, but something more—a glimpse of peace, of grace, of a shore where pain didn't follow. Rylan's chest tightened, longing to stay, to shatter that wall and run to the porch, but the barrier held fast, and Trickle's eyes met his—knowing, hinting at truths *she* couldn't voice. The sun sank, the silhouette flared, and the world faded black into *her* embrace, leaving him with a hunger he couldn't name, a vision of light *she'd* gifted him.

* * *

Rylan stirred, eyes fluttering open to the spring's familiar shimmer, the Kingdom's hum cradling him once more. Trickle lay beside him, *her* hand still pressed to his heart, *her* golden hair fanned across the grass, jade eyes watching him with a love so fierce it renewed his soul. *She* smiled—slow, radiant, a Queen's grace—and murmured,

"Where you been?"

He blinked, the park's glow lingering in his veins, and grinned, raw and unshaken.

"Somewhere... perfect," he rasped, voice thick with wonder. "Bubba's there, Trickle—fishing, happy. OG was too... and you... It's... it's home, in a way I can't explain."

"It.. It was your home.... It was where you come from....."

His hand covered *hers*, pressing it tighter to his chest, feeling *her* pulse sync with his—a lifeline forged in the Kingdom's depths. *She* nestled closer, *her* head resting where *her* hand had been, golden strands tickling his skin.

"Ssssshhhhhhh..."

She reached up and touched *her* finger to his lips.

"And now you know where Bubba is..." *she* whispered, changing the subject, *her* breath warm against him.

"He's part of us—a part of all of this."

The spring rippled, Rylan's chest swelled—reborn in love's wild grace.

* * *

Time was slowly claiming Rylan, and *she* knew that soon he would have to return. *Her* breath caught, and *she* grabbed his hand, as *her* lips crashed into his, a collision of first love's wildfire and a lifetime's devotion. *She* laughed softly into it, flirtatious, free, a sound that danced across his skin.

"King Rylan..." *she* whispered, *her* voice a passionate, longing thread, weaving into his core.

His body swelled—not a boy's anymore, but a young man's, chest broad with pride, heart pounding with the weight of *her* words. He leaned in, lips brushing *her* ear, voice a husky murmur,

"Queen Trickle..."

She pulled back, eyes flashing, correcting him with a playful,

"Princess..."

He pressed a finger to *her* lips... soft, silencing *her* with a man's quiet steel.

"You're my Queen. To you, I commit my everything—my Kingdom, my heart, and my soul."

Hours bled into what seemed to be only minutes, twilight creeping over the horizon, a purple bruise on the sky's edge. Trickle, was glued to Rylan's every word as he told *her* everything about where he had been, when he suddenly realized where the sun lay in the sky. Time was slipping, a cruel thief tugging him home. He pulled *her* closer, kissing *her* once again, tasting the bitter-sweet ache of farewell, his tears mingling with *hers* now, salt on their lips.

"Trickle," he rasped, voice quiet and gentle, raw with a man's strength and a boy's fear, "I gotta go..."

She nodded, eyes glistening, *her* hand gripping his as if *she* could tether him there forever. He stood, pulling *her* up, their fingers laced tight. OG lumbered over, nudging his leg with a wet nose—a drooling anchor to this moment. Rylan's heart tore—pride swelling, love roaring as he looked at his Queen, knowing he'd return to *her*...

Always...

Ride or Die

The twilight sky bled crimson and gold, with faint sparkles of silver scattered like dust throughout. The sun, a dying ember, kissing the horizon as the full pale moon stole the sky. Rylan and OG carved their path homeward, the creek's Trickle a fading hymn in their wake. Fireflies sparked alive, their frail glow a stuttering pulse against the encroaching dark, but the air thickened—heavy with damp moss, the sour tang of mud, and a creeping chill that prickled Rylan's neck. Trickle's kiss still seared his lips, *her* voice—the *Sound of the Water*—a tether to his soul, yet that gnawing pull deep in his gut roared louder now. It was a siren's wail, sharp and urgent, driving his steps faster along the creek bank.

They approached the dark pool—a gaping maw in the creek's belly, its surface a black mirror swallowing the last light. Rylan's stride faltered, his breath snagging as his hazel eyes caught it: a ripple, jagged and alive, slicing through the stillness. The sunset's molten glow struck it at a wicked angle, igniting a shimmer of copper—unnatural, unholy—bubbles spitting up from the abyss like the gasps of a drowning beast. He didn't see the Dragonfish, not yet, but its presence clawed at his spine, a shadowy glow stirring beneath the deep.

"SHHHHH!" Rylan hissed, voice a razor's edge, dropping low as he thrust a hand toward OG. "Stay here!"

The massive dog froze mid-step, obeying without a flicker of doubt, sinking to his haunches with a thud that shook the silt. OG's fur bristled along his spine, eyes glinting like twin moons, locked on Rylan with a soldier's focus, drool pooling in the dirt like blood from a fresh wound.

Lightning-fast, Rylan snapped into his warrior's stance—years of training coiled into a single heartbeat. One knee slammed the earth, grounding him like a rooted oak; his left hand clutched a fistful of four fiver loads from his pouch, smooth stones cold as death against his palm; his right arm cocked back, the first fiver load in the chamber, wrist poised for the twist that could slay a legend. He thought to himself,

I was not created in the spirit of fear, but of strength, love, and a sound mind.

He repeated it over and over again in his head until it found his voice, until it was the truth. He was a spring wound tight, every muscle singing with lethal intent, his chest heaving as he pointed upstream, finger trembling toward the pool's heart.

"There—" he pointed, whispering to OG, his voice was a thread of steel, "can you see it?"

OG's head whipped to the water, a low growl rumbling from his gut—deep, primal, a war drum rolling through the dusk. He mirrored Rylan's coil, sinking lower, haunches taut, a beast ready to unleash hell, his massive frame vibrating with pent-up fury. The pool answered—Dragonfish breath, like smoke rising from the surface, a swirl against the current, a violent churn, bubbles swelling into grotesque boils that popped with a sickening hiss.

* * *

The Dragonfish erupted through the surface in a geyser of black water and flame, its full, glorious evil unveiled—six feet of molten copper scales glinting like hellfire, black spikes raking the air like a crown of thorns. Its jaws gaped, teeth jagged like shattered glass, amber eyes blazing with a hunger older than time. Rylan staggered back, breath stolen, heart slamming against his ribs. It was his first true sighting, and it was monstrous—beautiful in its malevolence, a nightmare stitched from Bubba's ghost and Pops' rage. He could hear it clearly now; it spoke in an evil, whisper like groan that hissed.

"Miiiinnnnneeeee....."

He launched the first fiver load—wrist snapping, stone flying—*plip, plip, plip, plip*—four skips, a heartbeat shy of perfection, splashing uselessly into the pool's maw. He snarled, reaching instinctively for the second load. The Dragonfish's fire gland glowed with rage; a fire erupted and shot a column of flames at him... He dropped and rolled, silt exploding around him, a maneuver he'd drilled a hundred times in the Kingdom's wilds.

Springing up, Fiver reloaded, he locked eyes with the beast—its fire gland glowing again, cherry-red beneath its jaw, pulsing like a second heart as it reared, hissing, tilting for the kill shot. Flame licked the air, a warning of death's breath.

Rylan fired—*plip, plip, plip, plip, plip*—five skips, the twist flawless, the stone soaring high. It streaked toward the gland, a missile of hope, but the Dragonfish snapped its head, unleashing a hard gust of blue and scarlet flames—scorching, sulfurous, a wall of heat that singed his hair and knocked the stone wide. It screamed at him like a vicious promise,

"MIIINNNEEE!"

The air reeked of burnt earth and brimstone, sour—familiar. The pool's surface ignited with floating tongues of flame, dancing like will-o'-wisps over a grave. Rylan drew back, hand plunging for another fiver load, fingers brushing its edges, knowing only one remained after this—the last of his arsenal. He rose, a knight facing his dragon, feet planted firmly, staring into those amber eyes—they *pulled at him*—a trance, hypnotic, beautiful in the most evil way, whispering promises of surrender.

The beast didn't strike again with flame; it beckoned—its gaze a velvet noose tightening around Rylan's soul. The dark pool shimmered, flames licking higher, calling him to join it—to drown in its depths, to be reborn in its black heart, to become the Dragonfish itself, a vessel of generational ruin, a tragic mirror of Pops' buried scales.

Rylan's arm slackened, the fiver load slipping from his grasp, clattering to the dirt. His legs buckled, knees sinking as the trance sank claws into him—his heart slowed, a dull thud echoing in his skull, his soul peeling free like smoke rising from a dying fire. He floated, weightless yet anchored, eyes wide and unblinking, sleep tugging at him though he burned awake. The pool's edge loomed closer, his feet dragging against his will, the black water's cold fingers brushing his shins.

"Your Mine, Your Mine... You are Mine..."

The beast chanted as though it had won, twisting and contorting in ecstasy and evil.

"No..." Rylan whispered faintly, his voice a ghost, fighting the pull with every shred of his being, but his body betrayed him—paralyzed, lost to the beast's song.

"nnnNNNOOOOOOO!"

The scream rose from his gut, raw and defiant, shattering the trance's grip for a fleeting second. In that heartbeat, OG exploded—a blur of muscle and teeth, a roaring avalanche of fur—crashing into Rylan with the force of a tidal wave. The dog's massive paws slammed him down, pinning him to the earth, breaking the pool's hold. OG sprawled atop him, a drooling shield, his tongue lashing Rylan's face—wet, warm, relentless—snapping him awake with a jolt of life. The beast's amber stare flickered, its hiss faltering.

Rylan gasped, air flooding his lungs, the world slamming back into focus—the acrid sting of smoke, the damp crush of OG's weight, the creek's frantic Trickle pounding in his ears. He shoved to his feet, shaking, hand diving into his pouch, seizing a grip on his last fiver load—his final stand. He spun, crouching low, Fiver cocked, eyes blazing with a warrior's fire. The pool stared back—silent but empty. Nothing. No ripple, no copper gleam, no flame. The Dragonfish was gone, vanished into the deep, leaving only the soft lap of water and the fading crackle of dying embers.

Relief crashed through him, a shuddering breath escaping his lips, but disappointment gnawed at its edges—sharp, bitter... He'd missed. The beast had slipped away, unconquered. Yet Rylan stood alive, a miracle in itself, baptized in battle, sweat and OG's slobber. The last fiver load slipped from his fingers, tumbling back into his pouch with a faint thump, a promise for another day. Rylan straightened, bewildered, his chest swelling with the raw confidence of a soldier bloodied but unbowed.

He grabbed the dented canteen, glinting in the moonlight, and uncapped it, tipping back the final swig of Mamma's Lemonade—tart, sweet, a lifeline stinging his cracked lips. The taste grounded him, washing away the trance's echo. OG nudged his leg, grinning wide, drool swinging like a victory banner. Rylan ruffled his scruff, voice hoarse but steady.

"You saved me, ya big lunatic. Ride or die, huh?"

Supernova

Rylan staggered from the dark pool's edge, his body a battlefield—muscles screaming with every step, lungs burning as if he'd swallowed fire, the Dragonfish's amber gaze still searing his mind like a brand that wouldn't fade. His feet slipped in the mud, catching on roots, each stumble a fight to stay upright. The night closed in, thick with the acrid tang of scorched silt and the fading sweetness of Honeysuckle, fireflies blinking weakly against the void, their light too small to push back the dark. OG shadowed him, a drooling titan, his paws thudding softly but steadily as they climbed the bank together. Rylan's knees buckled once, twice, but he pressed on, driven by a stubborn spark he couldn't name.

Exhaustion crashed over him like a rogue wave, relentless, the adrenaline dump hollowing him out until he felt like a shell. His legs wobbled, turning to jelly under the weight of what he'd survived, his breath coming in shallow, ragged gasps that scraped his throat raw. He'd faced the beast and lived—its copper scales, its fire, its hunger—but the cost was sinking in, a heavy ache spreading through his chest. He glanced back at the pool, its black surface still rippling, spinning faintly, and shivered. OG nudged him forward, a low whine rumbling from his chest, as if he knew Rylan needed to keep moving, needed to escape that stare.

At the bank's crest sprawled the hollow tree—Rylan stumbled toward it, the ground tilting under him, and dropped hard onto its rough surface. The wood creaked, splinters snagging his patched overalls, but he didn't care—

he just needed to stop. OG settled in close, a warm wall of fur and loyalty pressing against his side, his massive head swiveling to scan the pool below. Those amber eyes—dull now, tired, but he would guard Rylan to his demise, always. The dog's breath puffed warm against Rylan's arm, steady and alive, a lifeline in the dark.

The battle had gutted Rylan deeper than he'd known, deeper than the bruises blooming on his skin. His hands shook as he fumbled for his canteen, fingers clumsy, slick with sweat and creek water. Empty. Not a drop of Lemonade left to wash away the bitterness, to tether him back to the light. He let it fall, the metal clinking softly against the tree, and tilted his face to the stars—cold, distant, shimmering like Trickle's eyes when *she'd* smiled.

"Just a moment..." he muttered, voice hoarse, barely his own. "Just a small rest..."

OG shifted closer, resting his heavy chin on Rylan's knee, and Rylan reached out, fingers sinking into the dog's matted fur. The tremor in his hands eased, just a little, grounded by that familiar warmth.

He thought of the fight—the Dragonfish lunging, OG's bark cutting through the chaos, the way he'd swung that branch like a sword. His eyes slid closed, the constellations of the Heavens blurring into black, and he slumped down against OG, his shoulder pressing into the dog's side. OG didn't budge, just stayed there, solid as the oak, breathing slowly and deeply. Rylan's chest rose and fell with his, syncing up, and the world faded—the pool's whispers, the night's chill, the ache—all swallowed by the slow rumble of OG's growl...

* * *

Pain ripped him awake—a brutal yank, half hair, half ear, hauling him upright in a haze of groggy terror. The world tilted wild, senses scrambling to catch up, but the sour stink of old whiskey and stale tobacco slammed through the fog—a smell that was Pops, raw and mean as ever.

"I told you, boy, I freakin' told you, damn it!"

The voice thundered, a storm crashing down, and Rylan's wits clawed back just in time—he ducked as Pops' calloused hand swung hard, clipping his forehead with a crack that sent him flying. It was Pops' last stand, crashing through Mamma's red line. Rylan tumbled across the Kingdom's floor, mud smearing his cheek, stars exploding in his skull—white-hot, relentless, a blow that might've finished him if he hadn't felt the wind shift.

OG erupted—a lion charging from Narnia's wild heart, jaws gaping, teeth flashing for Pops' throat with a snarl that rattled the ground like a war cry. Pops roared back, a beast himself, catching OG mid-leap, but the dog twisted fast, fangs sinking deep into Pops' shoulder, just shy of his jugular. Blood sprayed, dark and wet under the moon's glare, OG's bite locked like a vise. They crashed together, titan against titan, rolling down the bank in a tangle of fury, slamming into the dark pool with a splash that churned the night alive. The water burst—swirling, bubbling, steam hissing upward like the breath of a Dragonfish breaking free.

Pops grabbed OG's scruff, his biceps bulging with whiskey-stoked rage, and shoved his head under the black water, holding him down with a killer's grip. Bubbles popped up in desperate bursts, OG's paws thrashing, claws scraping the depths in a frantic fight for air. Rylan staggered to his feet, adrenaline burning away the exhaustion, fear torched by a fire Trickle had sparked in him—a man's fire, not a boy's. He wasn't the kid who'd ducked and hid anymore; he was a King, shaped by spring's tough love, fearless now. He bolted for the edge, feet slipping in the mud, hand clutching his last fiver load, ready to jump—

"LET HIM GO!"

His voice deep and sure, the shout of a man forged in battle. The Dragonfish breached—a molten nightmare tearing through the pool, six feet of copper scales blazing like fire, black spikes slashing the air like a jagged crown of death. Its jaws snapped shut on Pops, teeth punching through flannel and flesh, barbed tail whipping around him—a burning rope that lit the night red. The beast flared brighter, flames licking along its edges, and yanked Pops under in a vicious crocodile spin—water churning red, gold, and black, a whirlpool of fury dragging him down.

OG broke loose, clawing to the bank, shaking off water and blood, his growl rumbling like a drum as he squared up to dive back in. The beast surged again, rising with Pops locked in its coils, scales glinting like molten metal, its amber eyes blazing with a hunger that swallowed hope whole. It let out a shriek that rang inside Rylan's consciousness.

"MIIINNNNEEE!"

Pops thrashed, his fists pounding its snout, blood streaking the water, but the Dragonfish tightened its grip, jaws clamping harder, fire flaring from its throat in a roar that shook the trees.

Rylan froze, the world slowing to a single heartbeat, sound fading to the faint, eternal Trickle of the creek weaving through his soul like a lifeline. OG barked—a fierce, guttural call—haunches tensing, ready to leap. Rylan's mind went blank, a quiet nothing, his hand diving to his pouch, grabbing the last fiver load—his family's thin thread, the Kingdom's final shot.

He locked eyes on the beast, its fire gland throbbing with molten fire under its jaw, a glowing weak spot begging for his aim. The Dragonfish reared high, Pops now dangling limp in its jaws, its tail thrashing waves across the pool, steam billowing as fire met water. Time stretched thin, his breath barely there, the night holding still with him. He let the stone fly—plip, plip, plip, plip, plip—five skips, the twist perfect, the fiver load slicing through the air, dipping low then soaring back up off the water like a hawk breaking free. His best throw ever, a warrior's song carved in motion, climbing high under the moon's cold light.

The Dragonfish lunged, jaws gaping, flames spitting like a furnace, but the fiver load struck true—a pinpoint blow to its fire gland, erupting it in a searing blaze of molten light. The explosion tore through the night sky, filling it with a million sparks of darkness, a supernova gathering itself above, its unearthly scream clawing at the stars. The beast's copper scales splintered, its body convulsing in a final, frenzied surge of fire before collapsing into dark ash. Embers cascaded like dying sparks, sizzling into silence as the water claimed them. The pool roared to life, hissing, spitting, and spinning mixing it's potion of ingredients. With an explosion of obsidian, demonic lightning bolts that arced upward into the ashen fragments were swallowed by the beast within the skies abyss, a tempest of fury that flared one last defiant time, and then vanished, leaving only still, crystalline water trickling under a hushed sky.

* * *

Rylan and OG charged as one, racing to the tree's jagged end, leaping into the pool with a splash that broke the silence. The cold bite of the water was sweet, reclaimed. They found Pops—sodden, heavy, his flannel torn to rags, blood swirling like ink around him. They hauled him back, Rylan's arms burning, OG's teeth locked on Pops' collar, pulling with a soldier's strength. At the bank, Rylan slid his hands under Pops' shoulders, heaving him from the water like a baptism finished—mud and water dripping from their hair, silt sticking to their skin. Pops lay still—too still—his chest twitching faintly, whiskey breath a weak gasp. Rylan dropped to his knees, hands trembling as he grabbed Pops' shoulders, tears spilling hot and fast, cutting tracks through the mud on his face.

"Please..."

His voice cracked, raw and jagged, breaking on every word, the creek's Trickle faintly cradling his cries.

"Please save him. Give him back—we need him—he needs us."

The plea ripped out, a boy's voice to the sky. OG pressed in, his big nose nudging at Pops' ear. A cough; wet, rough, alive—shook Pops' body. Rylan watched in slow motion as a Crimson Lotus drifted down the stream and settled in the redeemed waters of the pool. In that moment his Pops' eyes fluttered open, sharp with pain, but something else glinted there—grief breaking through, a man climbing out of his own ruin.

"Ry..."

His voice rasped, thin as thread, hand jerking toward Rylan's, weak but trying. Rylan grabbed it, fingers clamping tight, a lifeline across years of hurt. The pool settled, its black surface smoothing to mirror the stars, the Dragonfish's ashes sinking deep—a grave for the monster, a bed for the man it let go.

OG howled—a long, victorious bay that rolled through the Kingdom, bouncing off the hollow tree, waking the squirrels to chitter in wonder. Rylan laughed through his sobs, head tilting back to the sky, tears mixing with mud. The fireflies burned brighter, a swarm of hope circling above, and the creek's Trickle grew—soft, clear, a song stitching their broken family back together. Pops' grip tightened, a quiet promise, and Rylan felt it: the dark was gone, the dawn was here, a Kingdom renewed in blood and grace.

Home

It had been a full season of life, and Eldergrove had aged... The Kingdom bloomed anew under a late spring sun, its golden rays spilling over the hollow tree like a blessing. Rylan sat shoulder to shoulder with Trickle on the weathered log, its silver bark warm beneath them, squirrel nests chittering faintly within its heart. *Her* golden hair danced in the breeze, brushing his arm, and *her* eyes sparkled with a mischief that set his soul ablaze. OG bounded nearby, a drooling whirlwind of tiger-striped fur, chasing squirrels with reckless joy—barking wildly, butt just wiggling away, his goofy grin a testament to the battle won and love unbroken.

Down on the bank, Mamma and Pops basked in the sun's embrace, a quilt spread beneath them, wildflowers nodding in the grass. Mamma's belly swelled with new life, a gentle curve beneath her sundress, and Pops laid beside her—doting, tender, his rough hands softened by grace as he tucked a daisy behind her ear, his laughter rumbling deep and free. They glowed together, a quiet miracle stitched from scars, and Rylan's chest tightened with a fierce, unspoken pride.

"Race ya!"

Rylan leaped up and sprinted to the tree's jagged pinnacle, launching into the air with a whoop. He flipped—once, twice—before slicing into the crystal-clear waters of the pool, now cleansed of its dark past, its surface shimmering like a hallowed spring. Trickle followed, a golden blur, outdoing him with a triple twist that sent water spraying in a triumphant arc, *her* laugh ringing out like bells across the Kingdom. They splashed and swam, voices weaving through the air—Mamma's giggles, Pops' booming chuckles, OG's playful yips—a symphony of joy that drowned out the ghosts of yesterday.

Mamma waved them to shore, pulling a wicker basket from the quilt's edge, its bounty spilling forth: Spam sliced thick, government cheese and butter sandwiches stacked high, Saltines crunching under eager hands. They gathered round, a circle of love unbroken, water dripping from Rylan's hair, Trickle's sundress clinging damp and bright.

Saltines crumbled from their mouths as they traded stories—Pops' gravelly voice spinning tales of nine-skip stones, Mamma's soft lilt recalling Bubba's first fish, Trickle teasing Rylan about his Fiver flops. Laughter erupted, loud and messy, crumbs flying like confetti. Mamma reached into the basket's depths, drawing out a gleaming canteen—new, redeemed, its silver catching the sun like a promise kept. She uncapped it, pouring her secret Lemonade into chipped tin cups, the tart-sweet sting kissing their lips, a taste of home that bound them tighter still.

The crickets struck up their twilight symphony, cicadas droning a velvet hum, bullfrogs croaking deep and rich—an ensemble glorious and wild, serenading the Kingdom as the sun dipped low. Fireflies blinked awake, filling the sky with a thousand tiny lanterns, their dance a celebration that stretched into the twilight. They lingered, voices softening, hands brushing, hearts full—time suspended in the glow of a family made whole.

* * *

Later that night, Rylan lay in his bed, the oil lamp on his nightstand casting a warm halo over the room, its flicker dancing across the walls. OG sprawled beside him, a drooling mountain of fur, his steady huff-huff a lullaby that eased Rylan's bones. The day's joy lingered, but a spark flared in his mind—a memory tugging at him. He rolled over, reaching for his satchel slung over the bedpost, fingers brushing the worn leather. He dug inside until he found it: Pops' old journal, its pages yellowed, edges frayed, a relic of the man he'd been and the one he'd become.

He flipped through it, the scent of tobacco and ink rising like a ghost, until a loose page slipped free—he slowly unfolded it for the second time forgiving of it's complexity the first time he came across it—a torn scrap from the back of a Bible where it says "*Notes*" on the header, its edges curling, words scrawled boldly in Pops' jagged hand:

I will renew your spirit, remove your heart of stone, and replace it with a heart of flesh...

Rylan's breath caught, the words sinking deep, a vow fulfilled in every laugh by the pool, every touch of Trickle's hand, every beat of OG's loyal heart. Tears pricked his eyes, not of sorrow but of something vast—love, fierce and eternal, a Kingdom reborn.

He pressed the page to his chest as he looked out the window into the future, his lamp flickering low, and he saw a storm forming in the twilight spinning in a familiar pattern that churned his stomach. Flashes of amber electricity illuminated the slithering clouds fueled by promise. OG nudged closer, drool soaking the quilt, and Rylan rubbed his belly while he watched the night unfold.

The Tree of Life

The Tree of Life

Something Brewing

The skies erupted with pure venom; the deep, dark, and evil storm raged with spite. Black clouds climbed straight into the abyss above, a towering inferno of shadow that spun like a serpent thrashing in cursed waters. The tempest took the shape of a monstrous beast, within its form, molten crimson fire blazed—not lightning, but a hellish inferno, as if the beast had swallowed a thousand suns and spat their fury into the clouds. Its eyes cast a scorching light that seared the earth below, while its serpentine coils churned the clouds into a maelstrom. This storm was not mere weather; it was a living nightmare and it hunted Zora Thornweaver down the cracked highway, with a hunger to bar her from destiny's call.

Zora peeked over the steering wheel of her 1955 Chevy Nomad, a silver and wood- grain relic that gleamed like a tarnished crown under the storm's infernal glare. She perched atop two tattered phone books—stacked beneath her like a throne for the pint-sized soothsayer. The storm stalked her, in fear of her foretelling, sure to wield a light that would unravel its ancient secrets.

It was late spring 1983. Zora was racing the storm toward her destination, packed tight with the relics of her wandering life: treasures and tomes, collected from magical journey's. Every inch of the wagon was stuffed, except for the front seat where she curled to sleep, saved by a patchwork quilt that shielded her against the world's sharp edges. For months she'd lived this way—between rest stops and YMCAs. She was a vagabond crone with a heart full of ether and a soul stitched with starlight.

On the cracked vinyl seat beside her sat a slew of beloved books—**The Alchemist**, a leather-bound **Bible,** and a tattered copy of **Leaves of Grass.** Other reads that Zora had forgotten about were strewn across the car: **Wrinkle in Time,** a journal of sorts by an Eldergrove seer named Elijah Starscribe, **The Wizard of Oz**, and an **Encyclopedia of Magical Herbs,** just to name a few.

The radio crackled to life, the notes slithering like a serpent through the Nomad's bones. Zora's creaky voice joined in, a warbling echo of Morrison's growl, her long silver braids swaying as she sang. Her words were a prayer of defiance against the fiery beast in the sky.

"Riders on the storm—Into this house we're born..."

* * *

Zora had grown up with parents who drifted like dust in the wind. They were gypsy spirits, chasing music and gatherings across the country. Their home was an old school bus, turned into a rolling home with curtains and dreams. In that creaky space, Zora learned life's hard lessons—no school, just the wisdom of the road. She quickly learned to fend for herself, reading tarot cards, and making up fortunes for the hippies, who would toss coins and egg her on. Soon, her sight began to sharpen and she'd predict things that came true. She knew names before they were given, and foresaw the undone. She figured it was just how things were, with no one to tell her otherwise.

In her teens, Zora helped her mom mix herbs and oils, their scents of sage and lavender filling the bus. They sold these magical tinctures, bottles filled with visions and hope. An old spell-weaver had joined their travels and taken Zora on as an apprentice of sorts. Her lessons held a shadow, but Zora pursued the light, learning to turn darkness into something special.

As a young woman, she met Ezekiel Moonchild at a **Dead** show. He paid for his fortune and she fudged it in favor of her deeper motive. Their romance was short but they stayed connected, always knowing where the other roamed.

When her parents passed, Zora traveled alone in the bus, gathering trinkets and treasures—old books and amulets with secrets. She traded them for fortunes told and spells cast under the stars.

After a particularly dark and harsh winter, Zora felt a pull that she had never experienced, speaking to her destiny, spirits whispering of a new path. Her friend Ezekiel sent a vibe about Eldergrove, a town he thought she'd love. She felt his spirit tugging at her soul with a story yet untold. He had promised her long ago that he had something in mind for her traveling shop and that whenever she was ready it awaited her. She had even seen visions of the sign he carved her—a crescent moon—for her Crescent Coffershop.

Soon after, fate called and she met a gypsy woman who offered a trade—the bus for a sparkly old Chevy Nomad. The name fit her wandering soul; its engine growling with promise. She agreed, packed it full of her treasures, and drove toward her destiny. A little town of throwaways and starting-over families awaited. Ezekiel Moonchild had saved a magical lair in the middle of it, perfect for all her fantastical books and treasures.

* * *

Zora's eyes glinted as she dodged a pothole, a faded sign loomed ahead—13 Miles to Eldergrove—its letters peeling but glowing faintly. The beast in the clouds roared closer and Zora sang louder, her voice a thread of light weaving through the dark. She squealed into Eldergrove, right about twilight, the storm's dark beast still spitting at her. She skidded sideways into a parking spot in the town square and sent gravel flying like shrapnel. Ezekiel Moonchild stood in front of the Old Church, shuffling a ring of keys, waving with a grin that belied the fear in his eyes.

They grabbed boxes from the Nomad, their glances darting to the storm now circling like a predator, tightening around the town. Ezekiel ushered her through the door—old wood and new dreams, its walls humming with potential. He and Zora hugged hard like old forevers...

"You just barely made it my old friend." he celebrated. "You had me worried sick that this storm may have found you and swallowed you up."

Zora stood proud and tall, all four foot seven inches of her, and she winked with a gleam.

"Don't you ever doubt me, Mister Zeke?"

They laughed and hugged again.

"Listen.... I want to catch up, but this storm is brewin something nasty, and I need to get back over to keep an eye on my Little Chapel." He winked and pulled his stocking cap down over his long knotty hair, "Here's the key and if you need anything, I'm just next door. Otherwise, get settled and we can catch up after the storm."

Zora winked back, smiling calmly, and assured him. "Zeke old friend, if I need anything, I will just twitch-wiggle my nose, and say it three times...".

Ezekiel smiled a patronizing grin and shook his head. Looking fearfully out at the storm, he was thinking she may have just dragged it along with her.

Then he scurried off out the door.

Zora lit candle after candle, their amber flames flickering to life as she placed them on the front windowsill, a glowing defiance against the looming darkness. She stepped to the doorway and stared at the sky. Her composure was a challenge, daring the beast to come, as the candles' light spilled onto the cobblestones, a whispered vow that her spirits would hold.

* * *

Eldergrove slept uneasily under a battered sky, its heartbeat a faint hum in the witching hour. The air spun thick, heavy with sourness and something meaner. The small town square sprawled untamed between the crumbling mill and the Old Church, a patch of jade grass and mud where the Tree of Life loomed. Beside it stood the Old Church, its old wooden bones kissed by grace and time. Across the way, the newly branded Crescent Coffershop crouched low, its windows glinting like eyes in the dark.

The Tree of Life wasn't just a tree—it was a beast of legend, a protector of Eldergrove. Its limbs twisted skyward, gnarled and proud, holding a canopy of multicolored leaves trembling with secrets only a pure heart, gold as the sun and brave as a King, could hear. Its roots plunged deep into the earth, drinking from the hidden springs underneath. Albino squirrels, white as ghosts, streaked through its boughs, leaving faint trails, their ruby eyes glinting, while birds sang, lilting and free, a chorus weaving through the dark like fireflies on a breeze.

The Old Church slept beside it, a sagging giant of supernatural grace, its walls silvered by years of rain and redemption. Once a stiff cage of sermons and starch, it had now been revived by old Ezekiel Moonchild. The whitewash peeled like old skin, revealing knots and whorls that pulsed with a quiet fire. The steeple, defying its weathered bones, soared above Eldergrove in quiet majesty, with a clock that once conducted the town's heartbeat. Above its stained-glass window and arched wooden door, a sign swayed lazily: **Jesus Loves Everyone**. The Old Church glowed faintly, a shell of hope too stubborn to die, its survival a whisper of something holy stitched into its bones.

Across the park, the Crescent Coffershop squatted, its shingles sagging under ivy that glowed faintly green in the dark. Zora, the shop's new guardian, stood resilient as a chorus of candlelight sang in its window. She leaned in the doorway, her patchwork shawl flapping, staring into the storm with a grin that said she'd seen this coming in the tea leaves she brewed under the moon.

The night had crept in early—soft, a hush that prickled the neck and set the heart thumping. Then the wind hit—a low growl tearing over the countryside, gathering venom as it roared toward Eldergrove. The sky churned black, clouds boiling with streaks of blood-red and violet, as if the heavens had been gutted and left to drain. The Tree of Life stirred, its branches creaking, leaves shivering as the storm loomed—towering and formless, its winds slashing like daggers.

The tree fought back, a warrior of light roused from its slumber. Its roots clamped the earth, while its leaves lashed out, cutting through the gale like a thousand skipping stones. The storm bellowed, a roar that shook the park, uprooting saplings and hurling them into the dark, but the Tree of Life stood tall, its canopy a shield of green fire, bending but never breaking. The albino squirrels chittered frantically, ruby eyes glinting like embers, while the birds' reggae hymns swelled—songs of defiance that danced with the wind's rage.

The evil in the wind struck harder, a beast with a hunger to claim the tree's heart. It clawed at the bark, peeling strips away in vicious curls, and sent gusts spiraling down, slashing at the roots like a keeper digging a grave. The Tree of Life groaned, its trunk shaking under the onslaught. The storm's howl deepened, a guttural chant that rattled the earth, promising ruin. The critters scurried deeper inside its veins, while the birds clung tight, their song faltering but unbroken. The tree's whispers turned to a growl, a call to fight, to conquer the Kingdom's soul.

The gale surged, a tidal wave of shadow crashing down, its claws sinking deep. The Tree of Life buckled, its branches thrashing wild, leaves tearing loose in a storm of their own. The evil pressed closer, the air thick with the stink of brimstone and rot. The tree's groan became a cry—begging the night for mercy. The storm loomed, spinning and dancing triumphant, ready to snap the titan's spine and claim its light forever...

CRACK!—At 3:16 a bolt tore the sky in half, a jagged spear of light that wasn't lightning but something more powerful. It attacked the Old Church's steeple, splitting the dark with a thunderclap that shook the cobblestones and rattled Zora's windows. The church blazed alive, its oak walls glowing as if lit from within, a slow pulse of jade and gold creeping up the steeple like a spirit searching for its mark. The clock hands snapped to 3:17 with a shudder, then froze—etched in time like a scar, guarding Eldergrove's deepest mysteries.

The steeple tilted, groaning under the weight of the strike, leaning toward the Tree of Life like a hand reaching out. The glow leapt—a shimmering arc of holy fire, jumping from the steeple to the tree, engulfing it in a blaze that didn't burn but sang. The Tree of Life ignited, with a luminescence vast as a thousand angels, a mystical magic pulsing through its veins. Its leaves shimmered silver, its bark gleamed gold, and its roots thrummed with a light that drove the dark back. The storm recoiled, its howl turning to a shriek, the evil within it thrashing as the Tree gnashed its wrath. The squirrels froze, eyes wide, while the birds erupted, their hymn soaring—a chorus of triumph weaving through the light.

The Old Church pulsed in tandem, its walls glowing softly, the **Jesus Loves Everyone** sign flailing madly, blazing red as blood. The steeple leaned closer, crooked now, tethered to the Tree by that holy arc, a bridge of light binding them together against the darkness.

The storm clawed one last time, a desperate swipe that tore at the air. The Tree of Life roared—a rumble deep as the creek's song, its leaves slashing back. The storm's serpentine coils dissolved into ash, scattering like molten embers sucked into the heavens, its molten eyes dimming to cold, hollow voids that flickered once before collapsing into the abyss above.

The gale died, a whimper lost to the dawn creeping over the horizon—a blush of gold and pink kissing the jade grass, banishing the night's last demons. The Tree of Life stood tall, its glow softening to a shimmer. The Old Church loomed quiet, its steeple unsure, the heartbeat of the Kingdom sitting idly.

Zora nodded to the dawn from her doorway as if she knew what others only wondered about... a wisdom in her grin, and she faded back into the shadowy depths of the Crescent Coffershop.

A Man's Mark

Rylan had never seen Pops so jittery—not since his day of reckoning when the creek ran red and Rylan yanked him free from the Dragonfish's jaws. The day the Blackened Beast had latched onto his father's soul, and embedded itself too deeply to ever escape. Rylan and OG had stood for Pops and faced the Monster that spun the dark waters, rebuking its attack by way of tooth and christened stone, reclaiming the sacred waters of the creek and its crystal pools.

Pops had been scraping his way back ever since, reborn from the ashes, swapping whiskey and the stench of old stale tobacco for a backbone hardened by steel. His hands trembled now, not from the bottle, but from something fiercer—a fear of falling back into its grasp again.

Trickle floated through it all, her secrets locked tight in silence. Rylan had pressed her about them, but she wasn't ready to share. She'd washed up with Rylan after the creek battle—mud-streaked, fierce, her song humming in his bones—and Mamma never let her leave. Days bled into weeks, Trickle in Rylan's room, while he sprawled on the porch with OG. Mamma and Pops had fallen hard for her purity, grace mirroring Mamma's, soft as Honeysuckle and fierce as a lioness. She'd sweep through the house, stitching joy into every corner with her caring hands. Rylan loved her relentlessly—two flutterbys twirling on the wind, hearts tangled tighter than the Tree of Life's roots.

Mamma's belly was on the verge of bursting, a baby baking in her oven that Trickle fussed over like a Mamma Hen. She'd learned the secrets of brewing Mamma's Lemonade, and how to blend the magic *Honeysuckle Lemon Sugar*. She would squeeze the Lemons and grind the Honeysuckle with a grin full of secrecy, her apron dusted yellow, while Mamma rested her aching feet.

On Wednesday afternoons, they would tromp into the heart of Eldergrove, bound for the Crescent Coffershop. Zora always greeting them at the door,

"Come, my doves,"

She purred, ushering them toward the *Daily Digs*—treasures and tomes collected from magical realms. They dove in, elbowing through clutter in a gleeful tussle, laughter bouncing off the rafters, until they landed, as always, before the old Radio Phonograph—Trickle's favorite.

Hand-crafted by a wood-shaping wizard. Naturally oiled with little carvings of musical notes and twirls, dancing on each of the twelve pedals that when joined together formed a beautiful wooden flower that bloomed with the sound of music. Zora claimed it had a special magic for the one it chose, and that it had been awaiting its destiny for years perched on the old end table. Mamma froze for a moment like she was searching her brain, and she looked at Zora with curious eyes.

"How long you been here, Miss Zora? Because I just can't remember a time that you weren't. Fact, I remember driving past your shop in the Hotel Chevrolet the first time we wandered into town. You stood in that door and waved that magic *Come and Visit me* wave you have, even though you had no idea who we were."

Zora smiled with a deep warmth, "Oh Lord... I think it's been well over a hundred lunar cycles now since I rolled in that very first night."

Mamma shook her head, thoughts running tattered, "Mmm—Mmm. If this old shop could tell its secrets..."

Zora nodded her head, smirking as if to say *it does...*

Mamma hefted *The Grimoire of the Saffron Veil*, its cracked leather shimmering faintly, and Zora purred.

"That's woven from a desert crone's sunlit breath—bites if ye pry too deep!"

Trickle snatched one of the jars of firefly wings, watching it pulse gold like a heartbeat, as Zora winked and wiggled her nose with a twinkle in her eye.

"Caught mid-dance, them glowers—light the dark when my candles weep dry."

A fist-sized crystal ball swirled mist on the counter, singing the creek's next tune, Zora leaned in,

"River's voice trapped in there—tells ye what's comin' 'fore it knows itself!"

Mamma cooed over a dented brass compass, spinning unhinged past north...

"Finds yer need, not yer path, if you hold the magic,"

Trickle walked past Zora over to Mamma and looked curiously at the old compass. Zora laughed, tossing a dried Honeysuckle Braid to Trickle,

"Wards off the Fish smell, sweetling. Rub it all over..."

They wandered, amazed, holding up tumbled stones—amethyst, quartz, obsidian—warm as sun-kissed creek beds, and crystals that unlocked all the secrets to the Magic of Eldergrove—but one special thing had snagged

Trickle's intentions...

* * *

Rylan was sticking to his place on the porch, stubborn as creek mud. Trickle had offered a hundred times to trade—her sleeping out with OG and him taking the room, but he'd just smile and shake his head.

"Trick," he'd drawl, "I'd be out here anyway, with or without you here. Ain't no place better than this porch, stars above and OG sawing chunks beside me."

She'd laugh and submit, letting him be—imagination running wild, underneath the night.

Rylan scrubbed up begrudgingly. He told Mamma he had just been swimming in the creek the day prior and swore he didn't smell, but Mamma was determined. He took an extended thirty-second shower, even wet down his hair and went so far as to swap his usual grimy overalls for the brand new ones Mamma had gotten at the second chances store. He even tugged on a shirt with buttons, but shoes? Wasn't happening. He'd seen plenty of the Bohemians and what they went to the Revivals in and he drew the line.

Pops had slipped him the Old Spice bottle, winking a man's wink, "Drives the women cuuuhhhrazy,"

Rylan laughed. Naturally, he figured more worked better, and he slapped it on till the whole Kingdom reeked of spice and bravado. He bounded down the stairs, feet thumping, when Mamma's voice sang out—sharp and sweet, calling him to the porch. They all stared. Mamma spoke while trying to hold back a choking noise.

"Oh Lord... Cuugh—Someone smells... good?"

They all turned towards town, laughing at Rylan's expense, with OG joining in. Life's goodness exploded in his veins, a dog-sized burst of joy that glued them all together. The Old Church loomed ahead, awaiting the celebration. Rylan's heart kicked—something big was brewing. They moved as one, a scrappy kingdom of their own, marching toward that weathered oak door, the air thick with redemption and the promise of miracles still to come.

* * *

The Old Church loomed ahead, Rylan could see the line of beatnik believers gathering at the door being greeted by an Eldergrove icon. Old Bohemian Johnny, better known by the townsfolk as Johnny Pocketwatch, had become the official timekeeper in Eldergrove, ever since the old clock had fallen ill. He carried around a magical old pocket watch which never needed to be wound. It had been handed down through his family lines, which were filled with clairvoyants and enchanters. All the parishioners would check their watches with his as they exited the old chapel on Sunday mornings where he was always there to greet and send them on their way, just like clockwork. He was real close with old Ezekiel, and his history within the town went way back. He knew most of the stories that had ever been told about their little Shangri-la, and he had become the official **Chronoseer of Eldergrove** as Zora and old Zeke would refer to him.

Rylan, Pops, and OG lagged behind a bit, tossing a beat-up football. OG bounded between them, sloppy joy stitched into his bones. Mamma and Trickle strode ahead, cutting a path to redemption's weekly call.

Pops slowed, boots scuffing the earth. Rylan matched him step for step with the football tucked under his arm. OG plopped down, panting, as Pops' voice rumbled, rough as creek gravel.

"Your mamma and I been talkin'. Trickle's burrowed deep in our hearts, same as yours."

Rylan froze, hazel eyes locking onto Pops'. Ahead, Mamma and Trickle strode on, their figures fading, oblivious to the weight settling between father and son.

"We want her to stay," Pops said, scratching his stubble, "but you two flutterbys can't be sharin' a room like grown folks—you ain't there yet."

Rylan's cheeks blazed red, a flush creeping up his neck at the thought. Pops chuckled—a rare sound—and he leaned in close. "I been thinkin'—that old shed out back? You and me could turn it into somethin' worthy of her. A sanctuary she can come and go from, make her own. She don't hafta, but it'd be hers if she wanted it."

Rylan's soul sparked, a firefly flare in his chest. His whole body thrummed, vibrating with a joy so fierce he could've lit the sky. "Pops," he blurted, voice cracking, "I'd do anything to take care of her. I'd be honored to build it with you."

Pops winked, his arm—scarred from battles with bottles and beasts—draped gently over Rylan's shoulder, pulling him close as they walked. "Let's keep it hush," Pops whispered, conspiratorial, "make it a surprise."

Rylan's grin split wide, soul blazing through his teeth, a secret binding them tighter than creek roots. The football dangled forgotten in his hand, clouds forgotten overhead, until Mamma's voice sliced through the humidity,

"Let's go, Carl! Ain't no stallin'—it's your turn today!"

Pops and Rylan froze, their eyes were wide with despair. Pops faced the milk crate pulpit, the town's weekly reckoning, volunteered this time to bare his sins before Zeke Moonchild's flock. They traded a look—half-dread, half-laughter—Then trudged on, OG loping beside them, oblivious to the weight. Mamma waited at the church steps, hands on hips, Trickle beside her, both queens of this scrappy kingdom. Rylan felt it: redemption's pull, the spark of a shed-turned-sanctuary, a family stitched anew by love and secrets, marching toward grace with fire in their veins.

Redeemed

Pops stood at the milk crate pulpit, a trembling king in the Old Church's weathered heart, sweat beading like dewdrops. The flock sprawled untamed—wedged into every crevice of the oak-walled sanctuary. No pastor ruled here, no printed hymns fluttered—just a scrappy tribe bound by faith, sharing broken promises and miracles small as firefly wings.

A murmur rippled through the flock—someone hummed an old hymn, voices catching it soft as creek water kissing stones. Music surged, untamed and holy—Mrs. Peesewell's gray curls bounced as she stroked the pipe organ's cracked keys. The Bohemian pickers joined in, a barefoot fiddler sawed a bow that growled with the wind's voice. A group of old hippies weaved beats on worn out chairs and crates, sparking a worship circle as the odd instruments thrummed to Eldergrove's heartbeat. Their sound wove grit and grace, the flock rose—feet stomping and hands clapping—dancing in a revival swirl, hips swaying as if the Dragonfish thrashed deep beneath the oak floor.

As the dance settled, the air stilled, and one picker cradled his guitar, easing into an earthy version of **Let It Be.** The notes drifted slow, a tender ache spilling from his strings, a gravelly whisper unraveling the prose into the church's hush. The flock leaned into the melody, their voices rising softly, the Little Old Chapel thrummed with mystical and electric vibes. Its walls and

Honeysuckle claws trembled as if the very spirit of Eldergrove had ignited a flame that flickered in every soul present.

Every Sunday, the flock gathered under the crooked steeple, a single soul stepping forth to lead and share an invite—create a spark to coax the embers of faith into a blaze. This time, Mamma had put forth a name, she had called upon Pops when they were seeking out a volunteer. She thrust his name into the circle like a gauntlet he couldn't sidestep. Her eyes gleamed with that inner light forged from years of storms, locked on him—a challenge, a lifeline, a vow that he'd stand and speak, no matter how his titan's heart quaked.

The flock held its breath, waiting for the storm to break. He froze, boots glued to the floor, sweat streaking his face like penance under the steeple's crooked shadow. Pops swallowed hard, throat bobbing, and stood trembling before the makeshift pulpit, his broad shoulders fallen as if the weight of the moment pressed him down.

All week he'd toiled—scribbling jagged confessions on scraps of yellowed paper, pacing the sagging porch of their Eldergrove shack, rehearsing the script that'd bare his soul. He'd planned every syllable, every plea—clutching at the poet's heart he'd buried beneath whiskey and rage, but as his boots scuffed the crate's edge, it all fled. Something foreign surged through him, a tide he'd never known, warm—feral, prickling his skin like the Kingdom's magic waking beneath the creek.

"I... I'm tryin'," his voice, a cracked thread. Tears traced dusty trails down his weathered face. The flock leaned in, their breath held, "I had it all planned," he rasped, a sob catching like a beast's whimper, "but it's gone...I'm lost... Most days...I'm lost..." He turned to Mamma, pleading. "I've fallen so deep—hurt you, hurt Rylan...failed Bubba...broke every promise I ever swore..."

Rylan's eyes welled as he watched his Poppa's hands shaking, gripping an old, crumpled yellow paper like it was a lifeline. A murmur rippled through the flock, soft as the creek's whisper.

"We hear you, Carl," Zora Thornweaver called from the back.

Ezekiel Moonchild nodded, his voice a low hum: "Lay it bare, brother."

The fiddler's bow answered with a single, low mournful note, Mrs. Peesewell's organ sighed, and Rylan felt Trickle's grip tighten, her golden hair brushing his cheek as he bit his lip, blood blooming.

"I was a thunderous fool," Pops choked louder, hands clawing the air. "Laid angry hands on my boy when I should've held him—chose the darkness over my Kin—the poison over Mamma's songs."

The flock stirred, a tide rising, "We've seen it," Mrs. Peesewell murmured, her fingers hovering over the keys.

"I drowned my poet's soul," Pops cried, voice swelling, "left you all with a titan's shell—regret's my shadow now, my dark passenger."

Mamma rose, her belly was round with promise, her chestnut hair spilling like a halo. "But You Are Here..." Her voice, a melodic thunder, rolling through the rafters. She stepped toward him, strong hands outstretched, tears shimmering. "You're ours, Carl—flaws and all."

"Praise be!" rang out from the flock as it surged closer, a living heartbeat embracing her torment "c'mon Mamma... Sang it!"

Ezekiel clapped a hand on Pops' shoulder, and proclaimed with a voice of triumph,

"*We-All-Have-Fallen-Short-of-the-Glory*-my-Friend!"

The flock rippled in fluid motions like holy water growing restless in the wind. "Speak brother Zeke!"

"I failed you," Pops roared like thunder crying, his knees buckling as he gripped the crate. "Left Rylan's dreams to rot, turned Mamma's lullabies to silence—forgive me!"

The air cracked. Ezekiel bellowed a warrior's cry, hands in the air, dreadlocks flaring, and the flock erupted—hands clapping like thunder, feet stomping the quilted floor until it shook. The flock parted like the Red Sea as Mamma waded through. She knelt beside him, cupping his face, fierce yet tender.

"Forgiven, my love," she whispered, voice a storm breaking.

The musicians unleashed a tempest—guitars wailed like the wind through Eldergrove's oaks, the fiddle screamed a redemption hymn, and Mrs. Peesewell's organ roared. Voices soared in a wild, ragged song, a crescendo of redemption and grace. Trickle squeezed Rylan's hand until it bruised, her jade eyes glistening with tears and awe. Pops wept raw and free, cradled by Mamma's love, as the Little Old Chapel pulsed with pride...

Tiny Castle

Rylan and Pops had hurled themselves into the old shed like wizards conjuring a realm from dust and dreams. Their hands danced over the weathered husk to weave Trickle's enchanted haven into being. Tucked behind their Eldergrove shack, where the creek's silvery song wove through the air like a whispered incantation, stood the shed. It had once been a graveyard of Pops' rusted relics—wrenches, hammers, and saws tangled in cobwebs, steeped in the sour stench of whiskey-drenched nights.

Ever since Pops' raw, soul-baring reckoning at the Old Church, where he'd traded the bottle for a backbone forged in redemption's fire, his creative spark blazed. Each evening, he'd shuffle home from the mill or the creek's edge, his poet's heart spilling forth in a torrent of ideas. Rylan matched him blow for blow, his lanky frame buzzing with love, wanting to build the perfect haven for his kindred spirit. Loping through it all was OG—the Original Gangsta—the beast with floppy ears and a grin wide as a jack-o'-lantern, turning their labor into a riotous, joy-soaked game.

The tiny house stretched twelve feet by ten, a crooked jewel perched at the Kingdom's whispering edge, its walls rising from reclaimed oak salvaged from a storm-felled giant near the Tree of Life. The wood shimmered with silver veins, etched with Eldergrove's secrets, sanded smooth by Pops' calloused hands. He'd stained it a jade-green that mirrored Trickle's gold-flecked gaze, each plank pulsing faintly under moonlight as if kissed by its grace. The roof slanted sharp, a cascade of cedar tiles. Pops carved them himself, with a craftsman's care, their edges curling like the weathered pages of an old book. Above the door, a dried Honeysuckle braid swayed, its sweet scent a ward against lurking shadows.

Pops and Rylan were finishing up the front porch, a six-foot sweep of weathered planks, each one a different hue of blues and burgundies that danced like twilight shadows. Rylan etched a tiny magical wind flute into the woodwork—its notes trilling soft and lilting whenever the wind sighed through it. Pops sealed the wood, causing a glimmer like creek glass beneath the starlight. Rylan had crafted a rocking chair as well, its frame twisted from willow branches he'd wrestled from the creek's banks. He'd sanded it until it shone, then inlaid the arms with tiny quartz shards that winked like fireflies. It stood majestically, a throne for the creek-born Queen, presiding over the waters where she could watch OG gleefully chase Mother Earth's critters.

Rylan would watch Pops work, a master with his hands. He revered his work ethic and tried to model himself in those footsteps. He also worried when he would see those strong hands shaking. He could see it in his Pops' eyes that some nights were still a struggle. It scared Rylan a bit, but he loved his father deeply, and had fought the darkness to save him and the family.

"Pops—you doing alright? Sometimes I see your hands shaking, and I feel like you're struggling..."

Pops turned, looked right through him—his eyes—empty. For a moment Rylan swore he saw the darkness—it was a menacing, soul-sucking look that scared him. Pops grabbed hold and swallowed it back into the depths.

"I'm good, Ry. Some nights I still struggle but I concentrate on where I am putting the next foot. Your Mom—she's a gem who carries my heart and wants nothing but the best. I need to honor that, and you. I haven't been perfect, but I can do my best in every given moment."

While Rylan and Pops worked, OG was no bystander—he'd turn the build into his own sprawling playground while they hammered away. He had mastered fetching seven tools by name—trotting off with a proud swagger when Rylan barked an order. It was a fascinating, indulgent game for him. He'd strut around with a 16-penny nail jutting from his jaws like a cigar, or he'd do battle with a freshly milled board, any size, trying to thread it through the shed's narrow door frame.

"OG, you big lug, it ain't a toy!" Pops huffed and puffed like a wolf, threatening to blow, "That dog's got more grit than sense."

When they tossed scrap blocks into the trash pile, OG would dive in, snagging them with a triumphant grin, claiming them as treasures. Rylan would get on him,

"That's junk, boy!"

Rylan would fire up the saw, and OG would stand at attention. Tossing the cut-off end through the air, Rylan would watch OG leap, catching it mid-flight. He'd flop down, tearing it to bits with savage joy, wood chips scattering like confetti, a one-dog demolition crew laughing at the naysayers who'd dare to call it work.

Inside the tiny castle magic blossomed. Rylan hung Trickle's magic mirror as he looked over their creation, a living enchantment. The finishing touches were in place. A loft bed perched high, accessed by a ladder. Above it a skylight—a circle of glass swirling with mist like Zora's crystal ball featuring a porthole to the Zodiac. The floor stretched with planks salvaged from the Old Church's discarded floorboards, shelves of rough-hewn knotty pine cradled jars of dried lavender, sage, and wild mint. In the nook by the window, draped by tie-dye curtains, a bench was piled with hand-stitched patchwork pillows, gifted from the flock.

In the corner, an old radio phonograph stood, its wooden horn curling like a blooming lily, a treasure Mamma had bartered for at the Coffershop. Zora claimed it would spin a song without a crank whenever Trickle sang, whichever songs she wished for.

Mamma had stacked a tower of Trickle's favorite old records, scratchy vinyls of psychedelic rock and hippie anthems from the '70s and early '80s. *Surrealistic Pillow, Pearl, Electric Ladyland, Uprising,* with Trickle's favorite **Zion Train** cued up. Each sleeve carried a note of her essence, a soundtrack for her sanctuary.

Her Queendom awaited her, crafted with love and Eldergrove's communal mysticism. Rylan walked out and leaned on his broom, curious whether it would fly. He watched OG down by the creek while pondering on Trickle's mysteries, yet content to know her heart. A cold breeze darted through the mist, and the creek rippled awkwardly. He shivered, sensing a dark stirring, but held fast to the haven they'd built.

* * *

Rylan, Pops, and Mamma perched on their sagging front porch, the late spring sun casting a honeyed glow over the jade grass. They sipped their Lemonades, but the fourth glass sat empty on the weathered table, alone—a silent prayer waiting to be answered. Mamma let one of her thoughts slip out, voice a soft thunder of love.

"I know you two are too young to be thinkin' 'bout forever, but it just ain't the same when she's not around..."

Pops pursed his lips tight, nodding with a tenderness that spoke of a titan reborn, his heart stitched anew by family.

Rylan leapt to the porch's edge, eyes scanning the road's end both ways. Trickle had wandered off earlier, taking OG on a hike through the Kingdom's whispering trails. She'd humored Rylan's plea to stay clear of the backyard—but the secrecy had left her adrift, a breeze-blown spirit wondering where her journey would lead, feeling the ache of being outside the family's whispered plans.

Rylan's heart kicked as he spotted her in the distance, her sundress a splash of sunlight against the dusk. OG loped along beside her, his big old ears flapping like banners of joy. Rylan spun back, looking at Mamma and Pops, their faces alight with panicked excitement, a shared spark of magic dancing in their eyes. Mamma poured the waiting Lemonade and turned on the garden hose for OG. The three stood at the porch's edge, a trio of conspirators, like children guarding a secret too big for their britches.

Trickle looked up, her jade eyes catching the last rays of sun, and giggled,

"What?" Her voice rang like a lilting song.

Rylan blurted out his words, nearly tripping over them, "We have a surprise!"

Her smile bloomed, curious and warm, "OK...?"

The silence stretched as she climbed the porch stairs, her fingers wrapping around the glass of Lemonade, its sweetness a promise of home. They all stood motionless, glowing with gaping smiles. Mamma elbowed Pops, a gentle nudge of encouragement, and Pops elbowed Rylan.

"We want you to stay here with us," Rylan said, his words filled with hope.

Trickle's gaze softened, her words a vow. "I... am... here with you all..."

OG nudged her hand, his eyes glinting with an invitation, and Rylan, tugging at his overalls, added, "We've been tryin' to create a place for you... somewhere to call your own."

OG tugged at her sundress, his tail thumping. "What, OG?" She followed him toward the backyard, hesitating at the hedgerow. "Wait, OG... I'm not supposed to..."

Rylan was right behind her his changing voice soft. "You can now, Trick—we're ready."

They stepped past the hedge, and there it stood, a crooked jewel glowing in the dusk, its jade-green walls shimmering with Eldergrove's magic. Above the door, a dried Honeysuckle braid swayed, and carved into the threshold were the words Love Lives Here. An address placard swayed lightly in the breeze, reading Trickle's Place.

Pops stepped forward, his calloused hand holding a symbolic key crafted from wood with the word Home carved into it, his voice thick with emotion. "It's yours, Trickle—if you want it, that is..."

Her eyes lit up, and she gasped.

"What... What is this?"

Her heart drummed with awe as she turned to the tiny home, gratitude shimmering in her gaze.

They all laughed, a sound of pure joy, and Rylan grabbed her hand, his touch a lifeline, leading her onto the porch that glimmered in the sunlight. Pops and Mamma followed, their pride a quiet fire, as they walked her through the enchanted haven they'd crafted. They pointed out each treasure and told its story. The loft bed with its willow ladder, thrumming with a creek-born chant; the driftwood desk inlaid with amethyst, quartz, and obsidian; the shelves of knotty pine cradling her favorite fresh herbs.

Trickle climbed the ladder to her bed, giggling as she looked at OG.

"It's too high for your muddy paws, boy,"

His mournful moan echoing broken hope.

"It's so comfy!"

She grabbed the patchwork comforter Mamma had made especially for her and wrapped herself in its safe haven. She peeked her head out, grinning, and froze—the giant wooden flower that bloomed with mystical music caught her eye. It waited for her in the corner below. She pointed asking,

"Is that..."

Mamma nodded, her chestnut waves spilling like a halo. "The one from Zora's shop."

The old wooden radio phonograph awaited her beckoning. Trickle gathered herself while sitting up and began to hum her and Mamma's song—a siren's call that spun the flower to life, unfurling it's blossom, baring sweet nectar—music fluttering through the air like **Three Little Birds.** She listened with her heart, clutching Mamma's newly quilted comforter to her chest as tears dampened the fabric.

"There's one more thing," Rylan's voice was soft as a prayer.

"There's more? " She gathered herself and climbed down the ladder.

Rylan grabbed her hand, leading her back out to the porch.

“I made this special, just for you.”

He pulled the rocking chair out from around the corner and placed it in the exact spot he’d planned over many evenings of crafting it—overlooking the Kingdom.

Trickle sat down, her breath catching. “I can watch the whole world from here...”

The creek shimmered below, its silvery song a mirror to her heart, the horizon stretching wide with the promise of forever. She sat, the weight of their love sinking deep, her eyes brimming with tears—she grabbed his hand, voice a trembling vow.

“My King... my Love...”

Rylan’s hazel eyes glistened,

“My Queen... my Love...”

The words hung in the air, a sacred bond sealed by fate.

Hypno-Spiral

Rylan woke to the rooster's crow, racing the sun as he launched down the stairs, taking them four at a time. He grabbed his pre-filled *Lemonade* canister from the fridge and dashed out the door.

Kneeling by the garden hose, he gulped the cold water straight. Rust and earth swirled gloriously on his tongue. With a rogue grin, he angled the hose at OG, thumb half-capping the end. He unleashed a wild arc of spray that glittered like diamonds in the dawn. OG launched skyward, laughing—jaws snapping, massive paws pounding the dirt like war drums—floppy ears flapping like a baby elephant's in a fairy tale.

Dropping the hose, Rylan swung a leg over his pride and joy: a battered PK Ripper with mag wheels and red knobby tires, a gift from old Ezekiel, who'd found it in one of his abandoned storefronts. To Rylan, it was freedom incarnate, sparking his urge to roam. He'd spent the morning scrubbing it clean on the front lawn between playful battles with OG, the chipped paint whispering tales of past glories. In his mind, he wasn't just a scrawny kid—he was Evel Knievel reborn, staring down a lake blazing with fire, teeming with man-chomping crocigators, the crowd roaring as he revved for the jump.

Patting his satchel, Rylan checked his supplies: a "just-in-case" dollar bill, as Mamma called it, tucked away safely for an emergency payphone call; five fiver loads ready for action; saltines with a Spam-and-cheese sandwich wrapped with love; and a canteen sloshing full with Mamma's pure affection.

"What's good, G?" Rylan squinted at his sidekick. "You ready to tear it up or what?"

OG's amber eyes blazed, his tail wagging so fiercely his whole backside shook the ground. He tiptoed forward, stealing a sly head start toward town—one step, then another—paws silent as a predator's promise, never breaking eye contact with Rylan.

"Oh, it's on, boy!"

Rylan slammed his feet onto the pedals, and they bolted like lightning, hearts pounding for whatever lay ahead.

They tore through the front yard and onto the old dirt road toward town, a blur of dust and determination. OG's massive paws pounded the earth, surging ahead like a runaway freight train, but Rylan gained fast with his legs pumping furiously. Veering off the road onto a path he'd carved through countless travels, he eyed the pit jump challenging his bravado. He launched, kicking out the back end, landing with a flow that set him up for the first turn—a sharp, unforgiving corner. He and OG had built a berm by piling dirt up against the old cedar fence, but with the speed from the jump, he always hit it flying. The force carried him high, almost over the top, riding the fence line until gravity yanked him down, shooting him out the bottom.

OG barked mockingly, leaping ahead, holding true to their challenge. Rylan pumped the pedals and yanked the handlebars, bunny-hopping the curb, tires chewing through Old Man Jeeter's patchy lawn. The old man squirted his hose at them and gave them the old number one sign, "cheering" loudly, hand raised high. Grass flew as he cut the corner to gain ground on his rival, the bike rattling beneath him, nearly catching OG.

Launching off the curb back into the street, Rylan locked eyes on his next target: a dirt ramp crossing the town's stream, a packed-earth launchpad promising glory or disaster. OG barreled ahead, hitting the launching pad with a primal growl. He soared skyward. His floppy ears flapped like battle flags as he sailed, only to crash midstream in a spectacular tumble. The water catching him exploded like a geyser.

Rylan didn't hesitate. Pedaling with every ounce of his scrawny might, he hit the jump full throttle. The bike soared—higher and further than ever—a streak of reckless magic cutting through the air. Below, OG shook off the wet, eyes glinting as Rylan flew overhead. He crossed up his handlebars mid-flight like Jumpin' Joe Hendrix at the BMX races—pure, reckless poetry in motion. His exit wasn't quite as graceful as he overshot the trail, crash-landing with a crunch into a tangle of bushes. He jumped up and wrestled himself free in a flash, yanking the bike with him.

Their eyes met—OG's knowing spark matching Rylan's wild gleam—and something electric crackled between them, a shared pulse of adventure. Without a word, they exploded forward, racing toward the Tree of Life, the ancient oak pulsing with Eldergrove's secrets. Tires screeched, paws thundered, and they shot into a sixty-yard dash to the finish line, neck and neck.

The Tree of Life towered ahead, waiting to whisper its forgotten tales. Rylan felt it—something alive in its roots, calling him. He leaned low, muscles burning, as OG's breath huffed beside him, a primal rhythm driving them forward. They crossed the finish line in a skid of dirt and fur, Rylan throwing his hands skyward, hollering, while OG hopped on his hind legs.

"CHAMPION!" Rylan claimed, grinning.

OG plopped down, cocking his head, matted fur dripping stream water, staring at Rylan like he'd lost his ever-lovin' mind.

Rylan's grin faltered as he gazed up at the Tree. A breeze stirred its leaves, and for a heartbeat, they shimmered with a light not born of the sun—something ancient, something waiting. What secrets did it hold? What magic hummed in its veins, ready to draw him into its shadowed embrace? The Tree of Life stood silent, daring him to find out, and Rylan's heart thumped with hunger for the wonders yet to come.

* * *

Rylan sprawled across the grass, chest heaving like a bellows, sweat stinging his eyes. The Tree of Life loomed above, its gnarled branches clawing the sky like a maze crafted specifically for him. Its roots plunged deep into caverns cradling Eldergrove's underground springs. Rylan had heard tales of vast networks of rivers and pools beneath the town, their entrance rumored to lie within a waterfall in the magical forest—his Kingdom. Despite days of searching, he'd yet to find it. OG plopped beside him, panting hard. The steam was curling from his matted fur in faint wisps, like the creek exhaling a spell.

The air under the oak's shade grew sharp, a chill slicing through summer's heat, alive with a hum that thrummed in Rylan's bones. He pressed his lanky frame against the trunk, bark biting his skin, and caught a flicker. An emerald light pulsed through the leaves, quick as a chipmunk's dart.

"Whoa, G," he said, ruffling OG's fur, fingers tingling with a static snap. OG's eyes glowed, guile stirring as he nudged Rylan's hand, a rumble in his throat like thunder dreaming of rain. Rylan's grin flashed, stubborn as creek mud—he wasn't one to ignore a sign.

His gaze snagged on the trunk: jagged grooves spiraling upward, glowing silver beneath the moss, a secret waking from its slumber. As he scraped the moss with a stick, his heart slammed like the mill's hammer. Ancient symbols bloomed—crescent moons bleeding light, eyes in triangles watching back—humming with power that tickled his spine, whispering like the Dragonfish's shadow or something older still. Ezekiel's voice echoed in his mind:

"*That Tree's got whispers, boy, but only for those with magic to hear.*" Rylan's soul sparked—he was no ordinary kid; he was a knight of the Kingdom, born to chase its riddles.

"Guard the ground, G."

OG huffed, floppy ears flapping. He paced back and forth like a sentinel raised by some fierce creature. Rylan scrambled up the two-by-four rungs he'd nailed the spring before, splinters pricking his palms, chasing the glowing magic. It wasn't carved—it moved, snaking into crevices that pulsed under his touch, a path to somewhere. He swung onto the tire-swing branch, then leaped higher, wiry limbs dancing branch to branch like a chipmunk acrobat. Below, OG tracked him, huffing support—or perhaps griping at being left behind—massive paws dancing on the grass like sledge hammers, mirroring Rylan's every move.

Rylan reached his crow's nest, a flat cradle where two mighty branches met—a natural tree fort, fortified by thick limbs sprawling like a rib cage. From this perch, he could see for miles, and to him, Eldergrove was a stage, teaching lessons Mamma wouldn't and Pops hadn't.

* * *

The tree pulsed with life and secrets. Rylan knew its rhythm by heart. Tuesday afternoons, the townswomen gathered in its shade, their gossip ablaze—tales of husbands storming bedrooms like gorillas, or tearing through bathrooms like bulls in a china shop. Their vivid words made Rylan's cheeks burn hotter than a skillet. He'd thought Pops and the men had colorful language, but the women spoke a different tongue entirely. They laughed, trading jam jars and love-hate vows, their voices weaving the Kingdom's song.

Fridays were the real circus, and Rylan ensured he was settled in fifteen minutes before showtime—the mill bell's 4:30 clang. Men would spill out like cattle charging through the gates—sweaty, broad-shouldered titans, shirts stained with grit, strutting around the Tree's base like cavemen claiming a kill. Old Milwaukee cans cracked open, red-and-white tin flashing in the sun, foam hissing as they guzzled—a ghost of Pops' old darkness before Mamma's love rekindled him. They punched each other's arms, hard enough to bruise, laughing as insults flew like sling stones. Some rivaled Pops in size—headlocks and wrestling seemed to be love's language among these untamed beasts.

The horseplay was wild: one man juggled cans like a circus bear, while a wiry fellow jeered, landing a punch that echoed like a hammer. From a battered knapsack, someone pulled a mason jar—Ezekiel's "Apple Pie," rumored to be brewed in the Old Church's shadows. They passed it quickly, secret as a vow, each man taking a slug, eyes watering as the fiery liquid revived their spirits.

"Zeke's pie'll make you see angels—or devils!" one coughed, wiping his mouth, and the circle roared, fists thumping chests like Planet of the Apes.

Talk turned to boasts, loud and primal—men crowing about the night ahead, plotting gorilla-like tactics, debating toilet paper direction, or marveling silently at their own daring. Their words painted wild nights with the women who claimed them.

By five o'clock, hot-rods and pickups screeched into the dirt lot, women swooping in to claim their property. The men whooped, beating on their chests while scattering to their queens, each couple peeling out as they left, tires spinning clouds of dust. One by one, they vanished into the dusk, leaving the square silent, his lesson adjourned.

* * *

The air crackled, urgent as a storm's first breath. An old hollow, once a knot, gaped in the wood, pulsing with magnetic silver light. Rylan felt it—a call in his bones, beckoning him closer. With bare feet gripping the bark, toes curling into its grooves, he stepped near. The light spun wildly, a hypnotic spiral like those on late-night Twilight Zone reruns he'd sneak-watch from the stairs when his parents thought he was asleep. It blurred into a searing swirl, and Rylan's breath abandoned him. Though clad in overalls, he felt unmoored, his soul teetering. His lanky frame shook, fingers clawing the bark, splinters biting like tiny fangs. The swirl spun faster, a vortex of silver and emerald, and a dark churn bloomed in his gut—a shadow's pull, fierce and ravenous.

A monstrous cloud, loomed on the horizon. Its edges pulsed with dark, laser-like flames in a hellish ballet. Black lightning crackled within, each pulse a snarl of power, and the flames—scarlet and blue, sharp as a demon's breath—licked the sky, hungry for ruin. The cloud's voice hissed, a rumble like thunder over the springs, a promise of destruction that churned Rylan's stomach with dread.

"Mine,"

His heart throbbed with excruciating pain as the cloud's darkness tore at him, its force a gale threatening to rip him from the Tree. The swirl in the hollow knot flared brighter, fighting back, and a vision bloomed in its core. The cloud surged closer, spitting dark flames like bad intentions. The banana-yellow school charred to cinders, the Old Church's crooked steeple melted under scarlet tongues, and the square—where families once gathered—burned to ash. The screams of Eldergrove's 1,260 souls swallowed by a lake of fire. Rylan's breath turned to poison in his throat, the vision searing his mind.

The swirl pulsed—a desperate cry—and the vision shifted. Flames parted like a curtain, revealing a wooden relic, rough as the Tree's bark, filling the hollow knot's glow. Four faces carved in its grain—Man, Ox, Lion and Eagle—pulsed with life, veins of light threading through their eyes, staring at Rylan as if they knew him. The faces turned, their carved eyes burning, and the Tree groaned, branches creaking like a banshee's wail.

The swirl blazed, fit to burst like a star, and Rylan's knees buckled. The cloud's voice screamed, its fiery claws reaching through the vision to claim him.

"MIIIIINNNNEEEE!"

The four faces flared, their light a shield against the inferno. The Tree's hum surged, a war cry, its roots thrumming with Eldergrove's soul, battling the darkness.

The swirl dimmed, its vortex fading, spinning into nothing. Rylan gasped, clutching the bark, the vision searing itself into his memory: the town's ashes, the four faces guarding him from the fiery cloud. The darkness retreated, its scream a fading echo, but Rylan's spark blazed—predator, not prey—ready to hunt the looming darkness.

North

Trickle danced through her cottage like a sunbeam caught in a breeze, her bare feet kissing the floorboards with every twirl. She'd been a whirlwind of whimsy, splashing color and life into her new sanctuary. The walls shimmered with tie-dye tapestries, while shelves brimmed with jars of wildflowers humming with the Kingdom's secrets. The air hung thick with the scent of Honeysuckle hope. The old wooden Radio Phonograph, a blooming flower of mystical music, spun its magic at her command, a loyal minstrel following her heart's lead. When words slipped her mind, she'd hum a melody, and the magic would bloom anew, petals unfurling to play the tune she longed for, as if the air itself knew her soul's cravings. "*White Rabbit*" swirled through the cottage now, its psychedelic riffs weaving a spell that set the walls aglow. Trickle sang along, her voice a siren's call, dancing with the notes like flutterbys on the wind.

"*Go ask Alice—When she's ten feet tall...*"

Outside, on the porch, the critters of the Kingdom gathered, drawn by the music and Trickle's celestial voice. Birds perched on the railing, chirping a chorus that wove into the phonograph's hum. Trickle giggled, her laughter a ripple of creek water over stones, as she hung a new treasure on the porch: a tiny house of weathered cedar, its roof a cascade of shingles painted with crescent moons, a gift from her morning jaunt into town.

* * *

Earlier that morning, Trickle had wandered down the cobblestone path to the Crescent Coffershop, her heart brimming with gratitude for the phonograph that soothed her spirit with its blooming melodies. Zora stood in the doorway, eyes glinting with a knowing that could pierce the veil of night.

"I had a feeling ye'd be showing your face, sweetling."

Trickle stepped inside, the shop's amber candlelight spilling over her like a warm embrace. Zora swept her patchwork shawl wide, her voice a lilting chant that danced with the shadows.

"Come, my little angel," she purred, her creaky voice a hymn to the wild, "I've somethin' special just waitin' for ye." From beneath the counter, Zora's gnarled hands pulled forth a tiny cedar house, its crescent moons glowing faintly, as if kissed by starlight. "Hang this on yer porch—it'll feed all the Great Creator's critters who hunger—all the feathered dreamers, squirrels, and chipmunks too, them scamperin' rascals. Ye won't need to fill it, never a worry—it'll always have just enough, a magic feast for yer court. They'll gather to hear ye sing, to hear ye whisper the world's secrets, and they'll never leave empty. That's charm—woven from the moon's own breath."

Trickle's jaw dropped, her jade eyes wide as the creek at dawn. "I love it, Miss Zora, but I can't afford this!" she gasped, her voice trembling with awe and worry, her hands fluttering like the wings of a hummingbird.

Zora's grin sharpened, a blade of kindness wrapped in mischief. She pressed a weathered finger to Trickle's lips with a gentle shush. "I didn't ask ye for no money, dove. This be my gift to ye, a little treasure for ye sanctuary." Her eyes twinkled, a constellation of secrets, as she twitched her nose thrice, a playful spell that set the shop's candles flickering like a chorus of fireflies.

Trickle tried to protest, her golden hair swaying as she shook her head. "But you already gave me the Ra—" Her words stumbled, caught in Zora's knowing gaze.

Zora's laugh cackled, dancing with the wind's own mischief. "Mamma gave ye the Radio Phonograph, sweetling, not I. Don't ye go mixin' up yer blessings!" She winked, her silver braids swaying like a pendulum, ticking to the rhythm of a lovesick heartbeat.

Trickle's smile bloomed, wide as the Kingdom's horizon. She couldn't recall a single time Zora had let her pay for anything—not the firefly wings, the Honeysuckle braid, nor the tumbled stones that whispered creek secrets. She wrestled with everything Zora's spirit provided, feeling as though she had nothing of value in return. Her heart swelled with gratitude, and she flung her arms around Zora, hugging her tight, as if she could squeeze the moon's light into her bones.

"Thank you so much, Miss Zora! You are such an amazing friend to me. I will always carry your love in my soul wherever I go. I promise."

Zora hugged her back, eternal love in her eyes, her patchwork shawl wrapping them in a cocoon of starlight. She pulled back with a grin, her nose twitching like a rabbit caught in a dream.

"I see ye've been usin' that Honeysuckle braid I gave ye," Her voice was a playful growl, sniffing the air with exaggerated flair. "Fish smell's all gone, ain't it?"

Trickle burst into laughter, her hands clapping with delight.

"All gone!"

She twirled around in place, her sundress a splash of sunlight against the shop's amber glow. The birds outside trilled louder, as if joining the jest, their song weaving through the Crescent Coffershop, a symphony of magic and mirth that sealed the bond between the kindred spirits, stitched by love and light.

* * *

OG led the charge to the cottage, his hulking frame a storm of delight, his butt a wiggling mess of pure, unbridled love, tail thwacking the air like a metronome gone rogue. His front paws danced a step-dancer's jig, hopping back and forth with the clumsy grace of a bear at a carnival, eyes glinting with mischief as he barked a serenade for his golden queen. Rylan power slid in on his PK Ripper right behind, the BMX a streak of lightning under his command. His tires skidded in a dramatic arc, sending a spray of earth scattering into the air.

"Trickle, you ain't never gonna guess what just happened!" His voice rang with breathless wonder, his chest heaving like the bellows of a mill fire.

The critters on the porch scattered in a flurry of wings and scampering paws, their furry and feathered court disbanded by the whirlwind of the arrival. Trickle's lips parted in a fleeting pout, her jade eyes dimming with disappointment as her critter choir fled. But the sight of Rylan's flushed grin and OG's dancing paws reignited her glow.

"What's goin' on, Ry? You okay?"

She rose from her willow rocking chair and gestured to the step beside her. "Come up here and sit a spell—I've got some of your favorite waitin', and OG—I trekked down with my trusty bucket earlier and fetched you some creek water, fresh and cool—here you go, big boy."

She set down a wooden bucket, its grain etched with the creek's own whispers, the water within shimmering like a mirror of starlight. OG dove in with slobbering gusto, sending droplets flying in a baptism of delight.

Trickle giggled as her gaze drifted back to Rylan, who stood barefoot and beaming.

"The Tree, Trickle," he said, his voice dropping to a reverent hush, "it showed me somethin'." His words crackled with the electric hum of Eldergrove's magic, a spark dancing in the air between them, as if the breeze carried the Tree of Life's ancient song.

Trickle's eyes locked onto his, wide and knowing, not a heartbeat of hesitation in her celestial gaze. "I know, Ry," she whispered, her voice a thread of light weaving through the dusk. "The magic's happenin' everywhere—dark and light—I can feel it, electric as a storm." She sat on the step, patting the spot beside her with a playful smile. "Come sit, Sir Lancelot," she teased, her tone a melody of mischief and warmth, her fingers brushing the air like a siren's call, beckoning him closer.

Rylan sat down next to her, and she latched onto his arm, her touch electrifying, sending shivers racing through him. Her jade eyes drank him in like he was the only star in her sky. "I wanna know everything."

Rylan spilled his tale like a river breaking free, words tumbling in a rush of wonder and fear: the Tree of Life's crow's nest, the hollow knot's silver glow, the fiery cloud on the horizon burning Eldergrove to ashes, the recurring hiss of, "MIIIINNNNEEEE!" and the vision of the wooden relic, its four faces—Man, Ox, Lion, Eagle—alive, spirit-filled, watching him with gazes fierce and holy. His voice trembled, raw as the earth after a storm.

"I don't know what any of it means, Trickle. Do you?"

She tilted her head, her golden hair spilling over her shoulder like cascading sunlight. A playful smile curled her lips, a secret dancing in her gaze.

"Nnnoooo..." Her voice softened into mystery laced with promise, "...but I know who might."

She squeezed his arm, her touch a vow, her smile a beacon of their shared light, as the electric air hummed with the Kingdom's magic, binding their hearts in a dance of friendship and unspoken love.

* * *

On the painted planks of blues and burgundies, Rylan sat cross-legged, a pencil gripped in his calloused fingers, sketching his vision from the Tree of Life with the fervor of an artist etching his destiny. Trickle nestled beside him, her breath hitched with each line, as if she were unraveling the secrets of his soul. OG loomed behind them, a hulking sentinel of love, his massive chin perched on their shoulders, floppy ears tickling their necks as he nosed his way into their conspiracy. His curious eyes glinted with dogged determination to be part of whatever magic they were brewing.

Rylan's sketch was a valiant attempt, but the Eagle, Ox, and Lion had morphed into a comical trio—a walrus with a drooping mustache, a zebra with wobbly stripes, and a Woody Woodpecker lookalike with a beak sharp as a mill saw. Trickle pointed at the Lion, her finger trembling with suppressed laughter, her voice a lilting tease of bubbling ripples.

"Is that s'posed to be Fred Flintstone, Ry?" she giggled, a melody of pure delight. "And that one"—she pointed—"Scooby-Doo, right?"

OG joined in with a rumbling bark, his tail thwacking the porch like a drumbeat of joy. Rylan's cheeks flushed a sunrise pink, frustration knitting his brow as he wadded the paper into a defeated ball, his shoulders slumping like a knight who had lost his sword. Trickle's laughter softened, her hand finding his arm, her touch a whisper of sunlight that melted his frown.

"It's okay, my King," she said, her words always knowing the right path.

"You just tell it to Zora and Old Zeke the way you told me—every shiver, every spark. I'm sure they'll unravel it, they always do."

The three of them hatched a plan to venture to the Crescent Coffershop at first light, where Zora and Ezekiel would be perched out on the shop's porch like two ancient crows, sharing town secrets and sipping their secret brew—a potion Ezekiel swore could wake the world with its smoky apple-flavored tang.

The critters had returned to the porch, their tiny paws tapping in rhythm to the songs blooming from Trickle's old phonograph, its wooden petals unfurling with the Birds' tune. OG tried to inject himself into the choir, his massive head tilting as he hummed along, but the sound rumbling from his throat was more like an old soul with a bad back groaning at dawn—a gravelly, off-key wail that made the birds flutter in protest. Trickle giggled, and OG glanced at her, shy as a pup, his amber eyes bashful beneath his floppy ears. She leaned over, ruffling his fur with a tenderness that could mend the moon, and cooed.

"That's beautiful, Old Feller, you just sing with everything you got. Ain't nobody in this world cares that you're the only one in tune—don't let us hold you back, Mister."

OG glowed under her encouraging white lies, his tail wagging like a metronome of joy, his heart swelling as he howled louder, a serenade for his golden queen.

Trickle slipped inside for a moment, her sundress a swirl of wild shadows against the setting sun. She returned with a small box cradled in her hands, a ribbon of crimson silk tied around it like a promise. She sat beside Rylan, who'd taken a too-eager gulp of his Lemonade, leaving a glistening trail down his chin and onto his shirt. Her fingers trembled with a love so pure it seemed to hum in the air as she wiped his chin with the loose end of her dress, the fabric brushing his skin like a whisper of devotion. Her touch was a vow that wrapped around his heart like Honeysuckle vines. Rylan's gaze flickered to the box, curiosity sparking in his soul.

"What's that, Trickle?" His voice was a soft plea, as if every word he spoke was a love letter meant only for her.

She placed the box before him, her eyes shimmering with a tenderness that could make the creek weep.

"I've got somethin' for you, Ry," she said, her voice a melody of gratitude, each note a thread of gold weaving their hearts closer. "It's a way to thank you for your eternal devotion, for lettin' me into your heart and soul, where I've found a home I never knew I needed."

Rylan's throat tightened, his hand resting on the box as he looked into her eyes, seeing her depth of love reflecting back.

"I'm the one who needs you, Trickle," he confessed, his voice raw with the weight of his truth. "You don't just fit into my world—you've changed it, made it brighter, bigger, better. You're my everything."

Her smile bloomed, and she grabbed his hands, her fingers trembling as she placed the small gift of pure love into his grasp. She leaned in, her lips brushing his cheek in a kiss that tasted of sweet, eternal summers.

"Open it, Ry,"

Rylan pulled back the crimson ribbon, his heart skipping beats as if he were unwrapping the first moment she'd ever appeared, the memory of her laughter and light flooding him with warmth that could rival the sun. Inside, wrapped in tissue, lay an old relic—a compass, brass worn by the years and scratched with the untold stories of a thousand journeys. Its hands spun wildly out of control, a dance of chaos that refused to settle on north, south, east, or west. Rylan's brow furrowed, a flicker of confusion in his gaze, but he masked it with a smile, not wanting to dim the light in her eyes.

"No, it ain't broken, Ry," she assured, her voice a velvet promise. "It'll never show you north, south, east, or west—but it'll point you toward findin' what you need."

Rylan's eyes widened, wonder blooming in his chest like wildflowers after the rain.

"So it's magic? "

His voice was a whisper of awe, as if the compass held the secrets of the stars.

Trickle's gaze softened, her eyes locking into his with a devotion that could tether the moon to the earth.

"I don't know 'bout all that," her voice was a lilting confession, "but I do know it'll always show you the way back to me."

The weight of her words settled into his soul—a compass not for the world, but for them, a talisman of their love, a promise that no matter how far he wandered, she'd always be his true north. He grabbed the compass and turned it over as it calmed from his touch, his fingers tracing its worn surface. He found an inscription on the back—Isaiah 30:21—etched in script as delicate as a whisper:

When you wander lost, your soul will hear the voice that will widen your path.

The compass slowed to a stop. Rylan's eyes followed its pointing hand. In his grasp it was fixated on Trickle, his gaze a question wrapped in adoration. She smiled, her voice a sacred vow. Rylan leaned into her, closer than he ever had, his heart swelling with the certainty that he was right where he belonged. The three of them sat on the edge of the porch, watching the Kingdom settle into rest. The sky was a canvas of twilight purples and golds, the creek's song a lullaby weaving through the air, while the compass held steady.

Secret Brew

Mid-morning sun spilled over Eldergrove, a golden tide kissing the jade grass and setting the creek's surface ablaze with light. Rylan pedaled his battered PK Ripper, its red knobby tires humming a hymn of freedom, while Trickle perched on the handlebars, her golden hair streaming like a comet's tail. The bike's front hubs sported pegs—mysterious stubs until Trickle claimed them, her bare feet curling snug against their metal, her lithe frame balanced on the padded crossbar as if it were a throne especially crafted for her tush.

"It's perfect, Ry!"

She stretched her arms wide, fingers splaying like wings, catching the breeze as if she could soar into the heavens.

"I'm flyin' Ry!"

She smiled with everything she had and took in a breath filled with the sweet taste of springtime. Rylan squinted to see past her, his hazel eyes dancing with effort and delight, the road a blur beneath their shared spell.

OG bounded ahead, a beast chasing a squirrel's fluffy taunt, his massive paws thundering across their path. The bike wobbled, tires kissing the edge of a bramble patch, and Rylan yanked the bars hard, laughing wild as Trickle's giggle rippled.

"OG, you big lug!"

Her jade eyes glinted with mischief and pure joy. Nothing could dim their happiness, not a near-miss nor the world's sharp edges. The plan that had hatched under last night's stars burned bright in their hearts. It was a vow to unravel the Tree of Life's secrets with Zora and Ezekiel's wisdom.

They rolled into the town square, the Crescent Coffershop windows winking amber in the dawn. As prophesied, Zora Thornweaver and Ezekiel Moonchild perched on the porch, along with old Johnny Pocketwatch standing behind them. They were sharing stories and the morning brew—Zora's smoky coffee concoction laced with a spill of Ezekiel's apple-pie moonshine. As always, Zora's silver braids swayed in the breeze, her smoked-quartz eyes pierced the morning haze, while Ezekiel's tie-dye shirt flared bright as his grin, knotty long locks tucked under his favorite tam, and old Johnny twirling his pocket watch and checking it against the sun rising in the east.

Rylan skidded to a stop and Trickle vaulted off, her sundress a swirl of wildflowers. She skipped the steps altogether, scrambling over the railing with a dancer's grace, claiming the lone rocking chair like a queen seizing her court. Rylan tumbled after, breathless, his lanky frame buzzing with purpose.

"We're so glad we found you!"

Zora and Ezekiel traded a glance, their brows arching as if to ask, Which one of us? Trickle's gaze flicked to the table, where three tin mugs steamed their brew a forbidden alchemy. She twitched her nose, a playful spell, and teased,

"Apple-flavored coffee? That's a new one."

Ezekiel coughed, feigning deafness, while Zora's laugh cackled like wind through the oaks.

"Child," she purred, her voice a lilting chant, "you get on with whatever it is that dragged you here at this hour."

Rylan stepped forward and spilled his tale like a river breaking free. Words tumbled wild, raw as the Kingdom's pulse—the Tree of Life's crow's nest, the hollow knot's silver glow, the fiery cloud's snarl of **MIIIINNNEEEE!** scorching Eldergrove to ash, and the wooden relic's four faces—Man, Ox, Lion, Eagle—staring fierce and holy, their eyes threading light through his soul. Ezekiel leaned in, his voice a low hum.

"I told you, boy, that Tree spins the supernatural—whispers for only them with magic to hear it, you got it..."

Zora sat still, her patchwork shawl pooling like a shadow, her dark eyes lost in thought, as if the ether itself whispered back. Silence fell, the air thrumming with the weight of Rylan's vision. Ezekiel stirred, leaning forward, his calloused hands clasping his mug, and Old Johnny paced back and forth mumbling something about rhythmic chaos unfolding, that nobody could quite grasp.

"Them faces in the vision, all lookin' different ways, sure feels like it means somethin' big." Trickle tilted her head, deep in her contemplation. "Maybe it's how they see—each from a different place, like they're guardin' somethin' together, each of them watching their specific direction."

Ezekiel nodded, his grin flashing. "Ox—strength, hard work, servitude. Carries the world's weight and don't flinch."

Zora's eyes sparked, and she leaned in, "Eagles—swift, vision, risin' above the earth's mess. Sees the divine, carries the spirit's truth."

Rylan bounced on his toes, chest swelling, and crowed,

"Aslan!"

They looked at him, puzzled, until he grinned wider.

"The Lion King—strength, courage, majestic as all get-out!"

Laughter erupted, a chorus weaving through the square, their joy a hymn to the Kingdom's wild heart, but the man in the vision stumped them, a riddle wrapped in light. What did he see? What was his role? OG nudged Trickle's knee, his eyes glinting with a bear-taught spark, a low whimper rumbling from his jowls. She patted him absently, her mind adrift in the vision's glow, until he nudged harder, insistent.

"What, OG, honey?" she murmured, glancing down. He met her gaze, head tilting as if nodding to a secret only they shared, and a bolt of knowing struck her like the Old Church's holy arc.

Trickle's eyes caught fire, and she whispered,

"It ain't a human."

Rylan, Zora, Ezekiel, and even Old Johnny froze, their breaths caught in the morning's hush, as she smiled, warmth radiating like Honeysuckle in bloom.

"It's a Cherubim."

The word hung in the air, a spark igniting the ether, the Coffershop's ivy trembling as if the Kingdom itself leaned closer. Zora's lips curled, a blade of wisdom in her grin, while Ezekiel clapped his hands, dreadlocks flaring. Johnny got back to his pacing and was now repeating "Time will tell, time will tell," over and over again. Rylan's soul thrummed, his heart a drumbeat of adventure, and Trickle squeezed his arm, her touch a vow. OG flopped beside them, tail thumping the boards, his floppy ears framing a grin that swore he'd known all along. The square pulsed with magic, the Tree of Life's whispers weaving through the dawn, daring them to chase the Cherubim's truth and whatever holy fire waited beyond.

* * *

The rag tag group sat spellbound, the Cherubim's echo a radiant ember in their hearts, each mind chasing its meaning through the ether. OG sprawled at Trickle's feet, ears twitching to the forest's sacred hymn.

Rylan's gaze drifted to the horizon, where the sky churned, no longer Eldergrove's golden cradle but a cauldron of malice. Swirling clouds coiled like a serpent's spine, their edges bruised with molten crimson and obsidian, pulsing with a hunger older than time. They mirrored the dark pool's wrath from his memories, its bubbling fury when the Dragonfish stirred, scales glinting like hellfire. The clouds seemed to see him, their gaze a cold claw raking his soul, whispering—"*MIIIINNNEEEE*"—that same guttural snarl from his vision. The sound of it slithering through his subconscious, beckoning him to a void where light and time drowned. Lightning crackled within the storm's heart, not mere bolts but a witch's brew of fire and chaos, imploding in bursts that birthed shadows with teeth. The storm was no natural beast—it was a hunter, a leviathan of smoke and flame, its coils tightening to choke the Cherubim's truth before it could bloom.

Zora leapt up, her silver braids flaring like comet tails, her eyes blazing with revelation. "I got it!" she cried, voice a thunderclap splitting the ether. "Hold fast, sweetlings!"

She vanished into the Coffershop, the door's creak a hymn to mysteries unveiled. In a heartbeat, she returned, cradling a tome ancient as the Tree itself—leather weathered, its edges glowing faintly, as if kissed by star-fire. Ezekiel's dreadlocks quivered under his tam, his grin fading to awe.

"What's that you got, Zora?"

She paused, her gaze a blade of knowing, and whispered,

"The Book of Truth."

The words shivered through the square, the cobblestones humming as if the Kingdom knelt. Zora opened the book, its pages exhaling a scent of myrrh and lightning, and her finger found the words etched in light. Her voice rang out as if the whole world was waiting.

"And after He drove the man out, He placed on the east side of the Garden of Eden a Cherubim, with a flaming sword guarding the path to the Tree of Life."

Rylan's jaw fell, they were on to something, his eyes wide as the creek at dawn, the words igniting his soul like the Tree's silver glow. Ezekiel sank back, astonishment carving his face, his tie-dye shirt dim against the verse's radiance. Johnny stopped in his tracks and blurted, "Father Time!"—while pointing to the old fractured clock on the church's steeple.

Trickle sprang up, her sundress a whirl of wildflowers, OG mirroring her, his massive paws dancing.

"You grabbed a Bible!" Her golden sparkles blazing, a prophetess in bloom. "That's in the Bible!"

Zora's laugh was a melody filled with starlight.

"One of the most magical texts ever scribed, sweetling—a Grimoire of the divine."

In that very moment, a monstrous bolt split the sky, not lightning but a serpent's fang, its electric hiss spitting out the clouds now roiling in above them. The Storm-Beast loomed, its crimson heart pulsing, scales of shadow and flame gleaming through the haze. Rylan wondered if it could still be hunting him as it had in the pool's dark depths. Its wind howled with incantations, clawing at his spirit, daring him to falter, to abandon the path that had been widened before them. The air crackled, heavy with brimstone, as if the leviathan's breath scorched the square, its coils weaving a cage to trap their quest.

Ezekiel's gaze snapped upward, his tam tilting as his dreadlocks flared.

"Sky's fixin' to bite, y'all—let's get hunkered down!"

Rylan stared, transfixed, as the clouds writhed, their copper gleam a predator's eye locking onto him, plotting his ruin. Trickle's hand seized his, warm as Mamma's prayers, her jade eyes fierce with defiance.

"Inside, Ry!"

She yanked him toward the Coffershop's glow, its ivy trembling as if shielding them from the beast's jaws. OG growled, hackles rising, a knight of fur and fang barring the storm's path.

The door slammed shut, sealing them in the shop's amber heart, where the Grimoire of the Saffron Veil flickered and the crow's skull rune hummed, as if the Kingdom itself stood guard. Outside, the leviathan roared, its lightning claws raking the sky, but within, the Book of Truth's verse burned bright—a flaming sword against the dark, daring Rylan and Trickle to chase the Cherubim's fire, no matter what hunted them.

* * *

Rylan placed his palms and forehead against Crescent Coffershop's warped window, its glass cool as the creek's depths. Zora's candlelight chorus blazed under him, painting his shadows alive with vibrations—a galaxy of handcrafted spells, each waxen flame a shard of magic: one for a fractured heart, another to fortify a spirit, one for strength, and another for wisdom. Their glow flickered in his eyes as he stared past the cobblestones to the Tree of Life. Above it, a vortex of clouds, swallowing the sun with a ravenous maw. Crimson lightning slashed the sky, revealing a serpent of shadow within, coiling tighter with a hunger that gnawed at Rylan's core. This wasn't just a storm—it was a living curse, a beast born of creek shadows and Eldergrove's bruised past.

Inside the shop, the voices wove a lilting spell, they scoured the leather-bound Grimoire, its pages crackling with magic and supernatural secrets older than the tree's roots. Ezekiel Moonchild leaned in close, while Trickle traced runes with a trembling finger. They hunted for whispers of a Cherubim in the text of the old book, blind to the sky's wrath brewing outside, their voices a soft hum against the shop's pulse—geodes throbbing, firefly wings flaring gold in jars. Rylan watched them and his mind flickered, conjuring Daphne, Thelma, Fred, and Scooby hunched over a magical tome, candlelight spilling revelations. He laughed at his interpretation, almost asking if OG needed a Scooby snack...

His breath caught, as if the air had tightened his chains. He turned back answering the calls from the storms breath and found himself locked into the grip of something far more sinister. He could feel his satchel pulsing, slung across his shoulder, thrumming violently—the five fiver loads, those sacred stones he'd carried since the creek battle, vibrated fiercely, a desperate call singing in his blood. They weren't just rocks; they were relics of his fight against the Dragonfish, each etched with a spark of the Kingdom's light, forged when he'd yanked Pops from those molten jaws. Their hum was a war cry, begging him to resist, but the storm's pull was stronger, dragging him into a waking nightmare.

His vision started to blur and it seemed as though he was watching himself from a distance—a hollowed out wraith of himself—climbing the Tree of Life, but it was no longer the titan of legend. Its leaves were ash, bark rotted to a sickly gray, branches dangling like fractured bones, stripped of the emerald pulse that once watched over Eldergrove's soul. This was a desecrated husk, defiled by the storm's venom. Rylan's shadow-self scrambled to the crow's nest, his perch above the Kingdom's ripples, but the view was gone—smothered by a void that devoured light and hope. The Fiver loads screamed louder, their vibrations rattling his ribs, a chorus of defiance against the serpent's lure. They burned hot in his satchel, five beacons of the boy who'd faced evil and won, pleading for him to remember...

At the tree's heart, Rylan's wraith knelt, fingers trembling as he offered his spirit to the coiled serpent. Its eyes—twin orbs of blood-red wrath—locked onto him, poised to strike promising poison, power steeped in ruin. The Dragonfish's essence pulsed within it, a primal malice whispering of dominion over ash and bone. Rylan's heart faltered, teetering on the abyss. The Fiver loads roared, their light flaring through the satchel's seams, searing his side as if to jolt him awake. But the serpent's hiss was a deluge, drowning their plea:

"MIIIINNNEEEE!"

Rylan accepted its invitation, reaching out, soul fraying, Eldergrove's lights snuffed out—every flame, every spark, gone. Zora's candles, those wards in every window, choked and died under the storm's dark breath. The town plunged into blackness, a silent grave save for the serpent's triumphant roar.

The climax surged, a battle for Rylan's soul. The serpent's claws sank deeper, its fire—scarlet and blue, sharp as a demon's fang—licking at his essence, promising to burn his dreams to cinders. The fiver loads wailed, their glow bursting free, painting his shadow-self in streaks of gold and emerald, a radiant defiance that stung the serpent's gaze. Rylan teetered, pulled taut between light and dark. The serpent's void offered strength, a titan's might to rival Pops' old rage, but it was cold, empty—a lie cloaked in glory. The fiver loads were vibrating, buzzing with Mamma's lullabies, Trickle's laughter, OG's sloppy joy, and memories of love that anchored him to Eldergrove's heart. His wraith-self wavered, fingers curling back from the serpent's maw, the stones' heat a fire in his veins.

A spark appeared in the distant window, faint but unyielding, a light no evil could smother. Rylan's wraith turned, drawn by a warmth that cleaved the void. There, cradled by the last candle's glow, a mystical orb, not quite human, and not quite not—woven of starlight, sparkles of jade flecked in gold. It was as vast as eternity, radiating a love that could mend the heavens. The presence was a vow that darkness could rage but never reign. The serpent shrieked, its flames lashing wild, but the Light reached for Rylan, a tether stronger than fate. The fiver loads spun in defiance, blazing, their song merging with hers, a crescendo that shook the dead tree's roots to life. Rylan's soul tore free, plummeting from the serpent's grasp, falling through the blackened sky, piloted by the light. The storm's claws slashed the air, as the Light carried him home.

He could see Eldergrove exhale, the Tree's roots re birthed, its shimmering leaves whispering, spells of grace. Rylan gasped, hands clawing the window frame relented, his heart thundering a knight's oath as Trickle's touch grounded him.... The fiver loads quieted, their warmth a steady pulse.

Rylan was regaining his sense of reality and he turned around slowly—looking deeply into Trickle's eyes—and he could feel the warmth of her devotion. He held back the looming fear of what he had just witnessed, and pulled her in close whispering,

"It's back..."

Trickle's arms encircled Rylan, a fierce tether of love and resolve, while OG settled at their feet, his steady gaze a silent vow to face any storm.

"We got you, Ry,"

Trickle murmured, her voice a soft hymn of loyalty. Rylan's eyes met OG's, the dog's defiant stare daring even the darkest shadows to test their luck. Beyond them, the team of steadfast disciples, huddled over ancient tomes, their faces etched with weary determination. Rylan's hand ruffled OG's brow, a tender ritual.

"I just need a day of rest and focus in the Kingdom," he sighed, "with my sweet Princess and my loyal OG-pottimus," a nod to OG's potato-like figurine.

Twilight draped its velvet cloak over the land, and their research hit a stubborn wall. They vowed to press on, to share any spark of discovery, as Rylan, Trickle, and OG turned toward home. The trio faded into the amber glow of the setting sun, Rylan pushing his bike, while Zora, Zeke, and Old Johnny Pocketwatch waved, their silhouettes rooted like oaks as the Kingdom slipped into a soulful slumber.

Dream Weaver

Rylan, Trickle, and OG ruled this sacred stretch of Eldergrove, their laughter a wild hymn weaving through the oaks, where moss dripped like emerald tears and willows whispered secrets to the breeze. The creek's ripple sang bold and free, its voice a silver thread stitching their joy to the heart of the earth, while dragonflies darted in sapphire flashes, flutterbys spun golden loops above the ripples, a crown of light for the Kingdom's keepers.

Rylan launched from the hollow tree's jagged peak, a boy-king soaring, his body twisting mid-air before slicing into the pool with a splash that sent rainbow-colored fish scattering like jewels. Trickle followed, a vision of grace as she soared from the rope, a flip outshining his twists with a defiant giggle that danced across the water.

"Beat that, Ry!"

Her eyes glinting with mischief, a sparkle that pierced his soul. OG bounded along the bank, stomping in the water, a drooling titan, his tiger-streaked fur gleaming as he chased the fish's flickering shadows, barking a joy so fierce it rattled the ferns.

Rylan and Trickle had waged war in the water, a playful rebellion against time's quiet theft. Rylan dove deep, chasing a fish whose scales shimmered like molten-hued rainbows, his hands grazing its slick flank before it slipped free. Trickle, not to be outdone, surfaced with an amethyst-colored gem she'd found on the bottom clutched tight in her grip.

"This one's mine, King Ry!"

Her grin was a spark, igniting his chest with a youthful fire—wild, reckless, a love so bright it hurt. He splashed her, water arcing like liquid starlight, and she retaliated, her laughter a melody that drowned the cicadas' drone.

Breath-Holding came next, a test of will beneath the pool's glassy heart. They sank together, faces inches apart, bubbles rising like tiny prayers. At forty-four seconds, Trickle's hand grazed his cheek, her lips crashing into his—a sudden, electric kiss that stole his air and sent his heart thundering. He surfaced, gasping, water streaming from his hair, and she popped up after, her giggle a flirtatious trill.

"Cheater!" His voice cracked, with playful outrage, his hazel eyes blazing with adoration. "You stole my breath!"

They swam on, Trickle clinging to his neck, her arms a warm anchor as they glided through the pool's depths. The water, once black with the Dragonfish's curse, now sparkled with forgotten wonders. The pool was alive, its currents whispering hints of the springs deep beneath Eldergrove, where Zora's tales at the Crescent Coffershop had spun threads of magic—light and dark, pulsing like a hidden heart.

They hauled themselves to the bank, sprawling on a quilt of sun-warmed grass, water dripping from their skin like liquid light. Rylan uncapped the canteen, Lemonade tart and sweet, a taste of home that wove their hearts together. He tore into Spam and Government Cheese sandwiches, Saltines crunching, passing chunks to Trickle. OG wolfed his share, his grin a sloppy salute. They ate heartily, crumbs dusting their chins, laughter spilling as they traded bites and tales.

The creek's song filled any moments of silence, its ripples a melody that stirred Rylan's soul. His gaze drifted to the pool, its waters sparkling with secrets—supposed springs that pulsed beneath Eldergrove like a hidden heart. A question burned inside him, born of the Crescent Coffershop's unsolved puzzle. He turned to Trickle,

"Do you think a seed could fly across the whole ocean?"

She tilted her head, eyes thoughtful.

"My father used to tell me a single seed could nourish all of mankind."

The words hung. It was the first time she had ever mentioned any of the tightly held secrets hidden in her heart. Simple yet vast, a truth Rylan felt in his bones because it came from her. He nodded, love swelling fierce.

OG stirred first, his massive frame snapping upright, ears twitching like tattered flags. A low "huff" rumbled from his chest—a greeting, warm and sure—his tail wiggling with that giddy spark, drool plopping to the dirt. Rylan and Trickle froze, then heard it: a bell ringing, clear and bright, slicing through the Kingdom's hum like a call from beyond. Their eyes met, wide with knowing, hearts leaping as one.

"Zeke!"

They scrambled to their feet; the three amigos tore down the Kingdom's winding path, a trio of wild spirits racing to meet Ezekiel Moonchild, their hearts pounding with the thrill of competition that stitched their every adventure. OG reached Ezekiel first, nearly toppling the old hippie with a storm of wiggles and glee, his tail thwacking the earth like a metronome gone rogue, drool flying in a baptism of love.

Rylan and Trickle skidded to a halt just in time to spare old Zeke from drowning in OG's slobbering serenade. Rylan, barefoot and fierce, grabbed the handlebars of Ezekiel's battered Stingray bike, its pink, purple, and green spray paint shimmering like a psychedelic spell under the late spring sun.

"Hey, Zeke! Let me take that load off your hands!"

Rylan's eyes gleamed proud with his boyish bravado. The bike, a relic of Eldergrove's quirky heart, bore no seat—replaced by a custom-configured bench rack, a sturdy lattice of polished driftwood and hemp cords, that groaned under the weight of Ezekiel's worldly goods.

A bamboo fishing pole, its rune-etched surface said to hook legends from the springs' depths, paired with a tackle box painted with a psychedelic mandala, its crystal-and-feather lures humming with charms. A dented silver canteen, engraved with a crescent moon and dusted with glitter, sloshed with apple pie-flavored Lemonade. A patchwork quilt, its turquoise, saffron, and crimson squares stitched with fragments of Eldergrove's soul, and a cedar flute, inlaid with mother-of-pearl stars, rested in a velvet pouch. A tie-dye satchel of river-smoothed stones and crystals was tucked beneath with a leather journal of Ezekiel's doodles and shifting prophecies.

A basket up front cradled the town's mail and Ezekiel's notebook, a tome of embellished rumors and secrets that pulsed with the square's gossip. The metal tag, etched with Stingray, gleamed faintly, and its bell—rung with a clear, bright chime on Ezekiel's pilgrimages through Eldergrove's cobblestone veins.

Ezekiel Moonchild was no mere mailman but Eldergrove's keeper of dreams and "secrets". He held a heart that overflowed with a servant's spirit, and pulsed with the Kingdom's soul. His wiry frame moved with quiet grace as he would push his psychedelic Stingray through the cobblestone streets. No soul had ever seen Ezekiel ride that bike—it was a chariot he guided on foot, catering to the town's womenfolk with unwavering devotion and attention to their details. He nodded and smiled, a flirtatious sparkle in his eyes.

He would give out hand-picked bundles of the season's blooming harvest, and craft compliments like it was his purpose. Having inherited most of the square's ramshackle dens, he was no landlord but a steward, tending to Eldergrove's spirit. Children would listen for that old bell ringing, and they would come running, eager for his magician's tricks—coins vanishing, scarves blooming—and pockets stuffed with honeyed candies.

As Zora's faithful disciple, part-time Holy man, and Miss Peesewell's poorly kept secret lover, Ezekiel's servitude glowed in mended shawls, whittled charms, and shared sips of apple pie-flavored lemonade, each act a humble offering, binding Eldergrove in love, mischief, and the creek's eternal song.

"I got news for you two young-uns,"

Ezekiel rumbled, his voice a low hymn laced with the tang of apple-pie moonshine. Rylan, ever the knight of the Kingdom, cut in, his voice crackling with hope,

"Y'all unravel the mystery yet?" Ezekiel shook his head, dreadlocks swaying like willow branches.

"Not quite, boy, but we're diggin' deep. Zora, though—she stumbled on somethin' 'bout them springs, and she sent me to fetch ya this."

From the Stingray's basket, Ezekiel drew a tome ancient as the Tree of Life itself, its leather cover weathered to a sheen that glowed faintly, as if kissed by star fire. The Secret Labyrinths of the Bohemians, its title whispered in curling script, pulsed with a magic that prickled Rylan's skin. Ezekiel's calloused fingers flipped it open, revealing hand-drawn maps that snaked across the pages like the creek's hidden currents.

"Check the one Zora marked," he said, his voice dropping to a reverent hush. "She don't bend pages—says it's a sin against a book's soul. Uses her reading tea leaves instead, you know that. This one's different though... be careful here..."

A single leaf marked the page, its scent not of chamomile or mint but a sharp, wild tang that stung the air. Rylan, OG, and Trickle leaned in, their breaths catching as they saw it—a poison ivy leaf, its edges curling like a warning etched in venom. Ezekiel's eyes darkened, his tam tilting as he leaned closer.

"Zora ain't never used that before. She said to tell ya to tread careful—real careful. This here's dangerous, maybe deadly. That leaf's her way of sayin' the springs hold secrets that could be catastrophic if you ain't ready."

Trickle traced the map's lines with a trembling finger. The page showed a labyrinth beneath Eldergrove, a tangle of tunnels and pools where the springs pulsed like the Kingdom's heart, their waters shimmering on the enchanted page with light and shadow. There were a total of four waterfalls marked on the map: one huge one that sourced the other three was half cut off at the page's end. To Rylan's knowledge he had only seen two of them. The dotted line marking a path stopped at the base of the third one which was marked with a skull and crossbones. Rylan looked at Trickle,

"Do you know anything about any other pools or falls?"

She put her finger on the second pool that showed the three waterfalls surrounding it,

"The second pool, where you found me the second time, is sourced by three waterfalls, but one of them has a flow that is sick, the one with the skull marked on it, the third waterfall. I have never climbed up beyond that, I have only heard of the fourth fall. It's the magnificent pool that sources all of the water in every old myth and legend."

Rylan looked down at the map again and he thought deeply for a moment.

"The path stops at the base of the third waterfall that no longer flows."

Rylan was puzzled, his heart thumped, a knight's oath rising in his chest. He pointed to a name at the bottom of the map that indicated its creator.

Elijah Starscribe, a Bohemian villager, was a nomadic seer whose intricate, hand-drawn maps of the Kingdom's springs and labyrinths pulsed with prophetic insight, guiding those brave enough to follow toward the creek's eternal truths. The old stories around Eldergrove were that he had been losing his marbles after he descended deep into the caverns one too many times, looking for treasures. He would wander around town talking to the chipmunks, and telling tales to the locals of secrets and relics he'd received as gifts from the Tree of Life. He supposedly had gone pretty mad in the middle of a big storm back in the 1980s when the church steeple got struck and started its lean. Just before he had disappeared he climbed the old tower and moved the clock's hands to 4:20 in the middle of an old hippie gathering. No one had ever seen him since, and that was years before. Town folk just figured he was playing a joke and no one had ever bothered to change it again... It was always 4:20 in Eldergrove, the old Bohemians would joke...

Rylan and Trickle stood baffled as to what it all meant. The air crackled, thick with Honeysuckle and mystery, as if the Tree of Life itself leaned closer, its whispers daring them to chase the springs' truth. OG nudged Trickle's knee, his bear-taught spark glinting, a low huff rumbling from his jowls as if he sensed the map's weight. She knelt, her sundress a swirl of wildflowers, and pressed a kiss to his forehead.

Rylan clutched the book, its leather vibrating in his grip, his soul blazing with love and adventure. The Kingdom's breeze stirred, carrying the creek's song and the poison ivy's warning, a tapestry of magic and peril binding their hearts as they stood on the edge of Eldergrove's deepest secrets, ready to unravel the labyrinth's call. Old Zeke pushed himself off with a "Bon Voyage," and shrank into the horizon, ringing out an invitation for all comers with his old rusty bell...

With the sun dipping low, they'd wandered to the *old wooden cross* overlooking the Kingdom, a rough-hewn sentinel marking the resting place of Rylan's baby brother. Rylan kissed his fingers, pressing them to the weathered wood, a silent vow etched in grief. Trickle mirrored him, her touch gentle, her jade eyes soft with shared sorrow. OG sank to the earth with a whimper, his faint cry a mournful echo that stirred the willows.

They stood in reverent silence, honoring the loss that scarred Rylan's heart. Trickle's hands slid around his arm, her warmth a balm against the raw sting that still burned, fierce and unyielding. Rylan knew the purpose—the divine why, woven into his brother's absence, yet he couldn't quell the hate for the evil that had stolen him—a battle, he sensed, that had only begun.

They walked slowly toward Eldergrove, clinging to each other's company, the creek's whisper and the critters' hum weaving a fragile peace. At the house, they parted with a kiss, tight and trembling, a seal of love against the night's uncertainties. Rylan watched Trickle glide across the property, humming a lulling tune that blended with the old radio phonograph's croon:

"Ooh, Dream Weaver, I believe you can get me through the night..."

Pebbles

Rylan was slightly nodding off, the memories of the day's events swirling thick in his mind. His legs twitched to the rhythm of OG's snores, who had so graciously made a little space for Rylan on the bed. He couldn't fall into deep sleep, due to the calling he had to chase the map's mystery. Trickle and he had agreed the map's labyrinth—marked by that ominous poison ivy leaf—would wait till dawn's first light. The decision was practical, but Rylan's spirit churned, eager to unravel the secrets pulsing beneath the creek's song...

As he was falling deeper into the oncoming dream about the day's event's, a sharp ping at his window jolted him from the haze. Dazed, he stumbled off the bed and over to the window, cracking it ajar, while peering into the moonlit dark. There she stood—golden hair aglow, a handful of pebbles poised like a mischievous offering. She waved, her grin ornery and wild, and called in a voice that danced with defiance,

"Can Rylan come out to play?"

His heart leapt and he slid the window wide open, the night air cool against his skin, and he leaned out,

"Trick, you're gonna get us both in a heap of trouble..."

* * *

That night in the witching hour, Trickle's heart had thrummed with a restless fire. Sleep was a distant stranger banished by the call of Eldergrove's springs. Her excitement danced in her veins, urging her to prepare for the moonlit quest she and Rylan had vowed to chase at dawn, but dawn was too far, and she was no damsel in waiting. When the main house fell silent, she slipped from her bed, a barefoot conspirator cloaked in mischief. Under the pretense of craving a midnight snack, she tiptoed into the kitchen, light as a dragonfly's wing, dodging every squeaky board and clattering spoon with a thief's grace.

With a giggle stifled behind her hand, she brewed Mamma's Lemonade—tart, sweet, and kissed by Honeysuckle magic—pouring it into a shiny, new, second hand canteen. She filled it to the rim, slung it over a chair, a talisman for their journey. She pilfered Rylan's satchel from the coat hooks Pops had mounted on the wall, its leather worn soft by adventures through the Kingdom. She opened it up and took inventory with a grin: the compass she had given him, seven fiver loads, Pops' old journal, fragments of fishing tackle, Rylan's journal—among the boy-king's treasures, a single baby shoe stood out, whispering tales of a lost prince.

Trickle wedged in Mamma's homemade bear repellent, a potion fierce enough to scare the stars. Her mind flashed to the tale of Rylan and OG's clash with a man hunting bruin in the very hollow they would most likely cross through before daylight. Two cans of Spam, a hunk of Government Cheese, a log of Saltines—and The Secret Labyrinths of the Bohemians, all wrestled into their nooks.

Trickle's eyes caught a pair of boots by the door, shiny as a new moon, barely scuffed, and two sizes too small for Rylan at this point. She thought to grab them and snorted out loud, laughing at herself, the sheer ludicrous thought of shoes on her king's feet, tickled her soul.

She rolled her eyes with a flourish, snatched the satchel, and glided out the back door. She gathered a handful of pebbles from the ground and ran around to the side of the house, the cool wet grass kissing her bare feet. With the satchel stocked and slung over her shoulder, she stopped below Rylans window and took aim.

* * *

Rylan teetered halfway out his window, one leg slung over the sill, wrestling his overalls over his skivvies with a clumsy urgency, Trickle's mischievous invite, still ringing in his ears like a siren's call. He glanced back at OG, sprawled across the bed in a slumber deep as a hibernating bear's, with snores that could rattle loose the Tree of Life's roots. Rylan's eyes flickered with doubt, and he leaned out, whispering to Trickle below,

"What about OG, Trick?"

She threw up her hands, a playful shrug that danced with the creek's ripple, and shouted in her loudest whisper, a conspirator's plea that tickled the night.

"If we haul him down them stairs, he'll thunder like a storm and wake your Mamma and Pops for sure! Let him dream, Ry—we'll be back 'fore long, and he won't even miss us."

Her big beautiful eyes glinted, ornery and sure, and Rylan, bewitched by her reckless spark, felt the world tilt toward her logic, as if the springs themselves nodded in approval.

"I gotta grab my gear,"

He started to turn, but Trickle hoisted his satchel high, her sheepish grin a spell that could hush the critters' chorus.

"Just c'mon, lazybones! I've got it all!"

Rylan's heart thumped, a knight's oath caught between duty and adventure. He stole one last look at OG, sawing logs with a drooling grin, and spotted a pad of paper on his bedside table. With a hasty scribble, he poured his heart onto the page:

Mamma, don't fret—Trickle and I slipped out just 'fore the sun, to chase a yonder journey. Back soon, promise. RY

A fib, sweet as Honeysuckle, for the sun was hours from rising, but he couldn't bear Mamma's worry. He pinned the note to his door, a fragile shield against her fears, and clambered through the window. The night air wrapped him like the creek's embrace, cool and alive with bullfrogs' croaks and crickets' trill, a symphony cheering on the rebellion. Trickle grabbed his arm, her laugh a melody that drowned the stars, and they tore off together toward the Kingdom.

* * *

Under the full moon's silver gaze, Rylan and Trickle ventured forward, the night cloaking Eldergrove in a velvet shroud pierced by the Milky Way's radiant path—a celestial river guiding them toward divinity's edge. No lantern flickered yet; the trail glowed with lunar whispers and star-fire, each step a pilgrimage through the creek's raw, discordant hymn. The sounds of nature's chorus—wove a fractured melody, as if the Kingdom itself trembled with secrets too heavy to sing true. A warning perhaps left unnoticed.

They paused where the Kingdom's first pool shimmered at their feet, its crystal waters aglow with moonlight, alive with translucent streaks of life darting like spectral fish through the depths. Rylan's heart clenched—this pool, his sanctuary, was but a tiny vein in the vast, life-giving springs pulsing through Eldergrove's hills, a truth that both humbled and haunted him.

Ezekiel Moonchild's counsel, delivered that day at the pool's edge, echoed in his conscience—a gospel of caution, the poison ivy leaf's venomous curl a vigil of peril.

"Tread careful," Zeke had warned, his voice a low hymn of dread. "Them springs hold secrets that could undo ya."

Rylan halted, his breath catching, the weight of the unknown pressing like a stone on his chest. He turned to Trickle, her golden hair a halo in the starlight, her eyes fierce yet flickering with the same foreboding that gnawed his bones. He was a bit overwhelmed at the words of Old Zeke and what might come of this journey.

"Trick," His voice thick with resolve and a lover's fear, "remember what Zeke said—them springs... they're dangerous. See I'm good if somethin happens to me, but I can't ask you to risk yourself for my quest. It would be the end of me inside, if something bad came about to you."

Trickle locked herself onto Rylan's arm, looking straight into his eyes, and hushed his humble heart,

"Don't you be silly Ry, I ain't missin' this journey for all the magic in the Kingdom..."

With a soft click she sparked the magical lantern, its amethyst-and-jade panes came to life. The fireflies within flared like captured stars, casting a trembling light that danced with the night's pulse. Hand in hand, they stepped forward, the Kingdom's breeze a mournful sigh, daring them to chase the Kingdom's treacherous song.

Endure

The Kingdom's dawn was a reluctant whisper, the sun barely stirring from its slumbering veil, its frail glow smothered by a sky still cloaked in velvet black. The air hung heavy, thick with a dread that clawed at Rylan's gut, for they neared the cursed hollow where he and OG had once faced the Demon Bear, with its very essence stitched with the Dragonfish's molten fury. The Kingdom's pulse, usually a hymn of critters and willow sighs, had fallen silent, drowned by a stillness that felt like the breath of a grave.

Rylan's hand gripped Trickle's, grounding him against the darkness that pressed in closer, sharper, alive. He swore he heard something—a faint rustle, like footsteps stalking them along the bank, paired with a low, guttural growl that wasn't bear nor beast but something ancient and hungry, claiming the path as its own. The fiver loads in his satchel began to thrum with a ferocity, a warning of the dark forces weaving their snare. Rylan's heart thudded, each beat a prayer he didn't know he was whispering.

Trickle moved beside him, her steps silent, her grace otherworldly, as if the Kingdom's oaks bowed to her passage. The Oracle's Lantern dangled from her free hand, the fireflies within flickering feebly, their glow dimming as if the darkness itself drank their light.

"It's watchin' us, Rylan," her lilting voice a melody that cut through the silence.

Rylan's throat tightened, memories of the Demon Bear flashing—its molten copper veins glinting beneath its loc'd fur, jaws lined with jagged shards of glass that could grind flesh and soul alike. He'd heard Pops speak of the Valley of Death, a place where shadows walked and hope withered, and this hollow, with its empty winds and bottomless dread, felt like its heart. Through the fear, something deeper stirred within them, a spark not their own, pulling them toward the caverns ahead, where the labyrinth's mouth yawned beneath the springs. It was a call, urging him to walk where angels feared to tread.

A snap cracked the silence, and Rylan stumbled over an old broken branch—he stopped and knelt down, fingers brushing the splintered wood, rough as the Old Church's oak door. It was heavy, warm, as if the Kingdom's pulse still lingered in its grain. A *staff,* he thought, hefting it, its weight steadying his trembling hands. He twirled it, slow at first, then faster, carving a vortex of faith and fight through the air, a shield against the rustling shadows. Trickle raised the lantern, its faltering glow spilling a shroud of gold around them. She watched Rylan and her smile bloomed radiant, not an ounce of fear in her eyes, only a love so fierce it banished the demons clawing at Rylan's resolve.

A rustle erupted before them, grass hissing as if tread upon by unseen claws. A growl followed, low and ethereal, not of their world, but of the abyss. It was a claim that vibrated in Rylan's bones, whispering,

"*MIIIINNNEEEE...*"

The fiver loads rattled, their pulse a war drum, and Rylan's hand dove into his satchel. The growl sharpened into a shrieking howl, a wind born of evil itself, gusting from the hollow's depths. It hushed the fireflies in the Oracle's Lantern, their light snuffed out, plunging them into darkness thick as tar. Rylan's staff faltered, the vortex collapsing, and the path seemed to narrow, a tightrope over a bottomless pit where empty winds wailed, tugging at his soul, urging him to flee back to the comfort of Eldergrove.

Trickle's grip tightened, not in fear but in resolve, her fingers a lifeline.

"We're chosen, Rylan," her voice melodic thunder, echoing perseverance. "The springs ain't just water. They're a door, and we're the key."

Her words kindled a fire in his chest, a light no shadow could quench. He took a step, then another, the staff steady in his hand, its wood humming faintly. The darkness pressed closer, its growl now a chorus of unseen beasts, fire-laden eyes singeing the air, staring into their souls. Rylan's every instinct screamed to turn back, but Trickle's love, held him fast, a shield against the valley's despair.

A few more steps ahead, the creek's hymn began to stir, faint at first, a silvery thread weaving through the silence. An awakening of critters, inviting the sun—chipmunks chittering in the fallen tree's hollows—their presence a defiance of the dark. Ahead, the sun peeked above the horizon, a sliver of gold piercing the hollow's shroud, painting the oaks in hues of hope. Rylan's staff thumped the earth, each step a vow, his hazel eyes fixed on the caverns' mouth, where the second pool awaited their reunion.

Though I walk through the valley and the shadows that have been banished to them.... I will persevere. Rylan's mind wrapped itself around the magic in his soul. **I fear no evil, for love is with me**.

His words were internalized, but Trickle's smile widened, her grip on his tightened, and together they crossed the threshold.

* * *

They stood together before the second Pool, marked on the tattered map, with a heart from Trickle's doodles. Its waters shimmered like molten starlight, a liquid mirror where fish traced spirals of light—angel faces seeming to glow in the depths. They stood agasp, beyond tempted to return to the waters that were enchanted with magical creatures. The pool's pulse was a lover's whisper, beckoning them to indulge, to surrender to its embrace and forget the labyrinth's shadowed trials.

For a moment Rylan fell deep into the vision of their first kiss—a memory carved in his soul—Trickle's lips soft, her breath a spark that set his world ablaze. She ran her hand through the back of his hair, her lithe fingers threading through his dirty blonde strands, each touch a current that jolted his lanky frame. Rylan felt the yearning from his stomach, a hunger he had not yet resolved and didn't understand quite yet how to satiate. It was new, and deep, and had only happened around her. He loved a lot of things in his life—OG, Mamma, Bubba-Hulk—even Pops in his darkest hours, but this was beyond that. This was a first breath of crisp air, after having been submerged in the depths of nothingness. This was a leap of faith without any inhibition. In his mind, it was the beginning of the never-ending.

Trickle tempted him, her voice a lilting melody, sticky-sweet as the wild-flower mead sipped at the Old Church's altar.

"We could go and swim just for a moment, you know—cool off and all."

Her golden hair cascaded like a sunrise over her delicate frame, her smile a crescent moon that kindled a fire deep in his soul. Rylan looked at her with a burning inside of his everything, and thought that even the springs' cool waters couldn't stifle the flames. He had thoughts at that moment, looking into her soul's windows, that he had surely not known before...

Those nights when Pops had chased Mamma around the house with intents toward hard love, their laughter weaving through the sagging porch like a Bohemian hymn, Rylan suddenly understood. They didn't even seem so gross when he saw the glow that engulfed Trickle, her radiance a halo glowing with love's secret.

He was beyond tempted to run and swim, to deter the path forward, to lose himself in the Crystal Pool's enchanted depths where time might pause, where their love could bloom untouched by the valley's shadows. Something sang inside him, a melody older than Eldergrove. Rylan grabbed her, his calloused hands trembling with a reverence that felt like prayer, and kissed her, lips fierce yet tender, a seal upon his heart that burned brighter than the sun's first rays. He pulled her tight, her frame pressed against his.

"Queen Trickle—you move me," His voice, was raw with longing, soft as the creek's sigh. Each word dripped like honey, molten and pure. "My soul aches for you even as you walk beside me. You are the answer to my dreams, but we must continue..."

Trickle glowed, not because of his admiration of her, but because of her adulation of him. His resolve was heartfelt in her soul, a gaining of her trust with his recurring pureness, a King's oath that danced like the water's ripples. She loved him, beyond this world, beyond the Dragonfish's molten claim. Her jade eyes shimmered, wet with unspoken promises, and she leaned into him, her lips brushing his ear, her breath a warm breeze that sent shivers through his spine. A whisper escaped her soul,

"I'm so proud of you Ry, your wisdom lies deep within..."

She lightly kissed his ear with a tenderness that set his soul ablaze. The air thickened, heavy with the Kingdom's magic, the pool's glow pulsing in time with their hearts, as if the springs bore witness to a love that could rend the veil between their world and eternity.

Race Horse

OG was stirring, his legs kicked like he was at the Kentucky Derby and coming out of lane number two. A hulking beast of love sprawled across the bed, he so graciously shared with the Boy King. His massive frame claimed the center, a furry titan dreaming of that purty girl he'd seen on the *tell-a-vision* named Lassie.

His floppy ears twitched at the scolding administered by the rooster's impudent call. A low grunt rumbled from his chest, a warning to the dawn that it dared disturb his slumber. Half-lost in a haze of sleep, he rolled onto his back, paws shooting skyward like gnarled oaks reaching for the moon.

A spark of magic tickled his soul, from across the shack, down the creaking stairs, around a corner, and up the hallway, a subliminal pulse hummed through his bear-taught senses. The crinkle of a food wrapper—peppered bacon, to be exact, sizzling with Mamma's love. It sang to him like a siren's call, a message woven through Eldergrove's ether, tugging him from his dreams. His head lay in the depths of his drool as his amber eyes snapped open, glinting with a joy that could charm the creek itself. Rylan's absence from the bed barely registered; bacon was a quest worthy of a Knight, and OG was no mere dog—he was a guardian of the Kingdom, a soul stitched with mischief and devotion.

With a thump that rattled the floorboards, he launched from the bed, his hulking frame a storm of wiggles and glee. He scootched down the stairs, paws skidding on the worn wood. At the bottom, his feet betrayed him, sliding out in a glorious skid that sent him spinning like a top, tail thwacking the walls like a garden hose gone rogue. He regained his footing, undeterred, and barreled around the corner, up the hallway, and into the kitchen. The air bloomed with the sacred scent of bacon and eggs, a feast spun from Mamma's boundless love.

OG planted himself before her, his grin a crescent moon of pure delight. He spoke with elegance, a cordial "Woof," a gentleman's greeting laced with the charm of a bear at a carnival. His tail swept the floor like a broom chasing stardust. Mamma turned with a smile that could mend the heavens, her skillet sizzling with offerings she surely crafted just for him.

As the bacon's aroma curled around him, a shadow flickered in his heart. He scanned the kitchen, his amber gaze sweeping the familiar corners. Rylan's chair was empty; the table, missing his lanky frame; the air, devoid of his rogue grin. A pang struck, sharp as the creek's coldest current. Rylan was gone, and OG, loyal sentinel of the Kingdom, had been left behind.

The betrayal stung, not enough to dim the bacon's allure, but enough to knot his furry brow with worry. He wolfed down two strips, his jowls working with solemn grace, each bite a vow to find his boy, to mend the rift in their trio's sacred bond, then, his eyes caught it. A glint of silver resting on the chair, Rylan's Lemonade canteen, slung over the back like a forgotten relic. Its presence hummed with urgency, whispering of trails untrod and quests begun without him. OG's heart thumped, his wiggles giving way to a restless pace. He circled the kitchen, his soul a tangle of loyalty and longing. Mamma paused, her spatula hovering, her voice a soft thunder of care.

"You all right, Old Feller?"

OG met her gaze, his eyes cloaked in concern, he strode to the chair, nudging the canteen with a deliberate sniff, its leather warm with Rylan's scent. The message was clear: his King was out there, and OG would not rest until he found him. Mamma's brow furrowed, her hand brushing his matted fur.

"Oh, honey, I know," her voice was a lullaby woven with worry. "he left a note—off on some adventure with Trickle, says not to fret. I reckon he let you sleep, thinkin' you needed it."

She tossed a biscuit at him that he let hit the floor, her words had done little to soothe the ache. Adventure without him? The Kingdom's trails, the creek's song, the Tree of Life's whispers—they were his to guard, his to share with Rylan and Trickle. He seized the canteen's strap in his teeth, tugging it free with a gentle growl. The weight of it, a talisman of his vow. Concern consumed him, a fire fiercer than the Dragonfish, urging him to track his knight through Eldergrove's wild heart.

He paced to the door, canteen dangling from his jaws like a knight's banner, his soul blazing with purpose. The kitchen's warmth, Mamma's bacon, even the promise of eggs couldn't capture him. Outside, the dawn stirred, the creek's silvery hymn calling him to the trails where Rylan and Trickle roamed. OG's amber eyes gleamed, his heart a compass spinning toward the Boy King. With a final glance at Mamma, her worried smile a blessing, he nudged through the door, a furry titan chasing love's eternal spark, determined to reclaim his rightful place beside Rylan and Trickle.

* * *

OG launched from the shack's sagging porch, his massive paws thundered against the earth, the Lemonade canteen dangling from his jaws like a knight's sacred banner. He hit the dirt road at a gallop, a bulldozer of devotion. Rylan and Trickle, were out there, and he'd tear through the heavens to find them. Yet, as the trail stretched before him, a flicker of doubt pricked his soul. Their scents—Rylan's rogue grin, Trickle's Honeysuckle glow—wove through the air, a tapestry of their presence everywhere and nowhere, scattering his bear-taught senses like leaves in a storm.

He paused, his hulking frame quivering, charting the Kingdom's pulse. A breeze stirred, cool and sharp, whispering secrets from the creek's silvery heart. It tugged him toward the town square, a call as primal as the Tree of Life's hum, urging him to seek out Zora. His eyes sparked, and without a heartbeat's hesitation he tore off, a storm of fur and fang hurtling toward the Crescent Coffershop.

In the square, Zora and Zeke perched on the shop's porch, sipping their ritual brew, its tang a tribute to their fellowship. They froze, mid-sip, as a tremor shook the cobblestones—a furry juggernaut was barreling down the street. OG's massive form was a tidal wave of love and urgency. Zora rocked back in her chair, the queen of secrets, her lips curling with a blade-sharp smile. Ezekiel leapt up, dreadlocks flaring, his voice a low hymn of awe.

"Great Creator's Critters, here comes the Old Feller!"

OG screeched to a halt, paws skidding in a spray of earth, the canteen swinging like a pendulum of fate. His chest heaved, and a mournful moan spilled from his jowls, a serenade of longing that could hush the bullfrogs' chorus. Ezekiel reached for the canteen, his fingers grazing its strap.

"You bring this for me, boy?"

OG's amber eyes narrowed, a low growl rumbling like thunder dreaming of rain, a knight guarding his quest's heart.

"Easy, Old Guy,"

Ezekiel chuckled, stepping back, but Zora leaned in, her shawl fluttering like raven wings, her voice a lilting chant that wove through the dawn.

"I knew you'd come, sweet beast," she purred, her hand outstretched, fingers trembling with the ether's pulse. "The wind sang your name at midnight, a vow carried on star-fire."

OG tilted his head, canteen still clamped in his jaws, his gaze locking with hers, wise and fierce, a silent pact between guardians of the Kingdom.

Ezekiel's eyes widened, a spark of revelation igniting his soul, and he crouched beside OG, his arm encircling the beast's hulking frame.

"Zora and I danced with the shadows last night, Old Feller," his voice, thick with moonshine and mystery. "We unearthed a whisper—a clue to what your boy Rylan seeks, tied to the springs' deep heart."

Zora vanished into the Coffershop, the door's creak a hymn unto secrets unveiled. She returned, cradling a quilted knapsack, it's patchwork glowed faintly, as if kissed by the Tree of Life's emerald pulse. With a tenderness that could mend the moon, she slung the knapsack around OG's neck, securing it with a knot. She knelt, her silver braids grazing his loc'd fur, and wrapped her arms around him. Her embrace was a cocoon of star-fire and love. Leaning close, she whispered a secret into his ear, a spell only a beast of his heart could carry. She cupped his big cheeks, planting a kiss on his forehead that shimmered like candles, and her voice rang out, a command that shook the square.

"Get, Old Boy! You know what to do! Find your King and Queen!"

OG's soul blazed, the Boho bag tied around his neck a mantle of destiny, the canteen a beacon of his vow. He launched forward, a furry comet streaking toward the Kingdom, tail whipping the air like a banner of joy. The cobblestones trembled, the creek's song swelling to cheer him on, a symphony of critters heralding his quest. flutterbys and Dragonflies exploded like fireworks under the sun. Zora and Ezekiel watched, their mugs raised in salute, their laughter a melody weaving through the dawn. OG tore toward the springs, full knowing of his sacred charge—to reunite with Rylan and Trickle, to guard the Kingdom's heart, and to chase the labyrinth's truth.

The Journey

Rylan and Trickle stood at the second spring pool, waterfalls on the horizon, flowing. Their crystalline veils shimmering under a sky bruised with swirling clouds. The pool, which had once reunited them stretched wide. It was a sapphire mirror vast enough to drown the stars. Its waters hummed with a magic deeper than the first spring that Rylan had claimed as his own.

The falls thundered in majestic splendor, pulsing with the elixir of life, their torrents free and fierce, as if the Kingdom's veins coursed with boundless vigor; yet the third one faltered, its flow a sluggish lament, as though the waters of life had been siphoned by some unseen hand. The sight left Rylan's heart heavy, with a whispered doom. That was where the map had beckoned their presence. He turned to Trickle.

"Have you ever ventured beyond this spring-fed pool?"

Her eyes, twin pools of starlit wonder, met his.

"No, I have only heard of it in rumors," she murmured, her voice a soft ripple, "tales of a sacred source unseen by any who still draws a mortal's breath."

The map from Ezekiel's tome, had marked these falls as fed by a hidden fount above. It was a wellspring none had charted, yet Rylan and Trickle knew in their bones it was the lifeblood of Eldergrove's waters. The faltering third waterfall with its sluggish drip, seemed to beckon them toward a truth cloaked in peril.

As they traveled the path to the third pool, the air grew thick with the scent of moss and menace, the distant roar of the falls a hymn of awe and warning. The journey ahead loomed like the Storm-Beast's maw, its dangers coiled in the unseen. Yet, the beauty of the spring's expanse—its waters a mirror of the heavens, its falls a chorus of eternity—stirred in Rylan a fierce resolve to face whatever darkness awaited.

* * *

Rylan and Trickle had reached the first of the falls, the silvery torrent a song of eternity cascading over ancient stone. The map had pointed to a shadowed path veiled behind the falls' shimmering curtain, a route carved by the hands of unseen spirits. Rylan's gaze lifted, and for the first time, the weight of their quest stood on his heart with its colossal truth. Destiny vast as the meadows sprawled below. The sun, barely risen, waged a frail war against the dark clouds on the horizon, their edges flickering with electric malice, illuminating shadowed figures within.

Terror clawed at Rylan's soul, and but for Trickle's radiant aura, he might have fled back to the Honeysuckle haven of her tiny castle. Her hands found his shoulders, and he rose into their strength. Her silent resolve brewed courage in his veins. In her eyes, he saw himself not as a boy but as a knight of the Kingdom, destined to defy the darkness. With a nod, he led the way, scaling the boulder-strewn path that flanked the falls, Trickle falling in step, their hearts a tandem drumbeat against the valley's ominous whispers.

They climbed until exhaustion gnawed their bones, finding refuge on a flat ledge kissed by mist, where the falls' roar beside them sang of purity and peril. Rylan's throat burned, , his longing for Trickle's and Mamma's Lemonade. He rummaged through his satchel, heart sinking as he found no canteen, only Mamma's Manna, useless without liquid to soften their salt.

"Trickle," he rasped, "did you pack the canteen? "

For the first time ever, her face crumpled into a mask of broken light, her eyes pools of disappointment as she realized her failure. The weight of her oversight—a forgotten canteen—still swinging from the chair, threatening to unravel their quest.

"It's alright," Rylan's voice was steady, "we can drink from the springs."

He leaned over the ledge, the falls' tantalizing flow, just beyond his grasp, its mist teasing his fingertips. To reach further was to court a plummet into the abyss below. Defeated, he sank back, gazing out over the Kingdom's meadows, a view he'd never claimed until this moment, majestic yet heavy with the dread of their forfeited journey. Clearing the dirt from the stone beside him, he beckoned Trickle to rest. Her heart was heavy with the shame of her forgotten task.

"Destiny wove this pause," Rylan assured her, his voice a soft hymn against the falls' thunder. "this moment is ours to hold, and this is exactly where we are meant to be."

They had resolved to knowing that they needed to turn back. Together they sat, perched on the pinnacle of their perilous path, peering over the Kingdom's sprawl. Trickle leaned her head on his shoulder, her wrist brushing away tears of embarrassment. For the first time, Rylan saw himself as her pillar, a fortress of fortitude to carry her through the unseen trials ahead.

They lingered, resigned to retreat until better prepared, when a faint, familiar sound—wild and passionate as all the critters of the Kingdom—pricked their ears. The Kingdom's call stirred anew, its magic a thread of light weaving through the dread, urging them to rise once more into the shadow of the falls and the destiny that awaited beyond.

***

Rylan and Trickle stood on their mist-kissed ledge, the wind swirling upon them like the breath of a beast. The earth beneath their feet began to quake with a primal, bone-shaking tremor. Whatever stalked them wielded a power vast as the springs, a force that roared louder with each heartbeat, and yet, their souls giggled like creek pebbles dancing in the current. In the distance, the forest quaked, trees along the path trembled as if bowing to an unseen force, their branches vibrating in a dance of awe and dread. Fear might have drowned them in its icy grip, but knowledge was their shield, and joy their sword.

The force surged closer, a spectacle ripped from the silver screen of the old town theater—a beastly charge that stirred the soul. Rylan and Trickle sprinted to the ledge where they'd rested, hearts alight, and peered into the unfolding chaos.

Like a bull rampaging through a china shop, the forest erupted—branches snapped, leaves spiraled skyward, and a trail of dust rose like a dragon's breath, marking a path of rumbling wilderness that barreled toward them. In a heartbeat, their eyes locked on the truth, and joy flooded their beings. They thrust their hands skyward, cheering with the fervor of the Old Church's revival, chanting,

"OG! OG! OG!"

A massive blur of thunder burst from the tree line—a blur of resilience and integrity, his fur a tapestry of loyalty woven by the Kingdom's own hand.

OG, the guardian of Rylan's heart, had chosen to hunt them, defying the betrayal of being left behind. He saw them, a hundred footsteps away, and suddenly halted. His amber eyes filled with a storm of emotions. He tucked his bottom lip and crinkled his snout, looking anywhere but directly in their path. Rylan called out, voice a beacon across the chasm, and Trickle waved, a banner of hope, but OG, weary from his chase, yawned and sank to the earth, dropping the forgotten canteen from his jaws.

Concern, that fleeting specter, had perished, replaced by a quiet rebellion. His heart wrestling with the sting of abandonment. He turned, facing the forest's embrace, and lay down to wallow in the silt of self-pity, his defiance a heavy chord in the Kingdom's song.

Trickle's smile gleamed, a star breaking through the storm, her eyes sparking as if a crescent-lit bulb had flared to life. She reached into Rylan's satchel, her fingers finding the Government cheese, slowly pulling at the plastic that encompassed it, its crinkle a siren's call. From a hundred footsteps away and above all of Mother Earth's chaos, OG's ears twitched, his head lifting as the unmistakable rustle of that sacred, salty treasure, pierced his sulk. The wind howled, the falls thundered, and the forest sang, but nothing could rival the pull of that unveiling, like a promise kept. OG's defiance crumbled, his massive frame rising, eyes locked on his King and Queen.

In that pinnacle moment, as the earth still trembled and the Storm-Beast's shadow loomed, Rylan and Trickle's chants and OG's rekindled charge wove a tapestry of unbound spirit. It was a crescendo that sang of loyalty, redemption, and the magic that pulsed through Eldergrove's veins. The Kingdom's call surged anew, pulling them all—boy, girl, and beast—back to the edge of destiny, where the labyrinths awaited, their secrets ready to test the fire of their unbreakable bond.

* * *

The three of them lounged upon the mystically entrenched ledge, the falls beyond roaring a silver hymn to eternity, their crystalline torrents mirroring the emerald sprawl of Kingdom far beneath. The trio savored the divine delicacies that were packed within Rylan's satchel, while the old canteen passed among them. A scarce rain began to drift down, too feeble to revive the farmers' barren fields, yet potent enough to paint a radiant rainbow across the expanse. The colors were a covenant of hope arcing over the withered lands.

Trickle sat close beside Rylan, her feet swinging over the ledge's brink, her eyes, twin pools of starlit wonder, followed Rylan's fingers as they tugged at the small Boho bag swathed in Honeysuckle-twined cloth, pulsing with the Crescent Coffershop's magic.

"What do you think it is, Ry?"

Trickle's voice a soft ripple, threaded with the knowing cadence of a seer who'd glimpsed the creek's secrets. Rylan turned, his laugh a warm chord against the falls' ceaseless thunder.

"Whenever you ask a question in that tone, it's like you've already waltzed with the answer..."

She pinched his arm, a spark of mischief fueled her grin, then leaned in pressing a fleeting kiss to his shoulder. Her head rested there, a sanctuary woven of warmth and starlight. Rylan's hands froze on the parcel, the mid-morning world holding its breath. He felt whole, as if the Tree of Life's roots had laced through his soul, and he'd trade every mystery in Zora's gift to dwell in this completeness. The sky above churned, mid-morning's golden promise darkening as storm clouds swelled, their edges flickering with a Hypno-Spiral of electric malice, repelling the sun's frail light with its darkened beauty. OG let out a booming woof, sharp and commanding, as if scolding the heavens themselves, snapping the spell of the moment. Trickle bolted upright, her laugh a crescent chime.

"Yeah, Ry! What he says—open the gift already!"

Rylan flashed a sheepish grin, his heart still tethered to her kiss, and tugged open the parcel. Its cloth unfurled like a lotus petal to reveal Zora's offering.

* * *

Dearest Rylan, Keeper of the Kingdom,

*The creek mourns your name, and the Tree of Life shudders with your valor, for you've glimpsed its wound—a fiery cloud to crush Eldergrove. Ezekiel and I, guided by the crescent's glow, plumbed the Coffershop's deepest vault, unearthing *The Canticle of Eldergrove's Roots*, a sacred tome thrumming with the Kingdom's dawn. Within its saffron-soaked vellum, we found the notes of Bohemian Elijah Starfinder, the seer we spoke of, whose soul once danced with stars until dark storms—spawned by the Dragonfish's master, a blackened soul cloaked in tempest—drove him to madness.*

His scrawl tells of the Arboreum Relic of the Tetramorph, the Cherubim of your vision, guardian of the descendants born of the Tree of Life's seed, more enchanted than the Original Garden, found by Elijah beneath its boughs after a storm's wrath (that beastly gale of old, when the skies warred with our heart). Maddened, he hid the relic within a chest of covenant—gilded with creation's law, its lid crowned by a Guardian's gaze—burying it deep in the third fall's labyrinth, his final act before vanishing.

Those storms, steered by the Dragonfish's master, choked the third fall, casting it from the Source's grace, and with its life waters stilled, Eldergrove's fertile lands—once lush with bounty for our people—withered, starving the Kingdom's soul. The Tree's roots fade, and time itself lies bound, frozen when the dark seekers' assault tilted the Old Church's steeple. Elijah's notes, etched in starlight and despair, sing of a secret: the Cherubim, locked in its sacred chest, must be returned to the Tree's blackened heart, where you saw its pulsing spiral. Only then will the Tree's power blaze, a tide of light to slay the Dragonfish's master and free the third fall's waters, reviving the lands and the Kingdom's heart. His last writing, dated to his vanishing, speaks of the chest's inner spark—a force of creation's dawn, veiled until the hour of reckoning.

I've sought the meaning of time's release, tracing whispers in the Canticle of a clock reset to 4:20, a cipher of renewal or judgment, perhaps tied to the Source's rhythm or Elijah's starlit visions, though its truth eludes us. The Angel of Darkness hunts you, its dark seekers a blade against time's hands, which will not turn until the Cherubim is restored completing the arc between the fallen steeple of the people and the Tree that watches over Eldergrove.

Seek the chest within the third fall's labyrinth, where the Source guards its riddle in stone. Your heart, braided with Trickle's starlit grace and OG's bear-forged loyalty, is the key to its seal. Enclosed is a gift, a crescent-wrought ember from Elijah's fire, to light your path through the labyrinth's mist.

Heed the creek's hymn, Rylan, for it carries the seer's echo when the storm's fangs gleam. The Tree of Life's fate, Eldergrove's lands, and time itself rest in your hands—carry them as you carry love, fierce and eternal.

With the Crescent's blessing,

Zora

Elijah

The name Elijah Starfinder lingered, a whisper of star-fire and madness that danced on the lips of the old Bohemians. He was a prophet to some, a lunatic to others. He was a free-spirited sage whose soul burned with the wild, otherworldly magic that birthed the town's mystic dawn. To Rylan, his stories were a shadow of awe and unease, a mirror of his own tree-whispering heart, a riddle wrapped in saffron and storm.

Elijah had been among the first to weave Eldergrove's tapestry, arriving in a swirl of dust and dreams alongside Ezekiel Moonchild, quite sometime before Zora Thornweaver's storm-chased get away on that dread-filled night. He had come from somewhere far in the West, named after a Saint called Rafael. It was supposedly drenched in worldly magic and healing lands.

His myth, spun from Ezekiel's breath, was a kaleidoscope of wonder. Tales of a Bohemian dream-speaker who read the stars' secrets, and foretold thirteen days of rain with the precision of a clock-smith. He even named the hours their drops would kiss the earth. Stranger still, he'd prophesied the blooming of a Crimson Lotus in the creek's heart, a flower unseen for a century, its petals unfurling on the eve of a harvest moon to herald a child of destiny. Elijah's magic was no mere parlor trick; it was a current of the cosmos, mystic and untamed, swirling through the town like the creek's silvery hymn.

He hunted the mushroom fields beyond the town, where the earth's pulse thrummed beneath velvet caps, gathering their meats for feasts that drew the Bohemians like moths to a sacred flame. Under full moons, they gathered in clearings kissed by starlight, their bellies, filled with Elijah's savory bounty; mushrooms braised in creek water and wild herbs, their flavors a spell that unbound the soul.

He wandered Eldergrove's neighborhoods, a barefoot prophet in patchwork robes, greeting chipmunks and townsfolk by name, spinning tales of the creek's dreams to wide-eyed critters and wider-eyed children. Ezekiel swore Elijah heard voices others couldn't—the whisper of the wind, the sigh of the meadows, the heartbeat of the Tree of Life itself.

"That old dreamer could talk to the roots," Zeke would say, his moonshine grin wide as the dawn, "same as you, Rylan, with that spark in your soul."

Those words haunted Rylan, a mirror he both cherished and feared, for what did it mean to hear the Tree's call? Was it a gift, or a madness waiting to claim him, as it had Elijah?

Long before Rylan's boots tread Eldergrove's trails, a tempest had roared through the Kingdom, the beastly gale that chased Zora Thornweaver to the Crescent Coffershop's door. That night, the Old Church's steeple tilted under the storm's wrath, its clock freezing at the click of 3:17. The next morning, as the town sifted through the wreckage, Elijah Starfinder prowled the square, his eyes wild with a seer's fever. At the Tree of Life's base, half-buried in windblown dirt and leaves, he found a relic, its four faces—Man, Ox, Lion, Eagle—carved in ancient wood, glowing with a pulse that whispered his name. The Cherubim of Rylan's vision had called to him, its voice a thread of star-fire woven through the storm's fallout. He clutched it to his chest, arms trembling, as if shielding a spark of creation's dawn, and from that moment, Elijah was changed.

The town watched, wary and wondering, as he grew distant, his laughter dimming, his eyes haunted by visions of a dying Kingdom. He spoke in riddles, his voice a cracked hymn:

"The water must be saved, the Source unbound, or the Tree's heart will wither."

The relic, bound to his chest, was said to glow in the moonlight, a beacon of dread and awe, though none dared approach to see its truth.

One evening, Elijah had sought Zora at the Coffershop, his plea urgent yet cryptic:

"A sacred chest, Thornweaver, to guard the Tetramorphs fire."

Zora searched her vaults but found no vessel to match his mystic demands. Undeterred, Elijah vanished into the haunted hills beyond the falls, chasing a chest worthy of the relic's keep—a gilded covenant, its lid crowned by a mystic gaze, dreamed in visions that tore at his sanity.

Elijah's quests grew fevered, his absences longer, his robes tattered by the hills' sacred thorns. The townsfolk whispered of madness, their faith in his prophecies fading, though the Bohemians held fast. One mid-morning, as Zora and Ezekiel shared their ritual brew, Elijah appeared at the Tree's base, his silhouette stark against the rising sun. For the first time, his chest was bare, the relic gone, his arms empty of its weight. Ezekiel called out.

"Where's that old chunk of wood, Starfinder? Common over, sip some brew!"

Elijah's eyes, once bright as smoked quartz, were clouded, his smile a ghost of its former blaze. He joined them on the Coffershop's porch, his voice low, trembling with awe and fear:

"I found it, an ancient chest, worthy of its keep."

It was the last they saw of him. Elijah Starfinder had vanished, swallowed by the hills or the creek's embrace, leaving Eldergrove to decay in a frozen heartbeat, time stilled, its soul snared by the Dark Master. Time turned to dust, the town's pulse fading, until the child of the Crimson Lotus, came rolling into town that fate-filled day with Mamma and Pops in Hotel Chevrolet.

Decay

Rylan stood on the mist-kissed ledge, his gaze sweeping over Eldergrove's sprawling Kingdom. In the light's tender caress, the land faltered. Its reflection was dimmed by a creeping decay, the once-lush fields of the outer families, now brittle and barren. Their bounties had dwindled at the hands of the third fall's choked lament. He wondered, heart alight with a prophet's fire, if re-birthing the third waterfall could heal the land. If it could weave a Kingdom vaster, more vibrant than its golden past. Could he, Trickle, and OG reign here, not as rulers but as guardians, their love eternal as the creek's silvery song?

OG, weary of Rylan's circling reverie, growled low, his jaws seizing the cusp of Rylan's trousers with a yank that jolted him forward. Rylan laughed, the sound a warm chord against the falls' thunder. He glanced up to see Trickle halfway up the trail, and vigor surged through him, kindled by the tart nectar of Mamma's Lemonade. He lunged after her, OG's hulking frame bounding at his side. Step, by sweat-soaked step, they climbed to a summit, the air thick with moss and menace. They stood a gasp, a new level of the Kingdom unfolding before them like a sacred scroll.

At their feet, the third pool danced, its sapphire depths alive with magic older than the springs—fish that soared on iridescent wings, their scales a kaleidoscope of dawn's hues, and multicolored fowl gliding across the surface, their plumage a tapestry of rainbows and shadows. Grazing in the meadows, he saw creatures that stood as tall as horses with racks of horns that climbed into the sky like trophies. Rylan's breath caught, his soul humming with wonder, for these were creatures of a Kingdom uncharted, guardians of a truth veiled by mist. He turned to Trickle, her eyes twin pools of crescent-lit awe, and whispered,

"The seventh pool, the one not on Ezekiel's map—it must be the Source that feeds the Tree of Life and all Eldergrove's waters."

His heart flickered with a memory, the vision that had come after Bubba's passing, a realm of light and meaning that had soothed his family's loss. Was that mountain fall the place he'd glimpsed, the heart of his destiny?

They traced the brim of the third pool, the falls' roar a hymn of purity and peril, until the water's edge blocked their path, a shimmering barrier between them and the hidden trail beyond. Rylan glanced at Trickle, doubt festering like a thorn in his chest.

"How do we cross?"

His voice was a fragile thread against the torrent's bellow. Trickle felt his fear, a weight she'd vowed to share. Her commitment to their journey, a flame to carry his load. She released his hand, and beckoned him to watch. With the grace of a creek nymph, she stepped onto the stones that crowned the falls' precipice, each slab a defiant stand against the abyss. OG followed, his jaws latching onto the hem of her tattered dress, a tether to his grounding, his amber eyes fiercely watching her every step.

Rylan watched, heart pounding, as Trickle seemed to float across the chasm, her bare feet kissing stones inches away from oblivion, the crashing waters far below a siren's call to doom. They reached a dry outcrop that split the falls' flow, a sanctuary where the torrent parted like a sacred veil. Trickle and OG turned, their silhouettes framed by mist and rainbow, and beckoned Rylan, their faith a beacon to his courage. Doubt clawed at him, the height a specter of his deepest fears, but their footsteps were a path laid by faith. He made his choice, a free spirit's vow, and stepped forward, one trembling foot at a time. He kept his eyes fixed on Trickle's glow, not the abyss below. Each step was a bridge, trust woven into stone, until he finally reached their side. Trickle's arms wrapped around him, celebrating his resilience despite the dread that had nearly unmade him.

"You're taller than your fears, Ry,"

Her breath was warm against his ear. They turned, hearts still racing, and saw the water's split path flowing downhill toward the fourth pool, its surface hidden by the cliff's curve. No trail descended, no path offered safe passage, only the torrent's wild embrace.

OG, undaunted, leaped into the stream, his massive frame slicing the water, swimming toward the decline with a woof of defiance. Rylan and Trickle locked eyes, their faces streaked with mud, bodies overheated and sweat-soaked from the climb. A shared spark passed between them—wild, reckless and alive. Hand in hand, they plunged into the pool, the cold shock a baptism of purpose, their laughter a hymn that drowned the storm's distant growl.

* * *

The current seized Rylan and Trickle, tearing their clasped hands apart as the waters surged. Rylan's heart lurched, not for his own peril but for theirs, as he glimpsed Trickle and OG swept over the edge. Their silhouettes had been swallowed by the falls' silvery veil. Panic sank its claws into his soul, a cold specter threatening to unmake him, but love—fierce and eternal—ignited a fire within him. He ducked his head, and swam with the might of Tarzan, embracing the current with a vigor that could rival the stars. The water's embrace propelled him toward the abyss where Trickle and OG had vanished.

The current hurled him skyward, a twenty-foot drop looming below. Rylan launched through the air, body arcing like Clark Kent soaring into battle. He plunged into the fourth pool's fresh waters, his body slicing deep into a depth that seemed to have no bottom. Below, shadows danced—fish with wings of star-fire, perhaps kin to the third pool's marvels—but Rylan's eyes sought only the surface, where light promised reunion. He arced upward, lungs burning, and broke free, gasping as he swam to the shore.

Trickle and OG sat on the rocky edge, their laughter a crescent-lit chime that banished the storm's dread. They applauded, paws and hands clapping in a rhythm that echoed the creek's hymn.

"Holy cow, Ry," Trickle's voice was a playful ripple, "I'd almost have to score that dive a ten!"

Rylan emerged, water streaming from his frame, his grin wide as an Olympic champion's, his stature swelling just a fraction—not in pride, but in the warmth of their shared triumph. The amulet from Zora's Boho bag, slung around his neck, pulsing warm against his chest. It glowed faintly, a crescent-wrought ember from Elijah Starfinder's fire.

Trickle knelt at the water's edge, her fingers sifting through the pebbles to gather a handful of perfect skipping stones. She pressed two into Rylan's palm, her touch a spark of mischief.

"Challenge," her smile a dare woven with love.

"Accept!" Rylan's voice was a warm chord against the falls' thunder. They stood side by side and cast their stones, counting skips with the fervor of children unbound by time.

"Seven!"

Trickle pointed to her stone's dance, but Rylan shook his head, grinning roguishly.

"You know darn well that was a six."

She fixed him with the look—a starlit scolding that could hush the bullfrogs' chorus.

"Alright, alright, alright," he relented, hands raised in mock surrender, "I'll give you the seven, but you know I hit that eight—twice, if I'm shootin' straight."

Trickle rolled her eyes, her defeat a playful veil over a heart swelling with love for the boy who held it, her laughter mingling with OG's contented "**woof.**"

Vulnerability

The trio sprawled on the rocky shore, their breaths still ragged from the falls' wild embrace. The expanded Kingdom's pulse thrummed, while above, storm clouds churned, their edges flickering with electric malice. Yet here, in this fleeting sanctuary, they gathered themselves, souls braided by love and purpose, poised to chase the labyrinth's call.

Trickle sat cross-legged, tracing memories long buried beneath mistrust's heavy veil. The moment pressed against her heart—a crossroads where love demanded courage, where secrets, held tight like seeds in winter, yearned to bloom. She glanced at Rylan, and OG sprawled beside him, both their gazes fixed on her as if she held the Kingdom's fate in her breath. Her heart thundered, a wildflower queen ready to bare her soul, trusting at last that Rylan's love would cradle her truth.

She drew a breath, the air cool with the falls' mist, and her voice emerged, a lilting melody woven with the creek's silvery song.

"Ry," she began, soft as a willow's sigh, "there's a story I've kept locked away, not 'cause I didn't want you to know, but 'cause life taught me to guard it fierce. Pain's a hard teacher, and trust... trust is a flower that doesn't bloom easy, but sittin' here, with you and OG, I know my heart's found its home. I love you, Rylan, deeper than the Kingdom's roots, and I trust you to hold my truth."

Rylan's eyes widened, every muscle stilled as if the world hung on her words. OG's ears twitched, his massive frame leaning closer, as if he, too, sensed the gravity of her confession. They sat, boy and beast, enthralled, their destinies tethered to the truth spilling from her lips, a tapestry of loss and magic that could reshape their path.

Trickle's gaze drifted to the pool, its ripples a mirror of her past.

"My story starts with a loss that cut deeper than any blade—my folks, taken when I was too young to understand why. I believe you've seen 'em, Ry, in that vision gifted from the creeks heart, when the Kingdom showed you its secrets."

Rylan, lost in a mystical trance, glimpsed the gypsy encampment beyond the glass wall, two figures sipping a glowing brew like Mamma's Lemonade.

"I've visited that place in my dreams, standin' before that glass wall, my hands pressed against it, tryin' to reach 'em—sittin' there, in that old camp by that huge spirit filled pool, biggest I've ever seen. They are just smilin' and wavin', like they know I'm watchin', but the wall... never even cracks."

Rylan's hand reached for hers, his fingers lacing through hers, a silent vow to anchor her through the pain. His hazel eyes, swirling green and brown, shimmered with empathy, urging her to continue. OG nudged her knee, his loc'd fur warm against her, a guardian's pledge to shield her heart.

"The darkness that took 'em was never explained to me. I was a child, passed from hand to hand, sheltered by kind souls who gave me bread and a bed, but never a home. I learned to hide my heart, to trust only the wind and the stars, 'cause people left as quick as they came. I just drifted through the shadows, until Grandma Sarepine found me. The old enchantress, livin' far out beyond Eldergrove's edges, in a land where the earth sings and the trees all whisper secrets older than time."

Trickle's eyes sparkled, a crescent-lit glow kindling within them, as she spoke of the woman who'd shaped her.

"She was good, Ry, her soul bright as the Tree of Life's heart. She took me in, not as a stray but as her own, and taught me the supernatural things of our world—how to read the creek's ripples, to hear the oaks' dreams, to weave light from darkness. She showed me how to navigate the shadows that'd hunt me, the kind of evil that twists the heart and chokes the springs. I was her prodigy, passin' every test she set—spells spun from Honeysuckle, wards carved in willow bark, dances that called the moon's grace. She told me, "You were born for a purpose, a tiny shooting star, a destiny tied to the Crimson Lotus ."

Rylan leaned closer, his breath shallow, hanging on her every word as if they were the map to the labyrinth's heart. OG's tail stilled, his amber eyes unblinking, a furry sentinel quenching his eternal thirst with the divinity in her soul.

"When I'd learned all she could teach, a miracle came—I was walkin' the meadows beyond her cottage when a herd of white horses with wings appeared, shinin' like star-fire, their eyes callin' me with a whisper of destiny. I felt it, Ry—a pull in my soul, like the creek's song but vaster, promisin' purpose. I ran to the old woman, scared, heart racin', and asked what it meant. She smiled and told me, 'Child, they're callin' you to your true path. You're ready.'"

Trickle's fingers tightened around Rylan's, her gaze locking with his, a spark of wonder passing between them.

"For seven days, we prepared— weavin' charms, brewin' elixirs and learnin' the horses' names by heart—Irijah, Bina, Eulabeia, Moreh, Paraclete, and Tokhechah. On the seventh night, I climbed Athena, her wings thrumming with light, and we soared through the heavens in a dreamlike dance. Stars spun above, the earth a quilt of shadows below, and when I awoke, I was in Eldergrove's valleys, surrounded by small mystical creatures—pixies and imps, with eyes like fireflies, who taught me to live off the Kingdom's blessings. They showed me how to find what I needed, following their lighted pathways—berries, creek water, shelter under willows—never more, never less. I lived like that, wild and free, waitin' for my destiny to unfold."

Her voice softened, a melody sticky-sweet as wildflower mead.

"Then came that morning, while I was fishin' in the creek, I saw you, Ry, playin' like a boy-king, your laughter dancin' with the ripples. I knew it then, in my bones— you were my fate, the heart of my purpose. The Kingdom had called me to you, to stand by your side, to love you fierce and true."

Rylan's heart thundered, his eyes shimmering with awe and adoration, every word etching her deeper into his soul. The pool's glow pulsed in time with their hearts, the Kingdom bearing witness to a love that could rend the veil between earth and eternity. Trickle's voice trembled.

"I've been hesitant to tell you this, Ry, 'cause trust don't come easy when life's taught you to fear losin' what you love. Every time I thought to share, my heart flinched, scared you'd see me different, or that the darkness that took my parents might find us. But here, now, with the *Sounds of the Water* hummin' and your love holdin' me steady—I know you're my home. My heart's fully yours, and I trust you to carry my truth, to stand with me no matter what shadows we face."

Rylan's breath hitched, his hand cupping her cheek, his thumb brushing away a tear that slipped free. His voice was raw, a knight's oath woven with love.

"Your truth, only makes me love you more. You've carried this pain all alone, and still you shine brighter than the creek's brightest star-fire. I swear on

Life itself—I'll stand with you, always, through every storm. Your heart's safe with me, and together, with OG, we'll chase your destiny, and heal the Kingdom's wounds. I ain't never lettin' go."

* * *

They all stood as an unbreakable trinity, their gazes fixed, overlooking the fifth pool's mucky sheen below, where waters barely trickled. Rylan's heart tightened, a quiet ache blooming as he pondered what choked the flow and whether its redemption also lay within their grasp. They started down the path, an easy trek through the wilds, unlike the perilous journeys before, this descent felt like a gentle whisper, the Kingdom's breeze coaxing them forward with a tender hum. As they drew closer, the pool's allure tugged at their souls, an invitation to linger in its haunting beauty—a sparkling obsidian that cradled their spirits in a darkened mystical embrace.

The waters of life had long forsaken this place, their absence shriveling the valley's farms, leaving portions of the land brittle and barren. But the darkness here was no mere blight; it glowed with an ashen essence of pearl. Its tempting magnificence woven with death's quiet despair. The forest encircling the pool, though steeped in decay, shimmered with an otherworldly light. Its skeletal branches gleaming like moonlit bone, whispering promises of solace to those who dared to stay. Above, the storm swirled, its vortex spinning backward as if unwinding time itself. Yet, in this cursed hollow, the tempest felt different—serene, almost assuring, its breeze blowing from all directions, carrying a strange peace that settled over the trio like a velvet shroud.

Rylan held Trickle's hand, her warmth grounding him against the pool's enchantment, but a vision seized him. He saw her—a spectral Trickle, floating across the pool's glassy surface, her golden hair trailing like a comet's tail, her jade eyes beckoning him to follow into the abyss. The sight was both beautiful and haunting, her form a wraith of starlight dancing on the obsidian waters, her lilting voice a siren's call that stirred his soul. OG, however, stood vigilant, all four paws rooted in the earth's truth. He sensed the dark magic's pull, his stillness a stark contrast to the pool's seductive glow.

A low huff rumbled from OG's chest, a warning as he nudged Rylan and Trickle. Sensing their daze, he circled wildly, his paws stomping the earth with a rhythmic thud that echoed through the hollow. His tail whipped the air urgently, as he ran back and forth, letting out howling barks that pierced the forest's gloom. The sound was a clarion call, sharp and searing, awakening the deadest spirits lurking in the shadows. Rylan and Trickle, half-lost to the dark magic, stumbled toward the water's edge, their movements sluggish, as if drawn by invisible threads.

OG lunged, his teeth gnashing in a fierce display, his massive frame a storm of fur and fang. A searing howl tore from his jowls, a sound so primal it shattered the spell that sought to claim them, echoing through the hollow like a thunderclap. Rylan jolted, his consciousness flickering back, his mind battling the forces urging them to surrender to the darkness's solace. The pull was relentless, a whispering promise of eternal rest, but OG pressed against Rylan, blocking the tendrils of magic that clawed at his soul. Rylan gripped OG's scruff, the coarse fur anchoring him to reality, while his other hand held Trickle, her lifeless form floating, ensnared by the pool's curse.

In the sky, a serpent of storm and shadow emerged, its molten scales glinting within the vortex, its hiss a desperate vow to halt their quest. The tempest spun faster, a maelstrom of fury, its winds whipping the forest into a frenzy, skeletal branches clattering like bones in a dance macabre. Rylan and OG edged to the dormant third falls' precipice, the pool's dark magic still clawing at their heels, and peered into the misty abyss below.

Rylan cradled Trickle's limp frame, wrapping his entire being around her, his love a blazing shield against the darkness that sought to claim her. Her breath was shallow, her jade eyes fluttering beneath closed lids, as if trapped in a dream woven by the pool's enchantment. The winds hurled mud, covering them in deceit drenched with the warmth of comfort. With one arm around OG, his loyal guardian, Rylan held Trickle tight in the other, his hazel eyes catching a phantom call of his name from behind—a ghostly whisper that sent a shiver down his spine. He turned, half-expecting to see the spectral figures from his vision, but the hollow was empty, save for the swirling storm and the forest's ashen glow.

Facing the abyss, Rylan steeled himself, his heart thundering with a knight's resolve. The falls' mist kissed his face, as the Kingdom's magic thrummed from below—Rylan drew his final breath, and stepped into the unknown.

* * *

Rylan, Trickle, and OG plummeted through the abyss, an endless descent that stretched time into a cruel eternity, the **Sound of the Water** fading into a hollow wail above them. Rylan's heart thundered, a frantic drum against the icy grip of fear that clawed at his soul. He clung to his trinity, one arm wrapped around Trickle's limp form, the other gripping OG's scruff. His very being, screamed to let go, to surrender to the unknown that swept through him like death's cold breath, but Rylan's love burned fiercer, a knight's oath etched in his bones, binding them against the darkness that tore at their unity.

They plunged into the darkened depths, a whirlpool of utter blackness, a hungry maw that swallowed them whole, sending them tumbling head over heels in a relentless spiral. The abyss was a lifeless tomb, its void a suffocating weight that pressed against Rylan's chest, stealing his breath. He held tighter to Trickle, her faint heartbeat a fragile melody beneath his trembling fingers. OG fought beside him, as his air escaped, paws clawing against the whirlpool's pull, a desperate swim against the depths that dragged them ever downward, his amber eyes beginning to fade.

The impact came sudden and brutal, a bone-rattling crash as they struck the bottom of the abyss. The whirlpool's force sucked them into its merciless core. Rylan's world spun, dizziness a relentless assault,yet, midst the chaos, they became a knot of defiance—entwined in the vortex, a trinity forged in love and resolve. The black waters towered around them, a cyclone of despair that battered their bodies. Its howl was a banshee's cry echoing pure wrath. The forces clawed at their bond, tendrils of shadow snaking through the water, but Rylan's grip was iron, his eyes blazing with a fire no darkness could quench.

At last, the vortex faltered, its rage spent. With a shuddering groan, it parted, the walls of water splitting like a curtain torn asunder. A shaft of light pierced the darkness from above, a celestial lance that illuminated the abyss, casting a golden glow that repelled the obsidian walls. The light revealed a shimmering trail of star-fire, that led to a doorway carved into the cavern's heart. Its archway was a gateway to the labyrinth foretold in Zora's tome.

Rylan's breath caught, as he dragged Trickle and OG toward the entrance, their unconscious forms heavy in his grasp. Trickle's glow flickered, her faint heartbeat a whispered promise beneath his touch. OG's massive frame slumped, his amber eyes dimmed, his drooling titan spirit quieted by the abyss's toll. Rylan never faltered, his love a blazing shield that carried them forward. The opening loomed, its frame etched with runes, Rylan stepped across the threshold with his trinity in tow, their destiny a shadowed enigma waiting to unfold in the labyrinth's depths.

The Labyrinth

The labyrinth's maw devoured the trio, sealing them in its depths with a shuddering groan. Darkness cloaked them, broken only by the ember-colored pulse of Elijah Starfinder's amulet, glowing like a solitary star in a moonless void. Rylan clutched the gem, fastening it around his neck. Its light erupted, bathing the cavern in deep rubies and smoldering lavenders, casting shadows that danced like forbidden lovers. His bare feet slipped on slick stone, his lanky frame straining as he dragged Trickle's limp form in one arm and OG's hulking bulk in the other. Their weight was a sacred vow, but the sixth pool's whirlpool had stolen their spirits, leaving their heartbeats as faint threads against the cavern's crushing silence.

Guided by the amulet's glow, Rylan stumbled to a small pool, fed by an unseen source, its crystalline waters weaving through the cavern like a silver vein. The spring, the lifeblood of this shadowed Kingdom, pulsed with faint bioluminescent light. Its glow triggered by the light of the amulet, weaved a path through stone and shadow. It seemed to Rylan that the waters used to flow freely and something had blocked them, noting the cavern walls, etched with scars of a time when these waters roared through, their dwindling theft starving Eldergrove above.

Rylan laid Trickle and OG beside the pool, their forms bathed in its radiant glow. He drank deeply, the water surging through him like star-fire, flooding every corner of his being with healing light. Certain of its power, he cradled Trickle, propping her head in his palm, his thumb brushing her cheek. The amulet flared, its warmth a lifeline against the panic clawing his chest. A ghastly vision struck in the ripples—Elijah Starfinder, hands raised as the small pool surged with light. This was no mere spring; it was a font of the Source, a sacred well to restore the broken.

Rylan scooped the glowing water, its touch electric, alive with flecks of light that danced like fireflies in a summer hymn. He pressed it to Trickle's lips, tilting her head as the liquid seeped down. The pool glowed with the spirit of renewal, and Trickle's chest rose, a gasp shattering the silence. Her jade eyes fluttered open, twin stars of wonder, her voice a weak but fierce melody.

"Ry... you didn't quit me..."

Rylan choked, "Never," tears blurring his vision as he pulled her close, her warmth a balm to his soul.

He turned to OG, splashing the radiant water across the titan's snout. The spring's magic surged, crystals above blazing like a cathedral's stained glass, their violet and silver light enveloping the beast. OG's ears twitched, a guttural grunt rumbling from his jowls. His eyes snapped open, sparking with wild joy.

He stood and shook his massive frame, spraying water like a tempest, and let out a booming woof. Lunging, he pinned Rylan to the stone, his tongue slathering devotion across his face. Trickle's laugh, rang out as she joined them, her arms encircling their trinity—a knot of love no labyrinth could unravel. The pool's glow pulsed brighter, its waters whispering of the secrets, hidden deeper in the maze. Rylan rose, Trickle's hand in his, OG's bulk at their side, their resolve a flame against the dark. The labyrinth awaited, its secrets trembling in the spring's sacred light, ready to yield to their unyielding hearts.

* * *

Guided by the Veiled Seraphines crystalline thread, they wove through the labyrinth's sinuous veins, their presence a whispered vow kept secret by the watchful darkness. The spring's faint glow led them through an endless maze of tunnels, sprouting in every direction, but they followed the bioluminescent beings that pulsed at the light within the amulet. Their ethereal light, a delicate teal and moonlit silver, kissed the cavern walls, where veins of quartz and fluorite bloomed in response. The stones were painted with haunting hues of amethyst, sapphire, and molten gold. Each chamber was a dream-scape, a cathedral of shadow and color, trembling with the earth's ancient treasures.

Their descent wound through coiling passages, jagged walls slick with condensation, the air heavy with the scent of mineral and mystery. Rylan's heart thundered, the amulet's ruby and lavender glow now a faint memory, its warmth a lingering promise against his chest. The path narrowed, the stone closing in like a lover's embrace, until it forced them to their knees. The tunnel ahead shrank to a crawl, a point of no return that gripped Rylan's soul with dread. There was no turning back—the stone had sealed behind them at the labyrinth's threshold.

They knelt as one, peering into the claustrophobic void. In the distance, a flicker of light danced, its source unknowable. Rylan's gaze darted to OG, his massive frame ill-suited for such confines. Crawling was no titan's art, and barreling through risked disaster. He met Trickle's jade eyes, then OG's amber sparks, and spoke, his voice steady as a knight's oath.

"Whatever you do, don't stop. Keep moving. I'll bring up the rear to see you through."

Before he could finish, OG surged forward, his hulking form wriggling into the tunnel, tail wagging like a banner of defiance, his rear a comical silhouette against the faint glow. Rylan and Trickle paused, sharing a fleeting smile, their bond a flame in the dark. Rylan unclasped the amulet, its ember light flaring, and draped it around Trickle's neck. She protested, but he pressed it into her skin.

"I'll follow the light. Just promise you won't stop." His eyes locked with hers, fierce with love. "Don't be afraid. You've got this."

Trickle's brows arched, a spark of defiance in her grin.

"Afraid? Get over yourself, Batman."

Their laughter, filling only a single moment, was fragile but true. She leaned in, her lips brushing his in a kiss, then vanished into the tunnel, the amulet's glow trailing like a comet's tail.

Rylan moved to follow, reaching to secure his satchel—only to find it gone. His heart lurched. He'd set it down by the first pool when reviving them, its contents vital for the mission. The water's faint glow, dimming without the amulet's radiant dance, barely lit his path. He glanced at the narrowing crawl, then back toward the darkened labyrinths. It would take only a moment to retrieve it if he hurried. There was maybe enough light within the water to reveal his path. The labyrinth's hymn pulsed, urging him onward, but the satchel, containing his worldly treasures called to him.

He hesitated, the spring's whisper mingling with the distant flicker in the tunnel. Trickle and OG were counting on him, their trinity bound by love and fate. The Relic and its ancient chest lay ahead, guarded by the labyrinth's heart. Rylan steeled himself, the weight of his vow heavier than stone.

He'd reclaim the satchel and catch them, guided by the faint glow remaining within spring's sacred song. With a final glance at the tunnel's beckoning light, he turned back, the labyrinth's shadows swallowing him as he raced into the dark.

***

Rylan raced through the labyrinth's twisting veins, each step a battle against an unseen force. A magnetic pull back to Trickle and OG, was dragging at his soul. The faint glow of the waters dimmed with every turn, its bioluminescent shimmer fading without the amulet's ruby and lavender fire to ignite it. Darkness crept closer, a living shroud threatening to snuff out the spring's sacred light. Doubt gnawed at Rylan's heart, his frivolous choice to chase the satchel—a worldly tether—now a betrayal of Trickle and OG, who were left alone in the tunnel's crushing embrace. The weight of his folly pressed against his chest, a stone heavier than the labyrinth's sealed gates.

The glow faltered, surrendering to an abyss so complete it swallowed all sound and hope. Rylan stumbled forward, his mind spiraling into the void of his own making. He had abandoned his trinity for a fleeting possession, and the labyrinth knew it. The air thickened, laced with a sinister whisper—a mocking laugh woven into the darkness, celebrating his unraveling. Had Trickle and OG emerged from the tunnel's maw, only to find him gone? Did they think him a traitor, their hearts pierced by his absence? Were they trapped, crushed by stone or lost in the maze's cruel heart? The thoughts were daggers, slicing his mind with blazing precision, each cut a hiss of the dark's delight.

Rylan dropped to his knees, one hand plunging into the spring's dwindling trickle, its cool touch the only guide in this blind purgatory. The labyrinth was testing him, a trial of faith and worthiness. Its secrets and powers were guarded by a darkness that hungered for his surrender. He crawled, just a boy teetering on the edge of destiny's abyss.

Despair nearly claimed him, his body sagging against the cold floor, when his trembling hand scooped a meager handful of water. He raised it to his lips, the liquid kissing his parched mouth, a spark of life piercing the dark. Rolling onto his stomach, he pressed his face into the sparse trickle, bowing as if to the Creator's altar. He drank, lapping the sacred stream like OG at Eldergrove's creek. Each swallow was a plea for redemption. The water surged through him, a faint echo of the Source's star-fire, stirring his warrior's heart.

Then, from the void, a sound—a soft, familiar buzz, like the critters' chorus that had shielded him in danger's shadow. It was a beacon, a hymn of hope that set his soul ablaze. Rylan rose, hands braced against the jagged walls, and stepped forward, counting each stride as the buzz grew louder. Forty-seven... forty-eight... forty-nine... The sound wrapped around his heart, pulling him through the dark like a lover's vow. The walls widened, the air shifting, and a familiar clacking echoed—the satchel's innards, singing their own defiant hymn.

Rylan lunged, fingers closing around the satchel's worn leather, its weight a triumph against the labyrinth's malice. He could hear and feel the fiver loads buzzing within as the darkness hissed, its laughter fading as the spring's faint glow flickered back. He clutched the satchel, his heart thundering with renewed purpose.

* * *

Trickle scrambled through the labyrinth's suffocating tunnel, the amulet's ruby and lavender glow casting frantic shadows as she caught up to OG. His massive form was wedged in the stone's unyielding grasp, his hindquarters a barricade lit by the amulet's fire, blocking their path with denial's cruel key. Unseen to her, OG's front had pierced a veiled threshold, bathed in a distant, radiant light. He writhed, his giant paws scrabbling, unable to find purchase to push forward. Trickle strained to glance back, but the tunnel's grip forbade it. Her heart seized as she called Rylan's name into the void, answered only by silence. The darkness, alive with malevolent intent, sank its claws into her mind, whispering that Rylan had been stolen—another loss in a life littered with abandonment. Hope flickered, frail against the cavern's sinister tide.

"OG? OG, are you okay?"

Fear gripped her, the dread that the titan's indomitable spirit had succumbed to the labyrinth's malice, sealing her fate in this stony tomb. Her hand found the magic spot just above his tail, where his hulking frame met his wagging joy, and she scratched, calling once more,

"OG!" SMACK! His tail lashed her face, a relentless assault of unrestrained delight, reigniting her hope. "You okay, boy? You stuck?"

Her voice a defiant spark. OG's wiggles answered, a fierce dance against the stone, but his paws couldn't anchor, his body betrayed by the tunnel's confines.

Trickle's resolve flared as she drew her knees beneath her, leveraging every ounce of strength, and she pressed her body against OG's bulk.

"On three, boy, I'll push with everything I've got. We'll crawl through this inch by inch if we got to!" OG's tail thumped, muffled by her weight. "One... two... THREE!"

She grunted, hurling her full force into him. OG groaned, his body inching forward, one massive paw breaking free. Trickle pushed, her muscles screaming, as he clawed the stone, anchoring with that single paw. His second paw tore loose, and he surged, butt wiggles a battle cry against the darkness's sneer. The amulet blazed, its light a beacon of their unyielding spirit.

Trickle poured her soul into each shove, the labyrinth's malice seeping into her fading consciousness, a black tide lapping at her mind. Her strength waned, her breaths shallow, when suddenly OG's body lurched forward, released from the tunnel's choke-hold. The passage opened, and a blinding light flooded in, a celestial wave that swallowed her whole. Trickle's vision blurred, the amulet's glow mingling with the radiant abyss ahead, and she slipped into darkness, her body collapsing as the light claimed her.

OG's triumphant woof echoed, a titan's roar against the labyrinth's heart. Trickle lay still, her fate teetering between the light's embrace and the dark's hunger, her last thought a flicker of Rylan—lost, but not forgotten, in the maze's shadowed depths.

* * *

Rylan stood alone, swallowed by the labyrinth's ravenous darkness, its weight a living force pressing against his soul. The faint pulse within the water had completely vanished, leaving him adrift, severed from Trickle and OG. He opened his satchel, fingers trembling as they sought the sacred stones, their clanking song having guided him back through the maze's cruel twists. Those stones, alive with defiance when danger stalked, had rattled him to this moment. He grasped one, pressing its cool weight to his pounding chest, certain it would blaze a path through the void, but the stone lay silent, its light dormant, as if content in his return.

Doubt slithered in, a serpent striking within the dark, yet a faint vibration stirred from the satchel's depths—subtle, yet achingly familiar. It wasn't the stones' defiant hum but a softer call, a memory woven from starlit nights. Rylan's mind flashed to Trickle's tiny castle, its porch a sanctuary where they'd shared heartfelt treasures under Eldergrove's watchful oaks. His breath caught as he reached blindly, fingers closing around the source: a broken compass, a relic of their bond, its needle spinning with untamed yearning. He drew it out, its metal warm, alive with a pulse that sang of home.

In the blackness, the compass trembled, its arms spinning in a frenzied dance. Rylan gripped it tightly, and the needle slowed, its chaos yielding to his will. He clasped it with both hands, pouring his soul into the act, until the spinning stilled, the needle locking with a quiet click. He traced its hand, now steady, pointing not to north but to destiny, to the one truth that burned brighter than the Relic: Trickle and OG, his heart's home. The compass hummed, its magic a thread tying past to present, their trinity's love a flame no darkness could quench.

A vision bloomed, unbidden yet clear—Trickle's jade eyes, fierce with defiance, and OG's amber sparks, alight with joy, illuminating his inner calling. The labyrinth hissed, its shadows writhing, but the compass's pulse ignited Rylan's warrior spirit. He stepped forward, blind yet guided, each stride a defiance of the dark's cruel test. The air thrummed with ancient magic, the waters faint trickle rising, as if stirred by his resolve. The compass glowed softly, its light a ghostly echo of the amulet's fire, casting fleeting glints on the walls, a promise of the light ahead.

Suspense coiled around him, the labyrinth's laughter a sinister whisper, daring him to falter. Had Trickle and OG breached the tunnel, or were they trapped, their spirits waning? The thought was a dagger, but the compass's steady hum banished fear, its needle unwavering. If they had met harm the compass would spin without resolve. Rylan pressed on, the stone beneath his feet warming, as if the Source itself blessed his path. The fiver stones stirred faintly, their clanking a quiet chorus, joining the compass's hymn. This was his pinnacle, a moment where past oaths, fused with the present's desperate hope, forged a resilience that could shatter stone.

The tunnel shrank, it's end loomed, a flicker of radiant light piercing the dark. Rylan clutched the compass, its pulse now a roar, guiding him to Trickle and OG, to the Relic's sacred chest. He was no longer alone—their trinity's heart beat as one, a supernova against the abyss, ready to claim their destiny.

Lost

Trickle and OG waited, unaware of the cavern that surrounded them. The air, thick with a longing that bore their grief, the tunnel before them—a shadowed vein—swallowed their hope. Its silence stung, a thief that had taken their king, Rylan, leaving only the echo of his vow.

Trickle perched on hands and knees, her eyes searching the darkness of the tunnel.

"He promised, OG," her voice low, trembling with a fear that gripped her heart. "He was right behind me, his hand in mine."

Her words were quiet, raw with love, no grand gesture but a truth born of their bond. The tunnel gave no answer, its stillness a weight on her soul. Beside her, OG slumped, his fur heavy with loss. His joyful bark was silenced—a mournful hum rose from him, a song of sorrow that stirred the cavern's walls, calling for its Kings return.

"RYLAN!" Trickle called, her voice sharp, a plea cutting through the tunnel's dark. "Rylan, where are you?" It cracked, heavy with despair, as she turned to OG, her eyes bright with unshed tears. "OG, where is he?"

OG's wail answered, a deep cry to summon the springs' song, begging the divine for light. It echoed through the rock, a tide of shared pain.

Time stretched, each moment a slow ache. Trickle's hands twisted in her lap, her heart clinging to Rylan's memory, while OG's gaze held the tunnel, as if faith could bring their king back.

Then, love stirred in Trickle, she stood, her shadow soft, and reached for the tunnel.

"I'm going to him, OG," Her voice was steady, warm with devotion. "I can't leave him in the dark."

OG rose, his bulk a steadfast barrier. His eyes, glistening and filled with sorrow, held a resolve as true as light. He blocked the tunnel, a guardian knowing the dark's hunger could take her too, wedged his whole back end inside its mouth.

"Move, OG," Trickle begged, her hands lashing at his defiance, not in anger but in desperate love. "He needs me—I need him." Her tears fell, quiet on the stone, but OG stood firm, his whimper a prayer for light to break the night. Trickle sank down, her grief spilling out. "Rylan, please." Her voice was a soft vow, aching for her king.

In that very moment, OG's eyes lit with a wild, secret joy. His hind leg twitched, a familiar rhythm of bliss beyond his control, humming like the springs' eternal pulse. Trickle looked up, her breath beyond her.

"You starting that Harley Old Guy?"

His tongue rolled out and drool sprung free, his smile broke through, real and warm. Trickle knew this sign: OG's secret spot, wedged in the tunnel's mouth, tickled by a hand only love could wield. The cavern stirred, shadows easing like a lifted veil. Trickle's heart bloomed, her love a spark undimmed.

"Get out of the way you big oaf!"

* * *

The tunnel's grip was a lover's jealous embrace, clutching OG's furry haunches with a suction that mocked their desperation. Trickle's hands, small but fierce, dug into his brindle coat, her fingers trembling with the weight of devotion. She yanked, her voice a melody of urgency slicing through the cavern's damp air.

"OG, come on, you stubborn beast!"

Her words echoed off the quartz-streaked walls, mingling with a muffled chuckle from beyond the wall of fur—a laugh that carried Rylan's unmistakable warmth, like sunlight breaking through a storm.

"Is that you, Ry?" Trickle's heart was lurching with hope. "Move, OG—MOVE!"

She pulled harder, her boots slipping on the slick stone floor, while OG wriggled with determination. His giant paws clawed, scraping runes into the ancient rock, each scratch a plea.

"Push, Ry! Push!"

Trickle's voice cracked, not with fear but with a love so fierce it could shatter mountains. She felt the tunnel's pulse, a living thing, resisting their reunion as if testing the strength of their bond.

OG's eyes met hers, and in that glance, she saw his soul, loyal beyond the stars. With a deep grunt, he planted his paws, muscles rippling, and Trickle leaned in with her whole being. Behind the furry barricade, Rylan's whole body pressed against OG's backside.

"ON THREE!" came a muffled voice, "One—Two—THREE!"

With a unified heave—the tunnel gave birth. OG popped free, tumbling into Trickle's arms, nearly toppling her. A heartbeat later, Rylan's hand broke through the threshold of darkness, the compass catching the cavern's violet glow like a captured star. She seized his wrist, while OG clamped his jaws gently on her dress, tugging with slobbery zeal. Together, they pulled against the tunnel, reluctant to release its chosen one.

Rylan emerged, covered in muck and slime, he was no longer just a boy he was renewed, forged in the crucible of the labyrinth, his spirit alight with purpose.

Trickle flung herself upon him, her arms a sanctuary, her kisses a cascade of relief and adoration. OG joined the fray, his tongue painting Rylan's face with joy filled slobber. They collapsed into a tangle of limbs and fur, laughter bubbling like the springs themselves. Radiance grew, pulsing in rhythm with their reunion, as if Eldergrove's heart beat within them.

The air shimmered, thick with magic, whispering their names in a tender cadence. The cavern, once a shadowed maze, awoke, its walls blooming with light—violet and silver veins threading through crystal, pulsing like the Tree's own arteries. As their laughter softened, the trio stilled, their breaths syncing with the spring's rhythm. They turned, and the sight before them stole their voices, chaining their souls to its magnificence.

* * *

A crystal-clear pool stretched across one side of the chamber. Next to it, spanned a bottomless pit. Between them a path of stepping stones that seemed to float on pure faith. Rylan had never seen such an odd pairing. Death shouldered with life, like siblings quarreling for the ultimate prize.

The pool's surface, a mirror of eternity, reflected the cavern's celestial glow. Its edges shimmered with emerald fungi, velvet heartbeats that throbbed in sync with the spring's pulse. It was laced with quartz veins that bloomed and withered like living stars. Above, stalactites hung like frozen tears, their tips adorned with delicate crystals that refracted light into fleeting prisms, dancing across the water's surface. The air crackled, heavy with enchantment, each breath tasting of ancient promises.

Water-sculpted rock formations rose like shadowed paramours, their surfaces glistening with moisture that captured the glow, painting the stone with blushes of sea-green and cobalt. In shallow basins, the light from the algae pooled, intensifying into halos that whispered of hidden passion. The pool's currents wove gentle eddies, threading emerald and sapphire through the water, as if the spring itself dreamed in color. A faint, melodic drip echoed through the maze, harmonizing with the soft rush of the spring, urging them forward with a lover's plea.

Above it all hung a forest of roots dangling from the cavern's ceiling. Most were brittle and gray, their tips curling in decay. Once, this chamber had been a bustling underground river, its waters nourishing Eldergrove's soul. Now, the pool was a remnant, its level receding, leaving the roots to wither. Yet one root, defiant and radiant, stretched across the void, its tip dipping into the pool's silken depths. It glowed with the same spiritual pulse Rylan had seen in the Tree's hollow that exposed the riddle. It was a beacon of hope, a lifeline to the Arboreum Relic of the Tetramorph.

Rylan's heart thundered with certainty. These roots were the Tree of Life's roots, their glow fueled by an ancient seed spawned of creation's dawn. If the waters continued to recede, the Dragonfish's master, the Storm-Beast's crimson heart—would sever the Tree's roots, snuffing out Eldergrove's light completely.

Trickle's arm entwined with Rylan's, her warmth a steady flame, gazed at the pool, her eyes wide with awe. OG pressed against Rylan's side, his fur warm and grounding, his amber eyes reflecting the spring's glow. They sat in reverent silence, three souls bound by love, mystified by the beauty they were chosen to witness.

The pool's radiance surged, its waters rippling with a summons that thrummed through the cavern's heavy air. The ember amulet dangling from Trickle's neck guided their gazes to the pool's glassy surface. A vision was blooming—a spectral figure rising from the depths—its form shimmering like moonlight on water. It was Elijah Starfinder, his eyes alight with sorrow and hope. His hands, weathered yet gentle, opened wide in welcome, one palm reaching toward the trinity, the other gesturing toward the gilded chest on its root-wrought pedestal. The Arboreum Relic within pulsed, a silent vow of salvation, urging them closer.

Rylan's heart stuttered, his instincts sharpened by the labyrinth's trials. The prophet's image wavered, its edges fraying like a dream half-remembered, and his outstretched hand seemed to point not only to the chest but to the pit of despair gaping beside the pool. Was this Elijah's spirit, or another snare spun by the Dragonfish's master? Rylan's grip tightened on Trickle's hand, her warmth grounding him, while OG's low growl vibrated at his side, his eyes fixed on the pit's hungry maw. Rylan approached the edge, and the pool's glow parted like a curtain, revealing the wound that bled Eldergrove and the Tree of Life dry.

The pit was no mere void—it was a ravenous whirlpool, a gaping throat that devoured the Kingdom's lifeblood. Once, these waters had surged through the cavern, a mighty underground river feeding the springs that cradled Eldergrove's now withered soul. The pit's pull was relentless, siphoning the sacred flow into its bottomless hunger. Its lip receded with the force of the water flowing over it, and soon it would fall, extinguishing any life fed by the pools waters. A waterfall plunged into the abyss, its roar echoing the premonitions Rylan had seen in the Tree's vision.

The pit's edge was a jagged scar, like teeth, biting at the surface. The falls were no sacred spring—they were a thief, robbing the Tree of Life of its nectar. The pit's darkness swirled, a vortex that consumed not just water but hope, love, the very souls of humanity. Its hunger was blasphemy against creation's dawn. The Tree's pulse, faint but defiant, thrummed through the single root still kissing the pool's surface, a lifeline fraying under the pit's insatiable thirst. Trickle's breath hitched, her amulet flaring brighter, as if Zora's wisdom whispered through its glow.

"Ry," she murmured, her voice a melody of courage, "it's devouring everything."

Her eyes, wide with the pool's reflected light, held a fire that matched his own. OG pressed closer, his spark flaring in defiance of the pit's shadow. The cavern's hymn softened, a tender drip harmonizing with the waterfall's lament, urging Rylan to act, choosing to trust Elijah's vision, or heed the pit's warning. The pit's whispers grew louder, a siren's lie promising ruin. Rylan's heart thundered, torn between love's certainty and the labyrinth's deceit. The compass in his hand a steady flame urging him ahead.

* * *

Across the chamber, rising from the pool's heart, stood a pedestal of gnarled roots, twisted like lovers' hands clasped in prayer. Atop it rested Elijah's chest, surrounded by a plethora of his secret treasured relics. Ancient scrolls and maps that told a thousand stories, jewels of every color, and multiple crystal balls. Above them all, a gilded coffer rested, its lid carved with an angels gaze. It was shimmering with stardust. The Arboreum Relic of the Cherubim lay within its grasp, a spark that could heal the fourth fall, restore the Kingdom, and defy the darkness.

The bridge of faith spanned the pit, each stone glowing with runes that flickered like fireflies—ancient glyphs of courage, sacrifice, and truth.

Below, the pit's belly rumbled, its depths echoing with tormented wails that hungered for the unworthy. Rylan's hand tightened around the compass, its needle steady, pointing to the chest. Trickle's fingers laced with his, her touch a vow that no pit could break.

Rylan stood, his resolve an unbridled flame,

"We've come this far," his voice was steady, "The Tree chose us. We're not turning back."

Trickle rose, the amulet pulsing brighter, her eyes a constellation of courage.

"My King," she whispered, her voice a thread weaving their fates.

OG's tail thumped, his spark flaring, ready to charge the void. The cavern's glow surged, as if the Tree itself watched, its roots trembling with hope.

The first stone awaited, its rune pulsing with a question of faith only their hearts could answer. Rylan stepped forward, Trickle's hand in his, OG at their heels, their love a shield against the pit's hunger. The spring's song swelled, a chorus of creation's dawn, urging them onward. The chest gleamed, promising salvation or ruin. With each step, the cavern's magic wrapped them tighter, dragging their souls toward destiny.

The bridge trembled, the pit whispered, and the Tree of Life held its breath.

* * *

They stepped onto the first stone, the runes flaring under their weight, the pit below swirling with voices of vengeance. The stones swayed, tilting, flames from within the pit spitting at them like a serpent's breath. Rylan gripped tighter to Trickle's hand, OG's bulk steadying them, his paws gripping the runes with the grace of a dancer. They hopped from stone to stone, a skill honed by the boulders at the Kingdom's creek.

Halfway across, the cavern quaked, stalactites crashed into the depths, sending waves of darkness that rocked the foundations of their path. A growl erupted—something ancient and hungry. Rylan could see a pair of eyes burning like molten copper watching them from within the pit. The Dragonfish's shadow, woven into the labyrinth's heart, had woken. Its molten scales gleaming as it slithered through the pool of darkness below.

Rylan's heart thudded. "Keep movin'!"

He pulled Trickle as OG barked, a searing howl that shook the crystals above. The beast lunged, its tail whipping in the falling water, sending another wave that nearly swept them into dooms grasp. Rylan stumbled, his foot slipping, but OG grabbed his overalls, his love a shield. Rylan regained his footing and OG spun, his teeth bared, leaping at the shadow. His massive frame collided with its scales, a titan's defiance against the abyss. The beast recoiled, its growl a banshee's cry, giving them a heartbeat to scramble forward. They leaped across the last step onto the ledge that held their destiny.

The chest's glow bathed them in warmth, gazing at them with eyes that saw through time. Rylan knelt, his fingers tracing the lid, the wood humming with Elijah's magic. The Tree's roots were ablaze with shimmering light. But the Dragonfish's shadow roared, its form surging from the pool, its eyes locking on the relic, a claim that vibrated in Rylan's bones:

"MIIIINNNEEEE!"

The bridge collapsed, stones plummeting into the darkness, and the beast charged. Rylan clutched Trickle's hand in his, OG's bulk shielding them. The cavern quaked, crystals shattering, the Source's glow faltering, but the relic pulsed, its light a lance that pierced the shadow's heart. The beast shrieked, its form unraveling, scales dissolving into a black coiling mist. The pit trembled with anger and fire.

Rylan, Trickle, and OG stood, the relic in hand, their trinity unbroken. The chest hummed, its runes fading, Elijah's magic spent but victorious. The labyrinth's walls slowly parted, revealing a blurry pathway surrounded by an electrified pulse that led to anywhere but there.

Portal

They didn't hesitate as they leaped through the shimmering portal, its edges snapping shut behind them with a crack that echoed like a thunderclap across the Kingdom's springs. They stood battered and breathless in the mouth of an ancient cave, its jagged maw overlooking a field stitched with the tattered old bohemian encampments. Muck and slime clung to them, black as the pit's hunger, streaked with the emerald sheen of cavern sludge.

This cave, whispered in Eldergrove's tales as the haunt of Elijah Starscribes darkened soul, had been a place Rylan shunned. Its shadows were rumored to cradle the seer's madness. But now, standing on its ledge, the trio knew the truth. Elijah's written words, his prophetic maps scrawled with creek-born insight, had guided them to the Arboreum Relic of the Tetramorph. Inside the chest that now traveled with them, heavy with the weight of destiny, was no cursed relic of a broken man, but a Cherubim for the Tree of Life. They gazed down at the winding path snaking toward town, the bohemian flag flapping in the breeze. Its colors were faded but defiant under the graying sky.

Their breaths came in ragged gasps, hearts still thundering from the battles they'd just fought. Rylan sank to one knee beside the chest, its carved surface slick with their grime. He wanted—needed—to pry it open, to see the relic that had cost them blood and faith, but the chest was sealed. Its lock was unyielding, no key in sight. Trickle knelt down beside him, her fingers tracing the chest's runes.

"What is it, Ry?" Her ocean eyes were searching his, glinting with the same mystery that had drawn them to the springs. "What's it mean? "

Rylan shook his head, slime dripping from his brow, his hands trembling as they probed the chest's edges.

"I ain't sure, Trick," his voice was raw from shouting defiance in the caverns. "Not till we see it—Not till it's free."

OG lumbered closer, his massive paw swiping at the lock against the ancient metal, a frustrated huff puffing from his jowls. The trio scoured the chest, their filth-stained fingers seeking hidden catches, but the relic held its secrets tight, as if the Tree of Life itself demanded one final test.

They rose, resolve hardening like the oak at Eldergrove's heart.

"Zora'll know," Trickle's sundress fluttered as she stood, "her and Ezekiel—they'll resolve this riddle."

Rylan nodded, hoisting the chest with a grunt, its weight a promise and a burden. They turned to the untraveled trail, its stones choked with weeds, leading down from the cave to the town's embrace. The air was thick with Honeysuckle's sweetness, a faint whisper of the springs' eternal truths, but it crackled too, heavy with a coming storm.

Rylan cast his gaze skyward. Storm clouds rumbled, their edges curling like the coils of a familiar foe gathering strength. His heart clenched with a knight's grim certainty. The battles they'd fought, the slime they wore like badges, were but the prelude. The final reckoning, the true clash for Eldergrove's soul, loomed ahead. They raced on toward the square, carrying the chains of hope..

* * *

The trio hadn't faltered since they'd bolted from the cave's ledge. They surged into the town, a wild symphony of shouts and barks. Their voices—slicing through the twilight, were calling for Zora and Zeke. The sun had just drowned beyond the horizon, its final glow smothered by darkness and a sky being devoured by the storm. No moon gleamed, no stars braved the toiling shroud above. The clouds stirred like a serpent's scales, their edges flaring with a crimson pulse that hissed with revenge. The air hung heavy, thick with the iron tang of rain yet to fall. The Honeysuckle's sweet smell now a fading wisp beneath the storm's creeping menace. A shadow of foreboding cloaked Eldergrove, as if the Tree of Life itself braced, its roots quivering beneath the soil.

OG charged ahead through the square, now filled with the flock. They were awaiting entrance into the vulnerable sanctuary of the Old Church in order to ride out the storm. Trickle shadowed him, billowing like a wildflower caught in a squall.

"Zora! Zeke! We're here!"

Rylan trailed, his strength taxed by the ancient chest—the Ark cradling the Arboreum Relic of the Tetramorph. Its carved surface, bit into his bare shoulders, each step was a pledge, his bare feet bleeding into the earth.

They passed beneath the Tree of Life, its sprawling branches arching like a cathedral's vault, its leaves flickering with a green fire that wavered against the storm's encroachment. Rylan's eyes lifted, his heart tightening at the sight—its trunk weathered yet unyielding, its roots pulsing faintly, as if crying for deliverance. In his soul's quiet, he whispered a vow to the Tree, his breath barely audible,

"I'm comin, I swear it."

The Tree responded—its glow surging briefly, a hum vibrating through its boughs—alive yet burdened by the storm now a breath away. The clouds above growled, their crimson eyes—the Storm-Beast's gaze—glinting closer. The air crackled, not with hope but with destiny's stern promise, the storm's shadow sprawling like the pit's hunger across the Kingdom's springs.

They skidded onto the Old Church's plot, with the chest thudding beside them. Zora and Zeke stood ready, framed against the square's flickering lanterns, carried by the families from the bohemian encampments. They had been helping Johnny Pocketwatch usher the flock, faces laced with dread, into the delicate embrace of the community chapel. Zeke's prophet-sharp eyes were fixed on the roiling sky.

"Y'all cut it mighty close," he said, his voice a low drawl, heavy with warning. "That storm ain't just comin'—it's the worst we've ever faced, barrelin' straight for us."

His words landed like stones, the square's murmurs—fearful whispers, half-muttered prayers—swirling with the wind. Zora, her moonstone pouches clinking, fussed over them, her hands tracing the slime and muck that clung like badges of their ordeal.

"Y'all alright?" she demanded, her voice a blaze of maternal fire and mystic calm. "What happened in them caverns? Lord, you're tore up—look at all this filth! Let's go, git on over to the Coffershop and we'll get you all cleaned up."

Her eyes softened on OG, his fur a sodden ruin, and she knelt.

"Go get Mamma and Pops, big fella,"

Her tone a command laced with love. OG's bark shattered the air, fierce and true, and he tore off toward the house, a streak of loyalty against the storm's dark veil. Trickle knelt, her dress pooling, her jade eyes catching Zora's.

"We got the relic, Zora," she said, her voice steady despite the quiver in her hands. "But the chest—it won't open."

Rylan, still heaving, set the chest down, its runes glinting faintly, as if taunting their efforts. Zeke's brow creased, his gaze darting to the Tree of Life, its glow now a flicker against the sky's wrath.

"Time's runnin' thin," he said, voice grim. "That storm's got the beast's mark—ain't no natural thing. We need to git inside, now."

They helped Old Johnny seal the door to the Old Church, and made their way to the Coffershop, dragging the chest along with them. Old Johnny watched them through the cracked glass window with a sense of dread building in his guts. He mumbled,

"It's 3:00 o'clock, 3:00 o'clock—Time—Ticking—Time..."

As they entered the candle-lit Coffershop, Zora's hand rested on the chest, her fingers grazing its lock, her eyes far-off, as if hearing the Tree's whispers.

"This lock ain't waitin' for no ordinary key," her voice was low, prophetic. "It's a truth—borne from light, like Elijah's maps."

The Storm-Beast's eyes glared from the horizon, nearer now, its coils tightening around Eldergrove's soul. The final clash was looming...

Contempt

Rylan paced across the weathered floorboards, his shadow weaving through the amber radiance that bathed the room in defiant warmth. Beyond the glass was a crucible of black clouds threaded with crimson veins, their glare a vow to snuff the Tree of Life's final spark. If the sacred riddle of the key remained unsolved, Eldergrove's heart would shatter, the Tree's roots would sever and the town would be swallowed by the pit's ravenous maw.

Rylan moved with restless urgency, watching for Mamma, Pops, and OG through the deluge. The chest, its wooden runes pulsing faintly in the candlelight, stood unyielding on the counter. The Arboreum Relic of the Tetramorph was still locked within its grasp. Trickle hovered nearby, her resolve was mystic and unwavering.

Zora glided among them, her presence a lodestar of calm, attuned to the Tree's fading whispers. The storm's wrath surged, its rain a torrential scourge, each drop a shard of the Storm-Beast's will, seeking to quench the Tree's emerald heartbeat and fracture the town's spirit. Lightning tore the sky, illuminating the Tree of Life's boughs, their radiance faltering, its heart teetering on surrender.

Rylan paused at the window, his breath clouding the glass, drawn to the Tree's waning light, a beacon bracing for the onslaught of an unholy flood. Its branches quaked with desperation, as if crying for the strength to restore its soul. The Storm-Beast's eyes were filled with malice, a weight that promised annihilation.

A roar pierced the storm's clamor—Hotel Chevrolet was careening around the square's corner, its engine a hymn of rebellion against the tempest. OG bounded out, his bark a thunderclap that rivaled the storm's roar. The old truck screeched to a stop at the porch and Pops sprang from the driver's side. Ezekiel, already at the door, swung it wide. Mamma stepped out of the truck, her hand braced on her back, her belly swollen with a miracle poised to break forth. Pops and Ezekiel flanked her, bearing the weight of her condition, their faces etched with love and dread.

OG charged into the Crescent Coffershop, his paws skidding on the floorboards. Mamma entered, her breath heavy, as Pops and Ezekiel guided her with reverent care. Trickle and Zora leapt to action, clearing a space on an old daybed in the corner—Zora's nook for reading and naps. They spread an old quilt and eased Mamma onto it. Her hand cradled her belly, the unborn child a spark against the storm's darkness. Pops knelt beside her, his calloused hand clasping hers, his voice a soft murmur:

"You're safe now, darlin'."

OG, wet as a wash rag, nestled in at their side, searching for a place to rest his head.

They had been waiting most of the night, watching as the beast gathered it's arsenal. Wondering when it would launch it's assault, while frantically trying to solve the riddle that would open the Arc embalming the Relic.

Rylan's light sparked and he turned from the window,

"Zora," his voice was raw from cavern-born defiance, "what'd you write in that letter 'bout the key to this chest?"

His words hung, a plea heavy with the weight of Eldergrove's fate, the storm's crimson eyes glaring closer through the glass.

Zora stilled, plumbing the mystic depths of her noggin. A flame kindled within her, her voice emerging low, prophetic, carrying the creek's eternal truths.

"Heart—Grace—Loyalty."

Each word landed like a star falling into a still pool. Rylan, Trickle, and OG stood before her, their muck-stained forms a testament to their trials, their bond a mirror of the Tree's interconnected roots. Trickle's hand grazed Rylan's, her touch a vow unspoken. OG's low growl rumbled, sensing the riddle's sacred weight.

The storm's contempt surged, a lightning bolt splitting the sky, revealing the Tree of Life's fading soul, its branches trembling under the torrent's assault. The Storm-Beast's eyes, now a blinding crimson, promising annihilation. If the key's truth remained unclaimed, the Tree would perish.

The Crescent Coffershop pulsed with magic, the candles flaring as Zora's words echoed, a mystic summons to the flock's faith. Ezekiel's gaze met Rylan's, his nod a silent charge, while Mamma's hand tightened on Pops', her unborn child a beacon of hope.

Rylan's heart thudded, not with fear but with a knight's resolve, his vow to the throne blazing within. The chest's runes shook, as if awakened by Zora's words, its mystic power awaiting the key's light. The ghost of 4:20 lingered, Elijah Starscribe's frozen clock a silent witness, whispering of a dawn beyond the storm, if only they could unlock the riddle before doom claimed its prize.

Armageddon

The Beast's wrath had the town in its jaws, it vowed to choke the Tree of Life's final spark. The Coffershop thrummed with whispered prayers, its weathered floorboards creaking under the weight of destiny. Rain lashed the windows, each drop a shard of the beast's malice, while lightning carved the sky. Inside, the air was thick with spices and Honeysuckle's faint sweetness, a defiant thread of the shops soul woven through the storm's brimstone stench.

Trickle and Zora fussed over Mamma, she had just awoken from her slumber and realized her feet were hurting, their hands a blur of care as they shooed Pops back with playful scolds. They eased her back onto the old daybed and slipped off her sodden shoes. Mamma let out a deep, guttural grunt. She had fallen asleep and forgotten to take them off.

"My dang feet are on fire," She began to cry, "they look like pink balloons stuffed in a girdle!" tears spilled down her cheeks, her gaze snapping to Pops. "You better be grateful, Carl. I did this for you."

Pops nodded with a sheepish grin, his eyes dancing with love and a hint of terror, knowing better than to poke the Mamma Bear. He retreated a step, hands raised in mock surrender, his silent plea for mercy drawing a chuckle from Zora and Trickle. Mamma's wrath pivoted, her spirit now focusing on the Trinity.

"And where in God's green earth were you three? We were worried beyond sick!"

Her voice cracked, a mix of fear and fire, the maternal storm within her rivaling the one outside. Trickle, quick as a creek's ripple, grabbed a cool, damp cloth and pressed it to Mamma's swollen feet. The effect was instant—Mamma's face softened, her eyes glazing over like OG's when Rylan hit that sweet spot behind his ears. She sighed, a whisper of relief escaping her lips as she looked at Trickle.

"Oh how I love you, sweet Angel."

The words hung, tender and true, until a sudden scream tore from her throat, sharp enough to pierce the storm's roar. OG, sprawled nearby, tilted his massive head, his huff a cautious vote to stay out of the fray, his spark-filled gaze flicking warily between Mamma and the door.

Zora glided to a weathered shelf and retrieved the old tome, its leather cover etched with the springs' ancient runes. Elijah Starscribe's writings, alongside where the map of the seven pools had laid within, a mystic guide forged in the Kingdom's dawn. She pressed it into Pops' calloused hands, her finger jabbing at the passage that held the key to the chest. Pops cleared his throat, his voice a low rumble as he began to read.

**A chest of roots, an angel's gaze,*
Holds light to mend the Kingdom's days.
A heart, pure as dawn's first flame,
Unstained by a shadows shame,
Step through storms where crimson eyes glare,
To claim the spark that banishes despair.
The grace of an angel, soft as creek's sweet song,
A tender vow where broken souls belong
Shall weave the light through roots that fray,

And guide the lost to dawn's new day.
A guardian's loyalty, fierce as oak's deep hold,
Bound by love, unyielding, bold,
Will stand as shield when darkness strikes,
To wake the Arc with sacred light.
Three as one, in mystic trine,
Heart, grace, and guard in truth align,
Touch the chest where star-fire dwells,
*Reveal the Relic's holy spell.**

The Crescent Coffershop shuddered, its candles snuffed out in a heartbeat, plunging Eldergrove into a void as black as the pit's maw. The Tree's faint glow, visible through the rain-smeared windows, flickered once, then dimmed, its roots trembling under the torrent's assault.

Ezekiel, who'd been pacing the floorboards, his loc'd hair twisted into knots before his face—a habit born of deep thought—froze mid-step. A spark of revelation lit his eyes, as if the springs themselves had whispered a truth.

"OG! Rylan! Trickle!"

His voice cut through the darkness like a blade. He lunged for the chest on the counter, its wooden runes now pulsing with a fierce, golden light, casting the room in a radiant glow that defied the blackout. Ezekiel turned the chest toward the trio, its orb-like center blazing brighter, a star born of the Kingdom's heart.

"Put your hands here," he commanded, pointing to the orb, his prophet-sharp gaze locking onto them. "Rylan, you're the heart—your bravery shines like a beacon through the darkest pit." Rylan, his chest heaving from the labyrinth's trials, stepped forward, his hand trembling as he pressed it to the orb, its warmth surging through him like the Tree's own pulse.

"Trickle," Ezekiel continued, his voice softening, "Trickle, you're beyond fair, sweet angel. Grace flows in your very essence. You were born of the springs' ancient song." He gently took her hand, guiding it atop Rylan's, their fingers intertwining, a silent vow sparking between them. Trickle's gaze met Rylan's, their bond a flame that burned brighter than the storm's fire.

"And OG," Ezekiel said, a grin breaking through, "our faithful guardian—none is as loyal as you, ya big mutt." OG let out a triumphant woof, his tail thumping the floorboards like a war drum. He reared up, planting his massive paw atop Rylan and Trickle's hands. The trio stood united, their muck-stained forms a testament to their trials, their bond a mirror of the Tree's interconnected roots.

The Storm-Beast sensed the shift, and it surged into a frenzied fit. The Coffershop's front door exploded inward. Splintered wood flew like shrapnel and the wind's howl was a banshee's scream. Rain and darkness poured in, the Beast's crimson eyes glaring through the breach, their malice a blade poised to strike. Pops, quick as a lightning flash, leapt into the fray, hurling the weight of his redemption against the door. With a grunt that echoed Mamma's, he slammed it shut, stifling the beast's advance.

The chest, untouched by the chaos, began to rise, as if lifted by mystic hands woven from the springs' eternal light. Its runes flared, golden and fierce, the air humming with a choir of Angels. A low crack echoed, not of breaking but of awakening, as the chest's lid parted. A sliver of golden star-fire spilled forth. Outside a bolt of lightning tore through the sky, striking the square with a deafening crack. The thunder screamed, shaking the earth, while hail sharpened like jagged teeth forged its attack. The light from the chest burst into the room, a radiant tide that stomped the creeping darkness, banishing the storm's shadow with a force that rattled the windows.

Rylan, Trickle, and OG stepped back, their hands still tingling from the orb's touch, their hearts pounding in reverence. The chest lay open, its interior a silken cradle of light. The Arboreum Relic of the Tetramorph pulsed within—the four faces engraved upon it were alive and radiating. A perfect circle, etched with angelic runes, its glow a promise of redemption. It beckoned Rylan forward, its hum a whisper of Elijah Starscribe's prophecy.

* * *

Rylan approached, his breath shallow, each step a prayer to the Kingdom's light. The chest's runes pulsed, their golden hum a hymn of the relic, and as he peered within, four faces gazed up from the cask's inner glow, etched in celestial light, just like he had seen in his vision.

A Man, his countenance brimming with wisdom and compassion, a celestial aura cloaking him, his eyes alight with love's unyielding purity—as if he carried the spark of humanity's hope. A Lion, noble and fierce, its mane a crown of Christened Royalty, evoking Aslan's spirit, its gaze strong and loyal, a sentinel of divine authority. An Ox, steadfast and humble, a beast of burden ready to bear the world's sorrows, its eyes gleaming with sacrificial servitude—and an Eagle, its feathers radiant with prophetic vision, its divine perspective piercing the veil of time.

Rylan swallowed hard, not with fear but with reverence, the Tetramorphs faces a mirror of the journey he bore—heart, grace, loyalty, wisdom—woven into Eldergrove's eternal truth. Ezekiel stepped beside him, his loc'd hair knotted from thought, his arm encircling Rylan's shoulders like a prophet's mantle.

"You know what to do young Ry,"

His voice raw with faith, his eyes alight with the springs' fire, his gaze locking with Trickle's across the room. Her face, framed by the candlelight's amber dance, held a smile laced with concern, her eyes shimmering with love and dread.

Rylan's hand hovered over the Ark, and he reached inside for the Arboreum Relic, but his fingers brushed something else. A book, humble and worn, lay within the chest. Its leather cover was rough and tattered, stained with creek water and ash. Rylan freed it from the ancient coffer and opened it. Elijah's writings, letters and prophecies, 777 entries numbered in their standing, *Wrinkles of Time*, hand sketched on its cover. Rylan's breath caught, a jolt of destiny sparking through him. He handled the script with care, its weight a sacred burden, and handed it to Pops, who stood nearby.

Pops took the journal, his calloused hands cradling it like a relic of the Old Church, and placed it reverently on a velvet cloth on the Coffershop's counter, its runes casting a faint glow across the wood.

Rylan turned back to the chest and reached in, his fingers closing around the Arboreum Relic, its warmth surging through him like a current of electricity. He lifted it high, the sphere blazing, its runes a tapestry of the spirits inside—man's compassion, lion's nobility, ox's sacrifice, eagle's vision.

Time stopped, the Coffershop falling silent, the storm's howl muted as if the Kingdom itself held its breath. Even Mamma's eyes were wide with reverence, the pain of her condition eclipsed by the Relic's glory. Ezekiel's gaze burned with prophet's fire, while OG let out a low huff, his spark-filled eyes fixed on the Relic. Trickle's hand grazed Rylan's arm, her touch a vow unspoken, her presence a melody of creek-born grace.

The Storm-Beast sensed the shift, its roar shaking the windows, its crimson eyes glaring closer, their malice a blade poised to strike. Yet the Relic's light held firm, a beacon that defied the pit's maw, its glow spilling through the glass to kiss the Tree's boughs, their jade pulse flaring in response. Rylan slipped the Relic into his satchel, the sacred fiver loads inside buzzing with purpose, and slung it over his shoulder. He turned to Trickle, his hands finding hers, their fingers intertwining as if woven by the springs' eternal thread. Her eyes, brimming with tears, met his, her fear tempered by a love that burned fiercer than the storm.

"It'll be okay,"

Rylan whispered, his voice a vow that carried a man's compassion and a lion's courage. Trickle's lips trembled, a tear tracing her cheek, but her smile was radiant and resolute.

"Your destiny awaits sweet Ry,"

Her words were a whisper that seared into his soul, a promise that would never fade, even in the pit's darkest abyss. Their foreheads touched, a sacred moment stolen midst the chaos, the candlelight dancing across their faces like a blessing. OG nudged between them, his massive head pressing against their clasped hands, his huff a pledge of loyalty, the ox's steadfast heart binding their trinity.

Trickle reached down and gingerly ran her fingers over OG's face,

"Take care of him Sir Lancelot,"

OG's smile was a promise that she would hold on to.

Ezekiel stepped forward,

"The Cherubim's light is yours, Rylan," he gestured to the Relic's glow. "Man's heart, lion's roar, ox's stand, eagle's sight—you carry 'em all." His words landed like a star falling into a still pool, rippling through the Coffershop, stirring the air with the springs' song. Pops nodded, his hand resting on the **Wrinkles of Time**, its runes flaring as if Elijah himself bore witness. "

Mamma, her breath steadying, clutched Pops' hand, "Don't you dare mess this up, Rylan," she teased, her smile a beacon that rivaled the Relic's light. "I'm countin' on you to give this beach ball growin inside of me a world worth livin' in." Her words, half jest, half prayer, wove a thread of hope through the room, her maternal fire a mirror of the lion's nobility.

Rylan and OG ran through the door, lightning split the sky, and shards of hail released from its grasp. The Tree's boughs were no longer faltering but defiant, their glow a challenge to the beast's wrath. The journal on the counter pulsed, its runes whispering of the clock's frozen hour. Rylan's heart thudded, not with fear but with a knight's resolve, fueled by love and loyalty. Rylan's resolve was strengthened by OG, and they were summoned into the battle that lay ahead.

Clock Tower

They had made it through the night, and the sun was rising high in the sky. It had joined the battle against the Storm Beast, whose wrath had Eldergrove in its coils, a half dozen crimson eyes blazing through the deluge, a serpent poised to crush the Tree of Life's final spark. The Crescent Coffershop shuddered under the tempest's howl, its windows rattling as hail shards pelted the glass like the pit's own teeth. Inside, the air thrummed with defiant sweetness, pierced by Mamma's agonizing screams.

"HOLY—"

Zora's hand clapped over her mouth, muffling the colorful outburst, her other hand pressing a bundle of fresh-cut herbs—plucked from the springs' edge—onto Mamma's chest.

"Sweetling!" Zora hollered, her moonstones clinking, "Water please?"

Trickle, rushed across the floorboards, her bare feet silent on the weathered wood. She grabbed a pitcher, its warmth a faint echo of the springs, and gathered clean linens while hurrying back to Zora. Mamma lay in a puddle of sodden towels, her belly a miracle straining against the storm's darkness. Zora's gaze softened, catching Trickle's eyes darting to the window where Pops and Ezekiel stood, their silhouettes framed, hands and faces pressed against the plate glass. The Tree teetered on the brink of collapse. Its roots clung to the earth by a thread. One side had torn free, its boughs swaying like a drunken prophet.

"Go, baby girl," Zora said, her voice a creek's murmur, releasing Trickle. "Watch over 'em."

Trickle shook her head, her eyes brimming with resolve. "Somethin' more powerful than me has got him wrapped tight—what can I do to help you, Miss Zora?"

Zora's smile widened, her hands guiding Trickle's to Mamma's trembling palm. "Just hold her hand, sweetling. Hold her hand."

Trickle cradled Mamma's hand between her own, her touch a vow of grace, anchoring the maternal fire that burned against the storm's snarl.

Pops and Ezekiel pushed open the Coffershop's door, the wind's wail surging through the gap, their eyes fixed on the square. The Tree's veins glowed, while hail battered the earth, its icy wrath aimed at Rylan and OG. The storm raged, waters flooding the streets in a torrential scourge, yet a pathway parted the flood, a dry ribbon of earth woven by the springs' song, shielding the duo from the beast's malice.

An unseen light, wrapped them in its embrace, deflecting the darkness, its essence a hymn of the Kingdom's truth. OG barked, his massive frame bristling, his spark-filled eyes daring the storm to strike. Rylan moved with a knight's resolve, the Arboreum Relic of the Tetramorph buzzing in his satchel. They reached the Tree of Life and the lower rungs of its ladder, once a path to its heart, lay splintered, torn away to a height just beyond Rylan's grasp. He leapt, fingers scrabbling for a hold, but fell back into the mud sucking at his feet. He tried again, his hands slipping, the storm's roar mocking his effort.

"I can't reach it, OG,"

His voice was raw, his shoulders slumping under the weight of the fire laden eyes—dozens of them now, fire-filled, glaring from the twisting sky, their malice a blade poised to strike.

OG growled, his back pinning against the Tree, blocking Rylan's retreat, his bark a fierce rebuke that shattered Rylan's pity. The guardian's eyes blazed, urging Rylan to rise. Clarity struck like lightning—OG wasn't just a shield but a ladder, a pillar rising in defiance. Rylan wedged his fingers into the Tree's crevices, and stepped onto OG's broad back. OG rose onto his back legs, lifting his King to the rungs reach. Rylan grabbed hold, his hands steady, and began to climb. The Tree's veins glowed beneath him, its canopy flickering with hope, awaiting its new heart.

The Storm-Beast shrieked, its coils thrashing the square, yet the light held, a radiant shield woven from the Tetramorph he carried. Rylan swung through the branches, his bare feet finding purchase, leaping from rung to rung with the grace of a Bohemian Knight. The Tree's rib cage beckoned, a small opening in the boughs leading to its heart, its pulse was a desperate hum that drowned the storm's wail. Rylan entered, the air electric with the springs' song, the branches curling around him like a father's embrace. A lightning bolt struck, its fury aimed at Rylan's resolve, but the Tree's boughs deflected it with green fire.

The Tree's heart lay before him, an abandoned knot, a void where light once flowed, now choking its veins. Rylan reached into his satchel, past the fiver loads pulsing with supernatural fire, and withdrew the Arboreum Relic. Its sphere of woven roots blazed, its runes a tapestry of the Tetramorph—humming with the Kingdom's truth. Rylan paused, the Relic warm in his palm, its glow like Trickle's touch—was a vow to save their Kingdom.

He stretched, barely reaching the void, his bare toes gripping the bark, his breath a salute to Elijah Starscribe's frozen hour. With a knight's vow, he placed the Relic into the Tree's heart, its light erupting like a supernova, flooding the Trees veins with jade radiance. The Tree came alive, its boughs surging skyward, its roots clawing deep, a heartbeat reborn that shook the Pit's maw.

An attack tore loose from the storm, striking at the Tree. A massive limb crashed lifeless to the earth, splintering like the pit's broken teeth. The impact raged within the Tree, and Rylan slipped, his footing lost in the quake. He tumbled through a crack in the boughs, branches clawing at his overalls, and barely caught a rung three levels down. OG below, howled in panic, racing to cover the ground beneath, his barks a guardian's plea.

Rylan pulled himself up, his bare feet finding the rungs, his resolve blazing. He slid down the final stretch, landing in the mud beside OG, who greeted him with a hero's welcome—slobbery nuzzles and a thunderclap bark that rivaled the tempest. The Storm-Beast withdrew, its assault faltering, but its vortex spun, regrouping with a terror that promised annihilation.

Rylan's gaze snapped to the Old Church across the square, its steeple starting to glow with the same radiance as the Tree, an angelic light that held the beast at bay. A sporadic pulse throbbed between the Tree and the steeple that couldn't quite bridge the abyss growing between them. The ground cracked open and Rylan could see flames shooting up from the Pit beneath, spinning with malicious and murderous intentions. A million tortured souls screeching without resolve. The church's steeple leaned further than ever, ready to falter, reaching out to the pull of the Tree's heart.

Rylan stood in awe and wonder as to why the storm still hunted them. He had thought for sure that restoring the Trees guardian would slay the evil, but the town of Eldergrove was still under attack. The storm had shifted to trying to destroy the Little Old Church.

Rylan smacked OG's flank, his voice strong,

"Let's go, boy!"

* * *

Rylan and OG crashed through the Coffershop's doors, they spun, hearts pounding, to face the storm's father—the Dragonfish's sire—lurking in the tempest's heart, coils weaving a noose around Eldergrove. The beast had paused, not in mercy, but to gather its wrath, a serpent coiling for the kill. Beyond the Tree of Life, the cauldron in the town's belly yawned wider, a maw of churned earth and shadow, swallowing cobblestones, spitting mud, and birthing an earthen fall that vanished into the abyss below. Each lunge devoured more, a hunger that gnawed at the roots of hope.

Mamma's scream tore through the shop, a primal wail from the back where linens soaked and candles flickered. Rylan's gaze snapped from the pit to Trickle, her silhouette racing through the dim, eyes wide with relief. She lunged, and he caught her, her warmth a fleeting shield against the dread.

"It's over, thank God," she gasped, but Rylan's voice cracked, heavy with sickening truth. "It ain't, Trickle. It's regrouping. That hole—it's gonna swallow the town if we don't stop it."

Trickle's eyes darted to the window, horror blooming as the pit devoured Zora's old Chevy Nomad, its chrome glinting one last time before the earth claimed it.

"Zora! It ate your car!"

Trickle pointed out the window. Zora rose from Mamma's side, moonstones clinking, her mystic face carved with grief.

"Fates be, I reckon... I liked that old car, and my Everly Brothers 8 track was still in the dash dang it!" Her voice trailed as Mamma's cry surged with a tide of pain. "Mystic Mother Earth, IT'S COMING!" Zora bellowed, and the room froze, breath held, caught between two forces—one universe stealing life, another gifting it.

Trickle sprinted back to Mamma, kneeling beside her, hands steady despite the storm's roar. Zora moved with ancient grace, while Pops hovered, careful not to crowd. Rylan, OG, and Ezekiel stood rooted, faces pale as if a ghost had whispered their names. Rylan's gaze flicked back to the window, where the pit's jaws crept closer. The Old Church's steeple reached for a lifeline, a jade heartbeat begging to touch the Tree, yet the gap mocked them, a riddle unsolved.

An Angel's voice cut through the Chaos.

"Rylan!" Trickle's hands cradled Mamma, but her eyes burned with a mystical spark born of creek songs and starlight. "Grab the book, Ry!"

Rylan blinked, then saw it—the **Wrinkles of Time**, its rustic leather glowing on the counter, runes dancing like fireflies. He vaulted over, snatching it, and ran to where Trickle's gaze held him.

"I got it," he panted, pulse racing.

"How many passages, Ry? They're numbered, right?" Trickle's voice was a blade, sharp with purpose.

Rylan flipped the book open, pages whispering. "Seven hundred seventy-seven."

Zora's cry rang out, fierce and joyous. "Oh my, we got a head—anyone got a plunger?"

They all laughed except for Mamma, her nails dug into Trickle's hand, her groan a low, earthen hymn, pulling life from the void. Zora's eyes met Trickle's, a question in her mystic stare. "Push?" Mamma's grunt deepened, a warrior's vow.

"Go to passage four-twenty." Trickle's gaze locked onto Rylan, unwavering. Rylan's fingers flew, pages blurring, heart afire. Trickle turned to Zora, voice steady as the springs. "You were there Zora, when Eldergrove froze. You remember the time?"

Zora, poised like a quarterback stuffed up in between Mammas legs, and Trickle giggled at the thought of it. Ezekiel leaned in, their voices a chorus.

"3:17..."

Trickle rose, pointing at the book in Rylan's trembling hands.

"Third paragraph, Ry." Rylan's eyes traced the page, he found it, breath catching. Trickle's smile bloomed, a crescent moon. "Count—seventeen words."

Rylan's finger moved along the page—"eight, nine, ten,"

He paused looking right at her, a smile blooming on his face.

"What does it say?" Trickle demanded with a light stomp of her feet.

"restore—, hands—, time—..." He stopped, eyes lifting again, his smile fully risin,

"Reset the clock." he whispered to himself as he looked down at his watch. It was 3:08—he had to go.

Zora shot up, taller than the steeple, her joy a thunderclap.

"IT'S A BOY!"

The room erupted—Mamma's final cry, a resurrected wail piercing through the storm, life defying the pit. Trickle laughed, tears streaming, as she cradled the newborn, its tiny fists punching the air. Pops fell to his knees, sobbing, redeemed. Ezekiel's prayers hummed, a creek's song, while OG barked, tail a whirlwind.

Trickle turned to show Rylan. She scanned the shop, the riddled journal laid on the floor, and he was gone.

She stood holding tightly to the hope that Eldergrove and their family had so desperately wished for. She looked toward the door that swung open in his absence and whispered.

"Run Rylan... Run."

Hands of Time

OG's heart thundered anger behind a sealed threshold, Rylan had left him behind again, and the betrayal stung sharper than a wasp's barb. His floppy ears twitched, catching the storm's sour wail beyond the plaza. He paced, claws scraping the shop's floor, his whimpers rising into a determined growl—Rylan was out there, alone, and the darkness was calling his name.

Ezekiel, with his prophet-sharp eyes, knelt beside him, peering through the shop's fogged window. The Old Church's steeple loomed across the square, its clock frozen, a mocking sentinel against the green fire of the Tree of Life.

"What do you think, OG?"

Zeke's voice was gravel and grace, his hand steady on the dog's trembling flank. OG's amber eyes locked onto Zeke's, a glimmer of foreboding flashing like crimson lightning. OG's demeanor screamed: **Rylan's in trouble.** Zeke's jaw tightened, reading the warning in OG's gaze, and he reached up opening the door.

"Well, what are you waiting for? Go find him!"

OG exploded forward, his paws leaving claw-marked scars in the wood. The Storm-Beast assaulted him, but OG's heart was untamed, searching for his soulmate. He tore across the plaza, his slobbery jowls flapping like war banners. The pit's maw yawned ahead, a gnashing abyss of shadow and flame, swallowing chunks of Eldergrove's soul, and now approaching the church. OG's nose caught Rylan's scent, faint but fierce, leading him toward the Tree of Life sitting at the edge of damnation. His growl deepened, a holy rumble that shook the earth, vowing to drag Rylan back from hell itself if he had to.

* * *

The Old Church loomed, its crooked steeple stabbing at the storm-churned sky, and Rylan's mind burned with one truth: he had to reach that clock, reset its heart, and stop the pit from swallowing Eldergrove whole. The Tree of Life stood defiant, its roots clawing the earth like a fist against the pit's ravenous pull. Smoke and fire rose from the abyss, thick with brimstone and fury, as cobblestones and memories vanished into its eternal black. The pit's voice screamed in unison with the Storm Beast, hunting them from the spiraling sky, a guttural wail that clawed at Rylan's soul:

*"*MMMIIIIIIINNNNNNNNEEEEE.*"*

Temptation was his old nemesis, a serpent's whisper he'd fought before. He tried not to look down, to ignore the heat licking his bones, but the pit's call was a lover's promise. His eyes betrayed him, plunging into the beautiful darkness. There, in the flame-wreathed void, the Demon twisted, velvet and venomous. Ten times larger than the Dragonfish Rylan had slain for Pops' soul. This serpent was an Angel of malevolence, its movements, a dance of beautiful ruin. Its fire-glazed eyes pierced the inferno, locking onto Rylan's soul, gripping it with a heat that numbed his will. Ecstasy ran through his veins, the same paralyzing bliss he'd felt in the battle for his Pops' soul.

Visions flashed: Rylan crowned in flame, Eldergrove bowing at his feet, the Tree's light his to wield.

Rylan's heart stuttered. Trickle's laugh—wild, free, like the creek's song—whispered in his mind, her jade eyes brighter than any crown. Could he trade her, OG, Mamma's fierce love, for this? The pit promised power, but her kiss, that Lemonade-soaked dusk, was sweeter than life. His fingers twitched and unknowingly reaching for a fiver load, for her.

The earth crumbled around him, grass and roots dissolving into the pit's insatiable hunger. Rylan slumped, his knees buckling, one foot inching toward the abyss. Smoky, serpent-like tentacles erupted from the depths, blackened and ghastly, curling around his legs with a lover's caress. They lifted him, his body levitating, drawn into the Demon's embrace. His satchel swung heavy at his side, the fiver loads inside calling for him, but his hands hung limp, his soul slipping. The Demon's eyes burned brighter, promising eternity, and Rylan's fight faded, his vow to Trickle and the Tree dissolving like ash.

A roar shattered the trance, primal and holy, as a great beast—ingrained with the Lion King's spirit—surged from the storm. OG's jaws clamped onto Rylan's overalls, yanking him backward with a force that shook the heavens. The tentacles tightened, pulling at Rylan's soul with a thousand barbed hooks. OG snarled, his teeth sinking deeper, his growl a deep, sacred thunder that echoed with the Tetramorph's might. The hound's amber eyes blazed, promising hell itself:

Not my King!

Rylan's trance broke, his senses began flooding back—the pit's sulfur stink, the Tree's emerald heartbeat, OG's slobbery warmth.

"I..., let, let go—LET ME GO!"

His soul reclaimed, he kicked and screamed, clawing at the earth, his fingers scraping dirt and root. His left hand grazed a gnarled root, latching on to it, one of the Tree of Life's anchors, tethering him to Eldergrove's soul. Instinct took over, honed by a knight's lifetime of preparation. His right hand dove into his satchel, wrapping itself around a fiver load, its smooth stone buzzing with purpose. The satchel tipped, spilling the remaining loads onto the grass, their amber glow flickering like fallen stars. Rylan perched up, his fist armed with the stone, and stabbed it into the tentacles' grip. Each blow was a knight's vow, a defiance of the Demon's lure. The tentacles writhed, their smoky forms fraying, but the Demon's eyes burned fiercer. Rylan struck harder, his arm a blur, each hit loosening the darkness' grip. OG's growl deepened, his paws digging into the earth, pulling with a loyalty that could shame angels.

A jade bolt erupted from the Tree's heart, where Rylan had restored the Tetramorph. The energy shot down the root he clutched, surging into his body, and then OG's, lighting them both aglow with a pulsing radiance that rippled like the Kingdom's lost springs. The light was living water, emerald and sapphire, a hymn of faith, grace, and loyalty. The tentacles froze, crystallizing into brittle obsidian shards, poisoned by the Tree's power.

The glow intensified, gathering above Rylan and OG into a winged orb, its essence carved with four sacred shapes—man, lion, ox, eagle. It swelled, enveloping the crystal serpents still tethered to Rylan's legs, drawing strength from the Tree's reborn soul. The orb pulsed, and redeemed the fallen fiver loads, shattering them into a thousand blades of stone, spinning in its grasp like a chainsaw. Without a sound, it whispered resolve, and courage back into Rylan, marking his soul as claimed.

The Demon's eyes flickered, its gold-amber scales dimming as the orb surged downward, a comet of jade fire, casting fragments of fiver loads into the darkness. It plunged deep into the pit, carrying the crystallized tentacles with it, their forms shattering into a million glittering fragments from the light's attacks. The pit's wail faltered, its flames stuttering, but the abyss still churned, calling for more. Rylan collapsed, gasping, his hand still clutching the one last fiver load, OG's warm bulk pressed against him. The Tree's boughs swayed, it's emerald heartbeat steady but strained, as if pleading for Rylan to finish what he'd begun. The church's steeple loomed.

* * *

Rylan rose, his spine forged like a knight of Arthur's storied Round Table. The Tetramorph's celestial beams sliced through the abyss, encircling the Tree of Life, where a mere whisper of Eldergrove clung to existence. The Tree of life's roots, charred and gnarled, clawed desperately for the waters of life that once pulsed beneath the town. Rylan's heart thundered with purpose as he gripped OG, his loyal sentinel, and he stood.

"Let's ride, Friend!"

OG surged forward, parting the howling winds and flames that gnashed at them like demonic jaws. Rylan tucked the last fiver load into his pocket as they neared the church. No ladder breached the spire, but the climbing Honeysuckle, woven through weathered wood glowed with ethereal pulses, ascending and descending the vines at the same time. He couldn't see an ending to how high the Honeysuckle ladder climbed into the Heavens, but he could see it held his pathway to the clock. Rylan knelt to OG, his voice steady yet heavy.

"Hold the line, boy. Keep them all safe, and carry my burdens if I don't return."

OG's eyes blazed, a primal roar erupting from his chest, rebuking Rylan's doubt with fierce loyalty. Faith swelled within Rylan, stretching his frame taller, a tower of resolve against the impossible. Without a backward glance, he climbed trembling as the pit below spat its wrath at him. Beneath him, the battle raged—flames and shadows defending their dominion from the light of the Tetramorph.

* * *

Old Johnny Pocketwatch, pressed against the church's window spinning his watch around his finger, hosting a fervent chant:

"Hands of Time, Hands of Time, Hands of Time... it's 3:09, Hands of Time... "—a mystic incantation weaving fate itself.

The pit surged closer, its edge kissing the Church's foundation, threatening to devour the flock within. The storm hissed, sending venomous lightning bolts of demonic fire striking at Rylan, but a jade firmament—radiant, divine—cloaked him, guiding each step with celestial precision.

The abyss claimed one final bite of earth, leaving the Honeysuckle ladder dangling directly over the oblivion spiraling below. From the square, Old Johnny glimpsed Ezekiel and Trickle approaching arm in arm, battling through a maelstrom of fire, hail and wind. He ran and flung open the chapel's sealed doors, letting the evil gusts invade the sanctuary. Undaunted, the flock followed, defying the storm's wrath, forming a sacred circle around Ezekiel, Trickle and him, where they met. They gazed skyward, watching Rylan's silhouette dance against the chaos, his hands grasping for the steeple's clock.

Fire-shards rained, searing the Honeysuckle on either side, leaving Rylan stranded mid-climb. The clock loomed, a distant sentinel, its hands frozen beyond reach—a leap of faith as daunting as walking on water. Trickle's anguished cry pierced the gale as Rylan stretched across the void. He glanced down, seeing the flock encircled by a Cherubim's glowing wings, their linked hands a bastion of light against the darkness. Closing his eyes, Rylan surrendered to the spirit within, his resolve a blazing star. He let go and with a leap of faith he jumped across the abyss, fingers catching the clock's rusted edge as the demons below shrieked in fury, pulsing with betrayed rage.

Rylan hauled himself onto the precarious gutter, held by a single, corroded bolt, trembling under his weight. The pit boiled beneath, but he knew the task: set the clock to 3:17, the hour of redemption. With surety, he reached for the hands of time, partially rusted in place, their ancient weight resisting his touch. The storm screamed, the Tree's light flared, and Rylan's heart sang with the Kingdom's mystic pulse, every moment a vivid circus of fire, faith, and fate, etching salvation into the soul of the the town.

* * *

Rylan faced the ancient chronospire, its hands heavy with the weight of Eldergrove's fate, and with a knight's resolve, he seized the hour hand, dragging it counterclockwise against its will, to rest on the sacred three. His fingers, trembling with purpose, forced the minute hand three notches past the 3. Locking eyes with Trickle below, he felt her radiant warmth surge through him, her gaze alight with love, passion, and a desperate hope that this was not their end. With one final click, he set the hand to seventeen, surrendering to the jade light flooding his soul. He released everything, becoming one with the Kingdom's mystic pulse.

The flock below held their breath, eyes fixed on the steeple, but the storm roared in mocking his proclaimed triumph. Nothing stirred. The pit churned into a vortex of death, spitting the Cherubim's light skyward to be devoured by the Storm-Beast coiling above—a writhing cloud of blood and fire, its heart pulsing like a Dragonfish's molten gland. It was gathering strength for its final, cataclysmic strike. The Church's walls lost their battle, and crumbled into the abyss, its sacred innards shredded by the wind's relentless claws.

Rylan, perched on the trembling gutter, cursing the clock, his voice raw with anguish.

"I've done everything! What do you want from me!"

He roared, resentment burning at his failure. The flock's glowing dome flickered, dissolving into black motes fleeing into the dark. The Tree of Life, its roots nearly consumed, dimmed, its soul-lights winking out as the pit's grip choked its life.

Rylan's gaze sought Trickle, standing fearless beside Ezekiel, Old Johnny Pocketwatch whispering urgently between them. Their eyes blazed as they shouted in unison,

"3:16!"

The wind swallowed their words, and Rylan bellowed,

"I can't hear you!"

Trickle, undaunted, broke from the flock's fading shield, her sacrifice a beacon of defiance. She sprinted to the pit's edge, almost tumbling in, leaning out over the abyss as far as she possibly could, her voice piercing the chaos:

"3:16, Ry! Johnny says 3:16. Set the hands, and then move time forward on the mark!"

Rylan's eyes lit up, his hand shot to the clock, pulling the minute hand back one sacred click to 3:16. He checked his watch, it read 3:16 and 49 seconds. Clinging to the quaking gutter, he counted down—57, 58, 59—at the precise stroke of 3:17, he thrust the minute hand into place.

A pillar of pure light erupted from the Tree of Life's heart straight into the Heavens, a jade spear piercing the Storm-Beast's veiled gland. The church awoke, its vibration a thunderous hymn of salvation, resonating with the Kingdom's eternal rhythm. The Tree unleashed a second surge, a radiant arc bridging the pit to the steeple, igniting the clock's face with celestial fire.

The church's spire rose, defiant, shaking Rylan, testing his grip. The light struck the storm's core, and a glowing hand of divine wrath reached from the pit, grasping onto the bridge of light formed between the church and the Tree. A searing scream tore from the depths—six hundred and sixty-six Dragonfish, their scales aflame, surging skyward, pursued by seven hundred and seventy seven winged orbs of pure, radiant light. The demon cloud purged crimson lightning, raging against the Tree's and Chapel's united assault, in an apocalyptic clash for all of their souls.

The battle raged on in the Heavens and Rylan felt the final fiver load humming in his overalls pocket. It was calling him. He withdrew it, loading it in his Fiver's sacred coil. The gutter quaked as demonic laser like flames struck, clawing at his footing. With the grace of a knight forged in the Kingdom's fire, he steadied himself, a boy against a cosmic giant. Aiming at the storm's flaming heart, he called upon every bit of strength he had ever drawn from. Trickle, OG, Momma and Pops, the new baby—Zora, Ezekiel, Johnny and the Flock. As he summoned their strength he felt the warmth of Bubba-Carlton-Hulk and felt his sweet Prince standing with him.

His soul exploded with faith as he suddenly knew the outcome. He cocked his Fiver, closed his eyes, and fired the load, filled with the spirits of light.

It streaked like a glowing, jade tinted comet, skipping through the sky with the perfect spin, steering it straight toward the beast's core. It rose just as Rylan knew it would, cornering the beast and striking its fire gland with a damning blow. The Beast writhed, its scream an eternity of torment, as the clouds collapsed inward, swallowing their own fury. The pit choked, expelling its last venom into the sky.

The Tree of Life and the Church stood unyielding, their light—born of the Tetramorphs Deity—and in one last explosion it shattered the Master of the Dragonfish into a million flecks of absolution and nothingness.

* * *

Through the lingering remnants, the sun began reclaiming the heavens, in the most radiant colors Rylan had ever seen. The golden rays penetrating through the flickering darkness reminiscent of a blooming Crimson Lotus. It bathed Eldergrove in redemption's pure pulsing glow. Rylan stood tall, a titan forged by faith, gazing down at Trickle and OG, steadfast at the bottomless pit's edge. He smiled as he knew the battle had been won for now, and he turned, surrendering to his descent. He locked eyes with Trickle's, and she smiled back, feeling her heart sink all at the same time, as she watched the final old rusted bolt holding the gutter give way.

The flock gasped, Trickle's screams echoed into the darkness as Rylans light faded into nothing below them. OG let out a huge bellow filled with pain, that shook the ground and echoed through out the sky. Without hesitation, he leapt into the depths chasing after his "Ride or Die."

Trickle stood at the heart of the flock's gaze, her soul unmoored, no solace to anchor her. Rylan had been sacrificed to the abyss for the Kingdom's salvation. Disbelief clawed at her heart, her only thought, to follow, to chase Rylan and OG into the void. What if they were lost forever? What if they were just—gone? What would she become? Ezekiel, ever watchful, had lunged for OG as the loyal beast leapt, but his hands grasped only air. He turned to Trickle, wrapping her in a steely embrace, halting her reckless intent.

"Let me go!"

She kicked and thrashed, her voice a raw hymn of grief. Ezekiel held firm, tears carving rivers down his weathered cheeks, as the flock gathered, their eyes peering into the pit's unfathomable dark. Trickle fought with feral desperation, cursing Ezekiel's restraint, her heart a storm of love and loss.

A ripple began to stir among the flock—slight gasps morphing into murmurs, Ezekiel, fearing their judgment, loosened his hold. As he did, he heard the *Sound of the Water.* A deluge thundering through the void like the Kingdom's own blood. He turned toward the sound and staggered, nearly collapsing in awe.

The waters of life that had once filled the caverns deep below Eldergrove were flowing. A miracle pure and simple. Within, Rylan and OG clung to a mighty floating branch, shed from the Tree of Life during the celestial battle, now rising on a tide of radiant waters.

Trickle, her senses reeling, stood and wiped her tear-streaked eyes, half-convinced they betrayed her. She blinked, and there they were—Rylan and OG, borne upward on the branch, cradled by the holy waters that now filled the pit, transforming it into a shimmering lagoon encircling the Tree of Life. She spun to Ezekiel, enveloping him in a fierce embrace.

"I'm so sorry, Zeke,"

Her voice was thick with gratitude. He smiled, a silent renewal of their bond, no words needed to mend their kinship. Trickle whirled around, and dove into the luminous waters.

Rylan, his spirit blazing, lunged from the branch, meeting her halfway in a collision of destiny. OG, ever steadfast, had bounded to the last slender bridge of earth linking the town square to the island, where the Tree of Life stood resolute. He danced, a circus bear dance, fueled by pure joy, his wagging rear, a riotous spectacle that sparked laughter through out the flock. Rylan and Trickle floated, entwined, the current carrying them to OG awaiting on the shore. They collapsed on the bank, limbs tangled, laughter bubbling like a sacred spring, the setting sun painting them in 7 shades of gold. OG pranced and howled, a newborn pup reborn in bliss, his song a wild celebration of the Kingdom's triumph.

Rylan gazed into Trickle's eyes, which were mirrors of the waters that saved them. He kissed her so deeply it wove their souls into the eternal tapestry of the Tree. She clung to him, her arms a vow, binding them tighter than any storm could tear asunder. The flock erupted in cheers, their voices a celestial choir celebrating love's victory over the abyss.

Trickle looked deeply into Rylan's soul,

"My King"

Rylan wrapped her in his arms, quenching his parched soul and whispered,

"My Queen"

Ezekiel, turned and hobbled toward the Crescent Coffershop, carrying the tale of miracles witnessed. Zora stood in the doorway, her smile a knowing beacon. Ezekiel met her gaze, recognizing the mystic wisdom glowing in her eyes, and he realized that she already knew every thread of this story, woven in destiny long before anyone had ever spoke it.

Restored

Eldergrove Square had morphed into a magical waterfront village bustling with life, ticking away to the beat of the newly revived clock that perched on the church's steeple. Progress in rebuilding the old chapel was moving along. The flock had met that morning in a form of worship that included raising a new wall for the old church. That was followed by fried foods and a buffet full of questionable endeavors.

As always, Momma and Trickle had brewed up a big batch of Lemonade, and that was always a huge hit. The afternoon burst forth and a groove of foot-stompin' music engulfed the air. Old Man Tucker's claw hammer banjo wailed like a hallelujah, while Sister Mae's guitar strummed salvation's promise. Brother Amos's washboard rattled revival's thunder, and his rhythms wove a tapestry of joy that set the Kingdom's flock dancing, boots kicking up dust into golden clouds.

The potluck table groaned from the weight of the feast. Cornbread, ham-hoc infused collard green, peach cobbler, and dew-kissed tomatoes, were all a testament to the farmers' reborn fields.

At the heart of the revelry, around a checkered-cloth table wide as redemption itself, Rylan Blaze, Trickle, and OG broke bread with Mamma, Pops, Zora, Zeke, and Johnny, the flock's voices rising in a halo of song.

A new soul now graced the tight circle—the baby boy, Grady Blaze. Momma and Pops had come to a truce on his name, but Rylan still called him Little Spidey. Trickle, sparkling like a star fallen to earth, doted on Grady, while fetching Mamma anything she desired with a tenderness that lit Rylan's heart on fire with visions of the yet to come. Her eyes met his, her smile as warm as the rising sun, and she slid across the bench, her warmth a soft magic that quenched his soul.

Rylan's gaze drifted across the water, gleaming like a mirror of heaven, to the Tree of Life. Its roots now drawing deep from the redeemed waters, its branches humming with whispered truths.

"You've never been up there, have you, Trickle?"

She squinted against the sunlight dancing through the leaves, then grinned, bold as a summer squall.

"I ain't afraid if that's what you're gettin' at."

Her voice was a spark of defiance and delight. They paused by the lagoon, its waters mirroring the Tree's reborn glow. Their laughter rang like church bells, and hand in hand, they ran, crossing the land bridge to the Tree. At it's base they paused, the newly birthed springs waters mirroring the Tree's reborn glow. Rylan squeezed Trickle's hand, her warmth an echo of their kiss in the abyss.

"We did it Trick," he said, voice soft. "The Kingdom's safe, and you're still my Queen."

She leaned into him, her breath a sigh of shared battles, their silence a vow to never lose this light.

OG caught up with them, his massive bulk shuffling along watching for fish in the newly formed shoreline, but he let out a gruff woof signaling his dismay as they began climbing.

"We'll be right back G," Rylan grinned, "you can have the rest of my chicken if you want."

OG pranced back, tail wagging, already sniffing at the leftover feast as he crawled up onto the bench next to Old Zeke.

Trickle scaled the old rungs nailed into the Tree, her steps light as a zephyr, Rylan close behind, heart pounding. At the Tree's heart, where the Tetramorph gleamed anew, Trickle looked back at Rylan, her smile outshining the shadows, and then she lunged upward, no more rungs, bounding from limb to limb like a spirit set free. Rylan laughed and followed, not surprised, but ready to catch her if she fell. She spun around, eyes glinting.

"Think you could catch me if I fell?"

She teased at him, her voice a ripple of mischief.

"How do you do that?"

Rylan hollered, his amazement bursting like a firecracker. She laughed, wild and free, and soared to the canopy's crest, where she perched, a celestial bird ablaze in the setting sun's golden fire.

Rylan joined her, breath stolen as the canopy parted to reveal a horizon burning with liquid jade. Three waterfalls, well nourished from the source of the fourth living waterfall far off in the beyond, nestled into the horizon below the setting sun. Trickle's hand clasped his, her whisper soft as a sacred breath.

"Can you hear that—the whispers riding on the wind?"

Rylan closed his eyes, and a distant call stirred within his soul. Trickle reached out and placed her hand on his heart, her touch a symphony of love, grace, and wisdom. The creek lands themselves sang of an eternal Kingdom waiting beyond their worldly vision. An adventure that called out to them. The breeze swirled, sweet with jasmine and redemption, and Trickle's radiance merged with his, their bond an eternal ember, igniting the Divine.

www.ingramcontent.com/pod-product-compliance
Lightning Source LLC
Chambersburg PA
CBHW070639310726
48982CB00001B/332
9798999715456